THE CURSED CARNIVAL AND OTHER CALAMITIES:

NEW STORIES ABOUT MYTHIC HEROES

Rick Riordan Presents Books You May Enjoy

THE PANDAVA SERIES BY ROSHANI CHOKSHI
Aru Shah and the End of Time
Aru Shah and the Song of Death
Aru Shah and the Tree of Wishes
Aru Shah and the City of Gold

THE STORM RUNNER SERIES BY J. C. CERVANTES
The Storm Runner
The Fire Keeper
The Shadow Crosser

THE THOUSAND WORLDS SERIES BY YOON HA LEE
Dragon Pearl

THE SAL AND GABI DUOLOGY BY CARLOS HERNANDEZ
Sal and Gabi Break the Universe
Sal and Gabi Fix the Universe

THE TRISTAN STRONG SERIES BY KWAME MBALIA
Tristan Strong Punches a Hole in the Sky
Tristan Strong Destroys the World

THE PAOLA SANTIAGO SERIES BY TEHLOR KAY MEJIA
Paola Santiago and the River of Tears
Paola Santiago and the Forest of Nightmares

Race to the Sun by Rebecca Roanhorse

City of the Plague God by Sarwat Chadda

THE GIFTED CLANS SERIES BY GRACI KIM
The Last Fallen Star

THE CURSED CARNIVAL AND OTHER CALAMITIES:

NEW STORIES ABOUT MYTHIC HEROES

EDITED BY **RICK RIORDAN**

WITH STORIES BY

CARLOS HERNANDEZ · ROSHANI CHOKSHI

J. C. CERVANTES · YOON HA LEE · KWAME MBALIA

REBECCA ROANHORSE · TEHLOR KAY MEJIA

SARWAT CHADDA · GRACI KIM

RICK RIORDAN

RICK RIORDAN PRESENTS

DISNEY • HYPERION LOS ANGELES NEW YORK

First Edition, September 2021
1 3 5 7 9 10 8 6 4 2
FAC-021131-21225
Printed in the United States of America

This book is set in Goudy Old Style MT Pro/Monotype
Designed by Joann Hill

Library of Congress Cataloging-in-Publication Data
Names: Riordan, Rick, editor, compiler, author. • Hernandez, Carlos. Calamity juice. • Chokshi, Roshani. Beware the grove of true love. • Cervantes, Jennifer. Cave of Doom. • Lee, Yoon Ha. Initiation. • Mbalia, Kwame. Gum Baby files. • Roanhorse, Rebecca. Demon drum. • Mejia, Tehlor Kay. Bruto and the freaky flower. • Chadda, Sarwat. Loneliest demon. • Kim, Graci. My night at the Gifted Carnival. • Riordan, Rick. My life as a child outlaw.
Title: The cursed carnival and other calamities: new stories about mythic heroes edited by Rick Riordan ; with stories by Carlos Hernandez, Roshani Chokshi, Jennifer Cervantes, Yoon Ha Lee, Kwame Mbalia, Rebecca Roanhorse, Tehlor Kay Mejia, Sarwat Chadda, Graci Kim, Rick Riordan.
Description: First edition. • Los Angeles ; New York: Disney-Hyperion, 2021. • Audience: Ages 8–12. • Summary: A collection of ten stories by authors from the Rick Riordan Presents imprint that remix myths for modern readers.
Identifiers: LCCN 2020050325 (print) • LCCN 2020050326 (ebook) • ISBN 9781368070836 (hardcover) • ISBN 9781368073219 (ebook)
Subjects: LCSH: Mythology—Juvenile fiction. • Children's stories, English. • CYAC: Mythology—Fiction. • Short stories. Classification: LCC PZ5. R4498 Myt 2021 (print) • LCC PZ5.R4498 (ebook) • DDC [Fic]—dc23
LC record available at https://lccn.loc.gov/2020050325
LC ebook record available at https://lccn.loc.gov/2020050326

Reinforced binding
Follow @ReadRiordan
Visit www.DisneyBooks.com

To reluctant, undiscovered,
and unsung heroes everywhere

Contents

Welcome to the Multiverse Mansion

IMAGINE A MULTIVERSE MANSION in which all the heroes of Rick Riordan Presents exist together. Think of it as like the Hotel Valhalla, only even bigger and stranger (in the best possible way).

You unlock one door and find yourself on an adventure with Aru Shah, solving riddles and zapping snakes with lightning bolts in the Grove of True Love. You unlock another door, and you're on a field trip with Gum Baby to the Mississippi Civil Rights Museum, which might be fun—except for a cantankerous ghost who's causing all sorts of trouble. You unlock a third door, and you are side by side with Paola Santiago, searching for magical meat flowers to cure her sick chupacabra puppy, Bruto. And we will do *anything* to help our chupacabra puppies!

The book you're holding right now *is* that multiverse mansion. All your favorite authors from the Rick Riordan Presents imprint have contributed stories about heroes on fantastic adventures—myths remixed for modern readers. I've contributed one, too—my very first foray into the wild world of Celtic mythology! This book offers ten doorways into adventure—ten stories that offer chills, thrills, and lots of laugh-out-loud moments from across the mythological spectrum.

It's impossible to pick a favorite. I got to see Sikander Aziz wielding Abubu, the sky-cleaving sword (magic shovel?) of

Gilgamesh. I got to hang out with Riley Oh and her witch clan friends at the Gifted Carnival, which was awesome until an evil spirit from the Hell of Infinite Ice crashed the party. I got to see Sal and Gabi again, along with their class-nine AI toilet friend Vorágine, as they dealt with stray unicorns, prank-universe versions of themselves, and the ever-present threat of the dreaded chicken universe. The beauty of this anthology is that you don't have to choose. In a single book, you get to see a bunch of your favorite heroes in new adventures, and you'll meet some new friends as well.

So go ahead and insert your master key, demigods. Zane Obispo has a cave of doom to show you, with countless horrors like reptilian doppelgängers and human tourists. Jun and Min, galactic fox spirits, are back in their first adventure for the Thousand Worlds' Domestic Security Ministry . . . except it's not quite the mission they were expecting. Nizhoni Begay wants to take you to the All-Nations Assembly powwow, which should be a nice break from monster-hunting . . . unless, of course, monsters show up. I've got to be honest—some of these situations, I'm not sure how even Percy Jackson and Annabeth Chase would handle them!

I hope you enjoy your trip through the multiverse mansion as much as I did. The real danger is that once you start exploring all the wonders herein, you may want to stay forever.

Rick Riordan

If a hero isn't ready to lose everything for a greater cause,
is that person really a hero?

—Jason Grace, *The Tower of Nero*

Calamity Juice

CARLOS HERNANDEZ

YOU KNOW HOW IT'S impossible to walk up to a rainbow? Like, you keep going toward it, and it keeps moving away from you?

Well, friends, I have been inside a rainbow. And I can tell you from experience that they smell like horse barf.

Gabi and I noticed it the second we started climbing the stairs to hallway 3C in Culeco Academy. "Why does it smell like horse hork?" I asked her.

"It just smells like hork to me," Gabi answered. "I haven't smelled enough hork in my life to be able to identify the species by aroma. Ugh!"

It was getting stronger the closer we got to hallway 3C. We both hid our noses in our trench coats.

Yes, trench coats. Also, hats. Gabi wore a fedora bigger than a flying saucer, and I had on this big-brimmed Italian number that I'd only ever seen on rumpled detectives from black-and-white movies. Oh, and on Papi, because there is a brand of Cuban dude who loves a fancy hat, and he's one of them. I'd borrowed it and American Stepmom's trench coat and Humphrey Bogart's speech patterns for the skit Gabi and I had just been performing in Mrs. Waked's Intermediate Theater Workshop. The sketch was called *The Malta Falcon.* I was playing gumshoe Dón Silva (which uses all the letters in *Sal Vidón*, even the accent!), tracking down notorious thief Ria Bágel (which uses all the letters in *Gabi Reál*), who had stolen the most valuable object in the whole world: the ~~Maltese~~ Malta Falcon.

The object was an empty bottle of malta—that sweet, thick malt beverage that so many Cubans love and I never drink, because it would mess up my blood-sugar levels faster than you can say *hyperglycemia*—with a brass falcon wine-stopper jammed into the top. It was going to be the cheese-a-rific visual-pun climax of our skit. Dón Silva was just about to crack the case wide open and catch the lousy crook when Principal Torres's voice came over the intercom and asked to see Gabi and me right away, in hallway 3C. Something in her voice told us to hurry. We left so fast, we didn't even change out of our costumes.

By the time we got to the top of the stairs and stood in front of the double doors leading to 3C, we could barely breathe. "Holy heaving pony puke," said Gabi.

"It stinks like halitosis pudding up here," I replied. From my trench coat I pulled out two N95 masks and handed one to Gabi. And then, Humphrey-Bogart-ishly, I added, "Here, dame, cover your mug with this before you take a big sleep."

"Thank you," Gabi said, as she took off her fedora—*boom* went her hairball!—and slipped her mask on over her head.

"Remind me never again to make fun of all the cacaseca you tuck into your drawers every morning." She put one hand on each of the swinging double doors, then looked back at me. "Ready?"

I poked the brim of my hat with my index finger. "Let 'er rip, dollface."

In response, I got a look that said *I'm going to feminist you into next week for that comment.* But for now she ignored it and opened both doors with a mighty push. "Okay, let's see what the fuss is all about."

"What the fuss!" I exclaimed.

I was pretty proud of myself. See, when you find yourself staring down a hallway that looks like the inside of a rainbow and smells like the inside of a horse's large intestine, limiting your vulgarity to *What the fuss!* is a pretty major accomplishment. Hallway 3C now looked like someone had set off a tie-dye bomb. The walls, floor, ceiling, light fixtures, lockers, and everything else were covered—I mean *piled*—with what looked like goopy, glittery rainbow paint.

"Still wet," I told Gabi, running my finger along the wall. The glitter goop felt thicker than the purple oatmeal Principal Torres had for lunch every day. It was heaped onto the wall like someone had machine-gunned the hallway with fifty thousand paintball rounds.

"Eww-ww-ww-ww-ww!" said Gabi, smacking down my hand. "Don't touch that stuff, Sal! You have no idea what it is!"

"Unfortunately, I do," I said, sniffing the chromatic cud on my fingertip. Yep, still smelled terrible.

"You do?"

I'd been queasy ever since we'd started up the staircase, and not just because the stench of stallion spew was so strong. It was like ants were digging a new colony in my bone marrow. And only one thing gives me that sensation. "Can't you feel it?" I asked Gabi.

She shrugged. "Feel what?"

"Try relaxing a little."

The word *relax* has a special meaning for me. It's how I describe being able to see into, travel to, and steal from other universes. Most people don't have to concentrate in order to stay safely snuggled inside their home universe. It's as natural and as thoughtless as breathing. But me? If I kind of let my soul go translucent, picture my mind dissipating like campfire smoke, and imagine my skin being as porous as a gold prospector's sieve, I can suddenly find myself between realities. There are an infinite number of universes out there, and most people only get to live in one. Not me. Not anymore.

Not Gabi, either. She knew exactly what I meant by *relax*. So she relaxed.

And instantly fell through the floor and into a different universe.

Luckily, we'd been training for just such an emergency. We'd learned from Fix Gabi (a somewhat evil but now mostly reformed Gabi from another universe) that everyone has a unique personal cosmic signature (PCS) that identifies you as the you who is you and not some other you from some other universe. The yous from different universes all have their own PCSs. So we'd been practicing being able to locate each other, anywhere in the multiverse, by concentrating on our PCSs.

Which is what I did then, in the middle of the colorful, glitterful, mile-of-vile-bile hallway. I said her name aloud: "Gabrielle Reál." I remembered her multicolored fingernails, her nutcracker smile, and of course her hairball, which is so massive that, if you stare hard, you can literally see it growing. Most importantly, I concentrated on her PCS.

And I found her. She was in the chicken universe.

Of course she was in the chicken universe. It must be the universe right next door or something. We are *always* accidentally falling into the chicken-processing plant that's on the same spot in their universe where Culeco is in ours.

And the locals there have decided that they don't like us. Get this: They think we're literal, actual devils from *H-E*-double-hockey-sticks who have come to torture them and steal their chickens.

Which is completely unfair. We've only stolen two. And we even returned them!

Whatever. Gabi and I had been practicing yoinking each other from other universes, in case one of us ever needed to be rescued. But this would be the first time that it wouldn't be practice. This time it was for real.

I took a breath and held it. I widened my stance, punched a fist into my palm, and closed my eyes. And then I willed Gabi back to this universe.

She popped into existence in the same spot where she had

disappeared. Her face was covered by her fedora, as if she'd been protecting herself. Also, there were many, many raw chicken limbs in her hairball. She looked like a Christmas tree decorated with poultry-part ornaments.

"Hey," I said to her. "You're safe now."

She lowered her hat and looked over the brim at me. "Oh. Good. Thanks, Sal. As your mom would say, *Phew, baby!*"

"You okay?"

She nodded, taking deep breaths through her mask. "They were even more ready for me than usual in the chicken universe. Like, armed and ready. They were already holding chicken wings in their hands like boomerangs when I appeared. They commenced firing fowl at me right away."

I pinched a drumstick out of her hairball. "You don't say."

For the second time in three minutes, Gabi said, "Eww-ww-ww-ww-ww!" She started pulling raw chicken out of her 'do and throwing it on the floor. "Don't! They! Know! I! Am! A! Vege! Freaking! Tarian! I swear, the next time I'm there, I'm going to . . ."

She trailed off when she noticed that the parts disappeared out of our universe the moment they hit the multicolored mess on the floor.

"I only relaxed a little," she said, slowly catching on. "But I fell into the chicken universe like I was riding a waterslide."

"And the second the chicken from the other universe touches the gunk," I added, "it disappears. Betcha anything it all gets zapped back to where it came from."

"Which means . . ." The realization left her speechless for

.035 seconds, which is a new record for anything leaving Gabi speechless. "Which means this sludge is full of calamitrons!"

"Yeah," I said, staring down the hallway. "It's, like, one hundred percent–pure calamity juice."

Gabi made a face. "Juice, shmuice. This stuff smells like a fake vomit factory decided not to fake it anymore. Who or what could have done this?"

I had a hunch. But Papi's always saying that scientists don't jump to conclusions. They let the evidence speak. I needed more evidence.

"Let's find Principal Torres," I said to Gabi. "Maybe she can help us get to the bottom of this. Where do you think she is?"

"My guess," she answered, "is behind that."

Gabi was pointing to the far end of the hallway, where my locker was. But I couldn't see it right now, since the area was blocked by a zigzag of blue dividers. They call that "cordoning off an area" in all the detective stories I'd been reading lately.

On cue, a loud but faraway voice proclaimed from behind the dividers, "I understand everything now! The universe! It's so vast! And so beautiful!"

The voice wasn't Principal Torres's. It was Yasmany's.

Gabi and I looked at each other. Then we ran to him.

"Thank you for coming," said Principal Torres, after we'd scooted behind the dividers and joined her. She wore her traditional pantsuit—today's was green with yellow polka dots, and if you stared really hard and crossed your eyes, a 3-D dolphin would pop out—and plastic bags over her sensible heels, and a nose plug, like the kind swimmers wear, which made her voice sound weenie and creaky.

Also, she wore a worried expression. I think it was more worried than I had ever seen her look before. And she's a principal. Her whole job is to look worried, all day long.

She was standing above Yasmany, who was sitting against the lockers, buried under a gloptacular mountain of the putrid rainbow slop. Only his face peeked out from the slime.

We had the word *euphoric* on a vocabulary study list a few weeks ago. It came in handy now to describe Yasmany's dazed-yet-joyful expression, mouth and eyes as wide as a Muppet's.

"He looks euphoric," I said.

"Yasmany!" Gabi yelled, squatting close to him. "Are you okay? Speak to me!"

He didn't look at her. He was staring into the middle distance, like an astronaut gazing slack-jawed out a spaceship window. "So many possibilities . . . So many ways to be Yasmany." Somehow, his little circle of a face became even happier. "MANY Yasmanys! Yas-MANY!"

"Do you have any idea what happened to him?" Principal Torres asked. "And the hallway, for that matter?"

We'd let Principal Torres in on our multiverse-traveling secret last fall, which is why she had called us here. Clearly, this had something to do with our "gift." She didn't look like she was blaming us for this mess, but her eyes told me she hadn't exactly found us not guilty yet, either.

So I took a breath before I answered. But Gabi, whose superpower is speaking first, spoke first. "We don't know where it came from, Principal Torres, and we don't know why it reeks so bad. But what we do know is that the stuff covering the hallway is concentrated calamitron juice."

Gabi and Principal Torres looked at me to see if I agreed. I did. "I think it's letting 'Yas-MANY' visit parallel universes, like Gabi and I do. He's seeing how other Yasmanys are living their best lives."

"It seems he likes what he's seeing," said Principal Torres. "But I would rather get him and this hallway cleaned up ASAP. Is that something you two can help with?"

Gabi and I nodded at the same time, and I said, "We can send this gunk back to where it came from."

The two of us faced each other, took a horse stance, exhaled, and imagined we were pushing extra gravity into the center of the Earth with our palms. We didn't need to do any of that—all we really had to do was relax. But it's way more fun to break and/or fix the universe when you're in *Dragon Ball Z* poses. So we'd worked up a whole kata of punches and kicks and *hi-yahhhs!* that we liked to go through before we relaxed a little and actually made things happen.

"The multiverse is ours to break or fix!" yelled Gabi.

"The multiverse is ours to boldly go!" yelled I.

"If anyone or -thing gets in our way—"

"¡Vamos a formar el titingó!"

I got that last line from Papi. It's a little hard to translate into English, but roughly it means *We're going to cause a tremendous ruckus, a veritable debacle of epic proportions!* Only, like, way cooler.

Anyway, then we relaxed, and a second later, not a drop of that rainbow cud crud remained on the floor or walls or ceiling. Only a few drops remained on our shoes and my finger.

The hallway still stank, though. I had a feeling it was going to take one of Mr. Milagros's custodial miracles to get the reek out of hallway 3C.

Gabi and I both stooped over to help Yasmany up—no easy feat, since Gabi and I put together weigh about as much as his big toe. But we managed to squirm under his armpits and hoist him vertical.

As his eyesight drifted back from whatever universe he'd been looking at, he slowly came out of his stupor. "Gabi," he said. Then, like, so fast he hurt himself a little, he turned to me. "Sal." Then, way too fast again, he looked straight ahead. "Principal Torres."

The best principal in Florida pressed the back of her hand against his forehead, the same way Mami used to take my temperature. "How are you feeling, Yasmany?"

He shook the gerbils out of his head. "Okay, I think. Where's the horse?"

"Horse?" Principal Torres looked at Gabi and me.

"Yeah," said Yasmany, brushing us off him like Socrates scratching fleas. He looked left and right, then back at us. "There was a horse. Right here. It barfed on Gladis."

"It barfed?!" asked Principal Torres.

"On Gladis?!" asked Gabi.

"Yeah," said Yasmany. But then he corrected himself. "Well, on one Gladis. The other Gladis was riding the horse."

"There were two Gladises?" I asked in the same tone I say *uh-oh*.

Yasmany still couldn't believe that there wasn't a horse in the hallway. "It was huge. And striped, like a zebra, but with all the colors." He stamped his foot. "It was right here! You ain't seen it?"

"No," Gabi said. She pulled her tablet out of her trench coat and opened a note-taking app. "Did you see where it went?"

"Naw. What happened was, the horse barfed on Gladis, and she yeeted through the floor. And the other Gladis was on the horse, but she couldn't control it. It was tryna buck her off, and she was all crazy-eyed and yelling 'Whoa! Whoa!' and hugging on its neck like it was her daddy."

Gabi nodded detectively. "Um-hmm. *Verrrrrry* interesting. So what'd you do?"

"I got scared for her. Thing was finna kill her. So I ran up and tried to pull her down."

"That was brave of you," said Principal Torres. Even with her nose pinched, she sounded sincere.

Yasmany lit up a little at the compliment. But just as quickly, he lit down. "But before I could grab her, it barfed on me."

We took a second to absorb all this. So, okay: two Gladises. One gets vomited on by an out-of-control rainbow zebra and then falls through the floor just like Gabi did a minute ago. The other Gladis was riding said out-of-control rainbow zebra down the middle of the hallway. When Yasmany tried to help her, it barfed on him, too.

But unlike Gabi and Gladis, Yasmany didn't fall through the floor and into another universe. Hmm.

"Yasmany," I asked, "after the horse spewed on you, do you remember anything?"

"I had the weirdest dream, yo!" he answered. "It was like there were a million of me. And they all were different, but, like, the same. Like, still me. But not me. And it's like . . . It's like . . ."

He choked up. Out of nowhere, he was fighting as hard as he could to not cry.

"What's it like, mijo?" asked Principal Torres, taking a knee in front of him. Always the best listener, Principal Torres.

Yasmany snuffled. "There was this one Yas. He was going to ballet practice. And his moms was driving him. And she looked happy. They were talking and laughing. Like, she was happy to take him to ballet practice."

In this universe, Yasmany's mami would never, ever, ever take him to ballet practice. She's got some cacaseca ideas about what boys are and aren't allowed to do. And she's messed up Yasmany pretty bad, the way she's treated him. That's why he was spending so much time with Gabi's family now. They even built him a mini house in their backyard so he could escape from his mami anytime he needed to.

And he needed to six days out of seven.

Gabi went over and hugged him. "In other universes, other Yasmanys live different lives. I'm sorry you had to see that."

Yasmany gave her an affectionate, brotherly noogie. "I'm

not. It's good to know." He looked up, his face serene, like he was posing for a coin they were going to stamp his face on. "It's good to know things can be better."

Huh. Yasmany seemed different, even from the way he'd been this morning. He had tried to bully me (tried and failed lol) on the third day of school, and over the course of the school year, he'd slowly been changing for the better. Now, though? Now it was like *download complete*. He radiated tranquility. Like, I could almost hear the hum of his growing self-confidence.

Principal Torres noticed it, too. "This is good, Yasmany. This is very, very good. I can't wait to hear more, later. But right now, we have an emergency on our hands. Gladis is missing. From what you're saying, it sounds like a horse—a horse?!—either vomited her into a different universe, or possibly ran off with her. Is there anything, anything at all you haven't told us that might give us a clue as to where she could be?"

Yasmany thought for a moment. Then he pointed to the floor behind him. "Well, there's that thing. I pulled it off Gladis just before I got buried in puke."

We all looked at what he was pointing at. A scarf.

On it was a knitted ojo turco, aka a ward against the Evil Eye.

There must have been something about my face. Or maybe it was the way I did a full-body shudder. Or the way I said, "Crap and cucumber sandwiches." But everyone turned to me.

"Sal?" prompted Principal Torres.

"Spill it, Bubba," added Gabi. "And no cacaseca allowed. This is a cacaseca-free zone. Thou shalt not caca in my presence!"

"I think he gets it," said the weirdly-now-mature Yasmany.

"What? Did you meet Sal yesterday or something, Yasmany? His two middle names are Caca and Seca. No offense, Sal."

"None taken, you jar of farts," I replied. "Look, I swear I will explain everything. But I think Gladis is in trouble. We need to move to save her, now. And there's only one person who can help us."

"Who?" asked Principal Torres.

"The smartest toilet in the world."

Culeco Academy of the Arts is a very special school. Every day feels like Comic-Con, the way everybody cosplays—even the teachers and staff. Almost all the kids show up early and stay for detention, because that's when you get to play games and build robots and act out your favorite musicals and, yeah, work on tomorrow's cosplay. Every single grown-up at Culeco loves their job. They're very helpful to us—but only when we ask for help. They let us make our own mistakes, because they respect us that much. I think I like the respect best of all.

Naw. I like our toilet best of all.

Its name is Vorágine, and it's a class-nine AI. That means it understands how the multiverse works better than even Papi does—and he practically invented calamity physics.

We had piled into the all-gender bathroom of hallway 1W, where Vorágine lived. I stood in the stall with it, while Gabi, Principal Torres, and Yasmany lurked just outside, peering in.

I used a piece of toilet paper to clean off the little bit of equine effluence that remained on my finger and shoes.

Then I dangled the toilet paper over the bowl. "You ready, Vorágine?"

"This is so exciting!" said Vorágine. It had a sweet, chipper voice, like a Disney-cartoon sidekick. "I can't wait to taste magic horse vomit!"

Three of the four humans in the room leaned against the stall and concentrated on keeping their lunches down. Yasmany actually had to go hug the sink for a minute.

I dropped the toilet paper into Vorágine. The second the paper touched the water, the AI said, "Commencing calamitous chemical analysis." It swished the sample around its bowl like this was a wine-tasting. It added a series of different chemicals into its bowl—a green one, a milky-white one, and a gritty-pink one—and swished them around, too. Then it flushed itself and had a little think.

"What you got, vieja?" asked Yasmany, returning to us.

It would take a team of psychologists to figure out why Yasmany always called Vorágine *vieja*. It's what some Cubans call their mamis—a lot like *my old lady* in English. And he and the AI had been spending a lot of time together. Yasmany needed a lot of tutoring, and Vorágine was programmed to never run out of patience. So hey, you want a toilet for a mom, Yas? You do you, m'dude.

And anyway, Vorágine seemed to like it. It giggle-bubbled before it answered. "Oh, you! How am I vieja, you cad? I am not even a year old! Anyway, I have good news. By studying the subatomic structure of the calamitrons in the vomitus sample, I was able to get a lock on the universe it is connected to. The unicorn's emesis creates a portal to the same universe that the portal in Yasmany's locker used to lead to. That's the one, Sal and Gabi, that you call the 'chicken universe,' I think?"

"Wait, wait, wait, wait, *wait*!" said Gabi. She gasped and added, "A who-nicorn?"

"A unicorn," confirmed Vorágine. "Somehow it found its way here from its home universe. Tell me, did anyone get a look at the majestic animal?"

"Yasmany did," said Principal Torres.

"Ah, great. Yasmany, you saw a horselike creature?"

"Yeah," said Yasmany.

"Colorful?"

"Yeah. Covered in stripes."

"And it had a horn?"

"Yeah."

"What?!" Gabi yelled.

Yasmany blinked. "What? It had a horn."

Gabi stomped over to Yasmany until she was directly under his nose. "And you didn't think that was an important little detail to tell us?! That we're dealing with a unicorn?"

Yasmany laughed straight down at her, like a troll laughing at Frodo Baggins. "Excuse me, Señorita San'weech, but there ain't no such thing as unicorns."

Three people and one toilet waited for Yasmany to get it. He was the newest addition to the Sal and Gabi Have This One Weird Trick That Lets Them Hop Around the Cosmos Club, so he was still getting used to the idea that stuff that's fake in our universe might be real in other ones.

Principal Torres leaned toward him. Gabi got on her tiptoes, nodding encouragingly. Vorágine glugged in the hopeful anticipation that Yasmany would figure it out himself. I farted.

Okay, no, I didn't. But I wanted to.

"Oh yeah!" said Yasmany. "It's one of those Spider-Verse things!"

"Multiverse," Gabi corrected, shoving her fedora onto his head.

But you can't put a hat on m'dude without him running for the nearest mirror—in this case, the one over the sink.

"Yasmango," he said, admiring himself, running his thumb and forefinger over the brim.

"Gabi," said Principal Torres. "Sal."

This was an invitation for us to huddle with her. When we were in range, Principal Torres, not moving her lips much, whispered, "Gladis's dad comes to pick her up from school every day at 3:40 p.m. on the dot. I would very much like today to be exactly the same as every other day."

"There were two Gladises," added Gabi, referring to her tablet. "We need to find them both to get to the bottom of what's going on."

"If we find PrankGladis," I said, "I bet she can lead us to our Gladis."

Principal Torres locked her lenses on me like an auto-turret about to commence firing. "Who's PrankGladis, Sal?"

"You know her?" asked Gabi, her fingers wiggling just above her tablet screen, ready to make a big fat note.

"This is her scarf," I said, pulling the ojo turco scarf out of my trench coat. "She, um . . . She let me borrow it for a while."

Gabi shook her head at me. "And now she's come back for what's hers."

Principal Torres bent her right eyebrow—that's her "thinking" eyebrow—into an arrowhead. "I remember that scarf. It caused some trouble at the start of the school year."

"Good people," I said, doing my fieriest impression of Patrick Henry, when he gave his famous speech in Congress called "Give Me Sandwiches or Give Me Death!" (Or something like that.) "We have less than two hours and a whole multiverse to search. Now, we can either stand around pointing fingers at one another—"

Both Gabi and Principal Torres pointed fingers at me.

"Or," I continued, moving their fingers aside as though they were uncomfortably close bayonets, "we can get to work."

Principal Torres knelt to get eye level with me. "You said you would explain everything, Sal, and I'm going to hold you to that. But for now, we focus on Gladis."

"Gladis*es*," said Gabi. "There were two of them. One got blasted into the chicken universe. The other one got kidnapped by a unicorn."

"Right. So, okay, we know where one Gladis is. Let's go get her first."

"Easier said than done," I said.

Borágine burbled cheerfully, kind of like politely clearing its throat. "If you are worried about creating a stable portal, Sal, rest assured that I will help you and Gabi!"

"Thanks, Vorágine. But creating a portal to a different universe is the easy part."

"Said no one ever," said Principal Torres. "But if that's the easy part, what's the hard part?"

"Surviving," said Gabi. "They hate us in the chicken universe. They throw chicken! Lots of it! Why do you think we call it the chicken universe? Anyone who goes into that universe is going to get salmonella-spanked by flying drumsticks."

"I'll go," said Yasmany, rejoining us. We broke the huddle to let him in. "I ain't afraid of no drumsticks. Plus, with this hat, they'll all just fall in love with me and give me whatever I want."

We all took a second to admire Yasmany. Even after everything he'd been through, dude had a very healthy ego. Maybe even a little *too* healthy.

That pause was a productive one, though, because it gave me two seconds to think. I smacked my forehead and dragged my hand down until it covered one eye. "I am such an idiot. I can just text PrankGladis."

Clearly, no one else in the room had been expecting me to say that. The three humans tilted their heads like the little white tree spirits from *Princess Mononoke*.

Vorágine, who had no head to turn, had to vocalize its confusion. "It's theoretically possible, Sal. But it would take years, perhaps decades, to create the infrastructure for a cell-phone service provider that worked across universes."

I brought my smartwatch to my face. "Luckily, Gladis's

universe already has multiverse cell-phone service." Using voice-to-text, I said, "Gladis where are you question mark I think you might be in trouble period We want to rescue you period Tell us your location period" and then stared at my watch, waiting for the reply.

"Look at you," said Gabi, "talking into your watch like Dick Tracy."

I looked up. I'd forgotten about the trench coat and old-timey hat I was wearing. It's funny how fast life moves. One minute, you're doing a skit for theater class, the next, you're trying to rescue a friend who's trapped in an alternate dimension.

Just then, my smartwatch rang.

I'd been expecting a text, so it startled me. But caller ID said it was PrankGladis, so I yelled, "It's her!" Everyone crowded their heads around my wrist as I answered. "Gladis! Quick, tell us where you are so we can come get you!"

It took a second for the video to appear. When it did, it was not the face of PrankGladis staring back at us on my smartwatch.

It was the face of Principal Torres.

She did not look happy. "Ahora los diablos me estan llamando por el telefono. ¡Esta cruz tremenda que tengo que cargar!"

"What'd she say? What'd she say?" asked Gabi, who doesn't speak Spanish.

Three humans and one toilet began to translate for her at the same time. The humans let Vorágine finish, because we all knew how much it loved to help out. "The woman said, 'Now devils are calling me on the phone. What a huge cross I have to bear!' "

Principal Torres replied through gritted teeth. I'd never seen her speak as angrily as she did to her look-alike. "Nadie quería hablar contigo. Robaste ese teléfono que esta usando como si era tuyo. ¿Qué hiciste con la niña quien es la dueña propria del teléfono?"

Orágine translated her Spanish, too: " 'No one wanted to talk to you. You stole that telephone you're using as if it's yours. What did you do with the girl who is the rightful owner of the phone?' "

"Yeah," said Gabi. "You tell her, Principal Torres."

The reason Gabi had had the time to hear the translation and say something to Principal Torres before the woman on the other end of the call responded was because the woman, who looked exactly like Principal Torres, was staring at Principal Torres. At first the other Torres looked confused. But then she went from uncomprehending to enraged. "¡Me robaste mi cara misma, súcubu hermosa! ¿Y me vas a hablar de robando?"

" 'You stole my very face, you gorgeous succubus!' " Vorágine translated. " 'And you're going to talk to me about stealing?' "

That made our Principal Torres laugh—a much more common reaction from her than the anger she'd started out with. "Gracias por el cumplido, aunque sé que te estás felicitando a ti mismo más que a mí."

"Si tienes que ser la criatura de Sataná, por lo meno elegiste a ponerte una cara bonita."

The Spanish was picking up speed, the way it always does when Cubans get going. Seriously, for my people, Spanish isn't just a language, it's a race.

My Spanish was pretty rusty, since I'd only spoken it when Mami was alive. I wasn't able to keep up with the two Torreses anymore. And Vorágine couldn't squeeze in a word between them, the exchange was going so fast. Only Yasmany seemed to be following them now. He alternated between cracking up and covering his mouth every time they cussed, which was like every fifth word, because Cubans. (PS: I understood the swears. Dude, please. I just didn't catch enough of the other words to get what they were saying.)

Also, they were cracking each other up more and more, which made them even harder to understand. Principal Torres and her clone were belly-laughing. Yasmany, too. And Vorágine was bubbling more than a Jacuzzi.

"What. Is. Happening?" Gabi asked, stomping her foot.

Principal Torres let her last laugh empty itself of energy and wiped a tear from her eye. "We have come to an agreement."

Gabi and I looked at each other. "You have?" I asked.

Principal Torres nodded. "She and the other workers will allow you to retrieve Gladis."

Gabi did a triple take. "They don't think we're demons anymore?"

"No. I explained it to them. They just had never considered visitors from another universe as an option. Because, really, why would anybody?"

"That's why I used to call you *hechicero*," Yasmany said to me. "Black magic, I get. But I don't get any of this Spider-Verse [*BLEEP!*]."

The *BLEEP!* part was literally Vorágine covering up the swear word with a loud, perfectly timed bleep. "Language," it reminded Yasmany.

"Detention," added Principal Torres.

Yasmany stomped his foot. "Hey! Why ain't you bleep Principal Torres? She just cussed like a hundred times in a row in Spanish."

Vorágine gurgled defensively. "Principal Torres was engaged in a sensitive hostage negotiation. My righteous bleeping would have endangered that delicate diplomacy."

"Negotiations are complete," said Principal Torres. "We can go in and retrieve Gladis."

"So where is she?" Gabi asked.

For an answer, Principal Torres pointed at my wrist. We all looked at my smartwatch again. The Torres from that universe was pointing Gladis's phone at a huge metal-covered door. An industrial-refrigerator door.

"She's locked herself in there," said Principal Torres. She wasn't laughing anymore. "We need to get her out before she freezes to death."

There in the bathroom, Gabi and I relaxed a portal to the chicken universe into existence. Vorágine would keep it stable as we went through.

But before we did, I asked Principal Torres, "Can you see it?"

She wanted very much to be able to. She squinted with all her might. But she had to answer "No."

I turned to Yasmany. "Can you see it?"

I could tell he could before he answered. "That thing floating there, looks like floating sandwich wrap?"

"Yes. Do you . . . ?" I turned to Principal Torres as I spoke, to see if she would give him permission. "Do you want to try to go to the other universe with us?"

"[*BLEEP!*] yeah!" said Yasmany, earning himself another week of detention. He didn't wait for us. He ran through the portal.

Only in this case, *through* doesn't mean *through the portal and into another universe*, but *straight through the portal and into this universe's bathroom wall*. He basically did a vertical faceplant, stuck there a second, and then peeled himself off like a sticker.

"Are you okay?" asked Gabi, going up to him.

He was rubbing his forehead and nose, each with a different hand, but he looked more irritated than hurt. "Why ain't I go through?"

"I think getting doused in calamitron juice has given you THE SIGHT." Gabi opened her eyes wide and made tiger-claw fingers at Yasmany when she said *THE SIGHT*. "But to actually go through a portal, I think you have to learn to relax more."

"Hold up a cacasec," said Yasmany. "Ain't no one more relaxed than me." To prove it, he pinched Gabi's hat (which he was still wearing) with his thumb and forefinger, just like I had earlier.

That reminded Gabi to snatch her hat off his head and rest it atop her hairball. "Don't worry, Yas. Now that you have THE SIGHT, we will begin your training. It will be rigorous and painful. I'll make sure of that. But soon, you will be able to traverse the multiverse as easily as I."

Gabi sounded about ten billion times more confident than I was about teaching anything to anybody. But now wasn't the time for a debate. "We gotta go," I said.

"Sal," Principal Torres said. "Blood sugar?"

"A-OK," I said, pulling up the screen on my smartwatch so she could see for herself. I had tested it right before we went to meet Principal Torres in the hallway. I appreciate all the adults and toilets I have in my life to help me manage my diabetes, but really, dudes, you should know by now. Sal Vidón takes care of himself.

"Okay, good," Principal Torres phew-babied. "Now, stick to the plan. Say you're sorry to Ydania and the rest of the chicken workers for all the pranks you've pulled on them lo these many months. Then find Gladis. If it's our Gladis, great! Come right back. If it's the other Gladis, get her to help you find our Gladis. You have until 3:40 p.m. Eastern time in this universe. Got it?"

"Who's Ydania?" asked Gabi.

"That's Principal Torres's look-alike in the other universe," I said. I had learned her name back when I'd stuck my butt in her universe.

"It's also my middle name," said Dr. Gloria Ydania Torres, aka Principal Torres. "Isn't that, like, the weirdest coincidence?"

I'd actually thought it was weirder that her clone's name wasn't the same as hers. In my experience, names match across universes, so I'd always wondered why hers didn't.

But again, no time to discuss. Gabi and I, on three, went through the portal side by side.

And bumped into Ydania, who had been standing too close to the portal. "Sorry," I said automatically. Then, remembering my audience, I said, "Perdónanos, por favor."

Gabi picked up where I left off. "We apologize profusely and categorically for having tortured you and made you think we were evil spirits. For my part, that was never my intention. And as for Sal"—she looked at me, searching for something honest she could say—"he's also very sorry."

"¡Sí!" I said, like the word itself was an exclamation point.

Ydania had on a yellow apron over a white coat. She wore rubber boots that went to her knees with jeans tucked into them, yellow rubber gloves, and a hairnet that made her look like a Mario mushroom. She had glasses, too, like Principal Torres, but they were under safety goggles. Also, she had a belt with three long chef's knives holstered in it.

"Te perdonamos," Ydania said, and just like that, we were forgiven. Now that she wasn't yelling, her voice sounded almost exactly like Principal Torres's . . . if Principal Torres spent seven hours every day yelling at people. "Y te pedimos perdón a cambio."

"She's asking for us to forgive them, too," I whispered to Gabi.

"¡Te perdonamos!" said Gabi, arms wide. I might have

mentioned this in the past, but Gabi is very quick on the uptake.

Ydania and the rest of the chicken workers laughed and cheered. Relief ran through the chilly chicken-processing plant. Everyone was glad this accidental war between us was over.

Ydania stepped aside. In front of Gabi and me was the industrial refrigerator. "Se encerró de firme," said Ydania, pulling on the handle of the refrigerator to show us it was locked. "No lo podemos abrir."

"Yo puedo," I said.

Unlike other times today, when I'd made a big show of breaking the universe, this time I just quietly relaxed. Then I grabbed the refrigerator's handle. If anyone had examined it carefully, they would have seen it was a slightly different handle from the one that had been on the door a second ago. A quick cruise through the multiverse had revealed a bunch of refrigerator doors in this exact spot in a bunch of different worlds. A bunch of those had handles that were unlocked. So I temporarily stole one of them and, presto change-o switcheroo, Gladis, you're now free to goo. I mean go.

I pulled on the handle. The refrigerator door opened. There was PrankGladis.

She was hugging herself, her teeth chattering. Luckily, it looked like her universe's Cuban Americans had the same habit of overdressing that mine did. In both of our Miamis, if the temperature ever drops even one degree below sixty-seven, Cuban Americans start breaking out the fur coats. Those poor sandwiches would freeze to death in a Connecticut spring.

But thank goodness PrankGladis had on one of those coats

that look like the Michelin Man and a trash bag had a baby.

I knew it was PrankGladis, by the way, by the color of her coat. It was black. I had seen our Gladis earlier today, dressed very similarly, right down to the ugly Uggs. But her coat was red.

"SAL!" said PrankGladis, running out the refrigerator the second she saw me and giving me a big hug and rag-dolling me around. "Jou foun' me! Jou safe me! Jou are my 'ero! Ay, I so col'!"

"Here," I said, breaking the hug so I could withdraw her long-lost scarf from my trench coat and wrap it around her. "You're safe now."

PrankGladis looked around, a little fearful, a little curious. "Ay, thees crasy people threw cheekun a' me quando ese unicornio maldito barf me here."

Gabi stepped forward and got face-to-chin with PrankGladis. "They won't be throwing chickens anymore, sister, so you got nothin' to worry about from them. But you got plenty to worry about from me if you don't tell us what you did with the other Gladis."

In response, PrankGladis hugged Gabi. Big hugger, that PrankGladis. "I ang so, so sorrie!" she said, squeezing Gabi tight. "I was tryee to be nice! I jus' wan' to show Gladita how beautiful la vida es! And also I wan' my escarf back. So I try to tra'e her a ride on un unicornio for my escarf. But i' all backfire."

"You can say that again," said Gabi, squirming like a cat to get free of the embrace.

Ydania nudged me, and when I looked at her, she was

holding out PrankGladis's phone. I took it and immediately dangled it in front of PrankGladis. "Now it's time to make things right. Will you kindly contact your Sal, so he can help us fix all this?"

It wasn't even a minute later that a portal to a new universe opened up right in front of us. But Gabi and I didn't create it. This one was courtesy of PrankSal.

PrankSal had vertical eyebrows.

They looked like hairy parentheses on his forehead. When he waggled them, which he did a lot, they didn't move up and down. They went side to side, like windshield wipers.

They were, to say the bare minimum, disturbing. Even though I was standing in a different universe, at a different Culeco, in a field where nine giganto unicorns were peacefully grazing, I couldn't take my eyes off PrankSal's face.

"Why do you have vertical eyebrows?" I asked him.

He brought them together until they just about made a hair-circle on his forehead. "You like them? I discovered this universe, like, a week ago, where everybody has vertical eyebrows! I traded eyebrows with the Sal there."

And if you're wondering, like I was, how you "trade eyebrows" with someone, I got my answer by relaxing a little. Suddenly PrankSal's face revealed a connection extending to another universe, a highway of light leading to unknown realms. It was the same kind of connection Gabi and I had made for Baby Iggy to help Gabi's infant brother survive his autoimmune disease. But instead of using it to save lives,

PrankSal had connected himself to another Sal to give himself funky facial features.

PrankSal moved his eyebrows like two caterpillars square dancing. "Pretty cool, huh?"

"No, i's gross!" said PrankGladis. "I ha'e it, jou bi' weirdo!"

Then PrankGladis went up to PrankSal, and they hugged. But not like a sister hugging her brother. When my padres hug like that, I threaten to use the hose on them.

"I was so worried about you," said PrankSal, totally seriously, utterly unprankily.

PrankGladis separated from PrankSal just enough so she could put both hands on his face. And then they just stared into each other's eyes like there was nothing else to see in the entire multiverse.

Gabi and I turned to look at each other, too, but only so we could make frog faces and stick out the tips of our tongues.

"Jes, we datee," said PrankGladis, smiling at Gabi and me, all proud and sassy. "We haff so many a'ventures!"

"Is that your girlfriend?" PrankSal asked, chinning at Gabi. "What's her name?"

"Har, har, har," said Gabi, crossing her arms. "You know exactly who I am, Bubba. Now, where's the Gabi from this universe? She can help me fix this mess."

PrankSal moved his left eyebrow even lefter. "I don't know anyone named Gabi. Do you, Gladis?"

"Jus' tha' one," Gladis replied, chinning at Gabi.

Gabi evicted all the gerbils in her skull. "What?! There's

no Gabi in this universe?! No wonder you two are so out of control. There's no one here to keep you in line!"

"Oh, you sound like a ton of fun," said PrankSal, making and breaking the eyebrow-hair-circle on his forehead.

"Fun's over," I said. "We need our Gladis back."

"No prob, homie from another uni. I know how to find her, anywhere in the multiverse. Well, they do."

He gestured toward the unicorns.

They were massive, like Bane after he juices himself with Venom. Some were striped, others were spotted, and still others were patchy like cows, but they all had every color imaginable on their hides. Their horns grew out of weird parts of their bodies: their ears, their stomachs, their sides, their right nostrils. When the wind blew our way, I caught their smell. Dry barf and horse hide.

That stink. It was just like I remembered. I'd encountered unicorns before, back when I lived in Connecticut and didn't know how to control breaking the universe very well. One time, when I was trying to get my Mami Muerta back, I opened a hole so big that, well, unicorns could fit through it.

So they did. Constantly. A never-ending stream of unhousebroken unicorns. Eventually, we'd had to move.

Ah, memories.

"All I have to do is mount this mighty steed," PrankSal continued, walking toward the nearest creature. "Unicorns are herd animals. So they can always find one another, anywhere in the multiverse. Therefore, if we ride this big fella, he can take us to the unicorn your Gladis is riding, and problem solved."

"Great," said Gabi. "We have no time to lose. Since there's no Gabi here, I am temporarily declaring myself the official Gabi-guardian of this universe, as per Article III, Section Two of the bylaws of the Sisterverse. That means I am in charge." She walked determinedly toward the unicorn. "And, as your new leader, I say we get on this beautiful creature and find Gladis, ASAP."

PrankSal body-blocked Gabi before she got any closer. "Whoa, whoa, whoa there, Sparky. One does not simply walk up to a unicorn." He looked exactly like the Sean Bean meme when he said that. It's always nice when memes match in alternate universes. Makes the multiverse feel like one big happy information highway. "I'm the president of Culeco's Unicorn Equestrian Club. It was I who attracted unicorns from all over the multiverse to come and graze upon these green pastures. And it's my responsibility to ensure the safety of the students and the unicorns alike."

Geez, pal. Lay it on thick, much? What a showman.

Gabi wasn't buying it, either. "Principal Torres let you start a Unicorn Equestrian Club?"

"She doesn' know abou' i' yet," said PrankGladis. "I's a sorpresa!"

Yeah. That sounded way more like these two.

"Yep," said PrankSal, breaking off a piece of Pensacola Bahia grass and sticking it in his mouth so he would look extra cowboy as he spoke. "Riding this mighty steed is an art form unto itself. You have to show them who's boss. Guide them with a firm hand."

He patted the unicorn on the flank. In response, the unicorn slowly turned its head to look at PrankSal. Gave him a solid once-over, up and down and back up again.

And then it puked on him.

Like a fire hose. A fire hose that, instead of water, shot out rainbow horse barf. That blasted you into random other universes.

PrankSal was totally and completely gone.

"Um . . ." I said, turning to PrankGladis for advice about how to handle this seriously bad turn of events.

She was just shaking her head. "I swear he doss i' on poopose sometime. I's goiee to ta'e him a few hours to feegure ou' how to ge' ba' here."

"We don't have a few hours!" Gabi, stomping up to PrankGladis, pointed out. "We need to find our Gladis now!"

From behind me, a voice said, "The girl who went riding off on Carmita? I can help you find her."

Both Gabi and I slowly turned around to face the person who was talking to us.

Who turned out not to be a person at all but the unicorn that had just ejected PrankSal out of this reality.

"You can talk," I said.

The unicorn reared up, made a shocked face, and brought its front hooves to its cheeks. "You can hear!"

Gabi looked at her watch, made a scrunchie-mouth, and

then decided something. "You were saying you could help us?"

"Sure. It's just like that other Sal was saying. I know where Carmita is. I can take you right to her."

I raised my horizontal eyebrows. "Why should we trust you?"

It looked down its long, long nose at me. "Why shouldn't you trust me?"

"'Cause jou jus' barf my boyfrien' out of thees worl'!" said PrankGladis.

"Oh, right. Good times. But I won't barf on any of you, if you show me the proper respect. Did you see how that kid spanked me? He's lucky I didn't kick a couple of new horseshoe-prints into his forehead."

Luckily, Gabi was here, because if there's anyone who was born to butter up a mouthy unicorn, it was her. "My dear Equi-Cornius Maximus," she said, walking toward the horn-horse stooped and subservient, and making twirling gestures with her hands. "It would be the honor of a lifetime to be allowed to ride upon thy back and tour the multiverse, all in the service of returning a lost girl to her rightful place and time. I know that helping those in need will appeal to thy heroic nature. Tell me, O champion of the downtrodden, what is thy name?"

The unicorn was positively prancing in place after being plastered with Gabi's flattery, and its horn—which came straight out of its shoulder blades—quivered in delight, like a golf-course flag after a hole in one. "My name, milady," it said, bowing its head low, "is Norberto."

"A gallant name for a gallant soul. Willst thou helpest ustest?"

"I could do no less and still be worthy of thy bounteous panegyrics." Norberto knelt on one knee. "Come, milady, and mount thine eager steed, and together we shall rescue the fair maiden Gladis!"

Gabi got on Norberto like she was born on the back of a horse. In her trench coat and fedora, and yet sitting astride the unicorn, she looked like the cover of a genre-remix book I would like to read. Fantasy meets hard-boiled detective novel!

But the line she delivered to PrankGladis and me was straight out of the here and now. "Get on, losers. It's time to find the missing maiden."

"Hold on tight, kids!" said Norberto.

PrankGladis, in back, held on to my waist. I, in the middle, held on to Gabi's waist. And Gabi held on to the three-foot spiraling horn that shot out from between Norberto's shoulder blades.

"We're ready," said Gabi. "Let us spirit away with all the alacrity thy mighty equine legs can muster, Norberto."

The unicorn, loving every word that came out of Gabi's mouth, reared up on his hind legs, whinnied mightily, and barfed rainbows into the air. "We ride!" he said. And then we rode.

Straight into the sky.

Up and up and up we went, faster than a polychrome comet. Gabi and I figured out quick that we needed to tuck our hats away or we'd lose them. But that meant that pretty much all I could see was Gabi's hairball. Well, and taste it, too. "Gah yah paantsing haarbaal ahh aaf mah maff!" I yelled, which is what *Get yer pantsing hairball out of my mouth!* sounds like when your mouth is full of hairball.

She yelled something back, but I couldn't hear it—too much wind was storming over my ears. We got buffeted by turbulence. Frost started to form on the collar of my trench coat. Every time I inhaled, my lungs felt like I had two solid blocks of ice in my chest. And it was getting harder to breathe. The air was thinning.

Just as I was beginning to wonder how survivable this ride would be for non-unicorns, we punched through the fabric of spacetime and ended up in a wholly new spot in the multiverse.

I knew this instantly because the sky changed. It wasn't blue anymore, but yellow as sunlight. Below us, a layer of toasty-brown clouds, as poofy as biscuits, proceeded with the slow grace of elephants. We couldn't see land beyond them, they were so fat and thick.

But Norberto didn't seem bothered, since he didn't even ask if we were ready before he dive-bombed straight through them.

PrankGladis screamed in my ear. "Ay! Este unicornio maldito is going to keel us all!"

Spoiler: He didn't kill us all.

We busted through the layer of biscuit-clouds. They were strangely warm and spongy, and their texture made the roof of my mouth feel funny. On the other side, the land raced toward us so fast I could barely focus. The tears streaming out of my eyes didn't help, either.

And then, gently, one-hoof-at-a-timedly, we alighted on the ground. Like a four-footed swallow on a twig.

We had landed in a small circular clearing in a field of never-ending sunflowers. They were about the same height as those in my universe, but the blossoms were, like, five times as big. Like amazing flying-saucer sunflowers. Bumblebees the size of beavers crawled all over them, getting drunk off their nectar. When those bees flew, their buzzing sounded like cats purring. The breeze that was blowing through the sunflower stalks said *shh* the way a mami tries to comfort her crying hijo when he's scared. I smelled pear juice and grain on the wind.

It was the most peaceful place I had ever found myself, anywhere in the multiverse.

"Hey, Carmita," said Norberto before we saw anyone. "How's tricks?"

"Good," said Carmita the unicorn, emerging from the stalks. Her hide looked tie-dyed. She came trotting up to us, a two-foot horn jutting out of her right front knee. "Just acquired a new rider. Please meet my new human, Gladis."

And there she was, on Carmita's back: Gladis Machado. Our Gladis.

But not our Gladis at all.

She sat straight on the back of her multicolored mount. Her hair caught the breeze like a sail. She had that lift of the chin that princesses learn in how-to-be-a-queen school. Her ojo turco hung from a leather thong around her neck like a royal amulet.

This was not the Gladis I knew. When I'd first met her, way back at the start of the school year, Gladis had seemed pretty funny, pretty cool. But then she started thinking I was a brujo. Like, really and truly a practitioner of the dark arts. And so she turned on me, snap-of-the-fingers fast. She'd look at me suspiciously and clutch her anti-evil-eye amulet anytime I got near her. And everything I did just made the tension between us worse. (Example: I freaked her out by switching the scarf she was knitting with one that had an ojo turco knitted into it.)

But worst of all was the day she spent with PrankSal in the prank universe. When she came back from that little field trip across space and time, she was different. She constantly wore a worried look on her face. She was always opening her locker carefully, expecting something—someone, PrankSal—to pop out. She startled so easily now. Everything scared her. She never joked around anymore. She didn't come early to Culeco or stay for detention or try out for plays or do anything extracurricular. Her dad picked her up from school every day at 3:40 p.m.

She didn't hate me anymore—she thought I was the "brujo blanco" who was protecting her from PrankSal's "magia negra"—but she was a mere shadow of the person she'd been.

Now, riding Carmita, she was a shadow no more. Her aura was so regal she almost gave off light.

She said nothing. She was too royal to speak first. She stared at us, daring us to say anything.

It was PrankGladis who finally dared. But she didn't speak to Gladis—she slid off Norberto and marched toward Carmita, pointing a finger. "Jou bro'e jour word, unicornia maldita! We ha' a deal! Jou say jou were goin' to be nice to Gladita! An' den jou barf on me an' stole her!"

I mean, was she asking to get rainbow-horsebarf-hosed into another universe, like PrankSal?

But luckily, Carmita just pulled her head back defensively. "Anyone who would ride upon the back of a unicorn must needs prove their worth. They must stay mounted upon the splendid creature's back, no matter how much the mighty beast bucks and kicks, for one minute. Only then will they have proven that they are worthy. That is the unicorns' way."

"That is *not* the unicorns' way!" Norberto snorted back. "You totally just made that up. No other unicorn does that. Stop trying to make that a thing!"

Even more defensively, Carmita said, "Well, it's *my* thing."

"Her body, her rules," said Gabi, shrugging.

"I stayed on Carmita's back for a minute without getting thrown," said Gladis. Was her voice deeper than it used to be? She sounded like Ursula from *The Little Mermaid*. "I have proven I am worthy. Now Carmita and I have entered into a sacred bond. I am her human, and she is my unicorn. And we shall never be parted."

"Yeah," agreed Carmita. "Never!"

"That's not how this works," said Norberto. "That's not how any of this works."

Gladis ignored him. "We'll go wherever we want. Won't we, Carmita?"

"Anywhere you want, babe!"

"And if someone or something threatens us, we can make them disappear."

"I'll barf them back to the Big Bang!"

"Or else we'll disappear, and leave all danger behind."

"Blink of an eye, baby!"

Gladis sat up even straighter and, with the serenity of a vampire slayer after a good day of slaying, said, "I don't have to be afraid anymore. I refuse to be afraid anymore."

"Why are jou so afrai'?" PrankGladis asked Gladis. But the way she said it, I think she was finally understanding a little of what she and PrankSal and I had put Gladis through. And maybe she was starting to feel as horrible about it as I had for all these months.

But Norberto interjected before Gladis could answer. "Do you have hooves for brains, Carmita?! You're going to let this girl ride you all over the cosmos just because she stayed on your back for literally one minute?"

Carmita snorted. "The bond between maiden and unicorn is as ancient as time immemorial."

Through my jeans, I could feel Norberto's hide ripple in annoyance. "Those are just stories! That humans made up! To enslave unicorns!"

Carmita turned her head from Norberto and closed her eyes. She had beautiful rainbow eyelashes. "For a unicorn,

Norberto, you're such a pig. I am no human's slave. I bonded with Gladis of my own free will."

"And I," said Gladis, "have bonded my heart to Carmita's." She leaned forward and hugged Carmita's neck with all the love she had in her. "Que Dios bendiga esta unión."

"Great," said Gabi. "May Dios bendigas us all. But it's time to go home, Gladis."

Still hugging Carmita's neck, Gladis asked, "Home?" She said it in the same way the Sphinx might ask, *Are you my dinner, puny human?*

But indomitable Gabi wasn't intimidated. "Yes. Home. Back to our place and time."

Gladis straightened up and laughed. It was a spooky, faraway laugh, like an oracle who gets the punchline before anyone starts joking around. "I'm not going back to that small, poisonous place."

"But you have to."

Gladis shook her head at Gabi with a little bit of humor and a whole lot of smug. She looked down and smiled at Carmita, who craned her neck and snorted in agreement to whatever idea Gladis had communicated with just her eyes. They both faced forward and stared at us, all creepy and knowing.

And then they vanished.

"Oh, no you don't!" whinnied Norberto. And he vanished right after them. With me on his back. And with Gabi and PrankGladis *not* on his back.

"We have to go back for Gabi and PrankGladis!" I yelled in Norberto's ear, as I clutched the horn between his shoulder blades for dear life.

"We will," he said. "Just as soon as we catch Thelma and Louise."

"Who are Thelma and Louise?"

"Geez, kid. Watch a movie, will you?"

We were having this conversation in the middle of traveling to twenty universes a minute. Carmita and Gladis would appear in, say, the universe that was always half day and half night, and then, two seconds later, we'd appear there, too, because Norberto could always tell where Carmita was. I'd have just enough time to yell something like "Wait!" before they'd vanish again, this time, say, to the universe where musical instruments are actually monsters in disguise.

"Stop!" I yelled to them in the universe where mountains come to life and try to punch you in the face.

"Halt!" I begged Carmita and Gladis in the universe where geomancers keep space stations in orbit around gas giants via the careful manipulation of ley lines.

"Just a moment of your time, friends!" I pleaded in the universe with so many different shades of green, I was just about to name it the greeniverse, until Norberto explained that it wasn't a new universe at all—it was just Ireland.

"¡Un momento, por favor!" I beseeched them in the universe where you could trap a ghost in spoiled honey.

"IT'S *SAP!*" yelled Gum Baby so loud that everyone in every universe heard her.

Fine. Whatever. A universe where you could catch a ghost with sap that looks and smells exactly like spoiled honey.

The point is, they didn't stop there, either. "For the love of everything that's holy, please listen to me!" I implored them in the universe with no stars or suns or any kind of light at all.

"I'm listening," Gladis said.

"Oh," I said. By this point, I was kind of expecting this chase would never end. "Okay. Well. Do you think we could go to a universe where there's a little more illumination?"

"It's here or nowhere," she said.

Here is *nowhere*, I thought. I could tell the lower half of my body was still there, since I had my legs wrapped around a unicorn. But the top half felt like it was guttering out of existence like a candle flame. I put my hands in my hair to keep my head from disappearing. "Mostly, I just wanted to say I'm sorry."

"Oh, no, Sal," she said. And she sounded a little closer to me when she spoke next. "You don't have to be sorry. You've been a good friend to me. You've been protecting me from the other Sal all this time."

"Not very well. That other Gladis came to see you, and I didn't even know."

Even closer. "She was trying to help me, too! And she did! She introduced me to Carmita. And Carmita"—I could hear her hugging the unicorn's neck again—"Carmita has given me the cosmos!"

"We're just getting started, babe!" Carmita answered her.

I could feel Gladis thinking, so I didn't interrupt, and a

little later she added, "I'm starting to get it. I'm starting to get you, Sal."

"Me?"

"What you can do. How you do your tricks. It's not black magic, is it?"

I rubbed my face. It was like I could make it reappear by touching it. "It's not magic at all. It's science. Science that nobody fully understands, but science."

She laughed. "This is a miracle, Sal! A gift from God! Unicorns exist." It was such an incredible thing to say that she had to say it again. "Unicorns exist."

"But," said Norberto, "we're way different from your made-up stories about us."

"Yeah," I said. "You're a lot barfier."

"I like human stories about unicorns," said Carmita. "I want to be more like those stories."

"Me too," said Gladis. "People in stories are brave."

"It's easy to be brave," said Norberto, "when you don't exist for real!"

Gladis's voice never wavered. "It's been so long since I've felt brave. That's why I can't go back, Sal. I can't go back to being that squashed, small person."

I didn't know how to answer that. So I just let my hands fall away from my face. Doing that made me feel like it was easier to channel Mami. And I needed her now. She always knew the right thing to say.

I eventually said, and I almost didn't know I was saying it, "If you don't go back, you'll always be afraid."

Silence. Deadness. Eternity.

And then, a still, small voice: "What do you mean, Sal?"

I took a breath and wondered briefly how breathable air could exist in a universe with no light, so no trees photosynthesizing, so no atmosphere. Ah well. "Running away is underrated. It can save your life so you can live to fight another day. I don't blame you at all for taking the first horse out of our universe and into the unknown. But you also have to think about what you're losing. What you're leaving behind."

She blew air out of her nose, hard. Like a horse. "What am I leaving behind, Sal? Being afraid all the time?"

I answered slow and simply. "Your dad."

Her answer was more a breath than a word. "Dad."

Gladis's dad loved her. I'd seen him lots of times when he came to pick her up at exactly 3:40 p.m. He always looked so worried about her. He'd come in so often, before school and after, to talk to Principal Torres. He must have known something big was going on, but he didn't know how to help. So he just loved her and was ready at any moment to do anything he could, as soon as he found out what that was. It's what Papi did for me when I lost Mami, and what American Stepmom has done for me since she became part of our family. And I knew, when you have someone who loves you that much, that the last thing you want to do is make them suffer.

"If you never go home," I said, "then your dad will never be happy again."

"Who are you talking to?" asked Norberto.

"Um, Gladis?"

"She and Carmita left right after she said 'Dad.'"

I slapped my hands over my useless-in-this-universe eyes. "Why didn't you follow them?"

The unicorn under me shrugged. "I felt like you were having a moment. Unicorns are very empathetic, you know."

"Well, that makes up for their lack of brains, then."

He tensed. "Don't make me barf you into the universe that is just one big sun."

I grabbed on to his horn. "Can we go now, please?"

He snorted. "Since you said *please*."

And then, *bink!* We disappeared out of the universe with no stars or suns or any kind of light at all.

And reappeared at home.

Specifically, we reappeared near Culeco's student pick-up area, where parents swing by to drive their kids home after school. It's one of those huge half-circle driveways, and it has a covered waiting area and outlets to charge your phone or computer at every bench. Also, right now, it had Gladis.

She was alone. Norberto and I could only see her from the side, and only if we peeked around the massive tree we were hiding behind. The unicorn had wisely chosen to make us materialize in a grassy area a good hundred yards away, in a copse of evergreen trees near the school building. The pine needles that carpeted the ground even hushed Norberto's hooves a little.

Whatever I had said about unicorns' lack of brains before, he was a pretty smart equine, that Norberto. And I told him so, patting his side.

"Thank you, Sal," he replied. "Sorry I snapped at you. You're all right, for a human."

I pulled a CIA-grade mini-yet-ultra-powerful surveillance telescope out of a trench-coat pocket to get a better look at Gladis. She was dreamingly gazing at her phone. "Well," I said, low-voiced, "Gladis is back where she belongs. But where's Carmita?"

"Here!" said Carmita, trotting up behind us on her tiptoes. Tip-hooves. Whatever. "And look who I brought back with me!"

It was Gabi. And PrankGladis. And PrankSal.

"The gang's all here," I said, a little confused. Why were PrankGladis and PrankSal here?

PrankGladis read my mind. "I brou' Sal wi' me so we can apologize to Gladita. I didn' realize how ba' we messed wi' her head. I feel terREEbleh!"

"Yeah," said PrankSal. "I thought it was all just innocent fun. I'm real sorry." And then he made his vertical eyebrows do a little cobra dance.

"I'm watching you, Bubba," said Gabi, sliding off Carmita and, feet on the ground, turning to face him. "Remember, I'm the duly-appointed Gabi of your universe now. You start pulling your usual cacaseca, you're going to have to answer to me."

He made his lips burst like a balloon. "Sal Vidón answers to no one."

Just then, his phone went off. Smugly to Gabi he said, "Oh, a thousand pardons, but I have a very important call." As he pulled it out of his pocket, he didn't even look at the caller ID.

He just answered it and pressed it to his ear. "Yellow, it's Sal. Who dis?"

"Is jour woman," said Gladis, talking into her own phone. "An' I telli' jou tha' jou betta leesin to Gabi, or jou goin' to answer to me!"

PrankSal slowly pulled the phone away from his ear. He looked at PrankGladis, who was nodding at him like he was her sandwich artist at Subway. Then he looked at Gabi, who breathed on her nails and polished them against the lapel of her trench coat. And then he kind of didn't know what to do with himself.

"Now that that's settled, Sal," Gabi said to me, "let's have a situation report." And then, sounding less like a general and more like a person, she asked, "Is Gladis okay?"

I saw then that Gladis's dad's car was pulling into the pick-up area. Instinctively, I started putting my spy telescope to my eye again. But then I handed it to Gabi. "See for yourself."

She took it and locked onto the car. And just like I knew she would, she started narrating. "Okay, Gladis's dad is getting out of the car. He's coming around to greet her—oh, but Gladis is running toward him. She's airborne! He catches her! Oh, it's like a movie! He swings her around once, and then he sets her back on the ground. Gladis is explaining things to him in a really excited way. Oh, she looks happy! And her poor dad is, like, stunned. Like, *Who are you and what have you done with my daughter?* But he's smiling. Okay, Gladis grabs his hand, and she's pulling him toward the school. He's pointing to his car like, *But my keys are still in there!* or something—I don't know; I can't read lips. But Gladis doesn't care. She's just pulling him back into Culeco. They're inside. And the doors have shut behind them." She slapped my telescope shut and handed it back to me. "And if you didn't know, now you know."

PrankGladis started to dismount. "Okay, well, we haf to go after her, to say we sorry."

Just then, I got a text on my smartwatch. It was from Gladis.

Sal? Are you back yet? I'm in detention. I want you to meet my dad.

"Gladis," I said to PrankGladis, "you know what? Maybe you can apologize tomorrow."

"Why?" she asked.

Somehow, Gabi got exactly what I was thinking. "Because we should ask Gladis if she wants an apology. If she even wants to talk to you. She gets to set the terms."

"Oh," said PrankGladis, deflating a little. "Jes, okay. Tha's fair. I' ma'e me sad, bu' okay."

"Hey," said PrankSal, "if she doesn't want an apology, fine with me. I'm not sure what I'm even supposed to be apologizing for. I swear, some people can't take a joke."

Gladis looked at Gabi, and Norberto looked at me, and Carmita looked at both of us, and Gabi and I looked at each other. At the same time, all five of us nodded.

Carmita bucked. PrankSal flew in the air. And Norberto lasered him out of this universe with a precision blast of unicorn barf.

We all stood for a moment, blinking happily at the spot where PrankSal had been. It was Carmita who finally broke the silence. "He didn't even last one second on my back. He is unworthy of riding unicorns."

"Well, I'll be," said Norberto. "The system works."

Carmita took a bow.

"Where di' jou sen' him?" PrankGladis asked Norberto.

"Did you know," Norberto replied, "that there's a Universe Where Every Single Person Is Gabi Reál?"

Gabi squeed like a piglet. "WHAT?! I WANT TO GO! TAKE ME THERE, PLEASE, PLEASE, PLEASE?!"

"You," said Norberto, "are worthy, milady. Hop on."

Gabi's legs couldn't run to Norberto fast enough. "Tell everyone in detention I had an emergency meeting that I simply could not miss, Sal!"

"I betta go, too," said PrankGladis, resigned. "I shou' bring wha'ever' lef' of Sal home, af'er all the Gabis tear him to pedasos. Gimme a ride, unicornia chévere?"

"It would be an honor, milady," said Carmita, taking a knee to make it easier for her to mount.

The humans waved their hands, Carmita waved the horn on her knee, and Norberto gave me one of those nods that former enemies who are now friends give each other. And then, with a *bink*, they vanished.

I turned toward Culeco and, as I walked, I texted Gladis.

b there in a min just gonna steal ur dads car

The response was almost immediate.

OMG please! Then we won't have to drive around in that old lady car anymore. Can you steal us a Tesla while you're out?

That was the first joke she had made in my general direction since the beginning of school. It made me smile, yeah. But the wash of relief that ran through me? That was the good stuff. That felt like a brand-new start.

Beware the Grove of True Love

ROSHANI CHOKSHI

THE MOMENT ARU SHAH stepped out of the portal and into the Night Bazaar of the Otherworld, she knew it was bound to be a bad day.

By all accounts, everything *should* have been fine. The split sky of the Otherworld was the same as always: half day and half night. From where she stood on top of a hill, the glittering valley below—full of kiosks and shops that might sell anything from expired luck to a string of dreams—looked like jewels spilled onto a blanket. As usual, a sense of magic wavered in the air. Sometimes it reminded Aru of the scent of blown-out birthday candles, the way the world is supposed to smell after a wish. Other times, it felt like the morning of every holiday rolled into one. Ordinarily, she felt like she could breathe easier in the Otherworld, surrounded by magic and wonder. . . .

But today was no ordinary day.

A loud *pop!* sounded next to her. When Aru looked to her right, her Pandava sisters Mini and Brynne appeared. Mini adjusted her glasses. Today, she was wearing elbow pads, kneepads, and a bulky brown hat that made her look kind of like a small moose. Beside her, Brynne was wearing football gear, and two black lines were smeared under her eyes.

"'Sup, Shah."

Aru frowned. "What's with the . . . getups? Am I missing something?"

"Don't worry, I brought a helmet for you."

"Uh—"

Before Aru could get out another word, Brynne pulled a shiny white helmet from her duffel bag and tossed it to her. The headgear caught Aru in the stomach and she wheezed. Vajra shimmered on her wrist, as if annoyed to have been woken up by the sound.

"It's game time," Brynne said, clapping her hands. "You guys ready?"

"Are we *ever* ready for this day?" Mini sighed and bit her nails, her foot tapping nervously as she scanned the split sky. "Seriously! We said we were sorry. Why do we have to keep doing this?"

By *this*, Mini meant the dreaded weekly Errand Day. It was punishment, the Council had explained, for the Pandavas' grave insult to Urvashi. What was the "grave insult"? Falling asleep in the middle of her lecture on love stories last month.

Urvashi, the most powerful of all celestial dancers, had *not* been amused.

"Oh, let me guess," Urvashi had snapped when the three of them had jolted awake. "You think that simply because I teach *dance* and *poetry* that these things mean nothing compared to swinging around weapons and jumping through obstacle courses?"

"What? No!" said Aru.

Urvashi glared.

"Maybe a little . . ." mumbled Aru, sinking into her seat.

Brynne, as usual, was the most vocal of the three.

"This is all super important and stuff," she'd said flippantly, "but we're supposed to be training to fight the Sleeper's *demon* army, which is ridiculously dangerous! No offense, but *love* isn't dangerous."

"We're so sorry!" squeaked Mini. "Please ignore Brynne! She . . . She hit her head."

No I didn't! said Brynne through the Pandava sisters' mind link.

One more word, and I *will make it a fact!* replied Mini.

Urvashi regarded them quietly. She arched one perfect eyebrow and folded her arms. "So you don't think love is dangerous?"

"I didn't say that," said Aru. "Brynne—"

But it was too late.

Urvashi was determined to teach them a lesson. And as punishment, the Pandavas had to complete five errands for her. Aiden, who had totally fallen asleep in the middle of the class, too, was excused from coming in on Sundays for Errand Day.

"*He* is of apsara descent," said Urvashi primly. "*He* knows the dangers at hand. It's *you* three who need to learn."

Rude.

At first, Urvashi's tasks had sounded pretty easy. Pick up some dry cleaning? No biggie. Deliver a bottle of perfume to a friend of Urvashi? Sure.

WRONG.

Turned out *everything* Urvashi owned was powerfully enchanted. When the Pandavas had gone to get her dry cleaning, they'd ended up getting attacked by the silks, which reared up into a fifty-foot-high ten-headed lizard. It wouldn't stop trying to strangle them until Brynne and Aru figured out a way to scare it with store-bought detergent. And that was just the first errand.

The next had led to a herd of mechanical bulls nearly stampeding them when Mini accidentally dropped a vial of ensorcelled perfume. Then there was the time they almost drowned while picking up Urvashi's special "vitamin water."

The fourth errand should've been easy. It was just replying to her fan mail, after all.

But even the letters were bewitched, which led to the Pandavas getting trapped in a room with envelopes that alternately professed their undying love, tried to gnaw on Aru's ankle, or ripped themselves to shreds because the beautiful apsara hadn't bothered to respond.

It.

Was.

Traumatizing.

Their demigod weapons had been useless, and they'd finished each errand beat up, tired, and, in Brynne's case, extremely hangry.

"I'm not taking *any* chances," said Brynne now, as they

faced their fifth and final task. "This time, *nothing* is going to go wrong. We are finishing this last errand within *one* hour and then we'll be done!"

"Knock on wood," said Aru.

Mini turned around on the spot, panicking. "We don't have any wood!"

"Just knock on your skull!" said Brynne.

"My skull is not made of wood!"

"GIRLS!" shouted a voice from high above.

Aru, Brynne, and Mini looked up to see Boo flying toward them. Their pigeon mentor landed on his favorite place: Aru's head.

He pecked her affectionately.

"Ow!" said Aru, batting at him.

"Haven't we been through *enough*?" demanded Brynne. "Urvashi has made her point! I get it! Every single time we've gone on an errand for one of her dancing things or love charms, we've gotten brutally attacked. Message received."

"That's hardly the message," said Boo drily. "Urvashi may be a touch petty—"

Aru coughed loudly.

"Fine, *more* than a touch when it comes to slights or insults, but don't forget that she is wise beyond belief. She is a Council member for a reason, and may understand things you do not. *All* of us are trying to prepare you for the threat of war."

"Maybe we can use all the poetry to bore our enemies to death," said Aru.

Brynne laughed.

Boo pecked Aru's ear, and she winced again.

"What is it this time?" asked Mini, taking a deep breath. "Don't tell me she has a pet snake we have to feed or something. . . ."

"Your mission—"

"Should you choose to accept it," said Aru.

"There is no choice here," said Boo sternly.

"I know that! It's from *Mission: Impossible*."

"I would not say this mission is impossible."

"It's a movie—" Aru tried to say, but Boo spoke over her.

"Urvashi's gunghroos have been sent for cleaning," said Boo. "Kindly retrieve them and return them to her."

Aru paused, waiting. . . .

"Is that it?" asked Mini.

"That's it," said Boo.

"Just grab her anklet bells?" repeated Aru, to be sure.

"Take the bells and bring them back."

Huh, thought Aru. She had seen Urvashi's enchanted gunghroo bells before, and of all the things the apsara owned, they were perhaps the least terrifying. The anklets did nothing except chime prettily. It was said they were made from the silver of moonbeams and the sound of shooting stars. They didn't lure in unsuspecting feral animals or turn into menacing shapes.

Aru looked at her sisters. Mini's shoulders sagged in relief. Brynne shrugged, pulling off her shoulder pads.

"Fine," Aru said to Boo. "Bring it on."

"Is this where we're supposed to be?" asked Mini, looking around.

An hour had passed since Boo had given them Urvashi's assignment, directions to the pick-up spot for her anklets, and a lotus flower that was supposed to grant them entry to the special shopping center.

"Yep," said Brynne, crossing her arms. "Trust me, I *always* know my directions."

Aru believed her, but the location still seemed a little weird. The Otherworld was a bit like a quilt of separate locations from all around the multiverse. This particular spot, on one of the forested edges, was far away from the familiar tents and kiosks of the Night Bazaar. Dark and cool, it lay deep within the stretch of land where the chakora birds roosted. The sky above was the color of dust, and dozens of bone-white trees jutted up from the ground.

The Pandava sisters stood before a little black pond. Mini held out the lotus flower Boo had given them. He'd said that it would grant them entrance to the mall, but it wasn't like there was anyone waiting for a flower.

"Maybe just drop it in the water?" suggested Aru.

"If it doesn't work, I can blow it dry and then we can try something else," said Brynne, tapping her wind-mace necklace.

"Here goes," said Mini. She stretched out her arm and plopped the lotus into the pond.

The moment the pink flower touched the surface, glowing concentric circles bloomed around it. The ground beneath their feet trembled and began to rotate. The white trees grew taller, arcing over the Pandavas like a birdcage. The Otherworld shifted around them like the gears of a clock whirring into place. One moment, they were by a tiny pond, and the next . . .

They were in a glamorous building that resembled a giant greenhouse. The white trees, now inside, formed a glittering net above them. From their silvery branches hung jewels in the shapes of various fruits. The floor was polished marble, and through the perimeter of windows, Aru could see into different lands. Some of the windows faced skyscrapers, some revealed jungles, and others looked out over sunny pastures or craggy cave walls.

"This way!" said Brynne. "I see the sign for the jewelry-repair shop!"

Down the center of the greenhouse was a neat row of boutiques. Above them, enchanted signs blinked in the air. Aru and Mini followed their sister, stepping around—or sometimes ducking beneath—denizens of the Otherworld who walked or floated through the mall. Most of them looked like members of the heavenly court of Amaravati. There were gandharvas with golden skin and wings like stained glass, and beautiful apsaras snapping their fingers at attendants who carried armloads of silks and perfumes. All the visitors seemed to enter and exit through an open window here and there, but there was one gaping doorway that stuck out like a sore thumb.

"What is that?" asked Mini, looking closer.

As they walked past, Aru read the little sign in gold hovering above it:

THE GROVE OF TRUE LOVE

What did *that* mean? Aru wondered.

She imagined that if they were to step through the archway, they'd find rows of candles and Hallmark gift cards. But when she peered inside, all she saw was a long, shadowy passage. Aru shuddered as a wave of cold washed over her.

"C'mon, Shah," said Brynne, yanking on her wrist. "I've heard of that place. Apparently, it's cursed."

"Whoa! Really?" asked Aru.

Brynne rolled her eyes. "I think that's all made-up."

"Um, cursed?" asked Mini in a small voice.

"Like I said, it's probably nothing," scoffed Brynne. "Who's ever heard of a 'grove of true love' being dangerous?"

"Love *can* be dangerous," said Mini. "People can actually die of broken hearts. It's called *takotsubo cardiomyopathy*."

"People are weak," said Brynne.

Aru frowned. She didn't believe that. With a sharp pang, she thought of all the things her mom had been through with her parents and the Sleeper. Her mom was definitely heartbroken, but Aru didn't think her mom's sadness made her weak. If anything, it made her the opposite, because, no matter what had happened to her, she chose to keep trying.

"What I *really* want to know is why anyone thought it was

a good idea to put some potentially dangerous grove next to a shopping plaza!" said Mini. "That's *got* to drive up their insurance premiums. What about liability?"

"I don't think they have lawsuits here," said Aru. "Complainers could get turned into a rock for ten years or something."

Mini looked shocked, but Brynne didn't seem to care. "Apsaras love this area, and they're ridiculously petty," she said. "They probably send their exes into that place as punishment."

"Then why do they call it the Grove of True Love?" asked Aru, staring over her shoulder at the dark archway.

The farther they moved from it, the more Aru felt like she was being watched.

Brynne shrugged. "Apparently, if you make it out, you'll get some hint of who your true love is or whatever. Honestly, I'm sure it's just a hoax. But it's not like we're ever going to find out. I *refuse* to set foot in there."

"Because you're scared?" asked Aru, smirking.

"No!" snapped Brynne. "Because it's ridiculous!"

What happened next was . . . honestly, totally, completely . . . an accident.

Getting Urvashi's gunghroos was easy enough.

Perhaps even too easy.

Which was all to say Aru Shah firmly believed that what happened next was absolutely *not* her fault.

The moment the repair yaksha saw them, he handed an ivory box to Mini and sent them on their way.

"That's it?" asked Aru. "No pit of vipers? No sudden quicksand?"

"There's *quicksand* here?" asked Mini, looking around nervously.

"Score!" said Brynne. "Last errand is officially *done*. No more punishment. No more attacks. No more getting up early on a Sunday!"

Aru eyed the box under Mini's arm. "That's not how Urvashi usually operates."

"Yeah . . ." said Mini. "I dunno, Brynne, I think we're missing something. What if these aren't really her bells?"

Brynne resolutely kept marching forward. She was almost past the creepy grove when Mini said, "What if this is a setup and Urvashi makes us go on *five more* errands?"

That got Brynne's attention. She stopped short, her shoulders sagging. "Ugh," she said, turning to face them. "So what do we do?"

"I say we look inside the box and just *make sure* they're Urvashi's," said Aru.

"Are we supposed to do that?" asked Brynne. "Last time I checked, Urvashi hates when people mess with her things."

"It's just a tiny peek!" said Aru.

Brynne scowled. "*One* peek."

"Just the one," agreed Aru.

Mini set the box on the ground, and the three Pandavas knelt next to it. The ivory container was the size of a laptop case and secured with a simple gold latch that popped open when touched. Aru held her breath, Vajra squirming on her wrist. Brynne drew her wind mace and pointed it at the box. Mini winced a little as she eased it open. . . .

A hint of magic rose in the air. It sounded like the moment after a bell is rung and the chime lingers in your ears. There, sitting on a bed of trim red velvet, were Urvashi's gunghroos. Aru recognized them immediately. From the two wide silver bands dangled sparkling jingle bells the size of acorns. Aru let out a sigh of relief.

"See?" said Brynne. "You worried for nothing! They're perfectly fine and definitely hers."

"True," said Mini.

"The *really* important question is . . . what do we eat after this?" asked Brynne. "Sweet or savory? I really want a falafel."

"I don't like falafel," said Mini.

"Who doesn't like falafel?" asked Brynne.

"I could go for some ice cream," said Aru.

The Pandavas were in the middle of discussing the merits of falafel versus ice cream when Mini's eyes went wide.

"Um . . . guys?"

"I *still* think—" started Brynne when Mini pointed at something in the distance.

Aru looked up. Fifty feet away, and drifting lazily toward the archway of the grove, were a pair of anklets.

"That's weird," said Aru. "Because they look a lot like . . ."

Aru glanced down at the box lying at their feet. She could've sworn Mini had closed it before they'd started arguing about food, but no. . . . The box was open.

And empty.

"Get those bells!" shouted Aru.

Brynne spun her wind mace, directing a jet of air toward the gunghroos, but that only made them fly away faster.

"Block them, Mini!" said Aru.

She tapped her wrist, and Vajra transformed into a lasso. Aru twirled her lightning bolt over her head, aiming it straight at the bells. At the same time, Mini used her Death Danda and created a shield, trying to block off the entrance to the grove. . . .

BOOM!

Aru's lightning whip smacked against the violet sphere of Mini's shield. Light burst in the air, disorienting Brynne, who nearly lost her balance while Aru fell and landed on her butt. She tried to look around, but her vision was filled with bright spots.

"Oh no," whimpered Mini.

Aru rubbed her eyes. At that exact moment, Urvashi's gunghroos disappeared into the Grove of True Love.

"Now what do we do?" asked Mini.

Aru's and Brynne's eyes met, and Aru realized that she and her sister were having the same awful thought:

"We have to get them back."

Aru couldn't see anything past the threshold. It was as if the entrance was obscured by a magical screen. On the other side, she could detect the shapes of huge figures. . . . Were those statues? Guards?

Demonic things that would slice her in half the second she crossed?

Brynne cleared her throat. "Who's going first?"

"NOSE GOES!" shouted Aru and Mini, simultaneously clamping their hands over their noses.

Brynne glared at them. "You guys are chickens."

"Yeah, well, you're the only one who can actually turn into one," muttered Aru.

"Come on," said Brynne, taking one step inside.

Aru followed. Vajra had twisted into a wriggling current of electricity that clambered up and down her arm.

Stop fidgeting, Vajra.

The bolt zapped her.

The moment Aru entered, the space took shape. It was a stand of Moringa trees. Encircling the trees were statues of women carved out of black stone. They stretched out their glossy hands, and Aru could hear them whispering.

Please, do not leave me. . . .

I would do anything for you. . . .

I love you. . . .

The sound raised the hairs on the back of her neck. She turned in a slow circle, her lightning bolt raised to defend herself, but no one attacked them. Over the whispering came the faint chime of Urvashi's bells.

"Hey!" yelled Brynne. "Give that back!"

A sharp hiss came from the branches overhead, followed by a crackly voice.

If you fix this tale of love gone wrong,
I will return this pretty song.

Urvashi's bells chimed loudly.

If you fail, then you will see
That from my grove you cannot flee.

"Okay, hold up a minute!" shouted Aru.

But her words were carried away in a strange wind that blew through the grove. One of the statues opened her hands wide. The ground beneath Aru, Brynne, and Mini rose slightly, tipping them toward the statue, which was now glowing brightly.

Into the tale of love you go!
Watch yourselves, or there'll be woe!

"THIS ISN'T PART OF THE ERRAND!" hollered Brynne, but the Grove of True Love didn't seem to mind or care.

Fix this tale of love gone wrong. . . .

Aru had no idea what that meant, but before she could puzzle over it, her consciousness was sucked elsewhere. She felt as though she were falling down a tunnel of emotions. *Scenes.* As if she were rifling through the book of someone else's life.

The first page:

A beautiful young woman with nut-brown skin was standing beneath a banyan tree in a dark and ancient forest. Beside her was a handsome young man with a crown. The girl wore clothes that Aru had only ever seen on ancient statues or in old paintings that her mom displayed in the museum.

"*I will return for you, Shakuntula,*" said the man. He took off one of his rings and gave it to her.

Shakuntula! thought Aru. Aiden had told them about the story ages ago, but now Aru couldn't remember how he'd said it ended.

The second page:

Months flashed by, and Shakuntula was in a remote hut surrounded by wild animals. A man with a long white beard approached her from behind as she sat on the threshold gazing at the open road. Aru recognized the man immediately. It was Sage Durvasa, a powerful holy man with a terrible temper.

"*Shakuntula!*" he called.

But the young woman didn't respond, seemingly lost in thought. The two attendants beside her looked around nervously and tried to get her attention. Shakuntula sighed, twirling the king's golden band on her finger.

Durvasa scowled. The shape of his body suddenly seemed outlined in flames. "*How dare you not greet me!*"

Shakuntula startled, turning around swiftly as if she had only just now noticed the sage. "*Oh!*"

"*How forgetful you are in your duties!*" said Durvasa. He raised his hand in warning. "*May the person you are thinking of forget you, too!*"

The third page:

Aru still felt as though she was falling, and now she felt *mad* too. So *what* if Shakuntula was daydreaming? She didn't deserve a curse like that!

Apparently the sage thought so, too.

After Shakuntula broke down weeping, Durvasa winced in regret. "*Perhaps . . . Perhaps that was a touch hasty.*"

Ya think? Aru wanted to say, but it would be like yelling at a memory.

"*Show him the ring he gave you,*" the sage said, "*and your husband, Dushyanta, will remember you at once.*"

Uh-oh. Aru had a bad feeling about where this story was headed.

The scenes flashed forward. . . . Shakuntula and her band of attendants made their way to Dushyanta's kingdom. She was dressed in all her finery, her husband's ring gleaming brightly on her finger. To reach his land, they had to cross a river.

"Make sure that ring is on super tight, lady!" Aru shouted, but it made no difference.

One moment Shakuntula was smiling at the water, absentmindedly dragging her fingers across its surface.

The next, she shrieked, "*Oh no! My ring!*"

The fourth page:

Shakuntula stood in the halls of a golden palace. Aru heard her pleading loudly, pointing at the empty space on her finger. Tears streamed down her lovely face. On the throne before her sat King Dushyanta, frowning.

"*That is preposterous!*" he said. "*If I had a queen, I am sure I would know it. I don't understand why you would attempt such a strange jest, but it does not please me. Leave my kingdom at once!*"

The page turned once more. . . .

Aru fell to the ground on her side, the sunshine slanting into her eyes. She blinked, then slowly righted herself. She, Brynne, and Mini were sitting on the grassy bank of a wide river.

"That was *so* depressing," said Mini, sniffing loudly. "I can't believe he just turned her away like that!"

"Um, we are *trapped* in a story!" said Brynne. "*That's* what's depressing! Although, honestly, I'd seriously like to punch that king."

Aru shook herself, her hand flying to her chest. For a moment, she had really believed she was Shakuntula. She had experienced the heartache of being forgotten, the rush of hot shame in her face as she was turned away. Aru felt as if all the color had been drained out of the world, and she would do anything to get it back.

"How do we get home?" asked Mini, looking around them. "Wait. . . . I feel like we've been here before."

Aru looked around, recognition falling into place. This was the same river Shakuntula had crossed. . . . It must be the spot where she had lost her ring! Aru stood up on her tiptoes so she could see over the rolling green hills. Sure enough, the king's palace gleamed in the distance. It couldn't be more than a half hour's walk away.

Fix this tale of love gone wrong. . . .

"We have to get the ring back!" said Aru. "That's how we fix the story! If we find the ring and give it to Dushyanta, he'll remember Shakuntula."

"Which will make the Grove of True Love give us back Urvashi's anklets," said Mini. "And then we'll get out of . . .

ancient India?" She tugged her collar over her nose, glaring. "What if there's some old, forgotten strand of pollen that makes my sinuses act up? Or what if there's unclassified bacteria in the water?"

"This whole thing is probably just one big illusion!" said Brynne, kicking at the dirt.

Just then, a wide shadow fell over the Pandavas.

Aru noticed that the river, just ten feet away, had stopped churning so loudly. Slowly, she turned to face the water. . . .

And that's when she saw a pale pink snake, at least a hundred feet high, rearing up. The monstrous creature tilted its head to the side and flicked out its forked tongue. Its eyes were bright as garnets.

"Just an illusion, right?" squeaked Mini.

"ATTACK!" yelled Brynne.

She spun her wind mace, aiming it at the towering reptile. The snake neatly dodged the jet streams. Then . . . it *giggled*, making the river bubble up around its belly.

"Play!" it said.

"Wait, what?" said Aru.

The snake's voice was oddly high-pitched. Like a child's. The creature flopped onto the riverbank and wove toward them.

"Shield!" shouted Mini, pointing her Death Danda at it.

A protective sphere formed over the Pandavas.

The snake didn't seem to mind—it just coiled around them. Its pink scales pushed against the shield, and small cracks began to appear.

"On my count, Mini, lower the shield and I'll blast the snake," said Aru, transforming her bracelet into a lightning bolt.

Mini nodded.

"One . . . two . . ." said Aru, aiming the bolt. "THREE!"

Mini dropped the shield. Brynne kicked up a cyclone of dust, which spun in the air. The next moment, Aru seared the snake's pale belly with Vajra.

"OW!" said the snake, flopping backward about ten feet.

In a burst of pink light, it shrank until it was the size of a garden snake. It sniffed loudly, then raised its head over a tuft of grass.

"That was mean," it said in a small voice. "Why did you do that?"

"You attacked us!" said Brynne.

The snake hung its head. "No play. I go. No one likes the river guardian."

Poor thing! messaged Mini over the mind link. *How could you, Brynne?*

You thought it was a monster, too!

Wait, thought Aru. *River guardian?*

The little pink snake was almost at the riverbank when Aru yelled, "Hold on! We're looking for a ring! Have you seen it?"

The snake turned around. It rose a little higher, tilting its head to the side again. It kind of reminded Aru of a toddler. A definitely magical, possibly deadly toddler.

"A shiny?" asked the snake.

"Uh . . . yeah," said Aru.

"If you want shiny, you must give shiny," said the snake huffily. It looked at them expectantly.

I think it wants a trade, said Mini.

Aru reached into her pockets, but all she had was a hair band she had forgotten about. *I'm coming up empty. . . . Guys?*

Brynne didn't have a backpack, but for some reason she still had packets of hot sauce in her pockets. She pulled one out and threw it to the snake. The reptile made a delighted sound and slithered closer to inspect it. After one whiff it hissed loudly.

"No shiny," it said ominously.

Mini swung around her backpack and pulled out her inhaler. "I have this?"

The snake blinked at her, bored.

"Or this?" she tried, showing it a notebook.

The snake yawned.

"What about . . . this?" Mini pulled out a whistle and demonstrated how it worked.

The snake hissed, growing a bit larger.

"Okay, okay, never mind!"

That's it, thought Aru. *Maybe we'd have more luck draining the river and digging around in the mud for the ring.*

But at that second, Mini pulled out an empty candy bar wrapper that was, admittedly, rather shiny.

The snake gasped, slithering closer.

"Shiny . . ." it said, as if hypnotized.

"Nuh-uh-uh!" said Aru loudly. "If you want shiny, you must give shiny."

The snake sighed. It turned around and stared at the river.

Seconds later, it shot down the bank and disappeared into the water.

"HEY!" said Mini loudly, waving around the candy wrapper. "I thought we had a deal!"

"Okay, now what?" said Brynne, flopping onto the grass.

But a moment later, the ground trembled. The pink snake—once more the size of a massive waterslide—burst out of the water and slammed down onto the riverbank. Waves sloshed up from the river, the cold water surrounding Aru's ankles. When she looked up, the pink snake was staring at her wide-eyed like a puppy.

"Shiny," it announced proudly.

It opened its mouth, and a small pile of glittering objects fell to the ground. The pink snake swiveled its head toward Mini. "Shiny?"

"Here," said Mini, laying the candy wrapper on the ground.

"Wait!" said Brynne. "We don't know if the ring is—"

Before she could finish, the pink serpent dwindled once more to the size of a common garden snake. With a happy squeak, it snapped up the candy wrapper and wriggled back down to the water.

"Thanks?" said Aru.

The snake lifted its tail and flicked it as if waving good-bye.

Aru walked over to the snake's hoard.

"Be careful, Aru," said Mini. "River water holds all kinds of bacteria, and you're not due for your tetanus shot for another few months!"

Aru knelt and started sifting through the objects. There

was a copper coin, a broken pair of rhinestone eyeglasses, a soggy beaded purse, and a tarnished silver belt buckle in the shape of a cow's head . . . but no ring.

She picked up the belt buckle and was about to chuck it in the river after the snake when she saw something underneath it, half buried in the mud. Something gold. Carefully, she dug it out. Once she had washed it off in the river, she could examine it more closely. It looked like a man's band ring, old and handcrafted, with an intricate engraved design. This had to be Dushyanta's!

She held it up in the air, grinning triumphantly.

"Woo-hoo!" said Brynne. "Story fixed! Victory is ours!"

As Aru climbed the bank, that familiar, crackly voice from the Grove whispered in her ear:

You've fixed the tale, but have you seen the cost

Of what can happen when true love is lost?

Aru put the ring on her thumb for safekeeping, but the moment she did, the world tilted.

Once more, it was like she was falling through the pages of a story, watching them whir past as if someone were flipping to the end of the book.

The next page:

Dushyanta clutched the ring to his chest and fell to his knees in the palace. The king looked much older than the last time Aru had seen him. There were bits of gray in his hair and lines on his face.

"Fetch my horse!" he shouted to his attendants. *"I must find my queen at once!"*

As he spoke, Aru could sense panic rising in her chest. And *anger* at being robbed of happiness. It made her feel trapped and cornered . . . and desperate.

The next page:

The scene shifted back to a banyan tree deep in the forest. Aru remembered that this was the place where Dushyanta had promised to return to his wife. Now Shakuntula stepped out from behind the trunk. She was older, but still beautiful. By her side was a boy about Aru's age. The king charged through the woods on his horse, and he did not stop until he was steps away from his wife and child.

"Ah, my love," said the king mournfully as he dismounted. He took her hand in his and knelt in front of her. *"How much time have we wasted?"*

Shakuntula burst into tears, and Aru wanted to scream. Wasn't this supposed to be a happy story? In a way, it was. . . . At least the family was reunited. And yet, underneath it all, there was a knot of pain. From so much lost time, left out in the cold and turned stale.

Aru could feel, in that moment, every bit of Shakuntula's loneliness. All the evenings she had spent staring out into the darkened trees. All the mornings she had waited in vain. Aru could also feel the king's heartache, as if it were a fire smoldering in her chest.

Turn back the clock! Aru wanted to yell. *Demand a refund from the universe!*

But the page turned again.

When Aru Shah opened her eyes, she found herself standing in the mall, by the entrance to the Grove of True Love. A thicket of thorny roses had grown over the arched opening, blocking any access. Urvashi's gunghroo bells hovered in front of Aru. Gradually, the sounds of the marketplace caught up to her.

"We did it!" said Mini. "Right?"

Aru turned and saw Mini swaying on her feet. Even Brynne, who normally would've pumped her fist in the air and gone back to talking about what she wanted to eat, looked . . . confused. Her hand moved to the spot above her heart. Aru knew how she felt—as if an ache had settled there. When Aru blinked, she could still see Shakuntula and her family. Also, she could've sworn that she'd heard an echo of a boy saying "*Happy birthday*." It didn't make any sense.

"Oh good!" said a familiar voice.

The Pandavas turned and saw Urvashi floating toward them. She snapped her fingers, and her gunghroo bells zoomed to her and clasped gracefully around her ankles.

"Your errands are now complete," said Urvashi. "You're free to run along. In fact, I think Boo has an ice-cream treat waiting for you back at the Night Bazaar."

Brynne brightened. "Ice cream?"

"Does he have any nondairy options?" asked Mini, clutching her stomach. "I feel queasy."

"You'll have to ask him, child," said Urvashi kindly.

That was weird.

Urvashi could be *nice*, but she wasn't exactly the warmest person. Which meant . . . she was feeling guilty. Aru recognized that voice switch from plenty of times with her mom.

"Shah, you coming?" asked Brynne.

"I'll join you guys in a second," said Aru.

She watched her sisters walk off into the sunlit shopping center. Behind her, Aru could still feel the chill of the Grove of True Love. Little by little, the intense feelings were fading, but she knew she would always remember what it had felt like to be left behind like Shakuntula, or to be tricked by something out of her control.

"You knew, didn't you?" asked Aru, looking up at her teacher. "You knew your anklets would go into that place. . . ."

Urvashi nodded.

"Why?" asked Aru. "Why did you . . . Why did you make us see that?"

At this, Urvashi lifted her chin. "When I tried to teach you love stories, you did not care. And why should you? You've seen some of the world's teeth, but you have not yet felt their bite on your soul. Perhaps you think that battles are started by hate and won by love, but sometimes it is quite the opposite. I wanted you to know what those people felt like so that someday you might understand the lengths people will go to out of love . . . for it is not always a kind emotion."

Aru frowned. She thought of how she felt about her sisters and her mom . . . and Boo. That was love, and it was nice and warm, like a fluffy Great Pyrenees dog.

Urvashi regarded her sadly. "There will come a time when you understand, Aru."

SHAH, BRYNNE IS EATING ALL THE ICE CREAM! said Mini through her mind link. *YOU BETTER GET HERE QUICK!*

Aru jolted. "I, uh, I—"

"Go, child," said Urvashi, smiling. "Go and have your fun."

Aru ran off to join her sisters. Finally Urvashi's awful errands were over with, and the Pandavas had their Sundays free again. But as she headed toward the light and felt the cold shadows of the Grove receding at her back, Aru could have sworn that she heard Urvashi say:

Have your fun now, child, for it shall not last.

The Cave of Doom

J. C. CERVANTES

I WANTED TO INCINERATE Bartholomew Butts III.

Technically, I've never met the guy. But he's the reason Brooks and I discovered the eyeless birds that saw us before we saw them.

Yeah, I know. How can birds with no eyes see anyone? I'll get to that and everything else.

But let's start with Bartholomew, the British dude who gave a one-star Tripadvisor review to Maya Adventures, the tour-guide business my mom and Uncle Hondo run on Isla Holbox. The three of us built the biz from nada, a lot of hard work, and mountains of hope. And guess what? It's now one of the top-rated tour businesses within a hundred-mile radius. We've gotten eighty-seven reviews, and we're on a five-star (kick-butt) streak! Or we *were* . . .

I'd only been back home from my summer godborn training for two days when Hondo blew onto the patio and shoved a laptop in front of my face so I could read Mr. Butts's review.

"¡Mira, Zane!" he began, right before spewing a string of cusswords and ending with "¡Este idioto no sabe nada!"

Brooks dropped her half-eaten guac taco onto her plate, wiped her hands on her shorts, and leaned closer to the screen. "Isn't that the point of being an idiot? Knowing nothing?"

I choked back a laugh. That's Brooks. Usually sarcastic, sometimes salty, and always nervy. But she's got a huge heart—really. She's also my best-friend-turned-girlfriend. Whoa—that's weird to write. Anyway, we've faced a lot together: bloodthirsty demons; arrogant, spiteful gods; insufferable calendars—the usual world-ending stuff. There's no one else I'd rather have at my side—or my back. Plus, she's a ha' nawal, a Maya shape-shifter who can change into a muy grande hawk and can also breathe underwater. How cool is that? Almost as cool as my mad fire skills. Okay, well . . . maybe it's a tie.

Hondo folded his arms across his chest and scowled. "Just read it."

I tipped the screen away from the sun's glare to get a better view. Okay, so not only did Bart the jerk give us a one-star, he also threw down a bunch of lies. The title of his review was "Vexing Visit to Isla Pájaros!"

Vexing? Who even says that?

I read the first part out loud. "'I was nearly murdered by a monstrosity, and this is no exaggeration.'" I looked up at Hondo, whose face was getting darker by the second. "This guy is loco."

"You've only read the first sentence," he growled. "Keep going."

Brooks nudged my elbow impatiently. "Scroll down. I'm dying to see how this guy was *nearly murdered*," she said, rolling her eyes.

The rest went like this.

The tour guide, Hector, or was it Horace? Regardless, this H person took our group to the island by boat, and since it's a protected ecosystem, we were restricted to observing the birds from a lookout tower. Good thing I had binoculars. Just as my wife and I were leaving the rickety—and might I say DANGEROUS—tower, the rain and thunder started. That's when we heard it. Now listen, I am not prone to exaggeration or hyperbole or any manner of such things, but what happened next was truly shocking. We heard a bitter, tiny cry, like that of a hungry newborn. It sounded so human my wife was sure an infant had been dropped into the mangrove. The rest of our group was already getting back onto the boat by this time and didn't seem to hear anything. I peered through my binoculars, searching. If there was a baby down there, we had to rescue it. The rain was coming down faster by then, which is why I can't describe what I saw any better than this: thick, slimy, human-shaped, and crawling on its belly through the brush. And before you tell me it was an alligator, let me ask you: Are alligators bone-white? Do they have human faces? I, being a brave sort, ran down to the boat to tell H. To rally the troops, so to speak. But no one volunteered to go back with me, because they didn't want to get wet. The nerve! The tour guide just laughed it off and said that the island is known to play tricks on people's minds. Rubbish! I know what I saw. We know what we heard! There is something awful on that island. Stay away! Do not give this horrible, unprofessional tour company one cent. Especially Mister Blooming H!

The second I was done reading, Hondo (correction, *Blooming H*) slammed the laptop closed. "Can you believe this crap?" He groaned. "This guy ruined our five-star streak."

"Mister Blooming H?" I couldn't help it. I busted up.

"That's all you got from that?" he said, still scowling. "Seriously?"

"Should we start calling you Horace?" Brooks asked with a totally straight face. "It has a nice ring to it, and you could even pass for one. Right, Zane?"

I thought Hondo was going to blow his carotid artery, but he didn't. Instead, his frown unfolded slowly like he was plotting something that involved pain and suffering for yours truly. Then he smiled really big. "Yeah, that's funny, Brooks. Almost as funny as the fact that you two are going to go to that island to scope things out."

"What?" I got to my feet. "Why?"

"Because, last time I checked, I'm your boss."

Brooks said, "You don't really think there's a baby monster with a human face living in the mangrove, do you?"

Hondo rubbed the back of his neck and let out a long breath. "Who knows? But I'm curious, and besides, I want to reply to this guy that we did our due diligence. I can't have potential tourists all freaked-out."

"It might bring more of them," I said. "People like that sort of creepy stuff."

People always love the promise of danger. They just don't like it when the promise is fulfilled.

Hondo gave me a stony glare. "Zane."

"Why can't *you* go?" I asked.

"It's Bird Island and"—he stabbed a finger at Brooks—"she's part bird, so maybe she could, like, talk to them. Find out if they've seen anything."

"I am not a bird interpreter, Hondo!"

She kind of is.

"So, you *do* think there's something out there. . . ." I said to my uncle.

Hondo grabbed the laptop and stuck it under his arm. "I think I'm tired of this convo, and I've got a plane to catch tomorrow, and I haven't packed yet, and if I'm late to meet Quinn, she'll murder me when I'm not looking."

Right. He and Brooks's older sister, Quinn, were a super-serious thing now, and they had decided to climb Mount Kilimanjaro together. Hondo wanted to make a he-man showing, because he planned to pop the question when they got to the summit. Which was the worst news of all time. I mean, I was happy for my uncle, but come on. I didn't want to be related to my girlfriend, even if it was only by marriage.

"Just say we checked it out," Brooks suggested. "Who's going to know?"

"I run an honest business, Brooks," Hondo said, "and that would be a lie."

She rolled her eyes. "Mm-hmm . . . like we've never seen one of those before."

Hondo threw me a look that told me I was definitely headed to Isla Pájaros and pronto.

Rosie, my three-legged boxer-dalmatian, lumbered out of the house just then and let out a long-winded yawn as she settled at my feet. I scratched her between the eyes, and a wavy trail of smoke floated out of her nose. I was still getting used to seeing her as a dog again. For about a year she had been a massive black hellhound thanks to Ixtab, the Maya queen of the underworld. But then, a few months ago, Ixtab decided that since me and my friends had pretty much saved the world and all the gods' butts, I deserved to get my dog back as a thank-you gift. The first gift I ever got from Ixtab was a letter opener. Sure, it magically morphed into a cane when I needed one because I walk with a limp, but still, a letter opener? Anyhow, this gift was way better—my Rosie, but with hellhound powers.

I kissed the top of her head. "See you soon, girl."

"You hope," Brooks teased.

Let me tell you, flying over the Caribbean Sea on a giant hawk's back is wild. It never ever gets old. But today, Brooks was coasting toward Isla Pájaros like we had all day. I mean, in Brooks's mind I suppose we did. She had no idea that I'd be taking off again next week for who knows how long. I needed to help my dad, Hurakan, return to his godly status. Get this—when my friends and I traveled back to 1987 to save all the Maya gods, the jefes had returned as teens. Some have gone back to their normal big-headed selves since then, but others, like my dad, are still, well, kids. Anyhow, I've never found a good time to tell Brooks. I guess I didn't want to ruin the one week we had together on the island. I just wanted it to be chill, ya know?

I really wanted to ask her if she could speed it up, but I thought she might "accidentally" dump me into the ocean, so I zipped my lip and just rode as her wingman. Literally. I'd done it loads of times, but every so often Brooks would zoom too fast or cut a turn so unexpectedly I'd hurtle through the air. Sometimes I think she did it on purpose just to keep me guessing.

Luckily for me, it had been smooth sailing so far today. The air was still and the sky was blue for miles. The only clouds were wispy threads of white.

So, I said, *you think we'll find anything?*

One of the benefits of being a godborn is that I can communicate telepathically with other godborns or sobrenaturals as long as we're touching. It really comes in handy when Brooks is in hawk form and not able to speak.

ANYTHING as in a monster that cries like a baby? she asked.

Or ANY monster.

Only one way to find out.

There were a couple of beats of silence and then . . .

Zane?

Yeah?

Why are you acting so weird?

I pulled the dumb card. *Weird?*

Like your mind is somewhere else. And that means you're not telling me something, so what gives?

I needed to tell her. Absolutely. But there were two good

reasons now wasn't the ideal time. One, I was two hundred feet in the air on her back, and if I made her mad, bye-bye, me. And two, a huge bank of threatening black clouds had suddenly appeared on the horizon beyond the island.

Crap!

Excuse me? she asked, all exasperated.

No, I mean . . . look. Storm ahead.

The clouds were moving at lightning speed, and if we didn't hurry, we'd meet all that twisted darkness head-on the second we hit the island.

Can you get us to the isla and back before that thing swallows us? I asked Brooks.

Really? You're really going to ask me that? Psh.

Yeah, it was a stupid question. During her training at the Shaman Institute of Higher-Order Magic this past summer, Brooks had become a speed maniac. As in almost not visible to the naked eye. It was seriously sick.

Hold on tight! she sang, like she'd been waiting for this moment.

I gripped her feathers, trying to prepare for off-the-charts g-force power as she accelerated. But, believe me, there is no preparation for that kind of speed. The world whizzed past. My cheeks flapped like loose chicken skin. Brooks tucked her wings and went even faster. I tried to yell *STOP!* but my skin felt like it was being torn off my face, my eyes were gushing tears, and I was pretty sure I had lost my ears a mile ago.

And besides that, my heart was ready to call it a day. I was still aware enough to know that I was going to black out in . . .

Three . . .

I saw stars.

Two . . .

I saw a kid in a trench coat and a funny hat riding a unicorn. Oh man, I really *was* losing it.

Brooks reduced her breakneck speed. I swayed dizzily.

What a rush! You okay, Zane?

Other than the fact that my brain was now meat loaf? I managed an affirmative that sounded like *uhhmmerm*, and then I blew chunks.

Ewww! Not on the feathers!

"Sorry," I groaned, wiping my mouth with the back of my hand. "But next time you decide to go all rocket ship on me, how about some warning?"

Would it have mattered?

"That's not the point," I muttered. As I righted myself, I saw that we were directly over the twenty-two-foot-wide island. By the looks of the storm, we had maybe six or seven minutes before we were in the throes of it.

Yeah, so much for a chill week.

Brooks floated closer to land—so close I could have jumped off her back and lived to tell the tale. *Be quiet*, she ordered.

I hadn't said a word. Probably because I was still trying to collect my stomach . . . and spine and eyeballs. Everything was a little fuzzy, but as we drifted, the isla came into better focus. Flamingos, pelicans, and ducks were rushing for cover from the storm.

I can't see through all the cacti and orchids, Brooks said.

Look, I insisted, *there isn't a monster down there. Just boa constrictors, iguanas . . . things that bite.*

We floated so close to the cacti, my sneakers grazed their tips. *Not so close!* I warned.

Then, unexpectedly, Brooks pulled up so fast I nearly tumbled off her back.

What are you doing? I shouted.

Did you hear that?

Hear what?

That voice. Brooks circled the lookout tower.

Like a big scary voice, or like a nice grandma kind of voice? This was a very important distinction.

Brooks ignored me. Then: *Like a strange voice.*

Define strange.

There. That's it.

I waited for her to share her discovery, because I heard absolutely nada. Well, except for the big tormenta racing toward us.

The birds, she said. *They're saying something . . . like in a chorus, and they sound scared.*

How does a bird even sound scared? Man, she really is a good bird translator.

Annoyed, Brooks nipped at my ankle. *You seriously don't hear it?*

Uh . . .

Shhhh . . .

I really wanted to point out that she had asked me a question, but whatever. I could tell she was in the zone and it was better for me just to let her tune in to whatever bird talk was going on.

I glanced up to see the massive black clouds gaining on us. We were now down to maybe three minutes.

Brooks released a cry, and I, not being able to speak bird, had no idea what she'd said. And then I heard it—a bunch of birds yakking and hollering like someone was severing their heads with a nail file or something. Whatever it was, it sounded ominous and terrifying.

They're only saying one word, Zane.

Welcome? What can I say? I'm super optimistic.

Danger! I think they're trying to warn us.

We should listen to the birds!

I expected Brooks to correct course, to get us away from the storm and, you know, the birds shouting *Danger*, but, as usual, she didn't listen. She just cruised even closer.

Brooks! Let's get out of here!

I just need to be sure. . . .

How about we be sure on a sunny day?

Holy K!

I seriously hated when she said that. *What's wrong?*

Zane—some of the birds, they don't have . . . eyes.

I didn't want to look down. I DID NOT want to see eyeless birds. I looked down. But all I saw were normal flamingos and a few pelicans flapping their wings furiously while they screeched their heads off.

Brooks's tone took on a whole new level of panic when she said, *They're trying to tell me something. . . .*

But I didn't understand what came next, because her thoughts were scrambled by the howling winds. The storm was close—too close. "We gotta bounce NOW!" I hollered.

Violent gusts rolled ahead of the tempest, pelting us with cold rain.

Brooks struggled against the headwinds. *I'm trying!* I could feel the tension in her muscles as she fought to climb out of the squall's reach.

Try harder!

It was too late. The tormenta gripped us in its unrelenting fury. I used all my godborn strength to hold on to the giant hawk. But I was no match for the storm, and neither was Brooks. She was knocked sideways into a vicious barrel roll. I was flung into the air like a puny stone fired out of a slingshot. And the last thing I heard was the earsplitting screeching of a thousand birds.

During the next few seconds of my probably-short life, I felt like a battered bottle cap spinning in a garbage disposal. Round and round, spiraling in utter darkness . . . But how? We had been flying only thirty feet above the island. So why was I still plummeting?

The impending bone-crunching *splat* on the ground had to be coming soon. The ground with cacti and boa constrictors. And screaming eyeless birds. All my muscles were tense, bracing for impact.

Brooks! Where was Brooks? She'd swoop in any second.

Anytime now.

ANY moment!

Nope. I was still tumbling to my death.

Suddenly, the air changed. It felt cold and damp. Peering through the dark, I saw a formation rushing past me—rocky and black. I was in some kind of wide gorge with wet, slick walls. And the place reeked of mildew.

Quickly, I released smoke from my fingertips. Long black trails streamed beneath me, taking the shape of a giant net. It wouldn't be strong enough to break my fall, but if I was lucky, it would at least slow my descent.

My eyes caught sight of images painted on one wall. I was going too fast and was too preoccupied with not dying to decipher the gold symbols that seemed to appear every few feet.

But I did see my salvation—a small outcropping to my right, if I could just stretch far enough to reach it. With a grunt and an all-out acrobatic swing, I managed to catch the ledge. My body slammed against the rock wall and a vicious pain ripped across my ribs as I held on tight. Then my fingers began to slip.

With godborn grit and determination, I heaved myself onto the mere four-foot-by-four-foot shelf. Exhausted, I collapsed onto my knees and wrapped an arm around my throbbing rib cage as I leaned over the edge to see how far away the bottom was.

Yeah, I probs shouldn't have done that.

Something thick and fleshy and nearly transparent was coiled on the sandy floor thirty feet below. I take that back. Not something—lots of things. Things that looked like albino viper boas. All intertwined in a fat, disgusting cluster of pinkish white flesh. PS: Viper boas *do not* inhabit this island. A ball of panic exploded in my chest.

Crap!

One half of me was thinking that I could incinerate the snakes, but how uncool would that be? I was the trespasser.

The other half of me was thinking, *THEY'RE BOAS! Do it!*

I created a small orb of fire to get a better look. The snakes hissed and writhed, unwrapping their fat bodies from one another as they shrank into the shadows.

Okay, so they didn't like light. Then I wondered, *Is this what Butts saw? A stupid snake?* I DEFINITELY wanted to barbecue the guy.

"Zane?"

"Brooks?"

My heart thundered with relief. I lifted the orb and looked across the thirtyish-foot chasm, scanning until I saw Brooks, back in human form, about fifteen feet above me on the other side, kneeling on a shelf skinnier than my own. Her eyes glowed amber and gold.

"Brooks! Are you okay?"

Just as she said, "I can't fly," my gaze fell to her right arm, which was cradled in her left hand. "I think it's sprained."

My stomach lurched. I quickly snatched my cell from my pocket.

"I already tried," Brooks said. "No service in here . . ." She glanced around. "Wherever *here* is."

I peered down at the gross-o snakes again. "Do you get the feeling they're looking at us?"

"They are definitely looking at us."

I threw down a small fireball, careful not to hit them. Their hissing grew louder, but a moment later they were all slithering into a hole in the wall, leaving a trail of goo behind.

A series of squawks sounded from above. I could just imagine a flock of flamingos and pelicans dancing around the rim of this dungeon and singing, *You should have listened.*

"It's a little late!" I shouted, my voice reverberating across the stone walls.

Brooks gasped and froze. "Did . . . you hear that?"

"The birds again?" I grumbled. "You'd think they could have been clearer. Like *Hey, cave of doom down there.*"

Brooks shook her head, clearly concentrating on whatever her hawk senses were picking up. Then slowly, in a stage whisper, she met my gaze and said, "They weren't warning *us*, Zane."

"What are you talking about?"

"They were warning someone—or something—else," she said. "They think *we're* the danger!"

Okay, I was so not expecting that. "That doesn't even make sense. How do you know?"

"Because the last thing they said was 'Blood. Intruders with magic blood. Call up the cave.' "

"Who the heck would know we're supernaturals?" And did she just say *Call up the cave*?

"Do I really have to list them all?" she huffed. "Other supernaturals, gods, monsters—"

"You mean Maya gods and monsters . . . ?"

"I mean—" She froze again, which was seriously starting

to freak me out. Then she said, "Zane, there's something else in here with us."

"Yeah, the snakes, but they took off." I was definitely in denial mode.

Brooks's still-burning eyes met mine, and even before she spoke the words, I knew I wasn't going to like what she had to say. "Something else," she repeated in a whisper-shout. "Those birds from earlier? I'm pretty sure they weren't real. My guess is that whoever sensed our true natures is someone we really don't want to meet. So—"

"Hang on. So those birds were, like, fake? How do you know?"

Brooks scowled. "Hawks have the keenest eyesight in the entire animal world, and—who cares how! Can you just focus on the immediate threat?"

Well, I thought *how* was pretty important, but this wasn't the time to argue. Brooks was right about one thing—we had to get out of there, like, muy pronto.

I looked up. Even with my killer 20/20 night vision, I couldn't see the opening above us anymore. The storm clouds were obscuring the light. So I lifted another fire orb, but its glow didn't extend very far. Only enough to remind me that the walls were sheer, slippery rock—impossible for us to climb, especially with Brooks's bum arm.

Brooks turned on her phone's flashlight and pointed it below, but the beam was too weak to show much of anything. "Throw another flame down."

"Why?"

"There might be some tunnels, a way out of here."

"But the snakes!" My voice nearly squeaked. I knew enough about viper boas to realize we weren't getting out of there without some bloodshed. They lie in wait, ambush you, and then coil their bodies around you, constricting more with each breath you take until it's adios, life as you knew it. "I'm not in the mood to be a snake snack."

"Well, I can't fly, and we can't climb to the top, and I'd rather not starve to death on this ledge. So it looks like we don't have much of a choice but to go down."

"You're a superpowerful nawal," I reminded her. "You'll heal, and then we'll wing it out of here."

"But for some reason I can't feel the healing. It's like . . ."

"What?" But did I really want to know?

"Like there's a power in this cave slowing it."

"Well, *un*slow it."

Brooks rolled her eyes. "Can we just please check it out? This place is giving me the creeps."

She got to her feet and stared down the steep rocky descent at the base of her ledge. No way could she scramble down it, either. "Listen, Obispo. You were trained in rock climbing, you've got killer fire skills, and don't forget your missile-accurate cane-slash-spear. Plus, I can still change into a hawk. I can pick my way down with my beak and talons. And last time I checked, snakes hate hawks. So . . ."

"So, we find a way out even if it's through the murderous

albino snakes," I said, knowing her logic was on point and I 100 percent hated it. "Wait! What if they're fake like the birds?" I wasn't sure if that would be a good or bad thing.

"The snakes are real."

"Oh." That was so not comforting.

"Listen," Brooks said, "it's not any worse than that time we fought those demons at Jack in the Box, or went head-to-head with the bat god, or"—she threw me a half smile—"when we saw those really bad eighties hairstyles. God, I'm still traumatized."

I forced a chuckle, but it came out sounding like I was about to hawk a loogie. I mean, this definitely felt worse, since that was then and this was now. But she was right. We'd survived a lot together. We could probably survive this, too.

As I started to get to my feet, I accidentally dropped my phone. It clattered below.

Brooks gave me a look.

"Uh . . . okay," I said, playing it off. "You've got farther to go, so just take it slow, and whatever you do, don't fall."

"I thought you were an eternal optimist."

"This is me being an optimist."

I surveyed the only path I had to the snake pit—a vertical wall with just a few outcroppings to grip. For the first time I was thankful for the crazy rock-wall exercises Hondo had put us through at SHIHOM—the ones where he'd blindfolded us and tied one arm behind our backs, because *strength isn't only in your muscles. It's in the mind and heart.*

I changed Fuego into a spear, and when I looked back up to Brooks, the air around her was shimmering a silvery blue as she shifted into a small hawk. She started making her way down before I could take another breath.

Right. Always a step ahead of me. Time to level up.

I lowered myself over the ledge, toe-gripping what little purchase I could find while stabbing Fuego into the stone as leverage. With each thrust my ribs mutinied with sharp spasms of pain.

That's when my cell phone rang from below. Once. Twice. Five times. But how was that possible if there was no service here?

I picked up my pace, thinking whoever was on the other end of that call could send help. I mean, if the cell was working, maybe the GPS was, too?

Stab. Grip. Balance.

Stab. Grip. Balance.

And then, while hanging from the wall, I came face-to-face with a strange symbol, like the ones I'd dropped past earlier. And I'm not talking a Maya glyph. This was like nothing I had ever seen before. A tight gold spiral made up of dozens of little circles. And at the center, a seven-pointed star. I'd started to trace it with my fingers when Brooks hollered, "Zane!"

I glanced over my shoulder to see that she was back in human form and had already made it down safely. Yay! But she was trying to keep her balance as pebbles bounced at her feet. The floor was trembling. Boo!

The walls quivered, too, as if the cave was . . . waking up. I raced down the final fifteen feet and leaped to the ground with Fuego.

Brooks snatched up my phone, staring at it with wide eyes. "What the . . . ?"

I glanced down at the screen. It was filled with a bunch of the bizarre gold spirals flashing in rows.

I was definitely going to have to change my number.

A sickening hissing filled the chamber.

"Dark or darker?" Brooks asked, pointing to our only two paths out of there.

I went with darker, since it was farther from the snake hole. Brooks and I ran down the narrow passage to our left. A glowing Fuego lit the way and would hopefully keep the monstrous serpents at bay.

The ground trembled harder now. Bits of rock fell from the tunnel ceiling. The hissing grew louder. Brooks stumbled, nearly face-planting, but she caught my outstretched arm and righted herself. And then we smacked right into a dead end.

"I guess darker wasn't the way out," Brooks said.

Catching my breath, I turned to her. "How do we always find ourselves in these predicaments?"

She gripped my hand and gave it a hard squeeze. "I definitely think you're bad luck."

"You wouldn't be wrong."

"I guess we're not going windsurfing today after all."

"Yes, we are."

She shot me a look that either said *I appreciate your confidence* or *You're bonkers*. "Glad to see you're still an optimist," she said. "It's a good way to go."

"Brooks."

"Zane."

I took a shaky breath. "We aren't going to die today. You said it—we can totally take the snakes."

"It's not the snakes I'm worried about."

The hissing stopped. The quivering floor went still. But something else was with us in the cave. I could feel it.

"I smell something," Brooks whispered. "It's nearby and—"

Putting Brooks behind me, I stepped forward. "Don't wanna know," I said, and I set the passageway ablaze.

White-hot flames shot from floor to ceiling, with a perimeter of a good five feet to keep Brooks from being charbroiled.

There was a cry, like a baby's. Small at first, and then an all-out wail. I cut the fire and peered into the smoky darkness. The hairs on the back of my neck were standing at attention.

"I hate that Butts guy for landing us in this stupid situation," Brooks said. It was a strange thing to say in the moment. Before I could agree, she added, "And for being right."

We were *definitely* not getting rid of that lousy review.

"You mean *bloody* right," I said with a smirk.

"Not funny."

"Kind of is."

Among the crackling embers, an eeriness wrapped around us. My heart pounded like an iron fist against my bruised rib cage.

"Zane?"

"Uh-huh."

Brooks's eyes blazed as she took a whiff of the thick smoky air. "It's here."

And then something charged. I felt the skin on my arm rip open. I couldn't see Brooks through the smoke, but I knew she had shifted, because her hawk screech pierced my ears. She was somewhere behind me.

I launched Fuego into the smoky void.

And heard a slurping sound.

"Brooks, stay back!" I ordered before I exploded into flames. The fire moved outward until my body was surrounded by a blazing blue ring. When Fuego flew back to me, its tip was dripping with a gooey, glue-like white substance.

"Show me your face!" I screamed.

A figure walked into the burning circle. Tall, lean. Familiar.

It was . . . me.

This version of me had blacker-than-night eyes. Its mouth was twisted into a creepy grin.

Look, I'd been around a lot of Maya monsters and supernaturals. I'd even seen myself cloned before. But this? This demented version of me wasn't Maya. I could feel it. It was something else entirely, something ancient and not of this world.

Cold rushed through me. Blood oozed from my arm, trickling to my fingertips.

I stepped back, trying to get a read on this thing's weaknesses. But so far? Nada. The thing advanced slowly. Like it had all day to kill me.

Brooks's hawk cry pierced the cave with a pitch so shrill I thought my eardrums might explode.

The fake me snapped its head back, eyes roving at a terrifying speed. All pigment drained from its skin, hair, and eyes. Suddenly it looked like one of those weird ghost fish that live at the bottom of the ocean.

When Monster Me looked back, its face was contorted into a mask of vicious anger.

No more time to think. I lunged, spearing it in the gut.

The thing staggered, gripping Fuego like a lifeline. I thought the abomination might collapse. Game, set, match. But no such luck. Slowly, sickeningly, the monster pulled out Fuego like my spear was nothing more than a half-chewed toothpick and tossed it onto the floor.

The same white glue-like substance leaked from its gut.

Okay, so it was immune to fire *and* a magic spear. My bag of tricks was getting leaner.

Brooks's cries reached new levels of panic and frequency.

Kee-eeeee-ar. KEE-EEEEE-AR.

I willed Fuego to return as Monster Me's face twisted in pain. The creature opened and closed its jaw slowly as it cupped ghostly-white hands over its ears.

"Brooks!" I hollered, seeing the effect her shrieks were having on the beast. "More! Shriek louder!"

What followed was a series of earsplitting, blood-chilling cries at a pitch that could turn bone to dust.

Brooks didn't let up.

Monster Me began to shudder like it had a bomb in its

gut ready to explode. Its eyes rolled to the back of its skull. I'd only had a chance to creep backward a few steps when the thing shattered into a million pieces. Not of flesh or bone or even ash.

But of—get this—white scales.

I cut the flames and looked up to see Brooks in massive hawk form clinging to a rocky ridge. She fluttered her wings, letting me know that she was healed.

And before I could blink, she jumped down and lowered her neck so I could hoist myself onto her back. With her wings tight against her body, Brooks zoomed through the tunnel and back to our entry point, where she went vertical.

Higher and higher Brooks sped, racing as though the opening was going to close at any second.

"I see light!" I hollered.

You asked me to warn you next time I go rocket ship, she said. *I'm going rocket ship.*

I'd barely had time to position myself when she tripled her speed. And just before we bolted into the storm-free sky, I caught a last whizzing glance of the peculiar gold symbols on the wall. I twisted my neck to get a good look at the chasm we'd been trapped in, but now there was nothing below but cacti and orchids. It was as if the cave had never existed.

Once we were free, Brooks took her speed down a couple of notches.

"Where did it go?" I hollered.

Hopefully straight into a million-foot grave, Brooks screamed telepathically. Then, in a less furious tone, she said, *What the holy K* was *that?*

I have no idea, but it looked just like me except way paler. And it was immune to fire and Fuego! But you . . . You blew it up. Into scales, Brooks. Scales! I clutched my chest as if my heart was going to parachute out.

That's so gross and disturbing and GROSS, and what the Xib'alb'a, Zane?!

With each word, Brooks increased her speed, as if she couldn't put enough distance between us and that hell cave. I clung to her back, gripping her shiny dark feathers, hoping I didn't barf again.

As we drew closer to Holbox, Brooks slowed to a pleasant glide. Maybe she was exhausted from so much rocketing.

How did you heal? I asked.

Every time I shrieked, I could feel my strength coming back. It's something I worked on in meditation class at SHIHOM*—a kind of centering technique for when I'm in a high-stress, life-or-death situation. But I had no idea it would speed up my healing.*

A few seconds later we landed on a secluded beach far away from any tourists. I slid off Brooks's back and sent an immediate smoke signal into the sky for my hellhound. Then, feeling dizzy, I collapsed onto the sand.

"Why are you calling Rosie? Is your wound that bad?"

Sure, my dog's saliva had the power to heal the gash on my arm, but that wasn't the reason I needed her right now.

Before I could answer Brooks, a wall of black smoke rose

from the sand, and out of it stepped my dog. Well, my dog in her hellhound form, which was a massive, black, muscle-packed beast that could breathe fire.

Rosie galloped over and sniffed me, grunting and snarling as smoke trailed from her nose and eyes.

"I'm okay, girl." I patted her chest as I got to my feet. "I need you to go to Xib'alb'a. Tell Ixtab I need to talk to her. I found some kind of monster on Isla Pájaros. Tell her . . . it wasn't Maya."

Rosie's brown eyes went all soft and she tilted her head to one side as if to say *Are you sure you want to do that?*

I leaned against her neck and nodded.

With fangs still bared, Rosie threw back her head and released a howl before she vanished to the underworld.

Brooks gave me a look. "Um, you really think that was a good idea?"

"What?"

"No one summons the queen of the underworld," she said, tucking a curl behind her ear. "She's likely to send her demons instead to rip out your spine."

"Brooks, that thing—it could withstand both fire and Fuego."

Brooks chewed her bottom lip and said, "Good thing I saved your life again."

"Yeah, who knew your screeching would come in so handy?" I said as I sent a thread of fire to my wound to cauterize it.

Brooks looked up and surveyed the perfectly blue sky. "A

sudden storm, a hidden cave, a creepy, snaky lookalike, and that symbol . . ." She rubbed her arms vigorously. "Is it still on your phone?"

I glanced at my screen, but the flashing symbols were gone. Using Fuego, I drew the shapes in the sand. Brooks paced around the perimeter of the really bad rendition like she needed to get a different view to be certain.

"You've seen it before?" I asked hopefully.

"Never."

"Are you sure?"

She looked down at me. "Are you sure you drew it right?"

Just then Rosie reappeared. And beside her? Ixtab, goddess of the underworld. She wore a fitted sleeveless dress made of what looked like chain metal (kind of extra, if you ask me) and a scowl that could disintegrate nations. At the center of her dark eyes, pale blue flames flickered.

"How dare you summon me, godborn?"

Okay, so we were back in nemesis territory. Just a few months ago she was thanking me for saving her and the other gods. Man, Maya gods' memories are epically short.

Rosie turned in a circle and settled onto the sand like we were getting ready to have a reunion picnic or something.

I began with "Er . . . we found something—"

"Rosie told me."

She seemed totally unfazed, so I started to give her all the nightmarish details. She interrupted with "I don't have time for this. Just let me see for myself."

I knew what she was asking, and I hated to do it, but I

couldn't risk leaving out any important details, so I took her hand and opened my mind to her.

After she saw what had happened—and after I lived through it *again*—she stepped back. Her dress clinked like armor as she growled, "You called me here for *that?*" Her perfectly sculpted face remained as rigid as stone.

Was she for real?

I glanced at Brooks for some moral support, but she was staring at the symbol in the sand. *Yeah, thanks a lot.*

Okay, here's the deal. Ixtab might have been playing her usual cooler-than-cool goddess persona, but there was no way she would have come to see me if the *that* in question was nothing.

"Um," I said, realizing that whatever words came out of my mouth next mattered a whole heckuva lot. They could either peck away at the truth, or reveal a lie, or bury both deeper. "I figured that if there's anyone who knows about the cave and that thing, it'd be you. Goddess of the underworld." I threw in that last part for effect, hoping it wasn't too heavy-handed. Ixtab hates false compliments, and I really didn't want to make her madder.

"You think I keep a catalog of cave-dwelling monsters?" she spat. "You think I don't have enough to worry about, what with running nearly ten levels of the underworld? Trying to figure out why some of the gods are still teenagers, thanks to your little excursion to 1987?"

Oh, you mean the excursion that saved you and all the gods? I wanted to say. But you've never seen fuming until you've seen the deadly blue fires of Ixtab. So instead I said, "And what about the symbol?" I pointed to my sand drawing as a reminder of what she'd seen in my memory. She consumed the image with cold, appraising eyes, glinting with annoyance.

Brooks inched so close to me our elbows were touching. *She knows what it is.*

Doesn't mean she'll tell us.

Ixtab drifted slowly around the image, and as she did, her gaze grew more intense. With a sigh, she said, "Do you think I cannot hear those little thoughts in your little brains?"

"But you do, don't you?" I said, risking my little-brained head. "You know what this symbol is."

I knew that if Ixtab denied knowledge she would look weak. After all, Holbox is where she first hid me from the gods. She had surrounded the island with her magic and even transplanted my favorite volcano here, complete with a passage to the underworld. Which meant she knew this area backward and forward, including any and all happenings on Isla Pájaros.

"That is of no concern to you, godborn." I swear, her penetrating gaze was like a death grip, and it didn't help that she was dressed like a murderous gladiator.

I was about to agree. *Yup. No concern here. Just tell me you'll destroy whatever's in that cave and I'll go windsurfing and call it a day.*

But then Brooks said, "Well, then I guess we'll just have to go back and find out for ourselves."

Ixtab forced a smile, if you could call it that. It was actually more of a sneer that said, *How delicious it would be to rip out your tongue.*

Brooks stood her ground, which was way impressive. Me? I was sort of cringing. But I managed to say, "We can't ignore what we saw."

A warm breeze swept across the shore. Waves rolled in and out. Out and in. Finally, Ixtab said, "Are you certain you want to know?" Why was she still wearing that creepy grin? It made me want to say *JK! We for sure don't want to know.*

But in the end, both Brooks and I agreed.

Ixtab waved her hands, and we were instantly in the thick of Holbox's jungle, where only a slice of sunlight poked through the foliage. Rosie came along for the ride and settled at the base of an enormous banyan tree.

"That's better," Ixtab said after a deep inhale. "I think so much better in the dark. Now, you asked me, the all-powerful goddess of the underworld, to tell you a story, a story you are certain to regret. So, for the last time, do you really want to know? And before you answer, remember that this knowledge could set in motion certain events—events that may prove costly."

Rosie let out a small stuttering whine that sounded part Wookiee.

Sorry, girl, I thought, *but Ixtab's bluffing.* No way could knowledge ever be so awful. What's the saying? *Knowledge is power.* As if in reply, a voice deep inside me whispered, *Curiosity also killed the cat.*

Brooks threw me a glance and gave a nearly imperceptible nod.

"We want to know," I said.

Ixtab clasped her long fingers together. In the shadows her silvery dress now looked rusty and black. "But first, a promise."

Naturally.

"You must promise to let this go," Ixtab said. "To never tell another what I am going to tell you. If you do, the punishment"—here came the awful part—"will be to serve six months in a Xib'alb'a prison of my choice."

Ouch!

I'd been to the underworld. I knew some of its nastiest places, like Pus River and Rattle House. Believe me, just one hour in either location would be too long. And with all the goddess's recent renovations, who knew what kind of sick and twisted slammers she had dreamed up lately? But what choice did I have? I couldn't *not* know the enemy that had tried to kill me and was living only a few miles from me and my family.

Brooks stood taller, and just when I thought she was going to say something like *No way. I'm a Maya spy, a powerful water nawal. My nature is to hunt*, she shook the goddess's hand and said, "I promise."

Ixtab turned to me. "And you, godborn?"

Crap! I hated making god deals. They were binding. Which meant I'd have to outsmart the goddess to get out of this one, and that's about as easy as licking your own elbow.

"I promise to let this go," I said, "and never tell anyone anything—if you tell us everything."

I knew, of course, that Ixtab would never tell us everything, and that was my nice little loophole.

Except she saw my escape clause right away, and the next thing she did was laugh. A cruel, hardened laugh that made me feel sick.

"Oh, son of fire. I see you have become more astute at negotiation. But no, I will not agree to your terms. I will tell you what I choose to tell you. That will be enough. Now, what is your answer?" Her hand floated in the dim space between us.

Rosie lumbered over and nudged me with her nose.

"Ah," Ixtab said, "the hellhound is smarter than the godborn."

"Define *enough*," I said. "Like, an all-you-can-eat buffet? Or more like a sample size?"

Ixtab narrowed her gaze. "My offer is going to expire in three, two . . ."

I shoved my hand in hers and sealed the deal, hoping *enough* really would be enough.

"Before time began, there was a war. . . ." She started slowly, like she was going for dramatic effect, but all it did was annoy me. "It was between the gods and a species of being that was nothing more than monsters."

Species of being?

"What happened to them?" Brooks said.

Ixtab threw her cold gaze to the nawal. "We gods pulverized them and banished them into the bowels of the earth as a reminder to their kind to never challenge us again."

Yeah, that sounded way too familiar.

"But how did it replicate me?" I asked. "I thought that was a demon thing."

"And what is your point?"

I came at it more directly. "Was that thing some weird species of demon?"

Ixtab's expression hardened, but there was a flicker, a ghost of something else hidden there. "I can assure you that is not the case," she said. "You probably just ran into one of the sole survivors. . . ." Then she mumbled, "Cockroaches."

Brooks folded her arms. "And the symbol?"

"The image represents an idea, not a word."

I gripped Fuego, leaning closer. "Which is . . . ?"

Ixtab's jaw clenched, and for a second I thought she wouldn't tell us. But then she said, "The initiation is near."

"The initiation of what?" *A cockroach club?*

Ixtab said, "I'll be sure to ask the next time I have them over for dinner."

There should definitely be a change to Ixtab's title, I thought. *Goddess of sarcasm.*

"Why would they paint that symbol over and over?" Brooks said.

"Wishful thinking," Ixtab spat. "Spending thousands of years in the dark will do that to you—twist your mind into imagining you have a fighting chance, make you believe your rise is close at hand, when in reality"—her voice took on a sort of growl that sent chills up my legs—"your DEMISE is what is near!"

"A species of monster with a written language?" Brooks asked in a tone that told me she wasn't buying any of this.

Blue fire raged in Ixtab's eyes. "You dare doubt me?"

Uh-oh. Time for damage control. "Ha! No one is doubting you, goddess. We're just curious, and it sounds weird, right? I mean, um . . ."

"Zane's look-alike had scales," Brooks said, "so it must be part snake or something, right?"

"Or something," Ixtab said.

Okay, so if I was going to believe the goddess, then the monster wasn't part demon or snake. But *did* I really believe her? There was no point in pushing her, or asking the same thing in a different way. Ixtab would only spill what she felt like spilling. Her so-called *enough* was no more than a lousy crumb!

I said, "So, what are you going to do?"

"Do?" the goddess said flatly. "The doing has been done, godborn. The monsters were banished, or did you not hear that part of the tale?"

"But the eyeless birds," Brooks argued. "They were some kind of warning system. Which means they are trying to protect the monsters, and—"

"And they knew we were sobrenaturals," I added. "They trapped us and wanted to kill us. And then there's Bartholomew Butts—a human tourist. He saw and heard something, too. So that means that whatever you think is underground . . . is aboveground, too."

Ixtab sighed, gathering herself. "I have real problems to contend with. And you, Zane . . ." she added with that familiar murderous sneer reserved just for me, "aren't you supposed to be traveling with your father, helping him find a solution to his teen woes?"

Brooks lifted her eyes to meet mine, and a wave of guilt swept through me, because all I saw in hers was hurt.

Crap!

I wanted to say to Brooks, *I was going to talk to you about it . . . soon—ish. I swear!* But no way was I going to let Ixtab in on that convo.

Instead, after clearing my throat, I said, "Ixtab, I need to know that the thing . . . that it won't—that it *can't* get off Isla Pájaros." It was a stupid thing to say. I was grasping for some sort of assurance that she was never going to give me.

"I'll send a few demons to investigate later," the goddess said, straightening up. "Now, please turn your attention to more important matters, like Hurakan. And above all else, remember our deal. I'd hate to have to explain to your father that I had to imprison you because you couldn't keep your promise. And, Brooks?" She turned to my girlfriend. "Zane's prison will be infinitely worse than your own. Do you understand?"

Brooks looked physically stricken, like the goddess had spit acid at her. She nodded her agreement.

And then Ixtab was gone.

Rosie growled, which was her way of telling me *BAD, BAD, BAD choice!*

"We had to, girl."

My dog turned up her nose and snorted.

"Rosie's right," Brooks said. "We shouldn't have made that deal. We didn't learn anything other than the gods were at war with some monsters before time began. Big surprise." She took a deep breath, and then she socked me in the arm. Hard.

"Hey, what was that for?"

"When were you going to tell me about your trip?" I didn't even get a chance to answer, because Brooks went on to say, "I mean, I totally get it—he's your dad. But we swore no more secrets from each other, Zane!"

I felt like the biggest jerk in the universe and beyond. "I know I should have told you, but I didn't want our last week together to be all weird. I wanted—"

"To go windsurfing?" She threw her head back nonchalantly. "I'm still game."

Okay, so maybe she didn't hate me. Phew.

"The day isn't over yet," I said. "We just need to circle Isla Pájaros one more time."

"What? Were you not there for the god deal?"

"Look, Ixtab didn't say we couldn't go back to the island," I argued. "I mean, we've been there dozens of times. It's not like she gave us a no-fly zone, right?"

Brooks shook her head. "Just let the demons take care of it."

Demons. The word hit me like an avalanche. I began to pace, with Rosie trailing my every step. "Ixtab didn't really answer my question about whether the monster was a kind of demon. Did you catch that?"

"She was pretty clear, Zane." Putting on her best Ixtab voice, Brooks lifted her chin and said, "*I can assure you that isn't the case.*"

I had to laugh. It was a really bad impression. "But her expression," I said, turning serious again. "There was something there, like a lie she was trying to hide. It was almost like she hadn't expected the question, and I think it unnerved her."

"No one unnerves the queen of the underworld."

I stopped pacing. "Do you know of anything else that can replicate someone?"

"Other than demons?" Brooks began to tick off the answers on her fingers. "Some nawals. Gods. Oh, and our godborn buddy Marco."

True. The son of war was a master at cloning, and so were the gods. "But none of those are made of scales, Brooks."

She cocked an eyebrow. "So Ixtab was lying. It's not like we expected her to tell us the truth, right?"

Rosie whined and pawed the air.

"See?" I pointed to my dog. "She's convinced Ixtab is hiding something, too. And think about it—if you wanted to hide something like a cave of doom, why not do it on a so-called eco-protected island, where no lookie-loos can sniff around?"

Brooks's soldier expression had melted into one of fear. "We aren't going back."

"What are you so afraid of?"

Brooks's wings appeared behind her back, stretching out toward the shadowed trees. "When Ixtab told me your prison would be worse than mine, it was code."

"Code for what?"

"It was a warning, her way of telling me not to let you do anything stupid. She knows I'll protect . . ." Brooks sighed. "Why risk ending up in some awful, dark, twisted prison of the underworld?"

"I've been in one before, remember?"

"I'm sure that was a piece of cake compared to the mental prison she has planned for you, Zane. It'd be something even worse than what poor Hondo went through."

Looking back, maybe Brooks was right. But I hated being lied to, and worse, being treated like I was too dumb to see through those lies. "You're letting her threats distract us," I said.

"Zane! She's the goddess of the underworld. She doesn't just *make* threats—she *delivers* on them!"

"And she's not telling us everything," I argued. "I mean, *the initiation is near*? What does that even mean?"

Brooks came over and took hold of my arm. "Fine, you want to go back? Then at least let's think this through. Make a plan. Do it on the down low, when Ixtab isn't paying attention."

But Brooks was missing the point. We had to check things out before the demons descended, because who knew what they might find or "clean up"?

Leaning on Fuego, I said, "The plan is to fly over the island. That's it. And then I'll let it go."

Brooks narrowed her eyes. "Just a flyover?"

"And you're the pilot, so we'll come back as soon as you say."

A minute later, we were airborne again. Ixtab's warning seemed to echo across the sky. *This knowledge could set in motion certain events—events that may prove costly.* I had no idea what the events or the cost could be. Still, something way down in my gut told me that I would soon find out.

The island looked exactly as it had the last time we had flown over it, minus the wicked storm. Lush, peaceful, undisturbed.

See? Brooks said cheerily. *All clear. Now can we go windsurfing?*

But something wasn't right. And it wasn't the goddess's half-truths or the hell cave or even the eyeless birds. It was that symbol, and how it had been painted on the walls, almost like a pattern.

Do you hear any creepy bird-speak? I asked.

Nothing.

Fly closer.

Why are you like this?

Come on. Just one more pass.

Brooks extended her wings and floated about twenty feet above the island. The flamingos, pelicans, and ducks pecked around like they weren't fake little monsters. And thankfully, this time they had eyes.

I don't get it, I said. *Why would they wig out before and not now?*

Who knows? Maybe the storm had something to do with it. Didn't Butts say something about rain?

You're right! Brooks was definitely onto something.

Weird, she said.

What?

The birds . . . They're real this time.

And then I saw it.

There.

Clear as day.

The bushes below had grown together in the shape of the strange circular symbol. The ten-foot-by-ten-foot section would be impossible to see unless you had a bird's-eye view and were looking for it.

Look! I pointed out the discovery.

Maybe that's the entry to the nightmare cave! she said. *But, umm . . . It looks like the demons are already here.*

It took all of half a second to spot the demon partially hidden in the brush, digging in the sand and, thankfully, totally unaware of us.

Brooks floated higher, trying to be inconspicuous, but how inconspicuous can a goliath hawk really be?

Ixtab said she was sending them later, I reminded Brooks.

Hmm . . . Just another lie in paradise.

The demon stood up, stretched its long bluish-gray arms over its head, then vanished in a cloud of smoke.

Let's go check out what it was doing!

Zane, the island's protected. No one's supposed to walk on it, remember?

I'll walk lightly.

You have HUGE feet! Just observe from here.

Brooks coasted closer. . . .

Close enough for me to leap off of her back unscathed.

"Be my lookout!" I rolled into the underbrush just as Brooks released a threatening *I'm-going-to-pummel-you* cry.

As I waded through the scrubs, I sent up a prayer: *Please no boas. Please no boas. Oh, and no demons, either.*

Brooks circled above, her massive outstretched wings casting a giant shadow over me. Quickly, I went to work, looking for . . . what?

With Fuego in hand, I explored the space, searching under cacti and straggly bushes. I cruised the general area where the demon had been digging. But I found nothing out of the ordinary. Frustration mounted.

Until . . .

Clunk.

Fuego's tip rammed into something. I dropped to my knees and swept the sand away until I found a rectangular slab no bigger than a shoe box. Digging a moat around it, I realized it was a container of some sort, but no matter how hard I tried, I couldn't tug it free. The rough-edged stone was cool to the touch as I carefully wedged my fingers beneath the lid and lifted it off.

Inside was a shiny black shell the size of my thumb. It was oblong, rounded, and impossibly smooth. Right, it's no big deal to find a shell at the beach. But this one was different, because that spiral symbol was flawlessly etched on its surface. My nerves buzzed as I flipped it over to reveal a slit-like opening edged with fine golden teeth, like the bristles of a toothbrush. It was the most beautiful shell I had ever seen.

Then my eyes caught something else. On the inside of the box's cover, there was a perfectly preserved image. I swallowed hard. The Maya and lots of other ancient civilizations told stories through pictures, but I had never seen a painting like this. The picture depicted what looked like two demons. They were holding hands in front of a fire, surrounded by lush yellow flowering trees. One of the demons wore a red flower wreath on its head. I'd only ever known demons to be fang-baring, claw-dragging warriors. Definitely not the flower-wearing type.

I waved to get Brooks's attention. She swooped closer,

touching down as light as a feather next to me. Her eyes went wide when they landed on the painting. "What is that?"

"Demons having a party?"

"No—*that*." She brushed away more sand and pointed at a third creature, which was not wearing flowers. "*That* isn't a demon."

I did a double take. Brooks was right. It had a much bigger head than the two demons, and kind of exaggerated high cheekbones. But it was the huge, animal-like violet eyes that set the creature apart.

Where had I seen those eyes before?

Brooks stooped over, peering closer. "It's got scales."

I had missed that little detail. Snakelike white scales covered the creature's face, neck, and arms. Muy gross.

Glancing around nervously, Brooks said, "We need to get out of here."

That's when a trio of demon runners appeared in a puff of silver mist about fifteen feet away. I could tell they were part of Ixtab's elite army by their sharklike skin and the thick white braids hanging down their backs. So then who was the demon that was just here?

Brooks and I dove onto our bellies, hiding in the brush.

Crap!

If they saw us, we'd be tossed into a Xib'alb'a cage of torment faster than we could scream *HALP!*

Brooks took hold of my hand. *Stop breathing so loud.*

They're going to smell us before they'll hear us.

And then I remembered we were about twenty feet from

the ocean. Demons hate water, partially because it messes with their senses. Brooks must have made the same realization at the same moment, because she asked, *Feel like a swim?*

We began to slowly belly-crawl backward. Silently. No breathing allowed. Man, twenty feet felt longer than Death Valley. As soon as we had shimmied past the breakers, we dove under. I swam furiously, trying to put as much distance between me and the demons, and seriously wishing I had Brooks's killer ability to breathe underwater.

And that's when I realized I still had the black shell in my grasp.

Brooks grabbed my hand. *Come on, slowpoke.* And then she was hauling me along at a speed I guess only ha' nawals can attain.

A few seconds later, I broke free and went up for air. Brooks was right behind me.

We were a good hundred feet from the island. Wowza! She was a really fast swimmer!

"Hey," I said, searching the beach. "I don't see the demons anymore."

"They probs went into the cave of doom," Brooks said, wiping her soaked hair from her face. "I told you this was a bad idea."

"You think they knew we were here?" But what I was really asking was *Is Ixtab going to find out and come for our heads?*

"Hope not, 'cause I'm not about to be locked in a terror chamber, thank you very much."

Brooks shifted into a hawk and I floated onto her back.

"If that thing in the painting wasn't a demon," I said as she took flight, "what was it?"

No idea.

Ixtab's words rang in my memory loud and clear. *A species of being.* But what *kind* of being?

I've never seen anything like it, Brooks said. *And I've seen a lot, Zane.*

The sun was beginning to set, casting a pale golden glow across the sea. And then it hit me. I remembered where I had seen those eyes. They were part of a logo for an alien-sighting blog, *Eyes in the Sky*, written by my friend Ren. She was the first other godborn I discovered, and we're pretty tight. And did I mention that on top of being a godborn, she's also a shadow witch? Yeah, she can bend shadows to her will, create anything from nothing. That skill, combined with the fact that she's learning to manipulate time, pretty much makes her the most powerful of all of us godborns. She's also a big believer in alien civilizations.

After I told Brooks my revelation, I added, *You don't think . . .*

That Ixtab is stitching our names into our prison uniforms as we speak?

I'm serious, Brooks.

So am I.

A memory flashed across my mind. I was in Xib'alb'a with Ren a few months ago and she was bold enough to ask the queen of the underworld, *Have you noticed how much your demons look like aliens?*

We had all laughed it off, but what if Ren had been dead-on? What if demons—or some demons, at least—were actually part alien?

I must have asked that last impossible question out loud, because Brooks said, *Then it'll be the greatest secret the gods have ever kept.*

I fumbled for my (thankfully waterproof) phone.

Brooks said, *Please tell me you're not calling Itzamna or Pacific or ANY of the gods to ask about this.*

I dialed the number.

One ring.

Two.

Three.

Ugh, voicemail.

"Hi, it's me. You know what to do."

Beep.

"Ren!" I practically shouted. "I hope you're sitting down, because"—I glanced at the shell again—"you are not going to believe what I found!"

The Initiation

YOON HA LEE

OVER THE LAST FEW MONTHS, my brother, Jun, and I had faced space pirates, a treacherous tiger spirit, and a planet of vengeful ghosts. We'd come out ahead, even if Jun himself was a ghost now, and I looked forward to having more adventures. Sure, I was only thirteen, but I knew I could handle myself, especially with my powers as a fox spirit and the magic of the Dragon Pearl, which rested in a pouch at my waist.

When I stepped into my handler's office to learn about my first assignment at the Thousand Worlds' Domestic Security Ministry, I could hardly keep myself from bouncing on my toes.

"You want to impress the handler, remember?" Jun chided me. He was fifteen—forever fifteen now—and had served as a Space Forces cadet. Even as a ghost he retained the regulation haircut and dark-blue uniform most of the time. I knew I could trust his advice.

I knocked on the door, since Jun couldn't. "Agents Kim

Min and Kim Jun, reporting for duty," I said. I liked the sound of that.

"Come in," said a deep voice from within.

I entered and took a seat in an uncomfortable metal chair before my handler's desk. The seat had clearly been designed for an adult, and I was in my accustomed shape as a thirteen-year-old girl, rather than my natural fox form. Jun was a little taller, but of course he didn't need to sit.

"What's the mission?" I asked eagerly.

"First things first," said my handler, Seok. His stern expression and the gray uniform of the Thousand Worlds' Domestic Security Ministry would have intimidated most people, but not me. "You aren't an agent yet. You could get in trouble for claiming you are."

"If we aren't agents, then what are we?"

He smiled sourly. "You, Min, are an agent-in-training. Your first 'mission' is to go to the Gray Institute."

I digested that. "You're sending us to *school?*"

"Min . . ." Jun murmured.

"It's not *just* a school," Seok said, his face becoming sterner. "It's a *spy* school, if you insist. You won't be learning the quadratic formula—you'll be figuring out how to decrypt secret messages and spot sabotage on spaceships, that kind of thing."

"That's different," I said, perking up again. "And after graduation, we'll be full-fledged agents?"

Seok hesitated. "You'll be issued a temporary license, on account of your age." He nodded at Jun. "I realize that your condition"—he meant that Jun was *dead*—"makes the question of licensure moot in your case, but in Min's—"

"That's ridiculous," I protested. "You know what I'm capable of." Hadn't I rescued the Dragon Pearl from a corrupt tiger captain? "Besides, I could always shape-shift to look older."

"That only works if no one catches you doing it," Seok said. "Many people in the institute have prejudices against your kind."

I wrinkled my nose. By *your kind* he meant gumiho, or fox spirits. Most people in the Thousand Worlds believe we are extinct, but the harmful stories linger. In the old days, gumiho had used their powers of shape-shifting and Charm to bewitch travelers and, usually, eat them. I come from a family of reformed fox spirits. Jun and I had known since childhood that we needed to hide our powers—our identities—to keep everyone safe.

Seok continued, "You'll have to pretend to be older in order to attend the institute. Unfair as it is, no one will take a thirteen-year-old seriously. And you"—he turned to Jun—"will have to hide your presence. People don't have a high opinion of ghosts, either."

I nodded with false meekness and called on my shape-shifting powers, making myself taller. Maybe taller than was strictly necessary. I narrowed my face and gave myself the figure of a sixteen-year-old girl. Even though I was the right size for the chair now, it still hurt my tailbone. Apparently, the Domestic Security Ministry didn't believe in spending money on decent furniture.

Jun sneezed twice, which I heard as a tickling sound inside my head. Foxes can tell when another one uses magic, while other supernaturals, like goblins or dragons, are largely oblivious to it. When we foxes sense magic, we sneeze. I would have to make sure that Jun didn't give me away if I had to use my powers in an emergency.

"How's this?" I asked Seok. My voice was lower, too—a more mature alto.

"Very good," he said. "The training course lasts eight weeks. If you survive it, we may be able to make use of you. One thing more . . ."

I leaned forward.

"You'll have to leave the Dragon Pearl behind."

I scowled. "Why?" I resisted the urge to pat the pouch where it rested, although I could feel its weight tugging at my belt. The Pearl, an ancient artifact that had the power to terraform planets, had chosen me as its guardian. That wasn't something I was going to give up lightly.

Seok shook his head. "It's for your own good, and that of the Pearl. There's too much potential for trouble to follow you to the institute, and we want to keep the Pearl's location a secret, don't we? Not to mention that your possession of it would give you an unfair advantage over the other trainees."

I could have argued with him. But Jun was looking at me with concern, and I knew that he and Seok were right. Simply by virtue of having a ghost brother constantly by my side, I would be carrying bad luck around with me. I refused to abandon Jun, especially after all we'd been through, but at the same time I couldn't let that aura of misfortune affect the Pearl's safety. I had to deal with the consequences of living with a ghost, including protecting it and others from our luck.

"We'll look after it for you," said Seok, "and return it upon your graduation."

"All right," I said in resignation, hoping I could trust the handler. Everyone in the Thousand Worlds coveted the Pearl. I removed the pouch from my belt. A soft, sea-colored glow leaked from it, like mother-of-pearl waves tipped with pale foam. Then I handed the orb to Seok, and the glow faded.

Seok smiled faintly. "Even you can only get into so much trouble in eight weeks in a controlled environment," he remarked. "You'll be ready for action before you know it."

He was wrong on one of those counts.

The journey to the Gray Institute passed quickly. The Domestic Security Ministry booked me a spaceship transport to the ringed world where the school was located. As we came out of the Gate through space and approached the institute, I pressed my face to the viewport to stare at the place that would be my home for the next eight weeks.

The world, a gas giant, was named Daeriseok, or Marble. It resembled the fine marble I had seen on holo shows, aswirl with bands of color in moonish gray, rust, and shadowy violet. Daeriseok was made of gases that grew denser at the core, so there was no land, or even sea.

According to the briefings, people dwelled in wondrous floating cities with magically reinforced domes to protect them from Daeriseok's storms and poisonous atmosphere. The institute occupied one such dome.

"I don't even want to think about how much geomantic magic it takes to keep those domes stable," Jun remarked. He wasn't visible at the moment, to avoid spooking the ship's crew, but I could hear him clearly.

I'd known other ghosts during my adventures among the stars. As the stories warned, most of them were motivated by vengeance or anger or unfinished business. But Jun was different. His unfinished business involved his wish to visit every one of the Thousand Worlds. I didn't see any reason his being dead had to change that, and I hadn't noticed any change to his personality. He was still my reliable older brother, bad luck or no.

Spurred by Jun's remark, I examined the Gray Institute more closely. The viewport obligingly zoomed in. It definitely lived up to its name. Despite the shimmer of the dome, the institute resembled an old-fashioned fortress, except built of dull metal. Bands of light indicated the docking zones. Supply ships and shuttles flitted between the institute and the other domed cities, occasionally interrupted by flares of light in the sky as interstellar ships Gated to other worlds.

The institute loomed larger and larger until all I could see was the dark chute leading to the ship's assigned docking bay.

"Passenger Kim Min," the pilot said over the intercom, "please report to the airlock for disembarkation." The pilot repeated the announcement a few times, but I was already in motion with my one small bag. I no longer had the Pearl, sadly, and there hadn't been much else to pack. Seok had told me that the school would provide me with uniforms in my size.

I walked at a steady pace, as if my arrival didn't thrill me. Admittedly, I wasn't keen on taking classes, even if they did involve codes and ciphers and sabotage. I'd asked Jun if it would be cheating to do our homework together, and he'd only chuckled.

A short-haired officer greeted me in the docking bay, clad in a uniform—all gray, of course. A pin on her collar indicated that she should be addressed as a woman. I had a similar pin on my shirt.

"You're Trainee Kim Min?" she asked, smiling. "Please, come with me. I'm Lee Bina, and I help orient new arrivals to the special safety rules at the institute."

Surreptitiously, I sniffed the air. Like all foxes, I had an excellent sense of smell. Bina was mostly human, but I detected a whiff of tiger ancestry. That would explain why she had such a strong build.

Jun whispered, "You're staring," and I hastily bowed in greeting.

Bina bowed back, at a slighter angle, since she was the elder. "You're the last from Class Twenty-Two to arrive," she said. "The others have already gotten settled in the dormitory. I'll take you there."

As we walked, Bina showed me a map of the building on her data-slate. It had seven levels—seven for heaven's luck. Level one housed the docking bays and was off-limits except when we needed to travel planetside. The trainees' dormitories were on level two, and our classes would take place on levels two and three.

Bina had only gotten partway through explaining the layout of level two when an alarm went off. I almost jumped out of my skin. Along with my excellent sense of smell, I had acute hearing. More than the blaring noise, however, the acid stink of her fear made me want to lay my ears back against my skull.

"Stay with me," Bina said, "and do what I say, since I haven't briefed you on emergency procedures yet."

"Understood," I said, determined not to cause trouble. Not this kind of trouble, anyway.

"This is my fault," Jun said, chagrined. "The timing can't be a coincidence."

I didn't disagree, but I didn't want to make him feel worse, so I said nothing. We'd just have to deal with the situation, whatever it was.

Bina checked a status report on her slate, then strode quickly to a duty station, where a nervous trainee who smelled human was jabbing at several blinking controls. "Instructor!" he said, flushing. "I'm getting contradictory reports. This says the environmental dome is down, but there's no atmospheric leak."

I shivered. I might be magical, but even foxes need breathable air.

A severe voice came over the intercom. "Command to all personnel. There is a dome leak. Put on vacuum suits and shelter in place. We believe this to be a mechanical problem."

The doors that separated this section from the rest of the institute slammed shut. We were trapped.

I swallowed. "What else could it be?" I asked Bina as she pointed me toward the suit closet.

"In theory, an enemy attack," she replied, "but that's highly unlikely. Suit up, please."

One of the advantages of having done a stint on a battle cruiser was that I'd undergone many safety drills with the cadets. I knew how to put on a vacuum suit and adjust it for my size, then check its air supply.

Or so I thought. These suits were more sophisticated than the ones on the *Pale Lightning*, and it took me a few moments to figure out the controls. My initial attempt almost got me squeezed like a tube of toothpaste, but I fixed it in time.

Bina and the trainee had already suited up. The instructor was reporting in to Station Command. "Readings claim the leak is *right here*"—she indicated the emergency exit near the suit locker—"and I've gone over it with my instruments. It's a false alarm."

"Please confirm, Instructor," Command replied. "Are you sure an evacuation of the section isn't necessary?"

Oh no. I wasn't even going to be able to *start* the course if they had to evacuate the student quarters!

"Jun," I whispered while Bina talked to Command, "could you lurk somewhere else?" Without his bad luck around, maybe I could rectify the situation.

"I can't do that indefinitely," he protested. "I'm haunting *you*. If I stray too far, I'll—" He fell silent.

"You're right. Never mind." I didn't want him to lose his anchor to the world of the living. Besides, his absence would only solve the problem temporarily, and we were *both* here for training.

Bina nudged aside the trainee at the workstation, and he relinquished the controls. Her fingers spidered over the buttons. "Okay," she muttered. "That should do it. . . ."

Just then, I heard a loud, sharp *crack* from the wall. Correction: We all heard it. A second alarm blared, even louder than the first. My ears were going to ring for the rest of the day, assuming I survived that long.

If it hadn't been for my audience, I could have changed myself into a sheet of metal or rubber and covered the leak until someone else came up with a better solution. But Seok had warned me not to reveal my true nature. I didn't want to destroy our future by leading more people to believe that all foxes were no-good sneaks and liars.

Bina winced. "Min and Hansoo"—that had to be the other trainee—"you're about to get a crash course in emergency dome repair. Follow me."

I nodded a quick greeting at Hansoo before accompanying Bina to the hand- and footholds that lined the walls.

There was an ominous hissing as the station's air escaped through a deceptively small crack. How much longer would it be before the wall disintegrated and we were sucked out?

You've faced vengeful ghosts, pirates, and a wicked tiger spirit, I reminded myself. I could deal with this, too.

Bina opened a supply locker and started tugging on a heavy piece of machinery I didn't recognize. It was engraved with the character for *earth*. She had Hansoo and me help her roll it out.

"This is a shield generator," she said. "It will buy us time to seal the crack."

"This is Command," the same voice from earlier cut in, and I almost dropped my end of the generator, which would have smashed my toe. "Status?"

"Commandant Paik," Bina said, straightening unconsciously. "Attempting a fix, sir."

"You assured me that the maintenance checklist was accounted for just two days ago," Paik said, and I could practically hear her scowling.

"With all due respect, sir," Bina said as she gestured for Hansoo and me to continue hauling the generator toward the afflicted wall, "perhaps we could discuss restorative measures *after* I've dealt with the situation?" Her voice sounded hollow through the suit radio.

The commandant didn't respond, which was just as well.

There was another *boom* as the crack widened. I could see the darkness of the poisonous sky beyond it. I felt a pinch of panic and wondered how long the air in our suits would remain breathable. It was hard not to hyperventilate.

Relax, I told myself. I was sure I had at least eight hours of air before asphyxiation would kick in.

"This generator is short-range," Bina said, "due to its small size. But that makes it portable for emergencies like this." She indicated where she wanted us to set it up, practically on top of the crack.

We anchored the machine in place. Bina powered it on, and it started up with an obnoxious hum. Its blue glow formed a hemisphere that covered the fissure. The hissing noise stopped as the leak was plugged.

I would have sagged in relief, except my keen eye had caught a worrying detail. "Instructor," I said, "is that one of the station's meridians?"

All major structures in the Thousand Worlds, from the smallest office to the most immense space station, relied on meridians. Geomancers used the shape of the architecture, the arrangement of decorations, and the placement of gardens to ensure that the people within those structures enjoyed good luck.

I'd seen geomantic sabotage before, and I remembered the stomach-churning sensation that came from a broken meridian.

"This doesn't look like an accident to me," said Jun.

Hansoo cleared his throat, which sounded odd over the radio. He'd seen it, too. "Instructor," he said tentatively, "could it be a meridian problem?"

"We're going to need a geomancer to fix this," Bina muttered.

"Status report," the commandant's voice crackled over the suits' comm systems.

"Temporary seal in place," Bina said. "We've bought time for the engineers to do a repair. But, sir, there's a bigger problem. Trainees Kim Min and Lee Hansoo need to come with me to report to you in person."

Fifteen minutes later, all three of us were standing in the commandant's office. I couldn't remember the last time I'd seen such an impressive room—maybe Captain Hwan's office back on the battle cruiser *Pale Lightning*? It felt like a lifetime ago.

The commandant herself was a woman with her hair pinned up severely and a dense, muscular build that suggested that she came from a world with higher gravity. Her unsmiling expression told me that she wasn't one to cross. Besides, my instincts screamed that Commandant Paik was dangerous, and not just to my grades.

The commandant seemed to like cleanliness and order and right angles. A master geomancer must have laid out everything from the imposing desk finished with red-black lacquer to the ornate bookcases. I snuck a glance at the artifacts on the shelves, which looked out of place and whose significance I could only guess. Chipped stoneware with illegible inscriptions scratched into the glaze. A huge fossilized jawbone—surely not a dragon's? A shaman's damaged headdress.

I fought my unease. My homeworld, Jinju, hadn't attracted many shamans, but I knew about them. The profession was frequently passed down from parent to child—mother to daughter in the old days, but that had changed over time. I'd never heard of anyone *collecting* headdresses to use as decorations rather than ceremonial wear, and I'd also never heard of a shaman practicing while in the military. On the other hand, I was only a trainee, and it wasn't my place to ask.

More worryingly, I smelled the stink of Hansoo's nervous sweat and Bina's acidic fear. Was the commandant the type to punish the messenger? Or was Paik going to blame us for the damage to the station?

"Report," Paik said.

Bina summarized what we'd discovered.

The commandant's reaction surprised me: She smiled. It didn't make her look friendlier. The whiff of fear from Bina increased. What was going on?

"Congratulations," Paik said, staring directly into my eyes. I lowered them instead of staring back, which would have been disrespectful. "You passed the test."

I choked. "That was a *test*?" Cold air blasted my face, a reminder from Jun, and I hastily added, "Sir."

Too late. Paik's expression had already turned icy.

"You set it up as an initiation challenge, didn't you, sir?" Bina said with a reluctant note of admiration in her voice. "I should have known."

"Indeed," Paik said, as though that explained everything.

"I realize you come from a sleepier background, Trainee Kim," Paik said. "You were expecting sedate, sensible drills and lectures. But here at the Gray Institute we aim to turn out the Thousand Worlds' best agents, not meek bureaucrats. You must be on your toes all the time."

"Yes, sir," I murmured, all the while thinking, *This might be fun after all!*

"We aim," Paik continued, "to identify every recruit's special abilities through such tests." Her eyes gleamed, and I couldn't help feeling as though she could see through my human facade to my native fox shape. "You don't have any unusual heritage that I should know about, do you?"

I shook my head. The shape-shifting might be acceptable.

After all, dragon spirits and tiger spirits took on human forms so that they could fit into standard-size furniture and didn't block human-size doorways. But foxes could shape-shift more flexibly, and our other power, Charm, allowed us to sway people into doing what we wanted them to. That was the biggest reason people didn't trust foxes.

"Only human?" Paik pressed.

"There's no 'only' about it, sir," Hansoo interjected, looking injured.

Paik ignored him. "In any case," she said, "you should settle in and prepare for your next challenge." She smiled her cold smile again.

We didn't salute, but when Bina bowed to the commandant, Hansoo and I followed suit.

Bina assigned Hansoo to show me to my assigned bunk in the dormitory. I had a room to myself, albeit a small one. After Hansoo left, I looked at the bunk and tiny desk and joked to Jun, "If I'd been thinking, I would have brought decorations."

"I can attach myself to the wall if that would help," he quipped.

I was silent for a moment. Then: "Jun, I don't trust the commandant. She smells power-hungry."

"She does," he agreed, "but Seok won't take it well if you stage a revolution. We have to stick it out for eight weeks."

I was brooding about that when someone knocked. "It's Hansoo," he said, and I opened the door. "Are you ready to meet the rest of Trainee Group Nine?"

"Of course," I said.

They were waiting for me in the mess hall, which had a high ceiling and featured forbidding statues of warriors in old-fashioned lamellar armor, their swords sheathed at their sides. I'd handled a blaster before, but I didn't know how to use a sword. Had the commandant decorated the place? The statues seemed like her style.

Hansoo led me to a table where three other trainees awaited us. I glanced at their collar pins so I'd know how to address each of them. "This is Min," Hansoo said. "She's human like me." He grinned.

I smiled politely, but I was squirming inside. I hated having to lie about my identity, even though I should have been used to it by now.

"Hello, Min," said the tallest one. Their long blue-tinted hair was pulled back from their face in a ponytail, and they had the strong sea smell that indicated dragon heritage. "I'm Duri. My mothers wanted me to go into terraforming, but I'm hoping to become a customs inspector. Hansoo is always telling me it's the world's most boring job, yet last week I caught someone with counterfeit phoenix eggs in their luggage. I'm just surprised anyone was fooled. No heat or glow at all. That was *my* test."

I blinked. "What good are *counterfeit* phoenix eggs, and who was going to want them?" Phoenixes brought good fortune. It seemed sacrilegious to *smuggle* them.

Duri shrugged. "There's always a sucker, I guess." They nodded at the thin-faced girl next to them, who looked up from her old-fashioned paper book. The small horn in the center of her forehead proclaimed her goblin heritage. "That's Chinsun."

"I'm good with computers," she volunteered. She had a shy but friendly smile. "And if you ever get hungry, let me know!" Chinsun pulled out a pair of worn wooden chopsticks, the focus of her goblin magic, and flourished them. A packet of green-tea chocolates appeared, which she passed around.

"And I'm Haru," said the last one, who wore a belt packed with oddments. She grinned, revealing uneven teeth. "I'm a crack shot with a blaster."

"We're hoping it doesn't come to that," Chinsun said, but she exchanged smiles with Haru. "It's not like the instructors trust us with real weapons anyway."

"Which is a shame," Haru said. "I was hoping for live-fire exercises."

Given my experience of the commandant, I was surprised to hear that there *weren't*. "What 'tests' have the rest of you been through?"

"Good question," Jun said in my ear. "It'll help us get a better reading on Paik. At least she didn't put us through *two* tests, which means she doesn't know I'm here."

Chinsun slipped her book into a pocket and yawned exaggeratedly. "Mine was a virus in the station computers, causing the lights to blink on and off all haywire," she said. "It could have become a safety hazard if there'd been a *real* alarm."

"You're leaving out the part where you discovered that all the emergency pods had been disconnected, too," Duri chided her.

"Yeah, that, too." Chinsun yawned again, but I detected a whiff of remembered fear. She wasn't as blasé as she wanted us to think.

I looked expectantly at the girl who'd said she was good with blasters. "You?"

Haru smiled at me with such enthusiasm that I smiled back reflexively. "Killer robots!" she sang out.

"They wouldn't *really* have killed us," Duri said, but they didn't sound sure.

"Killer robots," Haru repeated stubbornly. "I had fun! Did you know that if you target the control systems in their midsections, you can take them right out? It's the *best*."

Chinsun's lips twitched. "You're so lucky you're not in hock for the repair fees. We rely on those robots to help us do maintenance!"

"They were shooting at me with their welding lasers," Haru said with a sniff. "I don't know what it's like on whatever cybernetic planet *you* come from, but where *I'm* from, if something shoots at you, you gotta shut it down."

"Yeah, and I'll be doing repairs with you during our off hours this entire training course," Chinsun grumbled.

While the two squabbled, I turned to Hansoo. "What about you?" I asked quietly, wondering why he'd been subdued during the whole discussion.

He flushed. "It didn't go so well."

I was dying of curiosity, but my shoulder felt icy cold as Jun warned me off. He was right. Besides, if it was important, I could get someone else to tell me later.

"What's your specialty?" I added, because I didn't want the conversation to end on an awkward note.

"Administration," Hansoo said, a touch defensively. "Someone has to do the paperwork."

I couldn't imagine settling for that instead of adventures, but I guessed it took all types.

Training started the next day, in the auditorium on level three. The first two days consisted of lectures about "our glorious heritage" and the history of the Domestic Security Ministry, and then, more sensibly, safety protocols. Jun didn't even have to blast me with cold to get me to pay attention to the latter. After my "test," I wanted to be prepared, just in case.

One of the safety protocols intrigued me, because it was so unusual. "Most of all," Commandant Paik said, her voice sharpening in a way that piqued my interest, "avoid damaging the advanced geomantic artifacts around the station. Because of the number of moons in orbit, the Gray Institute requires special tuning in order to maintain its dome and habitability. I don't have to tell you what the negative consequences could be"—she paused dramatically—"and I doubt any of you want to be the one responsible for causing the entire station to crash into the planet below."

"That's not possible," Jun murmured in my ear. "It's a gas giant. We'd just go out the other side."

I shivered. Either way, it didn't sound like a good fate.

On the third day, we woke to messages telling us to report

to a designated area for a training exercise. We assembled in the hallway, since our rooms were all next to one another.

"Who's the group leader?" I asked Hansoo when he emerged, and he pointed at Duri. I wondered uncharitably if they'd been chosen for their tall height. Then again, Haru would have been a terrible pick, and Hansoo didn't seem very assertive, and—

"It's randomly assigned," Duri said in a self-deprecating voice, as though they'd divined my thoughts. "C'mon, we're on the upper level."

The other groups were already in motion, filing out of the hallway in an orderly fashion, which impressed me more than I wanted to admit. They looked so adult. I'd just have to prove myself, even if nobody knew that I was secretly younger than everyone else here.

We walked quickly through the silver passages of the station and took the elevator to the upper student level, three. I wanted to ask the others what was expected of us—I'd been given little information, which I assumed was intentional—but their subdued expressions told me this wasn't the moment for questions. Instead, I spent the time wondering how much I trusted the ministry to prepare us for real emergencies without accidentally offing us. Chinsun's story of the disconnected emergency pods and Haru's "killer robots" hadn't exactly been reassuring.

"What *is* the assignment?" I finally asked as we approached the area we'd been sent to, which lay beyond a strange, worn turtle statue. The site, complete with spaceship wreckage, looked like it had been bombed.

We'd been sent to a shuttle bay that was designated for evacuations. I thought again of the commandant warning us not to send the institute tumbling into the gas giant. As a steader, I'd had to scratch out a living by farming in poor soil on Jinju, but I'd never had to worry about the *planet being completely permeable*. It made me more aware of how precarious life could be on other worlds.

"This is like one of those murder-mystery party games," Duri said, becoming more animated as they spoke. "We show up and try to figure out what's wrong and how to fix it."

"I'm good at puzzles," Hansoo volunteered.

Haru brightened, too. "Maybe there will be more killer robots!"

Chinsun shook her head. "Why didn't you join the Space Forces if you think the solution to everything is shooting it?"

"Too much hierarchy," Haru said, making a face. "Not enough killer robots."

As Chinsun rolled her eyes, Haru winked at me.

When we were near the statue, Duri swayed, and Haru reached an arm out to steady them. "You okay?" she asked.

"It's nothing," Duri said, not very convincingly. "I get these spells sometimes. I think I'm allergic to something in the station's air."

"The environmental filters should purge any allergens," Hansoo noted, "and the hydroponics aren't even on this level."

He noticed my curious look and added, "I memorized the regulations relating to particulate concentrations."

I made a note to myself that Hansoo would make a great study partner for anything technical. I was good at fixing things, sure, but I was a hands-on sort of mechanic, not a theoretician.

Hansoo said to Duri, "You sure you don't want to see a medic?"

Duri waved off his concern. "No, I'm fine. It'll pass—it always has before."

As Duri spoke, I frowned dubiously at them. For a second I could have sworn their outline had wavered. I knew they were part dragon. It showed in the blue tint to their hair and the hint of scales along the backs of their hands. I'd known a dragon spirit once who'd looked more human than this one, but perhaps shape-shifting abilities varied among individuals. In any case, I could have sworn Duri had grown . . . even taller? It was subtle, if so—maybe a couple of centimeters. But it suggested that they had lost control of the magic that kept them in human form.

Keep an eye on Duri, I mouthed to Jun. *I think something's wrong.*

An answering breath of cold air tickled my hand.

We returned our attention to the assigned area. There was a crumpling noise as something fell apart. Haru reached reflexively toward her belt, then caught herself, scowling. "They relieved me of my firearm after my initiation," she explained.

"Is that how you did away with the killer robots?" I asked.

She nodded. "They said I wouldn't need Old Fiery for the course, and when I'm certified I'll have to use field-issue instead."

It would never have occurred to me to *name* a blaster, but it told me a lot about Haru's relationship with weapons.

Chinsun hadn't allowed the byplay to distract her. "This looks like an *ex*-shuttle," she said in fascination. "Like if you turned it inside out and put the pieces through a blender."

"And you say *I'm* morbid," Haru muttered. She paced the perimeter, peering this way and that. "No other instructions, really?"

Duri consulted their slate. "We're supposed to clean this up and determine the cause of the incident."

"'Incident,'" I said, shaking my head. "Looks bigger than an 'incident' to me."

"Oh," Hansoo said wryly, "but don't spook the civilians, remember?"

A nervous laugh ran around the group. There weren't any civilians in the Gray Institute except people who docked temporarily to transport passengers or supplies.

"I'm so glad my little sibs aren't running free in this place," Hansoo said, looking around in dismay. "I'm not sure it's even safe for adults."

I hid a grin. I wasn't about to confess how old I really was. But Hansoo had a point.

I scanned the metal shrapnel with my slate's camera and ran it through a program to reconstruct how the shuttle had originally looked. The program needed some assistance on my part, but one of the things my late father had taught me was to see how machines were put together. I'd made good use of the skill in the past—I just hadn't expected it to come in handy here. I compared the results against the specifications for the institute's standard evacuation shuttles.

"There's a problem," I said. "The engine's core is still active. If it's unstable and it blows up . . ."

Even Haru blanched at the prospect of being caught in an explosion. "Where *is* it? You'd expect there to be a glow."

I showed the others my slate. The core was cleverly hidden beneath a pile of twisted metal scrap and dirt. How did you get that much dirt in a space station? Someone must have been importing it by the truckload.

"It's not a fake, is it?" Chinsun asked, although she sounded dubious. "I mean, even Commandant Paik wouldn't . . ."

Hansoo shushed her, and Jun's answering blast of cold almost froze my arm. "Watch what you say," Hansoo whispered.

"Too late," Chinsun remarked, although she also kept her voice down. "They're taking video of us."

"You could have told us that before," I grumbled, though I should have thought of it.

"Nah, it's fine," Chinsun said. "I'm feeding it a loop that shows us talking about our favorite singers."

"You don't even know our favorite singers," I said.

"Don't I?"

Haru looked glumly at the wreckage. "I didn't sign on for this. Shooting is the *opposite* of what you want to do when there's a risk of things blowing up in your face!"

"Wow," Chinsun said. "Common sense. I never thought I'd hear it from you."

"I wish I could make it *rain*," Duri said, referring to the weather magic dragons could wield. "But that wouldn't do anything for an engine fire. Is there a risk of that?"

"Yeah, is there?" Jun repeated. His voice sounded staticky, as though it were coming over a garbled comm channel.

While the others began clearing an access route to the engine core, I whispered to him, "Are you okay? You don't sound so great." Not that I was any kind of expert on ghost health, even though I'd met more than my fair share of them—a story for another day.

A faint cold breeze drifted by my left hand, then faded. I strained to hear whatever Jun was trying to tell me, but no luck.

Oh no. Did the Gray Institute have some kind of anti-ghost defense that Seok had neglected to warn us about? The more I thought about it, the more I realized that it wasn't such an outlandish idea. After all, if a high-security station like this one couldn't risk having its operations interrupted by bad luck from misaligned meridians, stray ghosts would be just as bad.

Jun isn't just any ghost, I told myself.

Duri nudged me, their mouth pulling down in an anxious expression. "Min," they said. "I know this is stressful, but we could use your help."

I was torn between telling them I had bigger concerns and snapping to. But whatever was wrong here could be related to

Jun mysteriously fading out. So solving one problem might solve the other.

"Sorry about that," I said with a shaky smile. I sniffed the air involuntarily, worried by the faint metallic reek I associated with engines. "What do you need from me?"

"I'm good with code," Chinsun said, "so if there's a bypass to shut down the engine, I could try that. I'm kind of a klutz, though. . . ."

"That's not reassuring at all," Haru said. Still, she patted Chinsun reassuringly on the shoulder. "How do you get by on physical evaluations?"

"I hack my way into the assistant waldoes and robots," Chinsun explained, "and I can use them to be my hands. Here, though . . ." She looked around dubiously. We all stared at the wrecks of what had once been the kinds of waldoes she was referring to.

I smiled tentatively at her. "I've got steady hands," I said. All the repairs I'd done around our ramshackle house on Jinju had been good training. "Just tell me what to do."

Duri and Haru also had good hand-eye coordination, so between the three of us, we soon cleared the engine core. I'd never seen one without its protective casing before. Looking at it made me anxious, and I could smell the others' worry.

Duri said something impolite under their breath when they jostled what remained of the primary dampener.

"Whoa, there," I protested, reaching out to steady the engine.

I hadn't imagined it the first time. Duri had grown another few centimeters. "Jun," I whispered. "Do you see it, too?"

But there came no response, and I didn't have time to wander off looking for my brother, much as I wanted to.

"Duri," I said, despite my reluctance to distract everyone, "have you noticed that you're *growing*?"

"I'm normally better at staying in human shape than this!" Duri said, refusing to meet anyone's eyes.

"That's not all," Chinsun said. She pulled out her chopsticks, which served as the focus of her conjuring magic. They had merged into a single stick and swollen in size, more closely resembling . . . a club. In the days of old, goblins had all carried magical clubs instead of more modern items like chopsticks or sporks. "I always look like this—well, plus or minus the haircut—but my magic is being unruly."

"You, too," Hansoo ventured, waving his hand to get my attention. "Duri is getting taller . . . but you're getting *shorter*. And your eyes have gone amber."

We all glanced at one another nervously.

"So, as you can see, I'm not entirely human," I said, because I didn't want them to freak out over my eyes. But I didn't elucidate. Thankfully, no one seemed to have jumped to the conclusion that there was a gumiho in their midst, and I wasn't going to bring it up.

I could have used Jun's guidance . . . but my brother was nowhere to be seen or heard. " 'Scuse me," I muttered, because I needed to check for him. "My nose itches."

"I've got a handkerchief," Hansoo offered, but I waved him off and pretended I was about to pick my nose in front of everyone. He hastily averted his gaze, as I'd intended.

My entire right arm was so cold it had gone numb. "What's with you?" I hissed at Jun as I turned away from the others. "You've never been this *ghostly* before."

In answer, the blast of cold only intensified.

I bit down a yelp. "Would you cut that out?"

Jun's voice, when he spoke, sounded as though it were echoing in a cavern of infinite depth. "Sorry, sorry . . ."

"Don't 'sorry' me, just *quit it*."

If anything, the cold grew more bitter.

"I'm sorry!" he said again, chagrined.

This time I saw Jun's outline in the sepulchral colors of ash and moonlight, and his hair, which had grown out, hung down raggedly the way ghosts' hair always did in the stories. He looked less like a respectable former Space Forces cadet, albeit one who happened to be dead, and more like a specter that was apt to eat your eyes if you offended him.

I drew back reflexively when his fingernails grew claw-like and his hair shifted white from its usual glossy black. I tried to cover my reaction, but he had already seen it.

"Something's not right," Jun said, every word accompanied by icy air. "I'm going to get some distance and try to figure this out before I bring harm to anyone."

He smiled sadly as he drifted away, walking with his misty not-legs into the distance.

I turned back toward the other trainees.

"Are you done with your *personal business* yet?" Hansoo asked.

"Yeah, sorry." I wiped my nose with my sleeve just to sell him on the fib, and his face screwed up in distaste.

In the meantime, Duri now towered over me by a good thirty centimeters. "I'm large as a dragon," they said, their shoulders hunched, "so it's a good thing we're in a shuttle bay and not a more confined area."

"Should we report this to the commandant?" Chinsun asked. "Maybe this isn't part of the test."

"What if it is?" Hansoo countered. "We don't want to give our evaluators the impression we can't deal with unforeseen circumstances."

The next thing that happened took the matter out of our hands. Duri's hair sheened deep blue, and their eyes as well. Blue-green scales grew over their olive skin. They bent over in pain. Hansoo tried to rush to their side, but Duri waved him off. "Get back!" they growled in a distorted voice, deep and rumbling, like the roar of the sea.

Duri hadn't been kidding when they said they were a large dragon. After all, dragons were spirits of sea and storm, and the seas—on planets that had them—could support much bigger creatures than the land could. I'd never thought about this much, because Jinju had been too barren to have much in the way of rain, let alone large bodies of water.

Sinuous coils rippled around the shuttle bay, and Duri's head lengthened into a dragon's visage, complete with a snout and deer-like antlers. I sneezed at the briny smell of seawater that permeated the air.

The remnants of Duri's uniform fluttered comically to the floor. There was no way they could have fit into it now. Their shirt couldn't even have wrapped around one of their thick forelimbs.

"Sorry about this," Duri said to us dolefully. It was almost funny to see a dragon of such size trying to coil into a knot so as not to take up more space. They were practically the size of a hoverbus as it was. "I think I wrecked the site. . . ."

"Oh no!" I exclaimed. Among other things, they were atop the shuttle engine. Or former shuttle engine. It had collapsed in on itself like crushed origami, but without exploding—so far.

"It's a fake!" Chinsun cried. "Duri, would you mind shifting that bit of tail?" Obligingly, they did. Chinsun dug around in the crushed remnants of the engine's exterior and produced a tiny device. "This projector fooled all our scanners into thinking there was a real engine inside."

"All the readings looked real," I said.

Duri slithered aside so we could get a better look. "It's like sitting on caltrops," they complained.

"How could they trick us like that?" Haru wondered.

"Safer than actually leaving an unstable engine core here," I said. "Let me see."

It was a tight squeeze now that most of the shuttle bay was occupied by a dragon. I inspected the device, then looked at Chinsun. "Can you hack this?"

She poked at her slate, which had miraculously escaped

being crushed, and typed out some commands. After a few moments, she looked up and grimaced. "Holographic generator in combination with some sneaky code to fool all our software into thinking it was real. And they have all the specs for our software, so . . ."

"We don't need the gory details," Haru said hastily.

"Wait a second," Duri said, preoccupied with something else entirely. "If we're losing control of our magic and reverting to our natural forms, what about everyone else at the institute? Listen."

I kicked myself for not thinking of that earlier. I'd been distracted by the small (large?) matter of having an immense dragon crowding us out. Now that Duri mentioned it, however, I could hear a cacophony from the nearest corridor. Animal sounds—the kind that might be made by dragons, or tigers, or panicked humans.

Also, why was I tangled up in my uniform, and when had everyone become so much taller? I began to say something, but it came out as a plaintive yip.

"Min," Haru demanded, "you're a *fox*?"

I was about to reply, except my ear itched so badly I *had* to scratch it. Normally I would have used my right hand, and I tangled myself up trying to reach for my ear with a forepaw. Then I figured I could use one of my hind paws instead. In the process, I clawed my way out of the clothes. It was only after I'd taken care of the distracting itch that I looked up to see the others—dragon, goblin, and two humans—staring rudely at me.

"Sorry," I said. It came out as half a whine. I looked down to see that my uniform was in shreds on the floor. Ordinarily I could conjure myself a suitable outfit as part of my shape-shifting magic. I tried to reassume my human shape and had no luck.

I was forcibly reminded of how *small* I was as a fox. My tail thumped nervously against the floor as I tilted my head back to regard the others. I could smell the reek of their distrust.

"Does the commandant know you're a gumiho?" Haru asked suspiciously. "I didn't think foxes were allowed in the Domestic Security Ministry!"

"There isn't a regulation *against* it," Hansoo said, which made me warm to him.

I tried nudging them all with Charm, mainly to soothe their suspicions so they wouldn't get distracted by the trifling matter of my heritage. It was probably a bad idea, but it was so hard to think clearly, especially when my ears kept itching! I hoped I didn't have fleas, because that would suck. Besides, whoever heard of fleas on a space station?

To my dismay, my magic didn't respond at all. It was as though I was trying to pick a flower that wasn't actually there. I assumed this was related to the fact that I'd lost control of my shape-shifting, just as Duri had fetched up as the most doleful dragon.

"Fox or not, we need everyone we can get," Chinsun said, to my everlasting gratitude.

I was so tempted to say *I'm a good fox* and roll over to expose my belly and show how harmless I was. I didn't want to give up my dignity even for the sake of sarcasm, though, and besides, I doubted it would convince them. Instead, I said, "My handler wanted me to keep my heritage secret because he was afraid it would be a distraction." It was close to the truth.

Haru flushed. "Fair enough," she said. "You haven't done us any wrong. It's just . . . the stories . . ."

If I'd been in my human shape, I would have blushed, too. I'd lied to a lot of people in my previous adventures and caused my share of trouble. I didn't possess Jun's steady nature, and if my ancestors had been anything like me, it was no wonder we foxes had such a bad reputation. I wasn't about to admit all this to them, though. Surely even foxes deserve a fresh start?

"I'll behave myself," I said, crouching low and wagging my tail. "Promise."

"All right," Haru said, and nodded curtly.

I would have no trouble navigating through the halls as a fox—the silver lining of being so small—but Duri was another matter. They weren't going to fit through the shuttle bay's exit unless they battered down the wall. "You go on without me," Duri said glumly.

"We can't do that," Hansoo protested.

"I'm not in any danger here," Duri said. "I'll figure out an alternate route. Go!"

We must have looked a motley sight as we hustled through the halls: two humans, a goblin awkwardly brandishing her chopsticks-turned-club as if she'd never held a weapon in her life, and me, a small red fox. Haru cast a worried glance back over her shoulder. "Duri only said that to make us feel better," she said. "What if the whole setup blows up anyway? I don't remember them being any good at improvised engineering."

"No," I said, "that's my department. Except I'm sure fox paws are no good for holding a vibra-screwdriver or laser cutter." My words came out between yips and barks, but the others seemed to understand them. After all, fox spirits had been speaking human languages since ancient times.

Hansoo shuddered. "I'd hate for you to hurt yourself trying, Min."

The next scene we reached made us pull up short. A tiger was cowering precariously on a ladder while its teammates tried to coax it down. Meanwhile, a red-faced boy was shouting incoherently at it and waving a welding torch in a way that made me think that someone was about to lose a hand, or maybe a head, even if the torch was switched off. I had the unpleasant thought that I had yet to meet anyone in the medical department. What if the chief surgeon was currently saddled with paws like me?

"What's going on here?" a shrill voice demanded. It was the red-faced boy.

I'd forgotten that people always do a double take when they see a fox wandering around. The boy dropped the welding torch, and I almost had a heart attack. Fortunately, it didn't switch on when it clattered against the floor.

"And why do you have a dog?" one of the other trainees demanded of my companions.

I stiffened and drew myself up to my full height, which wasn't much. *I'm not a DOG*, I opened my mouth to snarl.

"Min!" Jun whispered in my ear. I could feel crystals of

frost congealing on my fur, and I couldn't help but whimper in a mixture of gratitude and discomfort at the chill.

I wagged my tail in relief. Jun was back! In fact, he was eerily visible in the way of ghosts—a pale figure sheathed in rags, white for death. His hair, grown to waist length, hung loosely around his wan face, stirred by a nonexistent wind.

Even though I'd known Jun all my life, living or dead, I scarcely recognized him. It didn't help that as a fox I relied more on my nose than my eyes, and Jun didn't smell of anything except winter winds and the tallow reek of bone. I didn't remember this even from my previous encounters with ghosts. It was as if something had stripped any semblance of humanity from him.

"I'm so glad you're back!" I said, tail still wagging, because I was desperate to remind him that I was his little sister.

I hadn't counted on my teammates' reactions, however. A fox spirit was bad enough, but a ghost was even worse.

"I'll slow the ghost down," Haru hissed. "The rest of you, make a run for it."

Oh no! Jun was visible to everyone. Of all the times . . .

My ears went flat. "He's not going to hurt you!"

"Uh, Haru?" Chinsun said, studying me and Jun as though she saw oddities like this every day. "I don't think a gun, which you don't have anyway, is going to slow down a *ghost*." She addressed me next. "How do you know he's not harmful?"

I hung my head. "He's my brother," I said. "He died an untimely death. But he's always had my back, and he was an honorable Space Forces cadet in life. Please give him a chance."

Chinsun bit her lip. "Well, I guess it's not like we have much of a choice. Nobody here is a shaman, so we can't exorcise him."

Not exactly the most ringing endorsement, but I'd take it if it meant they'd accept Jun for the moment.

The other group of trainees had clustered together as if to defend themselves against me, like a small fox outnumbered by the rest of them had any chance at taking them all out with elite martial-arts moves. I wished!

"We have problems of our own," the red-faced boy said, edging closer to the fallen welding torch. He gestured toward the tiger, who made an abashed whine. "If you insist on palling around with a fox and a ghost, that's your problem. Just get them *out of here*."

"Well, *that* was friendly," Chinsun muttered.

Jun and I had already hurried past them. I didn't want to be around if the red-faced boy decided to turn that welding torch on me after all. Chinsun, Haru, and Hansoo trailed in our wake. I glanced back and saw Haru's eyes darting back and forth, taking in our surroundings as if we were about to be jumped.

When we had gotten some distance away from the other group, Hansoo ventured, "I hate to bring this up again, but are we sure we don't want to call the commandant? I know she, ah, has a fondness for testing us to our limits, but this seems extreme even for her."

I nodded, which felt odd as a fox. Even hot-tempered Haru grunted in assent. "Worth reporting," she said, "just in case."

Chinsun used her slate to try to contact Command. After several tense moments, she looked up and shook her head. "I'm not getting a response, which is weird. Want me to try hacking my way in?"

Hansoo looked alarmed, and I whined in agreement. I didn't imagine the commandant would take *that* well.

Chinsun's mouth curled in a half-wry, half-disappointed smile. "I guess we soldier on, then."

We passed other strange sights as we made our way through level three. Everyone—instructors and trainees alike—had been affected by the transformations.

Soon enough, though, we had more problems to worry about.

"Why's the corridor flooding?" Hansoo wondered as his foot splashed into an inch of water.

One cluster of trainees, which included a bewildered celestial youth whose skin glowed faintly, was trying to calm an agitated dragon. This one was much smaller than Duri, with green-and-lavender scales like fine jade. And unlike Duri, this dragon appeared to have lost control of their weather magic, because rain pelted down all around them. I could even see thick, sodden clouds above their head.

I bit back a whimper. Getting my paws wet had sounded fun when I was growing up on an arid planet where it rarely rained. But in reality soggy paws were even worse than having squelchy socks, because I couldn't take them off.

"I don't think the elevators are going to work if there's

flooding," Chinsun said, and we all agreed. We rerouted toward the emergency stairs.

The water slowly rose as we splashed onward. If I'd been human, I would've barely noticed, but now that I was half a yard at the shoulder, it was a different story. I lifted my tail high so it wouldn't drag in the water.

Besides, I didn't know how to swim! I had this vague idea that you floated and paddled a lot . . . and hoped for the best? If I survived whatever had gone haywire at the institute, I resolved that I would celebrate becoming a special agent by taking swimming lessons.

Other groups we passed included all sorts of supernaturals. More celestials, who were descended from the cosmic attendants of old. Their star-colored glows reflected in the water, and at any other time I would have admired the beauty of the light. Goblins like Chinsun, their horns more prominent now, were weighed down by unwieldy magical clubs. One of them had conjured himself a soda and was sipping it while calmly contemplating his teammates. We saw two more tigers, one of whom was sheltering in a box like an overgrown cat. There were others kinds of creatures, too, that I didn't recognize, and I hunched down, nose twitching, at the overwhelming mix of unfamiliar smells.

I was sad, but not surprised, to note that I was the only fox and Jun the only ghost.

Everyone in the bewildering tableaux had one thing in common: Each of them was near an artifact. The pieces came in all shapes and sizes, from wooden totems with elongated human faces to gilt antler crowns hung with comma-shaped beads, from worn swords of bronze to ink paintings on silk. The stomach-wrenching sense of wrongness near the artifacts reminded me of geomancy gone fetid. My unease grew.

"I don't know if the rest of you can sense it," I said, embarrassed by the way my speech was punctuated with yips and barks, "but the magic in the Gray Institute smells funny. It's worst around all the weird artifacts scattered around the place. They've got to be connected to the chaos."

"I'm human and even I can sense it," Hansoo said, backing me up. "Like I'm about to puke."

"Don't do that!" I said hastily, because I didn't want to step in it, what with the flooded floor. "Chinsun, Haru, what about you two?"

Chinsun shook her head, but Haru nodded reluctantly. "No one's ever accused me of being sensitive to magic," she said, "but it does jinx firearms sometimes, and this feels like one of those times."

Someday I'd have to ask her to tell me more. "Chinsun," I said, "I think we'd better try to call the commandant again at this point. This is out of control even for a training exercise."

"You'd think someone would have called it in already," Hansoo agreed, "but in that case, why hasn't she made an announcement?"

"Everyone's preoccupied," I said. "I'd do it, but . . ." I lifted a paw and looked woefully up at the others.

"I never thought about how inconvenient it would be not

to have hands," Haru said in chagrin. "No wonder your people went in for shape-shifting!"

Chinsun cleared her throat, and Haru pulled out her slate. "Command," she said, "this is Haru from Trainee Group Nine. I have a report for the commandant, or for whatever authority is available to take it." She had a crisp, soldierly way of speaking that made me nostalgic for my former stint aboard a battle cruiser, even if *that* had ended in shenanigans. But that's a story for another day.

Haru repeated herself, then put her ear to the slate. "I even adjusted the volume and everything," she said crossly.

"No response?" I said.

"Nope."

"Time for hacking?" Chinsun said, perking up.

We were almost to the stairs, if I remembered the institute's layout correctly. "Can you do it while we head for level five?" I asked. That was where the command center was located, including the commandant's office.

"No problem," Chinsun said with a chirpiness that I would have found reassuring under other circumstances. She continued to walk while staring intently at her own slate, poking at it and muttering to herself. Before I could say that I was worried she would careen into a wall, Haru took her elbow to guide her.

We reached the stairs. They were slippery from more flooding. I placed my feet carefully, since I didn't want to drown. Jun slowed down to keep me company, and I yipped my gratitude.

"Got into the system!" Chinsun exclaimed suddenly when

we had nearly made it to level five. Her voice took me by surprise, and I almost lost my footing on the steps and skidded down. Fortunately, I was nimbler as a fox than I was as a human, so I caught myself in time.

"Commandant, beg to report!" Haru said, leaning over so she could speak directly to Chinsun's slate. There came a crackle of static, but no response. "Why aren't there any visuals?"

"Cameras seem to be offline," Chinsun said, a furrow forming between her brows. "Do you think the commandant's in trouble?"

"We're almost there," I said. "Be prepared to intervene."

Haru cast a skeptical glance in my direction. "I guess you could create a distraction—you and your brother the ghost."

I bristled, but she was right. We foxes didn't overcome our predators through brute force, considering our diminutive size. And I didn't have access to the magic that would have made me more dangerous if it came to a fight. I'd always done best with guile.

Ironic that I'd been told to keep a low profile, and here I was in a situation where my magic could help us all, if only it would come back. Maybe Jun could scare the enemy?

At a nudge from Haru, Chinsun shoved her slate back into her pocket. We paused at the doors that opened from the stairwell, listening. Ominously, the din was, if anything, even worse here. Roaring, bird noises, busted electronics, the works.

Haru, Chinsun, and Hansoo all exchanged concerned looks. It was all I could do to keep my tail from thumping against the floor in agitation. If the command center was under attack, or had been sabotaged, I didn't want to tip off any enemies that the cavalry had arrived. Even if the cavalry consisted only of a goblin hacker who kept tripping over her club, a trigger-happy girl without a trigger, a budding bureaucrat . . . and one fox with drenched paws.

"I'll take point," Haru said, barely loud enough for us to hear her over the noise. "Min, you're the fastest, so be ready to bite any evildoers on my signal. If you can get their ankles, it'll limit their maneuverability. Chinsun, see if you can hack any of the maintenance robots into helping us out. Hansoo, watch the rear so we don't get ambushed."

"I wish I'd spent more time in martial-arts class," Hansoo said with a shaky grin, but he nodded to acknowledge her instructions.

Haru hit the door's controls and darted through and to one side when they started to open. She was so fast she could almost have been a fox herself. "Find cover!" she shouted before I'd had a chance to do anything but inhale the confusing mixture of stinks—mostly fear and dust and strange magic. My fur immediately stood on end.

I dashed toward an upturned chair, taking in the situation as I did. No wonder no one had answered our calls. Everyone was—dead? All the staff were sprawled on the floor or slumped in their chairs. But the commandant herself was nowhere to be seen. At the far end of the command center I saw the door to her office, closed and distinguished with a fancy plaque of blue and silver.

I couldn't see what Haru was doing, as a bank of consoles

blocked my view. I crouched behind one of the chairs, my ears flattening at the continued racket, and nudged the leg of the officer who was slouched in the seat. They didn't *smell* dead, and—aha! I saw their chest rising and falling, however shallowly. Just unconscious.

"I'll grab the first-aid kit," Hansoo said from behind me. "Chinsun, help me make sure everyone's okay?"

That left Haru, Jun, and me to face whatever had taken out everyone in the command center. I discovered that I was snarling. No way was some unnamed monster from the depths of space going to ruin my chance to become a secret agent! Jun, hollow-cheeked and long-haired, looked like he was keen to haunt whoever was responsible for all this.

"Come to me!" Haru yelled, and I ran up to crouch at her side. From the staff she'd scavenged not one but two blasters, one for each hand. I had to admit, it looked impressive, if impractical. But maybe she really was good enough to use two at once.

Just as we approached the door to the commandant's office, it exploded outward as though a giant had punched it. Only pure chance, or maybe it was leftover luck from the station's geomancy, prevented the metal shrapnel from puncturing any of the hapless staff. I felt a splinter graze my head, and a tuft of fur sliced off and wafted away.

A howling monstrosity emerged from the office. It was so tall that it had to hunch over to clear the wrecked doorway. As a matter of fact, it wrenched the doorframe open with clawed hands so the opening would accommodate its girth. I'd never seen or heard of anything like it before, whether in the folktales that my mom and aunties used to tell me when I was a kit, or in the holo shows that we'd crowded together to watch.

I only got a blurred impression of its appearance, which shifted from moment to moment before it rushed us. It had stripes like a tiger, scales like a dragon, thick muscles like a goblin wrestler, a fox's white-tipped tail, and more besides. I dodged and snapped at its heels as it barreled past me. Ugh! It tasted foul, like socks that had been worn for a week with a side of sewage and kimchi gone bad. There was something naggingly familiar about its smell, though. . . .

I circled around for a second attack. As I did so, Haru fired at it one-two, one-two with both of her blasters in a punishing rhythm. The creature snarled and swiped at the bolts of energy, which charred its hide and left a nasty scorched smell in the air. Haru certainly had its attention, even though she didn't seem to be slowing it down.

Chinsun must have succeeded at her hacking, because a number of maintenance robots were helping her and Hansoo drag the helpless staffers to safety in the stairwell. It was up to Haru, Jun, and me to keep the creature from destroying the makeshift infirmary in its rampage.

"Jun," I said after my second foul-tasting nip, "can you fly right at it? Jinx it real bad?" I figured if just having a ghost in the vicinity was bad luck, having a ghost stick it right to you would be even worse.

Jun's hollow laugh chilled me, and I inadvertently tucked my tail between my hind legs. "Gladly," he said, and lunged toward the creature, his hair streaming behind him. The creature recoiled when he passed *through* it and then stayed stuck *inside* it, like a terrible case of supernatural indigestion. All I could see of Jun were occasional fluttering strands of his hair. Would he be stuck in there forever?

"Jun!" I inhaled sharply in alarm, and the creature's stench filled my lungs. This time, however, I recognized the smell. "It's Commandant Paik!"

"You mean it ate her?" asked Haru.

"I don't think so," I said. "I'm pretty sure it *is* her."

How could she have morphed into *this* monstrosity? I thought furiously. And then I heard a scraping sound *above* the Paik-creature. Something was coming through the ventilation and trying to claw its way out. Another enemy?

I breathed deeply, almost gagging on Paik's smell. But another odor accompanied it, this one more welcome.

"Haru!" I yipped. "Fire at that grate above Paik to open it!" I tried to point with my muzzle.

In her place I'd have demanded to know why, but Haru was like a soldier. She obeyed instantly. Her blasts vaporized the bolts that held the grate in place.

Metal screamed as an enormous dragon, bigger even than the Paik-creature, fell through the opening and landed on the commandant, squashing her flat. The dragon's dramatic entrance was accompanied by a torrent of briny water, salty but refreshing. The creature cried out in a voice that changed from tiger's roar to serpent's hiss, and then it went silent.

"Miss me?" Duri asked with a grin.

For my part, I'd figured out that some kind of foul magic was involved, and it had to do with all the artifacts that Paik was so fond of. I leaped into her office and glanced around. Sure enough, the objects on her shelves were thrumming and glowing ominously.

"In here!" I called. "We've got to shut down this magic."

"Allow me," Duri said, and more water rushed through to flood the room, knocking all the artifacts off the shelves.

I paddled for all I was worth until I made it out of the office. Duri remained sitting on top of the knocked-out commandant-creature. "Sorry, sorry," the dragon said, their contrite tone incongruous coming from a creature of that size.

The waters subsided, and I found myself washed up on a console. The stomach-twisting sense of wrongness had gone away, and the thrumming had stopped.

Tentatively, I reached for my magic. What if it didn't come back? I'd always be a fox!

But I needn't have worried. The magic swirled around me, and I teetered on the edge of the console, back in my human shape, complete with a new uniform and pair of shoes. Even if the uniform was drenched and I could feel my toes squelching in my socks.

"You can shape-shift now!" I told Duri.

"If you're sure it's safe . . ." they said. But they eased off the creature, which even now was shrinking into the more familiar human form of the commandant.

"What was *that* all about?" Haru demanded, still training her blasters on Commandant Paik.

"Those artifacts and all her 'tests,'" I said, scowling at Paik. "She's been stealing everyone's magic!"

"It almost worked, too," Jun said, drifting away from her fallen form to hover next to me. I was pleased to see that he'd resumed his usual appearance: regulation haircut, Space Forces cadet uniform. "Except she lost control of her artifacts and . . . well, things got out of hand."

"I didn't even know such a thing was possible," said Hansoo, who'd ventured out of the stairwell. "But that explains why she was so interested in supernatural trainees." *Unlike me*, he didn't add. He glanced toward the makeshift infirmary and added, "I called Medical, and they're sending people to take care of the staff. Everyone will be okay, I'm sure."

"That was more of a test than I was hoping for," Chinsun remarked.

We all laughed, mostly out of relief that it was all over.

I looked around the sodden room and wondered what my handler, Seok, would think of my performance on only my third day of training. What else would the next eight weeks hold in store?

"I'm afraid there's another trial we're going to have to face," I said to my new friends.

Everyone immediately sobered up and regarded me with concern.

"We're going to have to break in a new commandant."

It wouldn't be the first time for me, but that, too, is a story for another day.

The Gum Baby Files

KWAME MBALIA

ALKE IS A STORY.

Each of us carries parts of it—chapters, scenes, even just a few words. And when we come together? That magical world is brought to life. And as long as we continue to pass on the story of its existence to others, it can never be completely destroyed. Maybe, just maybe, word by word and line by line, we can rebuild that special place we call our own.

So . . . keep your eyes peeled.

And if you're Alkean—from MidPass, the Golden Crescent, the Grasslands, wherever—remember this:

I'm coming to find you and bring you home.

"Gum Baby, would you stop playing with that? You're going to get us in trouble!"

Gum N. B. Baby—former Alkean pilot with the self-described "fastest hands in any realm"—looked up to see

Ayanna frowning at her. The girl held out her hand, making a *Let's have it* motion, and Gum Baby shook her head and scooted farther back behind the giant yellow school bus with the words JACKSON MISSISSIPPI PUBLIC SCHOOLS on its side.

"Nuh-uh," she said. "Gum Baby just got her turn with the shouty stick—she gets her full five minutes."

"You're supposed to use it to try calling anyone from Alke! Not to listen to that message over and over. And it's not a 'shouty stick'—it's a staff."

The third member of their group, also hiding behind the school bus, and providing shoulders for Gum Baby to sit on, said, "Actually, you're both wrong—it's now a baseball bat." Junior, also known as Stone Thrower, the fifth son of Anansi, looked back and forth between Ayanna and Gum Baby and cleared his throat. "Never mind."

Gum Baby patted his head. Junior used to whine that she got sap in his hair twists, but where else was she supposed to sit? Eventually he stopped complaining. Gum Baby sighed. It was nice when people performed their roles without fussing.

Unlike that walking disasterix Tristan Strong. Boy stayed hogging all the credit. Getting in the way of Gum Baby's glory. Well, he wasn't here now, was he? Nope. And did Gum Baby miss him? Not one bit. Not his big head, not his silly-comfortable hoodie, and especially not the wild, ridiculous mishaps that followed him everywhere. No, Gum Baby was just fine with her replacement Bumbletongue. But maybe she'd better check Tristan's last words one more time, just in case. And not because the two of them worked well together. Gum Baby didn't want him getting any funny ideas about having adventures without her, that was all.

Just as she took a deep breath to shout at the shouty stick—or staff, baseball bat, whatever—to replay the message, a loud rumble shook the ground, and a thick cloud of exhaust smoke rolled over them. The large yellow bus pulled away and, just like that, their hiding spot had disappeared.

The stranded trio stood near the back of a wide black parking lot, faded white lines dividing the surface into small blacktop islands that shimmered in the heat. Three more buses followed theirs and pulled in front of a large building on the other side of the lot. A sign out front read MISSISSIPPI CIVIL RIGHTS MUSEUM. A flood of children who appeared to be around Junior and Ayanna's age poured out of the buses and onto the well-kept grass lawn that stretched around the modern brick-and-glass structure. They gathered in groups, two to three adults moving around each, calling out names and wrapping bright orange bands around their wrists. One adult, a Black woman with a yellow bandanna over her hair, counted every child and made notes on the clipboard she carried.

"All right, campers!" she called out. Her voice carried far in the still air, and Gum Baby winced at the loudness. Even Keelboat Annie, the giant ferrywoman from Alke, could learn a thing or two about shouting from this lady. "Follow your group leaders and head inside! Remember: This is a museum. And what are our three rules for the day?"

The kids and chaperones answered in unison. "Listen, learn, and be respectful!"

"Excellent. Here we go."

The groups began to move toward the entrance, and Ayanna turned to Gum Baby with a sigh. "That was close. Hand me my staff and let me see if I can get us out of here. There's got to be a way to contact the others."

Gum Baby pouted. "But Gum Baby didn't get to shout at the shouty stick."

"It's a *staff*! And I'll give it back, I promise."

"Okay, but you said that last time, and Gum Baby never got to finish her conversation with the nice lady." She folded her arms in protest, the staff/baseball bat cradled between them.

Junior looked up at her. "You were talking to an automated voice service."

"Well, she had good manners, and Gum Baby is tired of stifling her need for gross conversations."

"You mean *engrossing*—" Junior stopped when Ayanna elbowed him.

She held out her hand expectantly, and Gum Baby, grumbling under her breath, reluctantly gave up the bat.

Ayanna grimaced as she held up her recently transformed magical staff. "Gum Baby, you got sap all over it." Sticky splotches covered the golden wood, all the way to the grip. Back in Alke, the head of Ayanna's staff was a carved stern face, but this bat had a glaring visage painted on the barrel.

Gum Baby stuck out her tongue at the bat. Everything had changed since Tristan brought them into his world. Without even giving her time to pack! Rude. Okay, yes, he did it to save them from destruction. Maybe she could let it slide. But now she and Ayanna and Spider-Boy were stuck in the middle of nowhere, no heroes or goddesses in sight. They needed to find the others—without attracting *too* much attention—so they could figure out what to do next.

Junior's magical bag of throwing stones, which never ran out of ammo, was now a cross-body satchel. Ayanna reached into it, snagged a rock ("Hey!"), and used it to scrape the bat clean. When she'd removed as much sap as she could, she attempted to hand back the now-sticky stone.

Junior wrinkled his nose. "Um . . . keep it."

Ayanna rolled her eyes and shoved it into her pocket.

Gum Baby blushed. "Gum Baby gets nervous in strange places, and when she gets nervous, she saps." She turned her back so she wouldn't have to see Junior and Ayanna stifling their laughter.

Ayanna wiped sweat off her forehead and scowled at the sky. The sun hovered directly overhead, and there were no clouds in sight to offer a reprieve from the climbing temperature. It was hot. Silly hot. Ridiculously hot. So hot, every time Gum Baby lifted an arm, sap wobbled threateningly above Junior's head. One wrong move and he'd have some sticky extensions.

And yet the heat was the least of their problems, because at that moment, a shout echoed across the parking lot.

"Hey! You two!"

The woman with the bright yellow bandanna stood nearby, a walkie-talkie in one hand and her clipboard in the other. She stared right at them and pointed. "Why aren't you with your groups?"

"Well—"

"You see—"

Ayanna and Junior spoke at the same time, then fell silent as they looked at each other, at a loss for words. Gum Baby fell backward, grabbing one of Junior's hair twists at the last second, so that she dangled out of sight behind his back.

"We got lost," she called out.

The woman narrowed her eyes. A large white sticker stuck on her T-shirt read: MS. JAMES, CAMP DIRECTOR. "Trying to avoid the field trip, more likely. And what is that you're holding. A bat? Field day is next week, dear. Hand it over, now."

Ayanna hesitated, then gave up her disguised staff. The woman grabbed it, frowned at its stained condition, then turned toward Junior.

"And all bags were supposed to be left on the bus. You know the rules—I was very specific before we left camp. Now you'll have to check it in downstairs. Follow me, quickly. The tours are about to start, and I want you two at the front of every exhibit. You *will* be taking notes. Understand?"

Her tone left no room for discussion. As Ayanna glanced at Junior, then at Gum Baby peeking over his shoulder, it was as if they all had a brief exchange with their eyes.

We really don't have a choice.

Gum Baby ain't scared.

She's going to take my bag? With my stones?

Gum Baby said she ain't scared—can y'all not hear her eye-thoughts?

It'll be fine, Junior. We stay in here for a bit, wait until the coast is clear, and then fix my staff and use it to call John Henry or Mami Wata.

Fine, but the camp lady better not take any of my stones.

Testing, testing . . . Are Gum Baby's thoughts working? Testing . . .

Ms. James turned at the entrance to the museum, one eyebrow raised. "Well?"

Ayanna looked around one last time and then began to walk toward her. Junior followed, his hands in his pockets, turning his head left and right to try to free some hair twists that seemed stuck together. Gum Baby, still hanging on to one twist for dear life, glared at no one in particular as she tried to raise the volume on her thoughts. They hadn't covered this in pilot school.

Gum Baby was so focused on trying to be heard, she didn't notice that the door to the museum failed to shut all the way behind them.

Nor did she notice the figure that slipped through the gap. It wore a tattered gray cloak over its entire body, and every time the dirty cloth fluttered, rustling whispers rose and fell.

When they'd all entered the museum elevator, the camp leader pressed a button, stepped back as the door closed, and turned around just as a sticky tiny hand tore itself from Junior's twist.

"Ouch!" he shouted, cringing.

Ms. James narrowed her eyes. "What is that?"

Junior gulped. "What is what?"

But the woman was already reaching behind him. She

plucked Gum Baby off of his shirt and held her up like she was some sort of dirty sock. The nerve! Gum Baby was just about to fire a well-aimed sap attack at her captor's chin when she caught Ayanna's frantic, silent gestures to remain still. Or maybe Ayanna was just itchy?

"That," Ayanna began, trying to draw Ms. James's attention away, "is my field trip stuffie. Yes. For when I go on field trips. I get nervous sometimes, when I'm away from home, so I bring . . . her. My *stuffie*."

Gum Baby started to frown. She wasn't quite sure, but being a stuffie sounded awfully close to being a doll baby. And Gum Baby would never, not now and not ever, stand for being called a doll baby. No sirree.

"For the last time," Ms. James said, "you were to bring no toys, no bats, no pouches"—here she glared at Junior, who cradled his pouch of stones defensively—"and certainly no stuffies. This is an educational outing that not everyone gets a chance to experience."

She sighed. "This is history, children. *Our* history. If you don't learn and remember what people fought for in the past, you won't know what you need to fight for in the future. What you'll see here today is the culmination of decades—maybe centuries—of nonstop, backbreaking, dangerous, and necessary work to give Black people a foothold in the shaping of this country. The efforts weren't about getting a seat at the table, but fighting for the right to even walk into the room. We worked very hard to be able to bring your whole camp here, and I don't want to waste a minute of our time together. So pay attention. Watch. Listen. You might learn something. Got it?"

"Yes, ma'am," Ayanna said.

Junior nodded.

Gum Baby continued to sway in midair, still trying to figure out if she'd been insulted or not. Maybe *Stuffie* was a good thing, like a nickname you gave your top adventurer. A heroic nickname, like *Champ* or *Boss*.

Stuffie.

Yeah, Gum Baby could get used to that. About time everyone started recognizing her contributions to adventuring. She'd practically changed the game! Why, without her, Tristan would've been captured by old Fluff Face—whatever his name was. So it was only right that Gum Baby started receiving some recognition as an absolute icon. These two kids would probably be lost without her. In fact—

The elevator doors slid open, and Ms. James marched up to a tall counter covered with junk. She dropped Gum Baby, Ayanna's staff, and Junior's pouch underneath a faded sign that read BAG CHECK. Next to it was another sign: LOST AND (HOPEFULLY) FOUND. The pile of odds and ends shifted, then fell back in a heap.

Ms. James threw up her arms in disgust. "Now where is the bag-checker? Ugh, I don't have time for this." She dusted her hands and nodded toward the elevator. "We need to get you back upstairs."

"But—" Ayanna started.

"You can pick up your things at the end of the field trip," Ms. James continued. "Now, follow me and I'll get you reunited with your tour group." She marched Ayanna and Junior back into the elevator, ignoring their protests.

Gum Baby was just about to give the camp lady two pieces of her mind (one for now, and one to take home and enjoy later), but something distracted her and—for once in her life—stole the words right out of her mouth.

It wasn't Junior's heartbroken expression at leaving his beloved throwing stones behind.

It wasn't Ayanna's continued gestures instructing Gum Baby to stay put—as if that were going to stop her, as if she wasn't talking to Gum Baby, aka Stuffie, the greatest adventurer across the realms.

No, it was a dirty, fluttering creature with tattered cloth for limbs—limbs that were currently reaching for her friends from a dark corner of the elevator.

Ayanna and Junior were in danger!

Gum Baby had to save them. And stop that weird ghostie creature from attacking anyone else. And . . . and . . . Well, first Gum Baby had to escape from this dumping ground for thingies and doodads. She didn't know what a Lost and Found was supposed to be, but, like everything associated with Tristan's world, it didn't make sense.

"How can something be lost *and* found?" she grumbled to herself, kicking the child-size red sneaker that had fallen behind the counter along with her. "You're either something or you're not. Can't be both. That's cheating." She kicked the shoe a couple more times. The laces had been quadruple-knotted, and it looked like someone had chewed on the ends. She shook her head. The sooner she escaped this labyrinth of odds and ends, the sooner she could knickknack paddy whack that camp lady upside the head.

Gum Baby tried to climb the mountain of junk to get back onto the counter, but every time she approached the top, something would shift and she'd tumble back down to the floor.

"UUGGHH, Gum Baby ain't got time for this! She has to save the day!" She stamped her foot, which, unfortunately, landed on the red shoe and got tangled in the bewildering knots.

Gum Baby snapped. "GET! OFF! OF! GUM! BABY!" She punctuated each word with a kick as she tried to dislodge the shoe. Finally, after several attempts, the now-sap-covered sneaker flew off, soaring over another towering pile of junk and out of sight. Gum Baby straightened an imaginary necktie, briefly contemplated making a tie out of sap to accessorize her current outfit, then filed it away with her other wardrobe ideas and turned to attempt to climb up the counter again. She took a step forward—

"Who's throwing things around like they don't have any sense?"

The voice seemed to come from the mountain of junk. Gum Baby instantly dropped into a crouch, a ball of sap in each hand.

"Who said that?"

"I did," the voice said.

Gum Baby narrowed her eyes. "Gum Baby heard of talking *junk*, but not actual *talking* junk. Maybe she hit her head."

The voice sounded apologetic. "Sorry, dear. Have to be careful in here. It's a work in progress."

Gum Baby nodded. "So's Gum Baby. At least that's what Miss Rose always says. Anyway, nice to meet you, Talkin' Junk. But Gum Baby's gotta go save her friends. They're helpless without her."

The voice laughed softly. A tapping sound echoed throughout the space, and then a hand appeared. The objects tumbled backward, as if they'd been pulled by an invisible string, and they somehow ended up in small, neat piles, organized by category. Folded hoodies. A line of shoes, both left and right, though the pairs clearly didn't match. Several bowls filled with keys, coins, and half-licked lollipops. As the items put themselves in order, Gum Baby dodged one or two eager pieces that zoomed around the room. And when it was all done, a tiny Black woman with a twisted wooden cane stood above it all, wearing a wide grin.

"My Lady says we must always stand by our friends," the woman said, as the last of a mismatched pair of socks found a partner. She harrumphed. "Don't know how museum visitors manage to lose one sock, and it's always the tube kind. Something about the stripes, I think."

Gum Baby's jaw dropped as she stared at all the tidy piles, including a stack of lunch boxes that rose like stairs. The old woman gestured to it with a smile, and after a second, Gum

Baby—still suspicious—climbed up and sat on the counter with her arms folded.

"Gum Baby don't know which lady you're talking about, but you wouldn't happen to be related to a Tristan, would you? Head about this big"—she threw her arms wide apart—"and always getting into trouble? He's got weird magic, too."

"Hmm. Tristan who?"

"Tristan . . ." Gum Baby paused. She realized she didn't actually remember Tristan's last name. Were they required in his world? Would they kick her out if she didn't have one? Was Baby her last name? If it wasn't, what last name was she supposed to choose? Stuffie?

"No matter," the woman said, seeing her hesitation. "Been so long since I used it, I forgot my last name, too. Just call me Granny Z."

"Well, Granny Z, Gum Baby knows a thing or two about magic, so once she's done rescuing her friends, Gum Baby's gonna come back to learn that sorting trick. Miss Sarah's always getting on her about *Clean up this, Gum Baby* and *Clean up that, Gum Baby*. Gum Baby sticks things where Gum Baby will be able to find them later, but apparently you're not supposed to sap your outfits to chairs. How was Gum Baby supposed to know that was Nyame's throne? His name wasn't on it."

Granny Z nodded gravely. "Sounds frustrating."

Gum Baby started pacing the countertop. "It *is*! Everyone already thinks Gum Baby gets in the way. Like she's a nuisance. A *nuisance*! Well, new day, new Gum Baby. This is a different realm, and she's not gonna let anyone tell her she can't be great.

Gum Baby will be the best adventurer this world has ever seen, starting with the ghostie she saw going after her friends."

She punctuated the last sentence with a stomp of her feet, which sent a collection of mismatched bobbleheads all nodding at the same time. She nodded back, grateful for the show of support.

A sign next to her read EVERYONE WILL BE FOUND. PLEASE BE PATIENT.

Gum Baby pointed at it. "Don't you mean every*thing* will be found?"

"Not at all." Granny Z pursed her lips and stared at the tiny hero thoughtfully. "This is a Lost and Found, little one, but not for things, despite what you might see in front of you. This here is for people."

"People?"

Granny Z nodded. "You'd be surprised at how many people wind up lost in life. Especially the most vulnerable—children. The world is a confusing place, and sometimes we all need a little direction. That's what Granny Z's here for." She frowned. "At least, she used to be."

Gum Baby raised one sticky eyebrow, put her hands on her hips, and turned around, surveying the cramped room. "Yeah, Gum Baby don't see any people. All she sees is a whole lotta stuff."

"Exactly," Granny Z said. She slowly made her way over to a weathered wooden rocking chair partially hidden by three stacks of snapback caps. When she sat down, a giant sigh slipped from between her lips and she stared sadly around the room. "Used to be this was a waypoint, a safe haven for children who fell out of some problem and needed a place to stay. But now someone is collecting the lost before they can find their way here, and I can't figure out who it is. . . ."

Gum Baby sat down on the counter, crisscross applesauce, and nodded. Her chin rested on a tiny fist as she motioned for the old woman to continue. "Why can't you just go find whoever it is and sap 'em up one time? That's what Gum Baby would do. WWGBD."

But Granny Z started shaking her head before Gum Baby had finished talking. "Doesn't work like that, little one. For now I'm tied to this location, because that's Her purpose for me. My Lady needs me to do something, although normally she gives me some sort of sign." Again the old woman stared at Gum Baby. "Hmm. Maybe . . . Well, regardless, I'm here until the job is complete. And I think that 'ghostie' you saw might just be the job. But I can't be in two places at once, so maybe I can get the best adventurer in this realm to help me." She said this last part with a twinkle in her eyes.

Gum Baby puffed up. Though she didn't quite understand it all—like who the Lady was and why she was tying up old magical ladies—she knew that power had limits. Rules that had to be followed. She stood, dusted herself off (which meant getting more sap everywhere), and struck a heroic pose.

"Fine," she said. "Gum Baby will help. This is her chance. Find the ghostie, rescue her friends, and give you a break. You just keep rocking, Granny. This is an adventure that needs a heroine, and this Stuffie is ready to stick to her gums."

"*Guns*, you mean?" Granny Z smothered a smile. "I thought you might say something like that. If you really wanna help, you might need a few things. Let me see what I can rustle up."

Gum Baby wasn't lost. Nothing was where it was supposed to be, that was the problem. She stood in the middle of a long hall, lights illuminating a wall covered with infographic posters to her right; bathrooms, lockers, and a water fountain to her left. She'd had to hide three times already as several tour groups, each crammed with rambunctious children of all ages trying their best not to shout and failing miserably, passed by. Gum Baby nodded in approval as one boy, hands covered in sticky purple jam, smeared another child's face and the two giggled. You had to teach them young.

Now Gum Baby unfolded the museum map Granny Z had given her, shook a few drops of sap off of it, flipped it upside down, scowled, and folded it back up. Whoever came up with the idea of maps needed to take a one-way trip to Sap Town, and Gum Baby would provide detailed instructions on how to get there. Maybe even illustrate them. She was contemplating whether to include the history of Sap Town and its border expansions when a voice came through a door propped open just down the hall.

"That's the second complaint we've gotten in the last twenty minutes! First the water-fountain incident, and now the lights in the Evers exhibit aren't working."

It was a lady. Could it be Granny Z's lady? Or someone else? Either way, it was probably best to lie low.

"I feel sorry for those two new kids—it's like bad luck follows them around."

Gum Baby froze. *Two new kids.* Was she talking about Ayanna and Junior?

"I'll send someone over to investigate, ma'am," said a second voice, this one deeper. Another adult, and it sounded like both of them were coming her way. Gum Baby searched for a hiding spot, then sprinted across the hall to an open locker. She slipped inside just in time to avoid being seen.

A short Black woman with gray hair pulled into a ponytail and wearing a navy blazer walked out of an office, followed by an older Black man with a silver badge on his shirt. Inside the room they left, Gum Baby saw a monitor showing live video of different parts of the museum. She frowned. She'd have to avoid being caught on camera or she'd never be able to rescue her friends and capture the ghostie. She waited until the two adults had turned the corner down the hall and then she slipped out. . . .

Only to freeze as one of the kids from before, the one with the sticky hands, walked out of the bathroom. The boy's jaw dropped.

Gum Baby stared at him.

He stared back.

Gum Baby pulled out the map and held it up. "Can you read this?"

The boy shook his head.

"Me neither. All right, pretend you never saw me. Secret Stuffie business. Got it?"

The boy nodded.

Gum Baby saluted him, then took off down the hall. She had to find the Evers exhibit, where the lights weren't working. That sounded like the work of a ghostie.

The Medgar and Myrlie Evers Exhibition Hall was a giant rectangular space filled with shadows and flickering light. There were no kids in here, but a large cylinder rose high in the air. Pictures of Black people marching, riding buses, and holding signs slowly moved around it.

"'Home of Heroes,'" Gum Baby read the sign aloud. "What does that mean?" She tiptoed toward the cylinder, keeping to the shadows and looking out for cameras. Many different people were featured in the exhibit photos, but three appeared more often than the rest. Two Black women and a Black man. Gum Baby sidled closer, curious. The faces floated in a row, as if waiting for her. Were these the heroes? Maybe they could help Gum Baby find her friends and defeat the ghostie. She just needed—

All the lights cut off, leaving the room totally dark. Gum Baby froze. She listened. For several seconds all she heard was the occasional faint laugh or shout of one of the kids taking a tour elsewhere in the museum and the sounds of thunder and rain outside. Then . . .

Fwip. Fwip. Fwip.

That noise. What was it? Where was it coming from? Whatever it was, it didn't sound like someone from the museum. It sounded like . . .

Fwip. Fwip. Fwip.

The ghostie.

Gum Baby shrank even farther into the shadows. She could visualize the thing's quick, jerky movements in the elevator with Ayanna and Junior. It didn't sound like the ghostie was coming toward her, but she wasn't going to take any chances. As she started to creep out of the exhibition hall, her foot brushed the edge of the circular carpet.

Click.

A spotlight turned on, and three familiar faces popped up in its beam on the cylinder while a voice boomed out of a hidden speaker.

"Homegrown heroes. Three people whose legacy and impact does our state of Mississippi proud. Like Ida B. Wells, born in Holly Springs a few miles down the road"—a Black woman with her hair in a bun took the center of the spotlight—"who stood up against the terror of lynching. Or, standing at the forefront of the drive for voting rights, Fannie Lou Hamer and Medgar Evers. Evers's name now graces this exhibition hall."

The other two faces took their turns—an older Black woman with an elegant church hat pinned to her hair, and a slim Black man wearing a dark suit and a stern expression.

"These homegrown heroes are pillars of the civil rights movement in our state," the narrator continued, "and throughout the museum, visitors will find exhibits centered on key items representative of their contributions. They are powerful symbols of their courage and efforts, and they help tie our future to our objective of commemorating the past. Starting with the exhibit in this very room. You can see the symbols. . . ."

Gum Baby watched as three different objects appeared beneath each of the faces. An old-fashioned printing press for Ida B. Wells, a voting form called the Freedom Ballot for Fannie Lou Hamer, and a set of journals for Medgar Evers.

Powerful symbols? Gum Baby thought. She wondered if—

Fwip. Fwip. Fwip.

Right—the ghostie! It sounded close. Gum Baby started to tiptoe backward.

Fwip. Fwip. Fwip.

A faint gust of air, foul and rank, brushed her face. The ghostie was right here! The long tattered-cloak arms, the headless form—the image threatened to root Gum Baby to the spot. She had to escape. Go back to Granny Z and hide in her piles of junk.

Wait, what was she thinking? Run away? That's not what Gum Baby did. She was the Stuffie! The memory of Ayanna's and Junior's expressions as they left her in the Lost and (hopefully) Found popped into her head, and Gum Baby balled her sticky tiny fists. No. She could do this. She'd beat this ghostie by herself. That would show everyone she was the greatest adventurer in this world and any other.

"Hey!" Gum Baby stepped forward. The ghostie swirled around, the bottom edges of its cloak swirling like oil in water. "Ghostie! Listen up and listen good—clean your ears out. Do you have ears? Okay, pretend you've got ears and make sure you hear every word I say. Go away. You've scared your last victim.

You hear Gum Baby? You're done! Leave this museum alone and go brush your teeth. Coming in here all funky. Oughta be ashamed."

The ghostie fluttered there for a moment, then moved closer to her. *Fwip. Fwip. Fwip.*

Gum Baby raised her right hand, a ball of sap clutched and ready to throw. "Gum Baby's warning you! She was planning on turning over a new leaf, but she couldn't reach the tree and somebody swept all the leaves off the ground, so she hasn't done it yet. But it's the thought that counts, right? Hey, what are you . . . ?"

The ghostie had turned around and was hovering next to a set of journals on a nearby shelf. A dirty cloak arm reached upward and stroked the spine of one volume.

Gum Baby gasped as the leather book began to disappear into thin air. "Oh no you don't!" The sap ball whistled through the air and clipped the ghostie right on one of its twisted cloth arms. "Don't touch anything in here—that cloak is nasty! Don't you ever wash it?"

The ghostie whirled on her. The cloak fluttered near where a mouth would be, and a harsh whisper filled the quiet.

"Ffffffforget."

Gum Baby squinted. "What?"

"Ffffffforget." The ghostie returned to the journal. The arm reached out again.

"What did Gum Baby say?" Another sap ball whizzed out, then another. They pelted the ghostie, driving it backward and away from the shelf. "Hands off!"

The ghostie snarled, then turned, its attention focused on Gum Baby, and sped toward her. She flipped backward, sap flying from both hands as she twirled through the air. But when she landed, the ghostie seemed unfazed. It lunged, the arm of its cloak twisted like a locker-room towel, and snapped at Gum Baby like a cobra.

Crack! Crack!

Gum Baby cartwheeled sideways, just avoiding the attacks, only to throw herself backward when the ghostie unfurled its arm and threatened to envelop her. Somehow she knew that if she disappeared within that stinky embrace, she'd never be seen again.

Over and over the ghostie assailed her, forcing Gum Baby to move left, right, and always backward to avoid being hit. They fought their way around the cylinder, in the shadows and under the beam of the spotlight. Gum Baby began to pant from the exertion. Her sap attacks weren't working! The ghostie wafted in front of her, and she launched one more tired flurry. Three sap balls zipped toward it—and missed. Instead, they hit the spotlight, covering the bulb and plunging the room into darkness. An alarm went off somewhere. Footsteps sounded, and a flashlight pierced the gloom.

"What's going on?" someone asked. After a few moments the overhead lights came on, banishing the shadows to reveal the man with the badge on his shirt and an exhibit hall covered in sap. The ghostie was nowhere to be seen.

And the journals had disappeared, too.

Gum Baby sat inside a locker, her chin in her hands. It was the same hiding place as before, and she liked the way it was roomy but also had slits so she could see outside. Perfect for observing without being seen, like when a security guard, the museum director, and a custodian were meeting to discuss the chaos in the Evers Exhibition Hall.

"Can someone explain just what happened in there?" asked the woman in the blue blazer. She was glaring back and forth between the guard and the custodian, neither of whom seemed eager to answer. But after a few silent seconds, the custodian shrugged.

"Strangest thing I've ever seen," he said. "Whole room is covered in spoiled honey. All over—even the lights. Gonna take a week to clean up the place."

Gum Baby bristled at the *spoiled honey* comment. It was *sap*! She did feel bad about the mess, however. Maybe, once she rescued Ayanna, she could use the shouty stick's magic to remove it.

"We need it cleaned up sooner than that," the director said. "The two heroes in the exhibit are a big draw for the museum."

Gum Baby frowned. *Two* heroes? There were *three*!

"In fact, some tour groups are headed there *right now*," the director continued. "Larry, could you give Mr. Clyde a hand?"

The security guard, Larry, looked around. "What about catching the person who did this?"

"It was probably a kid," the director said. "I'll keep an eye out. I have to make my rounds anyway. I'll check on the other exhibits and let you know if I find anything."

The director left, walking close enough to the locker that Gum Baby could read her name badge: MS. FIELDS.

The guard and the custodian were left behind in the office, scratching their heads. Mr. Clyde shrugged and tossed a cleaning rag to Larry, who caught it and stared at it dejectedly.

"Might as well get started," Mr. Clyde said. "Because she's right—Hamer Hall gets the most foot traffic of all the rooms."

Hamer Hall? It was *Evers* Hall, wasn't it? It was! Gum Baby was sure of it. She pulled out the map and unfolded it, holding it up to the light coming through the locker slits. There was the exhibition hall, right across from the bathrooms and lockers. It was called . . .

She gasped.

Before her eyes, the words on the map began to swirl. Slowly, as if an invisible hand was swapping letter after letter, the Evers Exhibition Hall label was replaced. Now it read HAMER EXHIBITION HALL. It was as if one of the heroes had never existed.

Or had been collectively forgotten . . .

Gum Baby scowled. This was the ghostie's doing! She had to get to all the exhibits and protect the other hero symbols before the cloaked creature got to them. On top of saving Ayanna and Junior. Nodding decisively, she slipped out of the locker and scampered down the hall after the director.

Ms. Fields walked briskly down the corridor, only stopping twice to adjust framed posters that had shifted on the wall. Gum Baby followed, scurrying from shadow to shadow when they were available, and sprinting across open space in a sticky blur when they weren't. She hurried, and not just because she wanted to find her friends.

The Wave of Forgetting followed closely on her heels. That's what Gum Baby called it, anyway. It was the only way she could think to describe it. In front of her, she could see evidence of Medgar Evers and his contribution to the civil rights movement—leading the charge to gain Black people the ability to vote unmolested. But behind her, like an invisible tidal wave washing away the shore, evidence of his work slowly vanished. Posters illustrating his life changed to displays about the other heroes. Signs to exhibits featuring him rearranged their letters to spell something completely different. Photos faded until there was an empty space where he'd previously appeared. It was horrible. Scary even to a superior stuffie like Gum Baby. And it had all started when the ghostie took Medgar Evers's journals. Who would do a thing like that? That was low, even for a ghostie. Well, Gum Baby wouldn't let something like that happen to the other symbols of the heroes. Not if she could—

WHAM!

She was so worried about the Wave of Forgetting that Gum Baby hadn't seen the director pull open a door. Gum Baby slammed into it face-first.

"Who left this door here?" Gum Baby muttered. "Gum Baby don't even like doors. She needs space for her entrances." She peeled her face off of the wood, leaving behind an outline of sap. Then she rubbed her forehead and glared at the door, but before she could yell at it some more, footsteps approached.

"Hello?"

The director poked her head around the open door, scanned the hallway, and frowned. She looked at the back of the door and stared at the residue on it. Her eyes narrowed as she dabbed a finger into the sticky substance. Then she muttered something under her breath about kids not washing their hands and walked back inside.

When she was sure the coast was clear, Gum Baby descended from the ceiling on a strand of sap that was knotted around her waist like a harness. A sly grin crossed her face.

"Who says Gum Baby's inventions are silly? Gum Baby's gonna corner the adventure market with this one. All the heroes are gonna want her Sappy Taffy. Why, I bet even Bumbletongue will beg Gum Baby to come along on his silly adventures now. But he should've thought of that before he left Gum Baby to go have fun on his own. In fact—"

Gum Baby walked inside the room and froze. The director stood in front of an elevated stage with an empty marble pedestal in the middle. A banner hung from the ceiling above. It read: FANNIE LOU HAMER AND THE FREEDOM BALLOT.

Then, one by one, the letters began to disappear, until all that was left was a generic sign stating the exhibit was under construction. The Wave of Forgetting had gotten here before Gum Baby. But how?

The director slowly turned around, and Gum Baby saw that she clutched a large framed document in her right hand. Ms. Fields moved in stiff, jerky movements, and her eyes were wide and blank.

Fwip. Fwip. Fwip.

The ghostie was twining up the director's leg and down her arm toward the Freedom Ballot. It stopped and twisted one corner toward Gum Baby like it was staring at her.

"Ffffffforget," it snarled.

Anger swept through Gum Baby. Just as she was getting ready to charge and show that ghostie who ran things around here, someone—no, several someones—burst into the exhibit hall.

"Ms. Fields! Ms. Fields! I've got them." It was Larry, the security guard. He had a kid in each arm, and he pulled them into the light.

Ayanna and Junior!

"I caught them red-handed, Ms. Fields," Larry said. "They said they were trying to clean up a mess, but I think they were trying to get rid of evidence." Larry paused. "Ms. Fields?"

Gum Baby, distracted by her friends' entrance, had missed the ghostie's exit. It must have faded back into the shadows. When Larry held up the "evidence" and moved closer to show it to the groggy director, a chill crept up Gum Baby's spine.

It was the sap-covered stone Ayanna had used to clean her bat.

"Honestly, you two, I'm quite disappointed." Ms. Fields sat behind her desk and stared over the rim of her glasses. Ayanna and Junior were slumped in a couple of armchairs on the other side, both wearing dejected looks on their faces. Gum Baby, who was hiding behind the office door and peeking through the crack, felt her spirits sink even lower when she saw their expressions. How were they going to get out of this one?

"I'm sorry, kids," Ms. Fields continued. "But you leave me with no choice. As soon as Larry gets back here with your permission slips, I'm going to have to call your parents."

Ayanna and Junior looked at each other. "Our parents?" Ayanna asked.

"Permission slips?" Junior said.

Ms. Fields looked at them with narrowed eyes. "Yes, permission slips. The ones every camper had to have signed by their parent or legal guardian before they could attend this field trip." She stared at them both. "You two *did* submit permission slips, right?"

"Father Anansi would never—" Junior began to say before Ayanna kicked his shin. He clamped his mouth shut.

"Of course we did," Ayanna said, pasting on a smile. "But this is all a mistake. I don't know what . . ."

Gum Baby crept into the office, determined to free her friends. She'd break them out, then they could all go catch the ghostie and get back to trying to find everyone else from Alke.

When Ayanna spotted Gum Baby, her voice trailed off and her eyes went wide.

"Is everything all right?" Ms. Fields asked. She began to look toward the door, and Ayanna leaned forward suddenly.

"Yes! It's fine. Just . . . Yes, fine. *Everything is fine.*" She emphasized this last sentence through gritted teeth, jerking her head at the door while glaring at Gum Baby.

What was her problem? Something in her ear?

"Okay, that's it." Ms. Fields picked up the receiver of her office phone. "I'm getting Larry down here, and then we're calling your parents."

She dialed a number, then waited. "Larry? Have you found those permission slips I asked for? What do you mean you lost track of time? That's no excuse. I told you this was your last shot. I don't care if you're my cousin or not—you can't keep doing this." Her voice dropped and she turned her back to make her conversation more private.

Ayanna leaned over and hissed, "Gum Baby! What are you doing? We told you—"

"Gum Baby knows that, but she found the ghostie! And it's stealing the heroes' symbols and making everyone forget about them." Gum Baby practically bounced as she tried to explain everything in a hoarse whisper. "And Granny Z told me I could do it, and Gum Baby's on an adventure, so she has to finish this."

Junior shook his head. "Did you get any of that?" he asked.

Ayanna shushed him, glanced at where Ms. Fields was still arguing in hushed tones in the corner, and then turned a stern expression on Gum Baby.

"Listen, you *have* to get back to the Lost and Found. Leave everything to us—we'll take care of it. You got us in enough trouble already. Go hide, stick tight, and try not to cause any more fuss, okay?"

Gum Baby began to protest, but at that moment Ms. Fields hung up the phone in a huff and turned back to her desk. Gum

Baby threw herself back out the door, knocking against it in her haste.

Ms. Fields looked up. "Larry?" She got up and walked over to look out into the hall. When she didn't see anyone, she scowled and then pulled the office door closed. Gum Baby, clinging to the outside like a spider, swung along with it and dropped to the ground with an undignified *thump* when the door shut.

"Nobody thinks Gum Baby can do anything." The little adventurer sat with her arms around her legs, knees drawn to her chest, on the glass countertop in Granny Z's Lost and (hopefully) Found. A pile of trading cards slowly sorted and stacked itself next to Gum Baby. As she watched each card go exactly where it needed to be, she wished she had that kind of direction in her life.

"Seems to me you might be going about things the wrong way." Granny Z looked down at Gum Baby from her high perch. The little old woman stood precariously balanced on a stack of three chairs as she used her walking stick to maneuver a ceiling light fixture made of cell phones. "Silly things think they're a chandelier," Granny Z grumbled. She rapped the chairs with the cane and, in a breathtaking instant, they dropped into a stack. Then she gracefully stepped to the floor. "Still, they get the job done, don't they? I ain't had this much light in here since a year ago when a produce-truck driver forgot he was in reverse and backed that thang up through the museum wall. I had sunlight and strawberries for days, I tell you."

Gum Baby snickered in spite of her mood.

Granny Z smiled and winked. "Now I got me some light so these old eyes can see, and I can stream my favorite jazz playlist anytime I want. You think that's what them cell phone providers intended? No, little one, not at all. But sometimes we find our calling in life wasn't what we expected it to be."

Gum Baby nodded. "Gum Baby was originally supposed to be a fairy trap," she said. "That's the way the Anansi story goes—at least how Tristan tells it."

Granny Z chuckled. "A sticky fairy trap. Now look at you. One of the greatest adventurers I've ever seen."

Gum Baby picked at a speck of dust on her sleeve. "You're just messin' with Gum Baby."

"Nonsense. You figured out what was happening to the heroes when no one else in this place could. Don't belittle your accomplishments, tiny one—the world will try to do that for you every chance it gets. Stand up strong and do what you know is best, even if no one else is standing beside you. You've got something that no one else has, and it's going to help you come out on top, mark my words. You just gotta stick with it."

Gum Baby sighed. "But how is Gum Baby gonna capture the ghostie? It's so fast. And there's only one more hero symbol and—"

She broke off, her eyes widening. "Wait. *Stick with it.* Granny Z, you're a genius!"

The old woman sniffed. "Ain't nothin' new."

Gum Baby grinned and somersaulted off the counter. She blew a kiss over her shoulder (a sap bubble floated dangerously close to the stack of trading cards, which shuffled in annoyance) and dashed to the door.

"Thanks, Granny. Gum Baby owes you one!"

Granny Z chuckled, then grabbed a suitcase and placed it on the stack of chairs she'd been standing on. "I tell you, they make 'em younger and younger these days. Hey!" she called out to the cell-phone chandelier. "Play Erzulie's mix."

One of the devices blinked on, and a trio of saxophones began to belt out a jazzy tune. Granny Z started to hum and pack her bag.

"Stick with it.

"Stick with it."

Gum Baby chanted the phrase to herself as she raced down the museum's first floor corridor. She dashed across the entrance hall, not even bothering to hide from the cameras covering the wide space, but instead flinging a trio of sap balls with pinpoint accuracy.

"Sap attack," she whispered, because the man behind the information desk was snoozing in his chair, his head thrown back and fingers laced on his belly. She didn't want to wake such a peaceful sleeper.

Gum Baby reached the main stairwell and didn't bother taking the long way up. No time. She had to get to the third-and-final heroes exhibit before the ghostie did. She sprinted toward the guardrail and leaped over it, flinging two long strands of sap at the landing above her. She anchored the other ends to her waist, then backed up, stretching the strands as far as they could go. Then, *shoom!* The sap slingshot sent her racing upward. One floor. Two floors. Three. Her momentum slowed as she landed gracefully on the top guardrail, and she grinned. *Gum Baby needs to come up with a name for that move*, she thought as she slipped free and was off running.

At the end of the hallway, Gum Baby saw—and heard—the director. Ms. Fields appeared to be scolding Larry the security guard, who trailed behind her, and Ayanna and Junior, who walked glumly on either side. Gum Baby tiptoed closer as Ms. Fields unlocked the double doors leading to a rectangular room with a vaulted ceiling and a massive mural on the back wall. Above the mural in bright-blue block letters was the name IDA B. WELLS NEWSROOM, and a photographic collage of the journalist/activist writing, speaking, and reading stretched out along the walls. In the center of the room, polished and gleaming, stood the remains of an old-school printing press.

The final symbol of the heroes.

Gum Baby slipped inside behind everyone else, then stopped.

The ghostie.

The tattered cloak fluttered just behind the printing press, its arms rubbing the giant machine as if cleaning it. Gum Baby knew better. It wanted to make that symbol disappear. If it did, then so would the memories and legacy of Ida B. Wells.

If you don't learn and remember what people fought for in the past, you won't know what you need to fight for in the future. That's what Ms. James had said earlier that afternoon. Gum Baby didn't know much about Tristan's world, but she was pretty sure that losing the memories of such important heroines and heroes couldn't be good.

Ms. Fields stopped her lecture in mid-sentence when she finally noticed the ghostie. "What *is* that?" she said, stomping closer. "I'm going to have a serious talk with Mr. Clyde. Leaving his dirty cleaning towels all over the— Oh!"

This last exclamation was uttered because the ghostie rose over the press, stretching wider and wider to cover it, even as its twisted arms reached for the director's face.

"Fffffforget. Ffffffor—"

"Not this time!" Gum Baby shouted.

Ayanna and Junior, their eyes glued to the ghostie, whirled around at the sound of Gum Baby's voice. Ayanna's face grew pale, and Junior groaned.

"Oh no, not again," he said.

"Gum Baby," Ayanna said hurriedly, "what are you doing? You were supposed to stay put!"

Junior, meanwhile, was searching for someplace to hide. "She's going to sap everything," he mumbled to himself. "Still picking sap out of my hair. Sap in my ears, sap on my hands. I pulled a piece of gum out of my pocket to chew, except I remembered, oh yeah, I never bought any gum. It was sap! They should've never gave her sap. Now we're going to be kicked out of this realm our first day here."

Gum Baby, a giant cube of sap in her hands, let a sharp grin cross her face. "This ain't a sap attack. This is war art."

"That's not—" Junior began to say, but Gum Baby continued

to talk, getting more animated as her sap sculpture gained more definition.

"You ain't seen nothing yet," she said. She revealed her creation, and both Junior and Ayanna lifted their eyebrows. Larry the security guard and Ms. Fields didn't say anything—the ghostie had its tattered cloak arms wrapped around their heads.

Gum Baby held up her palms, the sap art balanced in the middle, and shouted. "Hey, ghostie! Gum Baby knows who you are! And she's faced worse, believe me! Get ready for the new-and-improved sap *attract*!"

Gum Baby marched toward the printing press with her sap sculpture aloft. Instead of a boxing glove, or sappy taffy, she'd made a replica of a journal. It looked eerily similar to those belonging to Medgar Evers, which the ghostie had stolen earlier. Gum Baby thrust it toward the monster, who snarled.

"Yeah, that's right. You thought you had it, huh?" Gum Baby shook her head. "You thought you could float in here and make everybody forget their history? Just wipe it from everyone's memory? Well, Gum Baby's like an elephant, thistlehead—she never forgets! Medgar Evers! Fannie Lou Hamer! Ida B. Wells!"

Each name, uttered in remembrance, was like a physical blow to the ghostie. "Ffffffforget?" It shuddered, its grip loosening as Gum Baby stomped closer, brandishing the replica of Evers's journal like a wizard with a spell book. Ayanna, picking up on what Gum Baby was doing, elbowed Junior, and they stepped forward as well.

"Medgar Evers! Fannie Lou Hamer! Ida B. Wells!" they all chanted.

Gum Baby held the journal replica high above her head as she taunted the ghostie, the shouts of her friends giving her energy and strength.

"Come on, you used bath mat. What are you, scared?"

"Medgar Evers!"

Gum Baby sneered. "You moldy dishrag, come see about these hands!"

"Fannie Lou Hamer!"

"You unraveled, grease-stained, one-ply, soup-stained stankerchief!"

"Ida B. Wells!"

The ghostie roared in frustration, releasing Larry the security guard and Ms. Fields before launching itself across the exhibit floor. Ayanna and Junior ducked out of the way, but Gum Baby stood firm, screaming a challenge.

"Gum get sooooooome!"

CRACK!

The ghostie struck Gum Baby, one of its snakelike sleeves whipping out as quick as lightning.

Junior winced and Ayanna inhaled sharply . . . but Gum Baby just smiled. The cloth had landed on her arm—and gotten stuck there. The ghostie tugged at it, then attacked with its other rolled-up sleeve. *THWACK!* But that bit of cloak stuck fast, too. The creature tried to struggle free but only managed to cover itself with more sap in the process. Finally it slumped in resignation. Gum Baby let a feral grin cross her face and leaned in close, a fistful of sap in each tiny hand.

"Gum Baby was built for this," she whispered, before she began to fire sap ball after sap ball at the ghostie from point-blank range.

"I really don't understand how that artifact got so filthy," Ms. Fields muttered to herself as she stood with Junior and Ayanna in the entrance hall. Gum Baby was holding still in Ayanna's arms as she'd been instructed. Mr. Clyde wheeled the defeated ghostie past them in a blue plastic dumpster. Mounds of sap covered the monster, leaving only a few strands of cloth waving feebly in the air. "At least I *think* it was one of our artifacts. Ugh, I feel so faint." Holding her forehead, she wandered off to talk to the camp counselors, who were rounding up the rest of the kids.

"Think you hit it with enough sap?" Junior asked.

Gum Baby jumped out of Ayanna's grasp and assumed a superhero stance on the floor. "No. Gum Baby was holding back. There are kids around, and Gum Baby needs to set an example. She's a role model."

At that moment the boy who had met her outside the bathroom walked by. He waved at Gum Baby. "Hi, Stuffie!"

Gum Baby saluted, then turned to see Ayanna and Junior looking quizzically at each other.

"Stuffie?" Ayanna asked.

"The *Great* Stuffie," Gum Baby corrected, climbing up to

sit on Ayanna's shoulder. "The best adventurer in two worlds."

No one (thankfully) had a chance to respond to that before Ms. Fields returned, shaking her head.

"Don't know why I'm so out of it today. Exhibits open when they should be closed for cleaning, another one closed that I didn't remember being on the list . . ." She sighed and looked at the three Alkean transplants. "And you two—and your stuffie. I'm not even sure who you're with, because none of the camp counselors have you on their rolls *and* we couldn't find your permission slips. So . . . start talking."

Ayanna and Junior exchanged a worried glance.

"They're with me," a voice called out.

Granny Z ambled out of the elevator on the other side of the hall. She carried Junior's pouch slung over her shoulder, and she leaned on Ayanna's staff/bat as she stopped in front of Ms. Fields. Two suitcases followed her like puppies. "I'll take the kids from here, Caroline. My time here is over anyway."

Ayanna opened her mouth, then closed it. Junior looked from the old woman to the director and back again, as if unsure what was going on.

Ms. Fields frowned. "Mrs. Z, I didn't know they were—"

"You were busy, child—it's fine. I'll get them to where they need to be." Granny Z looked at Ayanna and held out the bat. When Ayanna reached for it, Granny Z held on to it for a moment, making eye contact with the girl. "Finally got a message from your folks. Seems they're waiting for you."

She let go of the bat, and Ayanna stared at her, confused, for a few seconds before realization struck. Ayanna gripped the bat with both hands and the barrel began to glow slightly. A fierce look of joy spread over her face.

Junior leaned over. "Does that mean . . . ?"

Granny Z tossed him his shoulder bag full of stones. "Yes. They're waiting on you. We need to get going."

Ms. Fields, still looking a bit foggy-headed, just nodded. "Well, I'm glad that's sorted. But who will run the Lost and Found?"

Granny Z shooed her away. "Oh, I've got the perfect person in mind. Don't you worry. Now go on and get some water, child—you seem a bit faint."

The director smiled. "Well, if you're sure." She said goodbye to the children, then walked off, frowning slightly, as if she'd remembered something and then lost it.

"Now then," Granny Z said, her hands on her hips as she turned to Junior and Ayanna. "You two need to come with me. I'll take you to your people. I need to go that way myself. Funny things are happening around here, and my help might be needed elsewhere."

Ayanna hesitated. "How do you know where to go?"

The old woman laughed. "Still don't trust me? Good. Hold on to that feeling—you're gonna need it in the near future. But why don't you ask them yourselves?"

Ayanna and Junior stared at each other, and then Ayanna gripped the bat tight with both hands. She closed her eyes as she spoke to the golden face painted on the barrel.

"Tristan?"

A few moments passed, and then: "Ayanna?"

Her eyes flew open.

Gum Baby nearly cheered. It worked! But her smile faded when she realized that wasn't Tristan's voice.

"Mami Wata?" Ayanna asked slowly.

The face on the bat morphed into that of the water goddess. Even in the painted lines, Gum Baby could see the worry on her face.

"Yes, child, it's me," said Mami Wata. "Is everything okay? Where are you?"

"We're fine," said Ayanna, "but we were calling Tristan. . . ."

"Did Bumbletongue run out of minutes?" Gum Baby interrupted. "Tell him to stop lecturing everybody."

Ayanna rolled her eyes and Junior snickered, but everyone froze when Mami Wata spoke again, a clear note of distress in her voice.

"No, it's not that," said the goddess. "Tristan has gone missing."

The Demon Drum

REBECCA ROANHORSE

"WE WERE ALL GOING to die! Me, Davery, the kids in the Ancestor Club, and a whole arena full of fifteen thousand people, and there was not a single thing I could do about it. Unless . . . No! It was too much to ask. I couldn't do it. I couldn't!

"There I was, facing the most terrifying moment I'd ever encountered in my entire thirteen years of life, and all I wanted to do was run.

"But I couldn't. Everyone was counting on me. I wouldn't let them down.

"I gulped noisily and raised my head to look around. Thousands of eyes stared back at me, waiting impatiently.

"The expectant silence was so loud it hurt my ears.

"The heat of the spotlight scorched my face, and sweat slicked my hair to my forehead.

" 'Wait for it,' I whispered to myself. Just when I thought I might pass out from nerves . . . there it was!

"*Thump, thump, thump.*

"It was the powwow drum, the heartbeat of the dance. I listened closely, and then . . . I heard it. Yes, just as I suspected, this was no ordinary drumbeat, but one that went wrong at the end, like someone was dragging something heavy and rotten across the skin of the drum.

"*Thump-ksh, thump-ksh, thump-ksh.*

"'Okay, demon drum,' I murmured to myself. 'Let's see what you got.'

"I swallowed hard, took a deep breath, and did the only thing I could. I—"

"Wait, wait, wait," Toni said. "That's not how it happened. I should know. I was there."

"Uh, I was there, too," I protested. "I think I know."

"Maybe you should start from the beginning, Nizhoni," Davery suggested, adjusting his glasses and looking, well, not exasperated, but kind of concerned about my storytelling skills. Huh. I thought I'd been doing pretty well.

"So we can all follow along," he prompted, making his suggestion sound reasonable. My best friend was nothing if not reasonable.

"So you don't *lie*," Toni said, crossing her hands over her chest and narrowing her beady little eyes at me.

I ignored her. Toni had it out for me, and was constantly trying to start a fight. We'd had to let her into the Ancestor Club because it was open to everyone at school, but she was always saying something nasty or mean. I don't know why she even bothered to attend.

Davery's suggestion, however, seemed fair enough. Even though the whole group had been at the big powwow together, we had very different ideas about how we all had almost died.

"Davery's right. Start from the beginning," said my little brother, Mac, sitting up straighter in his bed, "so I don't miss anything." I was glad to see his busted lip had started to heal, and with all our freshly drying signatures on his brand-new arm cast, he was well on the road to recovery. "Don't leave out a single gory detail. And they'd better be gory!"

I could tell he was still bummed that he'd had to miss the powwow. Mom had made him stay home because of his injuries. But he should have been glad he avoided the near carnage.

"Okay," I said, "but you might regret hearing this. I know you have a delicate stomach."

My brother flipped his black hair out of his eyes and gave me a defiant look. "My stomach can take it."

I met my little brother's gaze. "It's your funeral," I said, and Davery winced at my word choice. Well, facts are facts. No one said monsterslaying was easy.

"And no more interrupting," I said firmly, glaring at Toni. "Or you can leave."

She rolled her eyes like I was the brat here, but at least she kept her mouth shut.

I cleared my throat. "It all started on a Thursday morning in Ancestor Club. . . ."

Just so you know, this isn't exactly how I told the story out loud, because there were certain things I couldn't say in front of the other members of the Ancestor Club. However, it is the truth and nothing but the truth. Monsterslayers are held to a very high standard of ethics.

I was running late because my mom and dad are still in what they like to call their "second honeymoon" phase. They were recently reunited after years apart, because my mom, who'd gone off to do some monsterslaying to keep us safe, had gotten trapped in some kind of divine lost and found. It's a long story.

Anyway, Mom is back with us now, which means a lot of mushy romantic stuff is going down in our house, including breakfasts in bed, and flowers, and notes that I keep picking up, thinking they're for me, but they say stuff like *Sole mates 4evah* with a picture of two kissing fish, or *You have a pizza my heart* with, yes, a slice of pizza on it. I can't believe adults are so embarrassing, but it seems to be working, because Dad, who's been so sad for so long, now has some pep in his step. He is constantly humming old love songs. I know they are love songs, because every time Mom catches him doing it, she blushes and looks down in her coffee cup, and he smiles even bigger, and that's my cue to leave the room.

I have to admit, it's nice to see them together and happy. A lot of kids don't have two parents, much less two still-blissfully-in-love ones. They definitely don't get second-chance parents like I did when I freed my mom from her prison. So I can't complain. Except when Mom and Dad are oblivious to my needs.

"What's the big deal, Nizhoni?" Dad asked as he pulled the Honda into the drop-off lane in front of school. He popped the last bite of a donut in his mouth. It had been cherry flavored with vanilla frosting that read I CHERRY-ISH YOU on top. A gift from my mom, of course. I would have been annoyed at how cheesy the message was if (1) my mom hadn't gotten me one as well, and (2) the donuts themselves weren't, in fact, delicious. "You've never cared about being late for school before."

"Ouch, Dad." I winced. "No need to call me out like that." I know I'm not always the hardest-working student, but wow.

"Sorry," he said, not sounding particularly sorry. "But you know what I mean."

"Today is special. Davery arranged for his dad to chaperone our trip to the All-Nations Assembly powwow. The whole Ancestor Club is going."

"Oh, is that this week? Did you know that's the largest annual powwow in the country? Hundreds of Indigenous people from all over North America and beyond come to Albuquerque to attend. It's a big deal."

"Yes, I know. That's why we're going."

He chuckled, and he swallowed his last bit of donut. "I used to powwow back in my younger days," Dad said. "Loved those Forty-Niners the best. In fact, me and your mom—"

"Gotta go!" I said quickly, jumping out of the car before he could start reminiscing. His stories take forever, and I didn't have time to listen to one right now, especially since I knew it was going to be long if it was about my mom. Like I said, I'm glad he's happy. Also like I said, I don't need to hear all the mushy-gushy details.

I went to the library to meet up with the other club

members—Davery, Maya, Darcy, Kody, and the new girl, Toni.

"Oh good," said Darcy. "Now all six of us are here."

"You're late," Davery said, giving me the look of tardiness disapproval over the rims of his glasses. "I specifically told you that you needed to be here at eight forty-five, sharp."

"Chill out, D," I said as I flopped down in one of the comfy overstuffed library chairs. I glanced at the clock on the wall. "It's barely nine. I'm not that late."

He sighed, all heavy like I'd disappointed him, but I was used to that. Davery and I will never agree on the value of punctuality.

I glanced around. "Where's your dad? He's not even here yet."

"He's pulling the van around. We almost left without you."

I gaped. "You wouldn't!"

"No," he admitted. "But you really need to respect other people's time." He frowned. "Is Mac not coming?"

"He broke his arm, remember? Mom said it would be better if he stayed home. No more adventures for a while."

He leaned in to whisper so only I could hear. "Monster-hunting?"

"No," I whispered back. "Skateboarding." Mac and I have been secretly on the lookout for monsters ever since we discovered that our Navajo heritage gives us unique abilities to see and track them. My mom enrolled me in martial-arts classes, and my brother has taken up swimming lessons and skateboarding. I am not sure how skateboarding is supposed to help him hunt monsters, but it's a pretty cool skill to have.

We've also been making more frequent trips back to the reservation so Mom can spend some quality time with Grandma, and my grandparents can share traditional stories with us. But a lot of what my grandmother shares is rules about things I should or shouldn't do to be a good person. I try to follow them, but it's a lot, and I've never been great when it comes to obeying rules. I much prefer just listening to her stories.

"Will Mac be okay?" Davery asked.

"He'll be fine, as long as he can survive my mom fussing over him." Mom had acted like breaking an arm was worthy of a call to the governor to ban skate parks, and she'd been treating Mac like he was made of eggshells. But she had basically missed his entire life up to now, and I knew he enjoyed the attention. It would have driven me nuts, but he and I are different people, and we have different ideas about our mom. "Four to six weeks in a cast. I promised him we'd all come by the house later to sign it and tell him about the powwow."

"Speaking of the powwow," Maya interrupted, "when are we leaving? I don't want to miss the Grand Entry."

"No need to worry about that," Davery's dad said as he hurried into the room. A set of van keys dangled from his hand as he checked his phone. "Do we have everything? Davery, can you please read the checklist?"

Of course there was a checklist. Davery pulled a piece of paper from his pocket and unfolded it. He cleared his throat and started reading aloud. "Sandwiches?"

Darcy held up a Wonder Bread bag full of premade bologna-and-mayonnaise sandwiches on white. "Check," she called.

Before Davery could continue, Maya said, "I've got the blankets for saving our seats." She patted the pile of rug blankets in her arms.

"Does everyone have their spending money?" Mr. Descheny asked.

I dug out my plastic baggie with a twenty in it and held it up. Everyone else did the same.

"Good, good," he said. "Don't spend it all in one place, kids. Now, let's go."

We filed out after him, all of us chattering excitedly except for Toni, who trailed behind, her face scrunched up like she was sucking on a sour pickle.

This was the Ancestor Club's first field trip. We'd been waiting months for this day, and now that it was here, everyone shared what they were looking forward to the most.

"I'm definitely getting a T-shirt," Kody said. "Maybe one that celebrates my Ojibwe culture."

"And some beaded earrings," Maya added.

"I heard there's going to be a hip-hop artist on the main stage. I don't care about powwow dancing. I want to hear some fresh beats." That was Darcy.

"I've never been to a powwow before," Toni grumbled. "Senecas don't traditionally powwow, and my dad said they're a waste of time."

"Navajos don't traditionally powwow, either," Davery said sympathetically. "But now you'll see a lot of Diné and other tribes partaking. It's really become an intertribal celebration, with people from all Native Nations participating."

"Still, it's probably stupid."

I exchanged a look with Davery. He shrugged as if to say *What can you do?* I wanted to ask her why she'd bothered to come if she was going to be so negative, but as I opened my mouth, Davery shook his head. He was right. Not worth it.

"It'll be great to just unwind and have a good time." I leaned close to Davery as we took side-by-side seats in the van and lowered my voice. "A day off from worrying about monsters and saving the world. I plan to listen to some good music, eat frybread that I didn't have to make, and relax."

"Sounds good to me, Nizhoni," he said, and then whispered in my ear, "A powwow is the last place I expect to see a monster."

And to think that Davery is usually the smartest person in the room.

The All-Nations Assembly was in the arena where they hold all kinds of events, from rodeos to basketball tournaments to rock concerts. It was the only place big enough to fit everyone who wanted to attend.

There were thousands of people, both Native and non-Native, wearing street clothes like hoodies and jeans and Western-style shirts. Lots of Native pride was on display on T-shirts and caps. Everywhere we looked, dancers were dressed in colorful regalia—ribbons and feathers and custom beading and embroidery in a rainbow profusion of hues.

And underneath it all was the constant beat of a drum. It was amazing—thick and heavy, and absolutely everywhere. It was as if the powwow itself was one huge living organism, and each person, whether they were there to dance, drum, rap, sell merchandise, or just observe, was connected through the same pulse.

I shivered in anticipation as I handed the guy at the gate my printed ticket and got my hand stamped.

"You feel it too, huh?" Davery asked.

"Like the heartbeat of a giant."

He grinned. "Pretty awesome."

"Okay, kids," Davery's dad said. His arms were full of blankets, and the bag of bologna sandwiches hung from his fingers. "I'll go save us some seats near the center of the arena. You all go check out the rest of the event and meet me back inside when you're ready. Don't forget to stay in pairs."

We all agreed, and Mr. Descheny headed into the arena, leaving the six of us standing in a fenced-off area just inside the gate. It was usually a parking lot, but now it was divided into three sections. The first section, where we were standing, was an alley of different food vendors. Even this early in the day, the enticing scents of fried foods wafted through the air, inviting visitors to partake.

"Is that roasted corn?" Darcy asked after a big sniff. She pointed at a booth with a green and yellow banner.

"And kettle corn," Davery said.

"And there's corn stew," I said happily. Next to frybread, corn stew was my favorite. There were also stands for burgers, hot dogs, cotton candy, turkey legs, and a half dozen other delicious delights. It was enough to make my mouth water.

In the second area, just beyond the food vendors, I spied a big stage with a sophisticated-looking lighting-and-sound setup. That had to be where they were having the hip-hop show. And just past the stage I spied a massive white tent. A sign over its open doorway read MARKETPLACE.

"That's where I'm headed," Maya said, noticing the sign at the same time I did. "I bet there's a ton of amazing Native art and jewelry to buy in there!"

"And T-shirts," Kody added.

It was overwhelming, and this was just the auxiliary section. The real powwow, the drums and dancing, was all inside with Mr. Descheny.

"This is going to be so great!" I exclaimed.

"What do you want to do first?" Davery asked.

He and I exchanged a look.

"Frybread!" we said at the same time.

"But it's not even lunchtime," Maya complained. "And don't forget, we brought sandwiches. That way I can spend my money on jewelry."

"Oh, live a little," I told her. "If Davery says it's okay to have frybread at ten a.m., then no rule is safe. Anything can happen!"

Davery frowned like he wasn't amused, but I shot him a grin to let him know I was teasing.

"You don't have to get a Navajo taco, Maya," he said.

"They're called *Indian* tacos," Darcy corrected him.

"Um, pretty sure Navajos invented them," I countered, backing up Davery.

"Um, pretty sure you weren't there when it happened," Toni quipped.

She was so annoying. I just rolled my eyes, and Davery went on as if neither of us had said anything.

"As I was saying, Maya, if you don't want a savory taco, there are options. You can get frybread with powdered sugar and cinnamon. Or strawberry preserves. It's even great plain."

"Oh, okay," she replied. "I guess I could try it like that, then."

"My dad said frybread is bad for you," Toni said. "It's greasy and fried, and we should be eating healthier because diabetes and obesity are problems in our communities."

"Your dad sounds like he's lots of fun at parties," I mumbled.

"I'm sure your dad is correct," Davery said. "But if you have it only occasionally, as a treat, he would probably be okay with that, right? Moderation is the key, after all."

Toni didn't say anything to that.

The crowd had started to grow, and we had to pick our way through lots of happy and excited people who were chatting noisily and greeting friends. Even out here among the busy throng, I could hear the drumming from the arena. It truly did permeate everything. Kody and Darcy walked beside us, bouncing to the beat. Even Maya seemed to have some rhythm in her steps. Looking around, I saw another kid bopping along, too. In fact, every other person seemed to be dancing just a little.

"It really is like this place is alive," I murmured.

"It's kind of cool," Davery said, hearing me.

Kind of cool, sure. But something about it was making me

uneasy. I wasn't sure what, so I kept my feelings to myself. I was determined to have a good time and put any thoughts about monster-hunting behind me for the day.

"Which should we pick?" Davery asked.

Before us stood three frybread stands: Auntie's Best, Frybread Palace, and New Mexico Original.

"That one," I said, gesturing to Auntie's Best. It had a colorful banner that proclaimed the frybread at Auntie's was the BEST OF FAIR and YOUR COUSIN'S FAVE, and there was a great illustration of a round-faced woman winking and wearing a big smile.

"Cousin's fave?" Toni grumbled. "That's ridiculous. She doesn't even know my cousin."

"Don't be so literal," Maya said, sounding exasperated.

Wow. Maya was the nicest kid I knew. If Toni was starting to irritate *her*, then the new girl really was annoying.

"I'm not all that hungry," Darcy said. "I had vegan fruit roll-ups for breakfast. I think I'll go save us a spot in front of the hip-hop stage before it fills up."

"Good thinking," Davery said. "But we're supposed to go in pairs. My dad said."

"I'll go with her," Kody volunteered.

"Do you want us to get you some bread, Darcy?" Maya asked.

"No, I'm good," Darcy said. "What about you, Kody?"

"Same."

"Okay," I said. "We'll catch up." Darcy gave a little wave as she and Kody headed to the stage.

The line for Auntie's Best moved fast, and before we knew it, it was time to order. Maya got a plain frybread, Davery got one with butter and honey, Toni passed—probably because she's way too bitter to like anything sweet—and I picked powdered sugar and cinnamon. The frybread came on paper plates, and each hot and greasy piece took up the whole thing. We found a good bench to sit on where we could keep an eye on the outdoor stage. I could see Kody's head moving to the drumbeat. Yep, it was still going strong.

"Oh no," Davery said. "We forgot to get napkins. Toni, since you're not eating, would you mind going to get some?"

"What?"

"Could you please grab us some napkins?"

"No way."

I frowned. "But you're not even eating."

"Yeah, but I'm busy."

"Busy doing what?" I asked.

"Anything, besides hanging around you losers. I think I see someone I know." And then she walked away, leaving the three of us behind.

"You're supposed to have a partner!" Davery called, but Toni didn't even look back.

"My dad is not going to be happy," he said quietly.

"What should we do?" Maya asked.

"Let her go," I said. "This place is fenced in, and she knows where we are. She'll be fine."

Davery shot me a look, but I'm good at ignoring his looks.

"We still need napkins," Maya said with a sigh.

"I'll go," I offered. I could see the napkin dispenser from here. "I'll only be a sec. Go ahead and start without me."

I set down my plate and hurried to the dispenser, ducking through the growing crowd. I grabbed a handful and was back in less than a minute. Davery and Maya had each already taken a big bite of their breads and were chewing happily.

"How is it?" I asked.

Maya gave me a thumbs-up, and Davery said, "Auntie's best!" around a mouthful of food. I tore off a corner of mine, my mouth already watering in anticipation of the sweet, greasy goodness. But as soon as it hit my tongue, I gagged. It was rancid, like two-day-old garbage left out in the hot sun. I spat out the bread, coughing. My stomach heaved.

My two friends stared.

"What's wrong?" Davery asked, concerned.

"It tastes rotten!" I exclaimed.

"What?"

"Here." I shoved the plate toward him. He tentatively took a small bite. I waited for his mouth to turn down and his eyebrows to go up, but nothing happened. He took another bite.

"It tastes okay to me," he said, handing it back.

Maya leaned over to tear off a piece. "Okay to me, too," she said after she'd chewed and swallowed it.

I held the plate to my nose. Now I could even smell the sourness under the coating of sugar and cinnamon, and it was enough to make me want to heave again.

"Seriously?" I walked to the nearby trash can and dumped my plate in. "You all couldn't smell that?"

"Maybe you just have a sensitive stomach, like your little brother," Maya suggested sympathetically.

"You're not getting the flu or something, are you?" Davery asked.

"My stomach was fine this morning," I said, thinking back to my breakfast donut. "That bread was just foul."

"Sorry, Z," Davery said. He popped the last bite of his bread in his mouth and wiped his hands with the napkins I'd brought over. "Maybe we can try another stand later and see if it agrees with you better." He gestured with his lips toward the outdoor main stage. "Right now they're starting the first hip-hop show. Let's go check it out."

Maya had finished eating, too, and she dropped her plate in the trash. Together we wandered closer to the stage. The crowd was already dense, but I eventually spied Darcy and Kody in the front. They waved us over.

"Where's Toni?" Darcy asked.

"She ditched us," Maya said. "Guess we weren't cool enough for her."

"We were supposed to stay in pairs," Darcy said.

"I know."

"So, who's the group?" I asked curiously. I could see a DJ setting up his deck and a woman setting up a serious-looking drum kit.

"This is MC ThundarKat," Darcy explained, "and the DJ is DJ KareBare. She's Apache like me. My big brother saw them at this festival in Toronto and said they were great."

Darcy's big brother was a musician who traveled throughout the world with his band.

We all stood and chatted for a while, but soon I started to get anxious. There was no shade by the stage, and the sun was getting hot. We hadn't thought to bring water bottles, so there was nothing to drink, and the bad frybread taste still lingered on my tongue.

"Wonder what that's about," Davery said. I followed where he was pointing and saw that MC ThundarKat and DJ KareBare were arguing. Their voices were pitched too low for us to hear what they were saying, but they were clearly upset.

"Looks like they're having some technical difficulties or something," I ventured.

"This is taking a long time," Kody grumbled.

"I'm bored," Maya said. "I'm going to go check out the vendors while we're waiting."

"By yourself?" Davery asked, alarmed.

"If Toni can go off by herself, so can I. Besides, like Nizhoni said, the area is fenced in, and if there's a problem I'll just text you." She held up her cell phone and waved it in our general direction.

We watched her disappear into the tent area.

A few notes grated through the air. I threw up my hands over my ears. "Wow, that sounds terrible."

"Don't be uncool, Nizhoni," Darcy chided me. "I thought you liked hip-hop."

"I do, but that's not hip-hop. That's . . . cats screeching."

Another off-note twang cut through the air. "Or nails on a chalkboard!"

"It sounds fresh to me!" Kody said.

"It's not my favorite," Davery said, "but it has a nice beat."

"The only beat I can hear is that powwow drum," I complained. "They must be piping it in through the speakers. It really clashes with whatever track DJ KareBare's laying down."

"I don't hear the drum," both boys said at the same time.

"How can you not?" I asked, surprised. "It's incredibly loud." And it had gotten louder. So much so that it really did seem to be coming from everywhere.

The boys shrugged. I exhaled, frustrated. I wanted to like the concert, but there was nothing appealing about the clashing sounds.

"I think I'll skip this and go find Maya!" I shouted.

Davery nodded, and Darcy and Kody were already lost in bouncing to the music.

I sighed and wandered over to the vendor tent. Shopping wasn't really my thing, but I thought maybe I could find Mom something made by a Native artisan. I wandered down the orderly aisle, looking at T-shirts and earrings. There were some cool decals and even a poster that I thought Mac would like, but nothing that looked quite right for my mom.

A commotion farther down the row drew my attention. In fact, a crowd was gathering. Someone was yelling at a saleslady in an almost-hysterical tone. I stopped, shocked. I knew that voice.

I shoved through the growing swarm, because I had to see

it for myself. Yep, I was right. Maya was there in the center of the commotion. Her face was blotchy with tears and she was thrusting a paper bag at the vendor.

"You said it was five dollars!" Maya yelled.

"I changed my mind. It's ten now!"

"Take it back or give me my change."

"You don't get no change, because it's ten dollars!"

I pushed my way up to Maya. "What's going on?"

She turned to me, looking wild-eyed. "I picked out a cool pair of beaded earrings that would go great with my Pueblo grandmother's corn necklace, and the lady said they were five dollars, but as soon as I gave her my ten-dollar bill, she doubled the price. I told her I changed my mind, because I only have fifteen dollars left for the whole day, but she said no returns!"

I frowned. That was weird. I glanced over at the lady. Her face was set in stubborn lines and her arms were crossed over her chest. She did not look like she was going to budge, and I didn't want to be stuck arguing with an adult about money, even if she had cheated Maya.

"Just take the earrings and let's go," I said. "Maybe Mr. Descheny can bring you back here later and get you your change. Or we can all pool our money and make up the difference."

"You would do that?" she asked through her sniffles.

"Of course."

Maya turned to leave, and the woman let out a snort. I gave the vendor a glare and wrapped an arm around my friend, leading her away. As we left the tent, I couldn't help but notice that the powwow drumming was loud even in here.

"They canceled the concert," Darcy said when Maya and I caught up with the other kids. The crowd around the stage was grumbling, and I could see DJ KareBare packing up her records.

"What happened?" I asked.

Kody shrugged. "They played half a song, and then ThundarKat got on the mic and said everything was all wrong and he couldn't perform under these conditions and just stormed off."

"Whoa!"

"So disappointing," Darcy said with a sigh. "They're the whole reason I wanted to come!"

"There's still plenty to do," Davery said, trying to sound encouraging. "The main reason to come to the powwow is to see the dances. Let's go inside and find my dad."

Everyone sort of grumbled their agreement and we headed back through the food alley and toward the arena doors. I took the opportunity to tug on Davery's shirt, motioning him to slow down and drop behind the other kids so we could talk. He let everyone else pass and looked over at me expectantly.

"You are not going to believe this," I whispered, "but I just had to drag Maya away from an irate earring vendor. I thought the two of them were going to throw down."

"Whoa! Explain."

"I guess the vendor took all her money and then wouldn't give her the change. The lady was definitely trying to cheat her, but it was just Maya's word against the vendor's. I told her we should just go."

"Should we tell my dad?"

I looked over at Maya, who was clutching the paper bag to her chest and snuffling loudly. "Yeah, maybe. But I think there might be a bigger problem."

"What do you mean?"

"Have you noticed how many things have gone wrong here? First the bad frybread, then MC ThundarKat storming out, and now the cheating earring vendor? Powwows are supposed to be a time to unite and have fun, but this one is anything but. I think it's cursed."

"Cursed?" Davery asked, his eyes getting squinty behind his glasses, which always means he's thinking hard. "As in there's a monster here?" He checked nervously over both shoulders, but there was nothing to see.

I sucked in a breath. It was the last thing I wanted to admit, but the facts were adding up.

Davery nodded, getting animated. "That would explain why you're picking up on things the rest of us aren't. The bread tasted fine to me and Maya, but not you. And the music sounded off to you, but Kody, Darcy, and I didn't notice."

"But what about the fights?" Because now I realized there had been two arguments—one between the DJ and the MC, and the other with Maya and the vendor. "I don't think a monster could be in all these places at once, causing so many different problems. I mean, it would have to be everywhere, and there's nothing everywhere except . . ."

We looked at each other.

"The drum!"

We both listened and there it was, still a steady heartbeat underneath everything.

"If the drum is sick, then everything else would be sick, too," I ventured. "Just like a bad heart pumps bad blood."

Davery nodded in agreement. "I think you might be onto something. We should investigate the drum."

"What about the other kids?" I looked over at the rest of the Ancestor Club members. They were walking ahead of us, heads down, not even talking to one another. No one was having a good time, that was for sure.

"Maybe they can help," Davery said.

"But they don't have any ancestral powers, so how can they . . . ?"

We had to stop talking because we'd reached the doors of the arena. Darcy was holding them open and waiting for us to catch up. Davery and I hurried in, and I immediately felt overwhelmed. There were thousands of people in here, and all the color and noise of outside was amplified by being indoors. It was chaos.

And there, in the center of the arena, was our real problem.

It wasn't just one drum—it was six!

We were going to need the other Ancestor Club members, assuming we could find Toni and she'd agree to help us.

Davery and I exchanged a look.

"No time like the present to come clean," I said to myself. I cleared my throat.

"Hey, everyone?" I said. "We need to find Toni, and then we need to talk."

"You're a *what?*" Maya said, mouth wide.

"A monsterslayer," I repeated for the third time. "I know it's a shock, but it's part of my heritage and, well, I'm good at it."

"You're nuts," Toni said flatly. We'd found her sitting by herself in the back row, scrolling through the internet on her phone. Now we were all tightly huddled in the rear so we could hear one another over the crowd. "Either that," she said, "or you have delusions of grandeur. Maybe it's both."

"What's *grandeur*?" Kody asked.

Davery opened his mouth to answer but I cut him off.

"No time for a vocabulary lesson," I said, "especially one about trying to dunk on me, okay? And it's fine if you don't believe me. Anyone who wants to can sit out this mission." I looked at Toni then. "But if you want to help, I could really use it."

"Does monsterslaying involve kicking ass?" Kody asked.

"Yes! Well, sometimes. It's not always about physically beating up a monster, you know. Sometimes you need to outsmart it or find a different solution."

Listening to myself, I realized how much I'd changed over the past few months. Funny how I'd learned that violence isn't necessarily the best answer only *after* I discovered my monsterslaying skills.

"Bummer," said Kody. "But since the concert is canceled, I guess I'm in."

"You believe her, Davery?" Maya asked.

My best friend nodded solemnly. "I've seen the monsters myself, and Nizhoni knows how to handle them. She's the real deal."

Maya exhaled. "I'm not much of a fighter, but I'm in, too." She hugged me, smashing her paper bag between us. "Anything for a friend."

"Great," I said, extracting myself from her embrace after a moment.

"I'm in, too!" Darcy said. "Sounds almost as exciting as a hip-hop concert!"

"So here's the deal," I said as the others gathered closer. "Davery and I are pretty sure a drum is causing all the problems here, but we don't know which one it is."

Everyone looked down to the arena pit.

"Which *drum?*" Darcy asked.

"Exactly."

"We'll have to split up," Davery said.

"There's six in all," I said. "If we each pick a drum, we can find the bad one quickly, before the next dance begins."

I glanced at Toni. She was the only one who hadn't said she was in.

"Me?" Her brown eyes narrowed. "No way."

"It would make things more efficient," Davery observed.

"I don't even believe in monsters. My dad says—"

"Toni!" I said, exasperated. "Who cares what your dad says? Are you in or out?"

Her expression flattened like a dried-up pancake. "Out!" She turned and walked away.

Davery gave me a look of extreme disappointment.

"Don't," I said, holding up my hand. "She's terrible, and you know it."

"You used to be pretty terrible, too," he said quietly. "Before you found your powers and got your mom back."

"I was never *that* bad," I scoffed.

Four pairs of eyes settled on me. "Was I?" Ouch! "Okay, fine. I'll apologize to her, but *after* we stop this drum monster."

"Any idea how to do that?" Kody asked.

"Yes," I said. And I explained my plan.

Now that I knew my monster-hunting instincts were helping me suss out the bad vibes, I noticed problems everywhere. People all around me were arguing, a girl walked by complaining that the bells she had meticulously sewn to her dress weren't jingling, and a boy was in tears because his regalia had been stolen. Stolen! Things were definitely escalating.

We had managed to make it through the crowd to the short safety wall around the arena floor. Behind us stretched rows and rows of benches and hard-backed seats full of people waiting to see the dancers. My plan required the Ancestor Club to separate and investigate each drum simultaneously. The sixth drum was supposed to be Toni's responsibility, but since she had bailed, I was going to circle over to it after I checked the one I'd designated as mine.

The only problem was that it was impossible to get close enough to the drums from this side of the wall. They were spread out across the arena, and the only people allowed onto the floor were the dancers. Without any regalia, we couldn't even hope to fake our way in.

Luckily, Davery knew that there would be a social dance right before lunch. It was strictly for fun, and anyone could join in, whether they had regalia or were competing or not. So that was our chance. We would just sashay our way over to the drums.

It had sounded like a great idea when I was up in the stands, but now that I was lurking among hundreds of actual dancers waiting to go in, I felt like an idiot. What had I been thinking? I would be making a fool of myself in front of thousands of people!

"And now, ladies and gentlemen," said a voice over the loudspeakers, "it's time for one of the day's highlights: the Intertribal dance! We invite anyone who would like to join us to come on down!"

It was too late to back out now. As we were swept onto the floor along with the other participants, my friends didn't seem too sure about this, either. We all took our places in a huge circle. I gulped noisily and raised my head to look around. From the stands, thousands of eyes stared back at me, waiting impatiently for the Intertribal to begin.

The expectant silence around me was so loud it hurt my ears.

The heat of the spotlight scorched my face, and sweat slicked my hair to my forehead.

Wait for it, I whispered to myself. Just when I thought I might pass out from nerves . . . there it was!

Thump, thump, thump.

It was the powwow drum, the heartbeat of the dance. I listened closely, and then . . . I heard it! Yes, just as I suspected, this was no ordinary drumbeat, but one that went wrong at the end, like someone was dragging something heavy and rotten across the skin of the drum.

Thump-ksh, thump-ksh, thump-ksh.

"Okay, demon drum," I murmured to myself. "Let's see what you got."

I swallowed hard, took a deep breath, and did the only thing I could do.

I . . . danced.

I watched the women around me, each one supple in her own way, and I gradually found my rhythm. I shuffled my feet, grounding myself to Mother Earth, and kept my arms tight and my body loose. Powwow dancing has various purposes, depending on the dance, but it's always about power and endurance, strength and grace. And to my surprise, I found that I wasn't half bad. A tiny-tot contestant whirled by me, her little shawl flying. Okay, I wasn't a natural like that little kid, but I'd developed a lot more physical control by taking martial arts. What's more, I was beginning to understand why people found this kind of dancing meaningful. Davery would've been proud.

Speaking of Davery, I looked over to see the Ancestor Club kids all moving into position, each one angling toward their designated drum. I set aside self-consciousness and focused on getting close to my target.

The drums were massive—oversize rawhide-covered

cylinders on wooden stands with nine big men seated around them. Each man had a drumstick that he beat against the hide in rhythm as he sang. Depending on the type of song, the men might sing lyrics in their traditional language or simply vocalize sounds. Sometimes women stood behind them and joined in the singing.

After the group introduction to the Intertribal, when all the drums were pounded at once, the drummers took turns playing. One drum group would play for a minute or a verse, and then the next one would take over. It was perfect for figuring out which drum was cursed.

I had briefed the team on what to listen for: that strange swishing, rotten sound at the end of what should have been a crisp, clean drum strike. I also told them to look for anything unusual.

"What's unusual?" Darcy had asked.

"Nizhoni means creepy," Kody had supplied.

"Right," I'd agreed. "Creepy. Glowing eyes, twitching, that sort of thing."

"What if someone just has to go to the bathroom," Maya had asked, "and that's why they're twitching?"

It was then I was grateful that Davery and Mac were my regular monster-hunting buddies. Because honestly? Ancestor Club kids were a lot.

"You'll know it when you hear it," Davery had said, saving me from an epic eye roll. "Or see it. Just observe and report back."

I watched Davery as he moved close to his drum. He listened

carefully, concentration showing on his face, and he made eye contact with every guy sitting around the instrument. After a moment he looked over at me and shook his head.

I gave him a nod back. One down, five to go.

Next up was Maya. I was a little worried she might miss something, but she had the same intensity as Davery, and her examination of the drum looked thorough. I waited for a yes or no . . . and it was a no.

Darcy and Kody each went, and they had the same results. That left only two drums—mine, and the one Toni had been supposed to investigate. As if my thoughts had conjured her, Toni danced past me. She was actually pretty good, and I was thinking positive thoughts about her until she looked over her shoulder at me and said, "I think this is stupid, but my dad said I should be a team player sometimes." She shrugged, making it part of her dance move.

"Listen for the weird sound," I hissed.

She didn't bother to acknowledge me, just moved toward the drum.

I knew immediately that she had found it. As she got closer, she stumbled over her feet and missed a step. She frowned and tried to find the rhythm again, but it was like the drum wouldn't let her focus. Did it know she was there to expose it?

I'd barely had time to contemplate the drum being sentient when it happened.

The drum started to transform.

Before, it had looked like every other drum, big and round and covered in rawhide. But now the stretched skin started to bubble and roll, as if something inside the hollow body was trying to force its way out.

The leather strips that crisscrossed around the base separated and knotted themselves into two sinewy arms, the ends fraying into six-fingered hands. The wooden stand elongated into two legs attached to a barrel-shaped body. And the skin cover bunched and re-formed into a pair of shoulders, a neck, and a head in the shape of a deer's skull.

The creature reached for Toni with its rawhide arms. Its fingers grazed her hair, and she screamed.

I gave up all pretense of dancing and ran.

I slid toward the beast on my knees, grabbing a drumstick that had fallen to the ground when the singers had backed away in horror, and I came to my feet swinging.

Bam! I struck the deer/human/drum monster on its back. A sonorous *thump* echoed off the creature. I swung the drumstick again, this time whacking the monster in the side. But the blow didn't seem to have any effect beyond making the ugly sound reverberate through the arena even more. Frustrated, I hit it a third time, but the same thing happened.

"I don't think hitting it is going to work!" Davery shouted as he joined me. He had a drumstick in his hand, too, but he hadn't tried to use it. "It's a drum, and it's meant to be struck. Beating it just makes it play more."

"Then how do we stop it?" I asked, feeling desperate. The thing was still half-formed, mutating into whatever creature it was meant to be, but its deer face was getting more distinct. I could see a long snout with two black nostrils, deceptively delicate ears that seemed to home in on my location, and two eyes, black as bottomless pits, blinking at me like a newborn fawn's, if newborn fawns had razor-sharp claws and teeth and poisonous heartbeats. I knew instinctively that once the demon drum reached its final form, it would be impossible to defeat.

"We're here to help!" Maya called, and she joined us, a drumstick in her hand, too. Alongside her were Kody and Darcy.

"Where's Toni?" I shouted. I looked around frantically but couldn't see her anywhere. I wanted her to be safe, but I couldn't help feeling disappointed that she had run away.

"I guess it's just us," Davery said as he watched the rest of the dancers flee in all directions. "Do you have any ideas? It's starting to look hungry."

"Maybe it's thirsty!" someone shouted.

We all turned. Toni had come back, with one of Maya's throw blankets draped over her shoulders. In her hands was an oversize water bottle with a squirt top.

"I don't think—"

"No!" Davery shouted. "Look!"

Toni squeezed the bottle with both hands. A stream of water arced through the air, soaking the drum. She kept aiming until water ran down the drum's arms and legs, drenching its wooden body and saturating its rawhide skin completely. Then she threw down the bottle and whipped off the blanket. She waved it in front of the creature like a matador teasing a bull.

The demon drum made a pitiful sound, flat and tiny, and we watched in fascination as it began to contract. It was like it was growing in reverse, its once-menacing arms coiling into its body, the wood frame of its trunk warping in double time, the skin wrinkling like a raisin. It became smaller and smaller until it was a miniature version of the original—about the size of a hand drum. I grabbed the blanket from Toni and threw it over the drum. Once I was sure it couldn't bite me, I wrapped it up tight. Now it was about the size of my head, easy enough to hold in my hands.

Then I—

"Wait, wait," Mac said, interrupting. "You mean it didn't eat anyone? Or even bite you? Did it at least drool poisonous venom on you? I thought you said people were going to die!"

"You didn't see Nizhoni's dancing," Toni said dryly. "That was pretty dangerous. At least for anyone around her whose toes she might've stepped on."

I should have been annoyed by her burn, but it was actually a pretty good joke. "I never did ask how you knew getting the drum wet would incapacitate it," I said.

"It was the water and then the drying—with the blanket," she said. "Rawhide always shrinks when it dries."

"Let me guess," I said. "Something your dad told you?"

She looked sheepish but nodded.

We both laughed.

Okay, maybe she didn't have it out for me, and maybe her eyes weren't actually all that beady. And maybe I'd been the one looking for a fight this whole time when I should have been looking for a new friend. She wasn't *so* bad. . . .

"Hey," I said. "If you ever want to help me fight another monster, I could use someone with your quick thinking."

Toni grinned. I looked over at Davery, and he was smiling, too.

"What did the crowd think of that drum-deer thing?" Mac asked. "I wish I could've seen it. . . ."

"Fortunately," said Davery, "everyone thought it was just part of the show."

"A few people even wanted to give Toni a prize for her new El Toro dance," said Maya.

Kody and Darcy started breaking out her bullfighter moves.

Toni laughed and joined them, swaying her hips and waving both arms up and down in front of her. "I think this should be the Ancestor Club's secret greeting from now on."

"So, did you bring anything back for me?" Mac asked me. "A souvenir or something cool?"

"I sure did." I pulled an object from my book bag. It was swaddled in a black-and-white blanket with stripes and a geometric pattern. I held it out across the bed.

"I brought you a drum."

Bruto and the Freaky Flower

TEHLOR KAY MEJIA

PAOLA SANTIAGO, TRAVERSER OF haunted cactus fields, destroyer of legendary ghosts, and brief onetime possessor of supernatural-void power, was bored.

Like, *really* bored.

Ever since she'd returned from her adventure into La Llorona's spooky lair a few weeks earlier, her mom had barely let Pao out of her sight. There were no more trips to the riverbank to stargaze with her best friends, no more junk-food picnics, not even the algae pranks she'd so loved to play on her best friend and neighbor, Dante Mata.

Pretty ironic, Pao thought, considering the Gila had probably never been safer than it was now.

But of course, her mom didn't know Pao had dispatched La Llorona for good and closed the entrance to her monster-infested palace. All *she* knew was that her precious, helpless little daughter had gotten lost among the cacti and should never be allowed to leave the house or see another human being again, to make sure it didn't happen a second time.

Pao flopped on her bed, huffing loud enough for her mom to hear from the kitchen.

No reaction.

Pao threw a shoe at the wall.

Silence. Not even a *What's all that racket?*

"Ughhhhhh!" she groaned, tossing around on her bed like a little kid throwing a tantrum. This at least got the attention of the one living creature Pao *was* allowed to interact with.

Bruto, the chupacabra puppy that had attached himself to Pao just before she'd entered the void, looked much more like a regular dog these days than a fearsome scaled beast from below. He was a little rottweiler-ish, Pao thought, but lankier. She had to look closely to spot the details that made him different from your average pooch.

He lay listlessly by the door of Pao's room, his too-big paws sprawled out at all angles, his floppy ears drooping even more than usual.

He raised one of his doggy eyebrows at Pao's outburst, but otherwise he didn't move.

Which is odd, Pao thought, righting herself on the bed and examining her pup. When she'd first brought him home, it had been almost impossible to get him to settle down. He'd destroyed several of her mom's shoes (the evidence was currently hidden under Pao's bed), refused point-blank to be housebroken, and gone into full cyclone-of-excitement mode if Pao so much as sneezed.

But today, even after her flailing tantrum, Bruto was uncharacteristically stationary.

"You okay, buddy?" Pao asked, sliding off her bed and padding sock-footed over to where he lay. "You don't seem like your normal monstrous self." No response. "Not that I'm complaining about all my personal property being intact."

Bruto rolled one eye up to look balefully at Pao, then sighed, a mournful sound that made his lips flap like he was blowing a raspberry.

"Wanna play ball?" Pao asked in her best rile-up-the-puppy voice, retrieving a mostly chewed-up tennis ball from behind her desk. "Come on, you know you love it." She bounced the ball right in front of his nose.

He barely blinked.

"Okay, how about a treat?" she tried next, grabbing a bag of Starbursts from the top shelf of her closet. She'd had to put her stash up there after Bruto had found another whole package and devoured it. Wrappers and all.

The crinkling of the bag didn't rouse him. Pao broke the zip-locked seal, hoping the smell of the fruity candy he loved would do the trick, but she was disappointed again.

"Come on, buddy," she said, sitting cross-legged on the floor and pulling the floppy pup into her lap. The fur on his back was still stiff and bristly, but under his chin and belly it was velvety soft. "You gotta give me something here."

She took a yellow candy out of the bag and held it up to Bruto's mouth, remembering her mostly futile attempts to train him in the cactus field with a nostalgic giggle.

Bruto sniffed the wrapper. Pao's heart jumped into her throat.

"You want it?" she asked him excitedly. "Seriously, you can have the whole bag. Even the pink ones! I won't even be mad this time."

Bruto seemed to consider it. He sniffed the candy again. The tip of his black tongue even poked out for a second, like he was tasting it on the air.

Then he dropped his head back into Pao's lap with another heavy sigh, all interest gone.

Pao's heart sank from her throat to the pit of her stomach. Something really *was* wrong.

She got to her feet and carried the boneless Bruto to her bed (where he wasn't allowed, according to her mom's strict instructions). Pao settled him among her softest pillows while she racked her brain for a solution.

Of course, during her long petition to get her mom to agree to a dog, Pao had done tons of research on puppies. Breed-specific health problems had been an important part of her investigation, and they all seemed to come back to her in a rush now.

Lethargy in a young, otherwise healthy dog could be serious, Pao knew. Her mind raced through the causes, her pulse getting faster and faster.

"Infection," she mumbled. "Lots of puppies get parvo, but that's probably not what's wrong with you, right?" She hopped up and started to pace. "Metabolic disease?" Pao wondered aloud. "Diabetes? Hypoglycemia?" There was no way to tell.

She didn't even know what kind of organs a chupacabra had.

"Ugh!" Pao groaned. "If you were an ordinary puppy, I'd just take you to the vet," she said. "But who even knows what they'd find if they got you on an examination table. You could end up in some Area 51 lab being tested for alien DNA or something."

Bruto didn't seem the least bit concerned, and all Pao's research had been on *dogs*, not void beasts, so she was forced to admit it was useless right now.

To make matters worse, Pao could hear her mom's footsteps in the hall.

"Paola?" she called, tapping on the door. "What are you doing?"

Pao said a word under her breath that probably would have made her mom's face turn purple, and tossed a blanket over Bruto before settling herself at her desk. She couldn't let anyone know there was something wrong with him. Not if she didn't want her whole vet-to-Area-51-lab scenario to play out in real time.

"Just doing homework!" she called before her mom opened the door, looking around suspiciously.

"School doesn't start until next week," she said. "And where's the beast?"

"Napping under the bed," Pao said casually. "He wore himself out licking the insides of Starburst wrappers."

Pao's mom rolled her eyes. "How many times do I have to tell you those things are bad for him? He's a dog, Pao, not a sugar-crazed middle schooler. Give him the turkey treats I bought him—they're in the fridge. Maybe they'll help him learn some manners."

"Roger that," Pao said quickly, eager to get rid of her mom. "Now, if you don't mind, I'm doing early research for school. They're letting me into eighth-grade science this year, since I did all the seventh-grade work for fun during lunch last year, and—"

"That's good, sweetie," her mom said, already distracted now that she'd confirmed Pao was present and nothing was on fire. "I have to go in for a shift at the bar. Please stay in the house and—"

"Señora Mata will know if I step a toe out the front door, and you'll have me chipped if I even make an attempt," Pao said in her best impression of *I'm just bored and not at all freaking out about the fate of my adorable hell beast.* "Did I miss anything?"

Señora Mata was Dante's abuela, and the neighbor who'd been tasked with keeping an eye on Pao during her mom's work hours. Fortunately for Pao, Señora Mata had drawn a line about Bruto. No beasts in her apartment—not now, not ever. And Pao's mom didn't trust the puppy alone in the house, so Pao had won back the first bit of her freedom without much of a fight.

"It makes me nervous when you're too compliant," Pao's mom grumbled. "Don't forget to feed that thing. And *not candy.*"

Pao bristled, like she always did when her mom called Bruto *that thing*, but this time she let it slide. "Have a good night at work, Mom."

"Mm-hm," her mom said, raising an eyebrow. "I love you, mijita. Please be safe."

"I always am," Pao said with a cheeky grin.

Pao sat still in her chair, listening intently until she heard the door close, the key turn, and her mom's footsteps pass under the window. Then she sprang back up to uncover her puppy.

He was right where she'd left him, his eyes not quite closed.

Pao resumed her pacing.

"Okay," she said. "Okay, we have to do something. But what?"

Bruto didn't answer, and there was no one else to ask.

"Why can't you talk to me?" Pao asked, at her wits' end. "Why can't you tell me what's wrong?"

At this, Bruto opened his eyes all the way, looking right into Pao's with an expression that looked almost pleading. A little whine escaped from him, and Pao felt a pang in her chest. He was suffering, and she couldn't help him. She threw herself down on the bed and wrapped her arms around him, feeling him slump against her.

Bruto was still looking at her with his strange bright-green eyes, his expression intent, like he was trying to tell her something even though he could barely hold up his little head.

Pao leaned in closer, putting her forehead right against his. "I just want to help. How can I help?"

That's when it happened. There was a little flicker, like a movie was starting in Pao's mind. She saw a series of images. The desert. The widest part of the river, its dark water deceptively calm in the center. A red cactus flower blooming near the bank, surrounded by strange rock formations.

Pao gasped, breaking contact with Bruto in her surprise. The movie disappeared, leaving just her slightly messy bedroom and her lethargic puppy.

"What *was* that?" she asked Bruto, who only looked at her with those pleading eyes, as if begging her to try again. "Were you showing me something?" Bruto had gotten so good at playing the part of a regular dog lately that she'd almost stopped thinking of him as a supernatural creature.

Bruto whined, pushing his snout into her hand. It looked like it was costing him vital energy just to move his head a few inches.

"Okay," Pao said, taking a deep breath. "Show me again, boy."

She placed her forehead against his again, and this time the images came immediately. The riverbank, the dark water, the red flower. But there were more flowers, and they were massive. Each petal looked as thick and juicy as a steak with a long tonguelike pistil sticking up from the center. And maybe it was Pao's imagination, but she could swear the flowers smelled a little like raw meat. . . .

As if he could smell them, too, Bruto whimpered a little, but Pao kept their foreheads pressed together as the scene changed. From behind the flowers, shadows loomed. Shadows that looked a lot like Bruto before he'd lost his tentacle-like spines and his glowing green eyes.

More chupacabra puppies! Pao realized with a thrill. And they were advancing on the flowers like they were starving. . . .

The connection broke then, and Bruto whimpered more

insistently. But it didn't matter. Pao already had a plan. She just had to get out of the apartment complex first.

September wasn't any cooler than August in Arizona, which wasn't great for Pao's stealth-outfit selection.

She settled for khaki shorts and a weird beige T-shirt Señora Mata had once brought her from the flea market. On the chest was a rhinestone heart with an arrow through it, but considering how well the color of the shirt would blend into the desert landscape, Pao could ignore that glaring flaw for now.

The next issue was Bruto, who seemed to have used his last bit of energy to show Pao the strange meat flowers. His eyes were closed, and Pao would have worried that he was dead if it weren't for the little snoring whine escaping regularly from his nose.

She would have to carry him—there was no way around it. Pao thought she knew the spot near the river she'd seen in the vision. If she was right, it was about two miles from here, maybe a little more.

Pao grabbed a fanny pack she'd won in an end-of-year raffle at school, a hideous hot-pink-and-green thing she never would have been caught dead in normally. But desperate times called for desperate measures. Her backpack was too heavy and bulky to wear while carrying Bruto, and she'd brave anything—even tragic neon fashion—to help her puppy.

Into the fanny pack went a granola bar, a water bottle, a half sleeve of Starbursts, and the little knife Pao had received from the leader of Los Niños de la Luz during her adventure this summer. It didn't look like much, but it had helped Pao make it past things far worse than meat flowers.

"Okay," she said to Bruto. "Here goes."

It was tough to ease the door open silently with him in her arms, but Pao managed it somehow. The late afternoon heat was brutal, the sun growing heavier and redder in the sky as it descended.

Pao tiptoed past the windows of her apartment, praying to all the santos she didn't believe in to keep her footsteps quiet. Bruto sagged in her arms. She hitched him up on her hip like a baby. Even as a puppy he already weighed as much as a sack of flour.

"Hang on, buddy," Pao whispered to him. "Just a little farther and we'll be out of Señora M—"

The sound of a creaking door on the landing above interrupted Pao's reassuring speech.

"Paola, is that you?"

Pao swore under her breath for the second time that day. "Hello, Señora," she called up, as innocently as she could manage. "Just taking the dog for a walk. Mom said it was okay!"

Señora Mata leaned over the balcony railing. She was dressed in a quilted dressing gown and her chanclas—one of which Pao knew was secretly so much more than a smelly house shoe.

The old woman's eyes were narrowed in suspicion. "You expect me to believe that?" she barked, her voice sharp as ever. "You think I'm too old to know a sneaking out when I see one?"

Pao's heart sped up. She could run for it. Señora Mata was scary, but she didn't look fast. Sure, Pao would be in huge trouble by the time she got back, but at least Bruto would be better. . . .

"If you're going to make a run for it, head for the side of the building," the old woman said. "Pero you don't look strong enough to carry him all the way to el río."

"I . . ." Pao began, hitching Bruto back up as if to prove the señora's point. "How do you always *know?*"

Señora Mata's face split into a slightly evil-looking grin. "Someday you'll get used to it. Anyway, children with coddling mothers grow up to be weaklings." She made a dismissive gesture. "Go on. Have your adventure. You need to have some good stories to tell by the time you're as old as me."

Pao shouldn't have been so surprised. Señora Mata had been the one to send her and Dante off to the void entrance, after all. But Paola was still getting used to living in a world in which weird supernatural missions existed, let alone a world in which formerly strict adults encouraged you to go on them.

"Thanks, Señora," Pao said, trying to keep the uncertainty out of her voice.

"I don't love los brutitos," she said, turning up her nose. "But I suppose every creature deserves a fighting chance. Keep your wits about you, Paola."

"What's going on?" came a voice from behind the old woman.

Dante appeared behind his abuela, his usually messy hair

stuffed under a baseball cap. He was holding a soccer ball, and a gym bag was hanging from his shoulder.

On his way to practice, Pao thought, trying not to be bitter about it. But she had no time for him anyway. She had to get Bruto across the desert before it was too late.

"I gotta go," she said. "Have fun at practice."

She mentally patted herself on the back for not rolling her eyes at him.

"Wait," Dante said, dropping the bag and jogging down the stairs to Pao. "What's going on? I thought your mom wasn't letting you out?"

"It's Bruto," Pao said flatly, not daring to hope anything had changed since their adventure. Between Dante's soccer schedule and Pao's complete lack of personal freedom, they hadn't spent much time together in the past couple of weeks.

"What's wrong, little guy?" Dante asked, leaning in to scratch behind Bruto's droopy ears before meeting Pao's gaze.

"He needs something," Pao said, feeling silly now that she had to explain it out loud. "He's . . . fading. And I saw this vision." She hesitated, waiting for Dante to question her sanity, and was emboldened when he didn't. "There's a patch of freaky flowers a couple of miles from here that I think can help him, but I'm worried. I gotta get there fast."

"Well, then what are we waiting for?" Dante asked, smiling his crooked smile at Pao before holding his arms out to take Bruto. "Let me carry him, though. I should use my dumb meathead muscles for something, right?"

Pao felt her face heating up over his reference to an old insult of hers, but she handed over Bruto, grateful (though she'd never admit it) that she wouldn't have to carry him all the way on her own.

"Fine," Señora Mata said. "But be home before the end of bingo, ¿entiendes?"

"Yes, Abuela," Dante said, securing Bruto in his arms like he weighed nothing. He turned to Pao. "Let's go find some freaky flowers, huh?"

But Señora Mata hadn't finished with them yet. "Espere," she said, bending over. "You'll need this." She took off one crusty yellow chancla.

The first time she'd done this, Pao had been confused, and honestly a little grossed out. But this time Pao watched the slipper in awe as Señora Mata tossed it down in a perfect arc. Dante caught it.

"You sure?" he asked.

"Go," his abuela said, rolling her eyes. "Always so chatty, this one. Como una chismosa."

Dante laughed, shaking his head as he stuffed the slipper—now navy corduroy—into his back pocket. "Gracias, Abuela. Buena suerte en el bingo, okay? I hope you win big."

Dismissing his comment with a wave, Señora Mata disappeared back into her apartment, leaving Pao, Dante, and Bruto on their own.

"Which way?" Dante asked, and Pao found herself feeling hopeful for the first time since she'd discovered Bruto's malady.

Together, they could save him. They saved Emma, after all. This would be a piece of cake in comparison.

Right?

She pointed west, toward the river. "That way."

"Familiar," Dante said, and Pao was worried for a moment, remembering how upset he'd been the last time she dragged him along on a mission like this. But he was smiling, so Pao smiled, too.

Dante set out in the direction Pao had pointed, but Pao found herself hesitating. Was she really leaving again so soon? With her mom already a worried mess? Wasn't there some other way?

Up ahead, Dante stopped and waited for her to catch up. Bruto peeked feebly over his arm, his expression bringing the phrase *puppy-dog eyes* to life. Pao's reservations melted away in that moment. She had no choice but to do this. She had taken responsibility for Bruto in the cactus field when he'd had no one else to rely on.

She would make sure he was okay. She had to.

Her resolve intact, Pao took off at a jog toward Dante. "Magical meat garden, here we come."

Pao spent the first leg of their journey bringing Dante up to speed on Bruto's behavior, and the strange vision she'd seen when she pressed her forehead against her puppy's. If Dante thought this was weird or embarrassing or anything, he didn't mention it, which Pao appreciated.

She talked a little too much, trying to distract herself from the feeling she'd had ever since the vision: that she could somehow feel Bruto's heart slowing, his life force fading. She hoped it was just her overactive imagination, but she stopped to check on him every few hundred feet anyway.

"Pao," Dante said the next time she did it, when the Riverside Palace's exterior lights were still mostly visible behind them. "I know you're worried, but we should probably keep going. He's starting to feel . . ."

Dante trailed off, and Pao's heart sank. "What?" she asked. "Starting to feel what?"

"Cold," Dante admitted.

Pao put her hand to the little puppy's forehead and was alarmed to find that Dante was right. Bruto was usually a furnace (Pao hadn't had to use a comforter in weeks), but the skin beneath his spiny fur was cooling despite the heat outside and Dante's arms around him.

"Let's run," she said, and Dante didn't question her, just matched her pace as they made their way toward the river.

It didn't take long before Dante was visibly out of breath, even his newfound soccer stamina apparently reaching its limits with Bruto weighing him down. Dante was doing his best not to show it, but Pao could tell, and though she would have loved to talk to him and distract herself from what was happening, she kept quiet.

All she could think about was Bruto—she was racking her brain for *any* idea to give him more time. But she forced herself not to check on him again. During her trip into the void, she'd learned that a little faith could have a lot of power. She would have to remember that now.

A stitch in her side, her lungs burning, Pao used her mom's loopy-sounding *visualization* technique for the first time. She pictured her puppy alive and full of energy. She smiled as, in her mind's eye, he jumped and bounced and grinned at her in his hilarious snaggletoothed way. She tempted him with high-fructose-corn-syrup snacks that would probably be the end of a regular dog, and he did tricks for her—sitting, lying down, even balancing a soccer ball on his nose. . . .

Okay, maybe Pao had taken a *few* liberties with the visualized version of Bruto—but if visualizing was supposed to "manifest a new reality," couldn't she get a few training perks in, too?

"How much farther?" Dante asked, slowing down a little to rearrange Bruto in his arms. "Not that I'm complaining, just . . ."

Pao understood. But the daylight was already fading around them, and she didn't recognize anything in the landscape ahead.

"I don't know," she said. "I'm sorry, I only saw a place where the river is wide and there are some rock formations and these weird flowers. I don't know anything else. We just have to keep going."

If Dante was thinking the same thing Pao was—that her dreams, as always, were inconveniently short on useful details—he had the good manners not to say so.

As the sun began its nightly performance of painting everything above the horizon line in vivid reds, deep purples, and dusky blues, Pao and Dante continued at a slower jog.

"He's not doing so good, Pao," Dante said after a little while longer, as the darkness began to gather. "He hasn't moved in a while and . . ."

Pao's heart was a block of ice. She stopped, breathing heavily, feeling like someone had given her lung a really bad papercut and it stung with every inhale.

Dante stopped, too, and they came together, Pao touching Bruto's forehead, feeling how cold he'd grown. His eyes were closed, his little chest barely rising and falling.

"Do you think he's gonna—" Pao began, but Dante interrupted.

"Remember when he stole your mom's work apron when she was already late and he ran out the door with it?" he asked, his eyes sparkling.

Pao felt herself smile a little, almost against her will. "It always smells like the peanuts she keeps in her pockets at the bar," she said. "He made it all the way to the parking lot before she caught him."

"With curlers in her hair," Dante said, laughing. "Oh, and the time Abuela left that flan on the windowsill?"

Pao chuckled. "He barely left the plate."

Dante looked at her, still cradling Bruto gently as a little unconscious whimper escaped the chupe's lips, breaking Pao's heart.

"I have to save him, Dante," she said. "I don't know what I'll do if . . ."

"You will," he said, securing Bruto. "We've done more with worse odds, right?"

Pao nodded, taking a deep breath, steeling herself to run again.

This time, whether it was the short rest or the memories of her puppy's antics, Pao's feet flew across the hard-packed ground. Dante didn't look tired, either, keeping pace with her despite the burden of the unconscious Bruto.

Before long, they could hear the river's current up ahead, and Pao's relief battled with the fear flowing through her veins. Even though she knew La Llorona was gone, and the other monsters had been swallowed by the void, it was hard not to feel their presence here.

Cacti loomed along the riverbank, reminding Pao of everything that had befallen her this summer, every wrong turn and strange twist that could have resulted in the deaths of her friends and family, even herself. She'd been lucky so many times. What if she wasn't as lucky now? With Bruto's life hanging in the balance and Dante along for the ride again, she couldn't afford to fail.

Pao had forgiven herself for a lot as she passed through the throat of the void, but she knew she could never forgive herself if something happened to either of her boys.

"I think it might be close to here," she said to Dante, trying to banish her fears—both of the river and her own weakness.

"The Gila definitely looks . . ." She was going to say *wider*, but the other adjectives that came to mind weren't as helpful.

Ominous.

Terrifying.

Just as haunted as ever.

"Let's go," Dante said. And then to Bruto: "Just a little farther, buddy. Hang on."

Pao didn't know if Dante was right, but there was something about hearing him say it that made the burden of all this worry feel lighter. They pushed on, running until they were panting again and the lights of town were no longer visible behind them.

They kept going until they crested a low hill and all they could see was the inky river, the last stripe of sunset, and the rock formations ahead.

Formations that looked strangely familiar . . .

"This might be it!" Pao called, stopping before the rocks she'd seen in her vision. "Is this the place, pal?" she asked Bruto when Dante joined her.

He didn't stir, but when Pao scratched his ears, she thought maybe they felt warmer.

"It's pretty awesome here," Dante said, and Pao agreed. The landscape was spectacular in the purple twilight. Interesting rock formations weren't uncommon in this area, but these were different somehow. They looked almost alive. . . .

"Let's keep going," she said to Dante, walking down the steep decline to the river. She kept her eye out for any other landmarks that looked familiar.

The air grew more humid as they got closer to the water,

Pao noticed. And it had a strange odor, not like the usual river smell. Similar to the carnicería down the street. . . .

She'd never been so thrilled by the scent of raw meat.

"Look for a big red flower!" she called to Dante. "You won't be able to miss it!"

Dante didn't answer, but as they scoured the place together, the air was as thick with hope as it was with moisture. Sure enough, a few seconds later, she saw it. A cluster of massive, meaty petals forming the exact flower she'd seen in her vision.

In fact, she realized as they drew nearer, there was more than one blossom. There was a whole patch of them. Hopefully plenty to cure whatever was ailing Bruto. Then she and Dante could get back home before Pao's mom returned from work at midnight.

Pao whooped with joy and heard Dante's echoing shout as he spotted the flowers, too.

"Is it just me," he called as he raced down the bank, Bruto tucked under his arm like a football, "or do they smell like the meat counter at the taquería?"

Pao laughed, but she didn't slow. There were only a few rock formations between her and salvation for her best furry friend. She leaped over one that had club-like arms and landed heavily on the other side. Dante was right behind her. The flowers were almost close enough to touch.

In her desperation, Pao tripped over a rock she hadn't seen and sprawled on the pebbly ground, skinning both knees.

"Pao!" Dante called, skidding to a stop beside her. "You okay?"

"I think so," she said. Her knees were throbbing, and her hair had escaped its ponytail and was falling into her eyes. Her right ankle, which had caught the rock, stung viciously.

Dante pulled her up while she cursed her clumsiness. She'd almost gotten her bearings when she heard Dante gasp, a sharp sound that set off her alarm bells. Just then something hit her hard in the ribs, sending her toppling over again.

"What the—" Pao began, spitting out desert grit as she took another hit, this time to the thigh. There was no question about it—they were under attack. But by what?

Pao rolled over and over in the dirt, trying to create space between herself and her unknown assailant. She didn't stop until she collided with something furry. Bruto. He didn't seem to be hurt, but he wasn't moving, either.

And if Bruto was on the ground, where was Dante?

"Come on." Pao gathered up Bruto and got to her feet once more. "We're going to be fine, okay, buddy? Everything's going to be fine."

She might have believed it, too, if at that moment she hadn't gotten a glimpse of what they were up against.

The rocks littering the landscape weren't just rocks. They were *alive*, pushing out of the ground in little clouds of dust and charging toward Pao and Bruto with stone fists the size of grapefruits raised and ready.

"Of course," Pao groaned, backing up and half dragging her listless puppy along with her. "It can never be easy, can it?"

"Not for us!" Dante was beside her again, dirt-covered but otherwise none the worse for wear.

"Okay," Pao said, thinking fast as at least ten of the little rock monsters headed for them, while even more formed a semicircle around the cluster of flowers. "They're blocking the flowers, obviously, so we need to find a way to pass through them without getting—"

One of the rock creatures, about ten feet away, pulled back its arm and launched its stone fist like a baseball straight at Pao, who had to duck to avoid it.

"Pummeled," she finished as the small boulder smashed into the ground behind her. It definitely would have crushed her skull if it had made contact—a thought that didn't bring Pao much comfort.

"Are you okay?" Dante asked as another projectile soared in his direction, narrowly missing his left shoulder.

"I'm fine," Pao said, her mind still racing. There were at least twenty of the creatures moving toward them now, blocking every route to the flowers.

Well, every route besides the water. And La Llorona or no, there was no *way* Pao was going in there.

If it were anything else at stake, she might have considered giving up. She would have prioritized her bones (which had never seemed quite so fragile) and tried to find another way to accomplish their goal.

But it was Bruto, and she was losing him. She had to get through, and sooner rather than later.

"One of us should take Bruto somewhere safe," Pao said. "And the other—"

Another rock was launched at her, and she had less time

to dodge than before. The thing glanced off her funny bone and Pao jerked away yelping as it buried itself in the dirt behind her.

She felt it in the air before she turned—the strange shimmer and wave of energy that came when a magical weapon, or Arma del Alma, took on its true form. Dante's slipper had always transformed into a club quickest when Pao was in danger, and today was no exception.

The energy wave pushed the closest rock creatures back about ten feet, but they were mobile again in no time, ready to continue their single-minded assault on the intruders.

Turning to face Dante with her moment of borrowed time, Pao couldn't help but feel a twinge of her old envy. He looked heroic, there was no doubt about it, with his iridescent otherworldly weapon in one hand and a helpless puppy in the other.

Pao shook herself. Envying Dante his hero status had never gotten her anywhere.

"Here," she said as three more rocks sailed in their direction. "Let me see."

She reached for Bruto, but Dante (looking indecisive for a brief moment) handed her the club instead. Pao took it, feeling a hum of energy in her sore, tired limbs.

Pao had been sure he would give her the defenseless creature and send her off to keep Bruto safe while he did the heroic work of killing monsters. So sure, in fact, that her brain wouldn't quite catch up to the reality.

"Are you just gonna stand there and gape at me, or are you gonna find out how many of these things you can crush at once?" Dante asked, smiling without a trace of resentment in his features.

"Are you . . . sure?" Pao asked, though she was already itching to take action. "Because it's your weapon and—"

"Pao, we've got a sick puppy and some bizarro rock creatures and—in case you haven't noticed—very limited time on our hands, so why don't you do less talking and more pulverizing, okay?"

Pao grinned back. With the Arma in her hand, the prospect of tangling with the projectile-launching rocks seemed much less scary, and almost . . . fun.

"I'll be back once I get him somewhere safe, okay?" Dante said. "Do your thing."

"You got it," Pao said. "And thanks."

"Repay me by not getting your bones shattered," Dante replied, as Pao narrowly dodged yet another flying rock the size of her head.

This time, Pao didn't answer. She just turned back to the onslaught of stone creatures while holding the club like a baseball bat. Seconds later, a rock monster drew a bead on her, winding up its little arm to throw.

Pao beat it to the punch. The club made solid contact with its body. Pao had expected the weapon to crush the stone, or at least push back the creature—but instead it made the rock explode on impact and left behind nothing but a cloud of fine gray dust.

"Whoa," Pao said. "Cool!"

But there was no time to admire the effect. That creature

had only been the first to reach her—there were plenty more behind it, already cresting the hill. Pao managed to take out three with one swipe, the dust swirling around her like fog, making it hard to see.

She swung until her arms were sore and she could feel the grit of rock dust in her eyes and between her back teeth. She swung until she was out of breath, and the monsters were still coming. . . . Pao almost regretted taking the club instead of the puppy.

Dante still hadn't returned. Pao had hoped to create a path through the creatures so she could get closer to the flowers, but she'd barely moved besides the shuffling and pivoting necessary to keep up with the onslaught of monsters.

Where was Dante? she wondered. Was it bad that he hadn't come back? Did it mean Bruto was . . . ?

She batted as fiercely as she could, taking out four rock creatures at once this time. A new record. How many of these things could there possibly be?

Before the dust could settle enough for her to find out, Pao heard a bone-chilling howl. It was an earsplitting, goose-bump-raising sound that echoed through the desert like a siren.

But who did it mean to warn?

The answer became clear as the rock creatures—at least fifty of them that Pao could see—stopped moving for a second. Then they changed direction, as if attuned to the high-pitched call. Pao cast her eyes around, hoping to find the source of the howling, but saw nothing.

"Pao!"

She could barely hear Dante's voice over the cacophony, but she shouted back with everything she had. "Dante!"

He reached the top of the hill, breathless again and clutching a stitch in his side. "Pao," he said, gulping down air. "It's . . . They're—"

But he didn't even have a chance to get out the words before Pao saw them. Coming from the riverbank. The pinpricks of at least ten pairs of glowing green eyes, and above them, phosphorescent in the moonlight, rows upon rows of tentacle-like protrusions.

"Chupacabras!" Dante finally managed to wheeze. "Like, a lot of them."

"Yeah," Pao said, gripping the club still tighter. "I see. Where's Bruto?"

"He's safe," Dante said, finally catching his breath. "I stashed him in an old hollow cactus a half mile or so from here. He's . . . the same, Pao. He's still breathing."

A sob caught in Pao's throat. A cactus husk was exactly where Pao had first found Bruto—a helpless little thing separated from his family, just like she'd been at the time. They'd made each other less afraid. Become family on one of the longest nights of Pao's life.

She couldn't lose him now.

"Listen," she said, talking fast while the rock creatures were still distracted. "They just keep coming. I got as many of them as I possibly could with the club, but they're everywhere, and they're not stopping. With the chupacabras, too, I don't know how we'll ever . . ."

Dante had stopped listening. Pao knew that distracted look well enough by now. He was staring somewhere over her left shoulder, like he always did in the tiendita when there was a fútbol game on the old TV.

She was about to tell him exactly what she thought about his garbage manners when she heard something new. A playful yipping had replaced the howling, and it was a sound she was all too familiar with.

"Bruto?" she said, not daring to hope.

"It's not him," Dante said, his voice full of wonder. "It's . . . like, *twenty* of him."

The moon, almost full and absolutely brilliant, was cresting the horizon behind them, bathing the scene in an eerie glow. Below them on the riverbank, more than a dozen chupacabras had arrived on the scene. But not the full-grown ones Pao had fought this summer. These were puppies, too. None bigger than Bruto, and some considerably smaller.

They'd clustered between the rocks and the river, and they were *playing*. Crouching down in pounce position and wagging their little tails.

"They're gonna be crushed!" Pao said in alarm, raising the club to go protect them, forgetting in her haste that they might be predators.

"Wait!" Dante said, putting a hand on her arm. "They're not!"

He was right. As they watched in awe, the rock creatures tucked themselves into balls and rolled down the incline toward the tail-wagging monsters, which (much like Bruto had done the one and only time Pao tried to give him a bath) jumped out of the way at the last second. All ten of the rock monsters that had attempted to crush them ended up splashing into the water.

They didn't come back up.

"The chupes are tricking them into rolling into the river!" Pao said, giggling as if Bruto himself were pulling the prank. A new wave of rocks descended the hill and crashed into the water while the pups scampered away, their tongues hanging loose like they were laughing, too.

After only a few minutes, the puppies had cleared the area of rock creatures, and the path to the flowers was wide open.

The blossoms' scent was strong, and their petals shone with some sap or nectar that glistened in the moonlight. Every cell in Pao's body told her to run down there, grab one of the massive things, and carry it to Bruto.

But the chupacabra puppies were still there, clustered on the other side of the flower patch, peering warily into the center as if the flowers were scarier than the monsters they'd just outsmarted in minutes.

"I'm going in," she said to Dante, clenching her hands into fists. "We can't afford to wait anymore." Before he could say something cautionary, she stared right into his eyes. "*Bruto* can't afford to wait anymore."

He sighed. "I've learned better than to argue with that look."

"Wait here," Pao said, eyeing the suspicious chupacabra pups. "If anything happens to me, go get Bruto and . . ." She stopped there because she actually had no idea what Dante should do if anything happened to her. This vision, the flowers—they were their one shot.

"Don't worry," he said, though Pao was sure he didn't have any more idea than she did. "I'll take care of him."

Always the valiant hero, Pao thought. She nodded and handed Dante the club, feeling its warmth leave her. "I won't be able to carry the flower *and* the Arma," she said. "And I can't transform the weapon on my own anyway."

Dante looked truly afraid now, but he nodded once, his jaw clenched tight.

Before Pao could change her mind, she turned, unarmed, toward the flowers. The venomous eyes of the chupacabras shone in the moonlight, flashing their monstrous warning.

Pao took off at a run.

It happened immediately. The chupacabra puppies started to growl. It was a sound Pao had seldom heard from Bruto, and, amplified by twenty or more, it was even more haunting than the howling. It sounded like the time one of Mom's old hippie friends had played a musical saw in the living room.

Pao knew better than to think she could subdue the pups if they decided to attack her. There was no guarantee they'd take to her the way Bruto had, either—she'd always assumed he was one of a kind in that regard.

But she charged forward anyway, thinking of nothing but her cold, listless puppy and how she meant to save him no matter what the cost.

She was twenty yards from the flowers.

Fifteen.

Eight.

The growling grew louder, the saw sound oscillating until it seemed to be coming from everywhere at once.

When she was three yards away, one of the chupacabras gave a sharp yip, nothing like the playful sound they'd made when romping with the rock creatures. This one was unmistakably a warning, and it sent a thrill of fear down Pao's spine.

She didn't slow.

The chupacabras didn't move to stop her, either—though Pao was close enough now to see their razor-sharp teeth, the jet-black lips curling over them, and the green eyes wide with menace.

In front of her, the meat flowers were only steps away—and even more humongous up close. The closest one was at least the size of a hubcap. Pao hoped it wouldn't be too heavy to carry on her own.

She leaped, closing the rest of the distance between herself and the flowers. The smell was overwhelming here, like hot metal in her throat, and she braced herself for a dozen chupacabra bites.

But they never came.

What happened, in hindsight, was so much worse.

Just as Pao reached for the stem of one of the massive blossoms, the ground shook beneath her feet. The growling around her turned to snarling, and for the first time Pao noticed that the pups' eyes weren't on her at all. They were on the flowers.

Pao's hands were locked on the stem, which was the size of a baseball bat and covered in toothlike thorns. She pulled with all her strength, too aware of the tremors intensifying, pebbles jumping and dancing between her sneakers.

The flower wouldn't budge.

Just a few feet away, the chupacabras' eyes were wide with terror and malice. They snapped in her direction, but they didn't dare move closer. Not when the ground was still shaking.

"Come *on!*" she shouted with one last sharp, upward tug.

All it did was cause her left hand to slip, and one of the thorns tore her palm wide open.

The chupacabras went into a frenzy at the smell of her blood. They pushed closer to the invisible barrier they seemed determined not to cross as the earthquake threatened to knock Pao to the ground.

Stubbornly, she clung to the flower, refusing to abandon it even though she could hear Dante screaming at her from the top of the hill.

With the jostling of the earthquake to focus on, Pao almost didn't notice when she began to rise. At first, it just seemed as though the chupacabras were getting smaller, and the vibrations of the ground were changing slightly—lifting her rather than shaking her.

By the time she realized what was happening, it was too late.

Pao and the flowers were two feet, then five feet, then ten feet in the air, and the chupacabras became the least of her worries. Because the place she'd been standing wasn't just a patch of meat-scented plants. It was a patch of meat-scented plants growing on something's *head*. The head of a giant creature that was emerging from the ground with Pao as its unwilling passenger.

When she was fifteen feet in the air, clinging desperately to the thorned flower stem, Pao screamed. She didn't love heights on the best of days, and this was a new level of scary.

She was twenty feet up by the time the monster stopped rising. Below her she could see stone arms extending from the sides of its body. When it took its first step, the head Pao was perched on so precariously tilted, and she screamed again.

"Pao!" Dante's voice echoed from below.

"I'm okay!" she called back, not at all sure why she'd said that when she'd maybe never been *less* okay in her life.

"What do we do?" Dante shouted up to her. "How do we get you down?"

"Don't suppose you have a parachute?"

She heard Dante laugh, a panicked, tight sort of laugh, but it made Pao feel a little better. Better enough to close her eyes, steel herself, and say, "Just get the club and start smashing!"

"But what if you—" His question was interrupted by the monster taking a step back and jabbing its massive fist in Dante's direction. Fortunately, it missed.

Pao held on for dear life, her stomach turning as the gigantic thing pivoted, almost sending her flying off its head and far away from the flowers. *I just need to pick* one, she told herself when things had steadied. One and then she could jump off and hope for the best. But she wasn't leaving without a chance to save her puppy—even if it meant risking herself.

She felt rather than heard it when Dante took his first swing with the club. This monster was far too gigantic to turn to dust on impact—and what would it mean for the flowers if it did?—but it certainly staggered, resulting in another alarming list of its head.

Pao barely caught herself at the edge this time and looked down from her dizzying height at the scene below. Dante, moonlit and fierce with the glinting club in his hand, waited for the right moment to strike again. The chupacabras slavered in their terror, eyes glowing green.

The creatures hadn't yet joined the fight, and the question was—which side would they be on if they did? Would Dante be in even more danger when they decided they wanted the flowers more than they wanted to keep their distance?

Would Pao?

When the monster steadied itself this time, there was a permanent slant to the head on which Pao stood. Dante had done some damage with the club, but not enough to keep the giant from swatting at him again.

Pao knew her only option was to retrieve the knife from her garish fanny pack and use it to cut through the flower's stem, but she'd need both hands to do it, and the monster wouldn't stay still for long enough.

"Dante!" she yelled. "Try to keep it calm!"

His laugh was a bark this time. "Yeah, no problem," he said. "I'll just sing it a lullaby!"

"I just have to . . ." Pao said through gritted teeth as she let go of the stem and wobbled dangerously on the tilted surface as she reached for the knife. "Almost there . . ."

The knife wasn't sharp enough to cut the stem easily, so Pao began the laborious and dangerous process of sawing away at it. When she broke through the root's cortex—thinking absurdly of the biology class in which she'd learned plant anatomy—a gooey red liquid began to bleed onto her hands.

"Ew!" Pao screeched, in a way most unbecoming for a scientist. But the stuff was, for lack of a more technical term, completely icky.

Still, she was making progress. She got more than halfway through the stem, and then finally the massive flower released with a sound like a plug being pulled from a drain. At least a gallon of the gross red goop splashed all over Pao's hands and shoes.

She'd expected the smell and even the off-balance feeling she'd have when she no longer had the implanted stem to cling to. What she hadn't expected was for the monster to let out a strange grinding scream and throw itself backward, sending Pao and her hard-won prize flying into the air. . . .

And plummeting toward the ground.

Pao instinctively turned her body to shield the flower—or was it part of the giant's head?—as she fell. *Bones can be mended,* she thought as the wind whistled in her ears, *but this* thing *might be Bruto's only hope.*

She hit the ground on her left side and curled around the red tentacle flower in an almost fetal position. The pain of her jarred bones was instantaneous, and it knocked the breath from her lungs. The process seemed to take several minutes, though Pao knew logically it could only have been a few seconds.

Finally, she was still, her heart pounding, her ears muffled to the chaos still happening around her.

She moved carefully, first her toes, then her fingers, then the rest of her body parts one by one. Somehow, miraculously, she was whole. And so was the flower.

Pao struggled to her feet and spat blood, still clinging tightly to the massive growth, which weighed almost as much as Bruto. Its smell had already started to turn rancid, and Pao knew she didn't have long to get it to her dying friend.

On her feet, if a little shakily, Pao searched the landscape for Dante. He was still doing his deadly dance with the monster about a soccer field's length away from Pao. That giant had really tossed her.

After a vicious crack to the creature's right leg, Dante scanned the area for Pao. He smiled and whooped when he saw her standing and holding the flower.

Pao was torn. She wanted to stay and help him fight, but the organism's vivid red petals had begun to brown at the tips. She had a feeling it wouldn't be any good to Bruto rotten.

"Go!" Dante shouted, as if he were reading her mind. "Go get him!" He pointed upriver, where he'd stashed the unconscious Bruto.

Pao didn't need him to tell her twice—she took off in a flash. Every step was agony on her tender, battered body, but she didn't let the pain slow her down. She just ran with all the energy she had left, lugging the flower like it was the most precious cargo on earth.

Behind her, the chupacabras' growls echoed, combined

with the sound of smashing rocks. Pao hoped it was Dante delivering the hits, and not the other way around.

Within a few minutes, Pao came across a cactus husk lying on the ground, and her heart sped up. She was on her knees in a second, the meaty flower beside her, wilting still further with the accompanying smell of a potluck buffet table at the end of a long celebration. The point when you're not sure you'd eat the leftovers anymore.

But maybe you'd feed them to a dog. . . .

Please, Pao pleaded to the santos her mom lit candles to, to the universe, even to the ghosts. *Please let him be alive*.

Pao reached into the cactus and felt Bruto's cold body, his listless limbs. Even the bristles of his fur felt less poke-y than usual. With tears in her eyes, she gently pulled him out, not sure he was still breathing. Was she too late?

"Bruto!" Pao said, pulling his little body to her chest and burying her face in his fur. "Please, buddy, please wake up!"

Nothing happened. No rise and fall of his chest. No snore in her ear. Nothing.

Pao cried harder, squeezing him to her like she could press some of her own heartbeat right into him. Every ache and pain from the rock fight and her fall came back tenfold as she held him, the reality of losing him too enormous to process. Like a dying star, or a black hole . . .

But then, just when her grief had reached a fever pitch, Pao heard something. A tiny snuffle of breath. She'd never gone still so quickly.

"Bruto?" she asked, her voice barely a whisper.

He snuffled again, one of his eyes opening just a fraction, and Pao collapsed around him, hugging him, sobbing into his fur for an entirely different reason now. He was alive! She hadn't been too late. There was still a chance. . . .

Still hiccuping around her tears of relief, she set Bruto next to the red growth he'd showed her in the vision. There was no doubt about it now—he was sniffing, both eyes open, moving toward the smell of it.

"It's for you, pal," Pao said, her voice breaking. "I got it just for you."

The first bite Bruto took—just a feeble little nibble—made a dramatic and obvious difference. He got to his feet and ate more voraciously, avoiding the petal tips that had gone brown in favor of the vital red pieces in the center. He ate until his tail was wagging and his eyes sparkled with the mischief she had feared she would never see again.

Finally, once he'd had his fill, he ran to Pao and threw himself into her lap, sending her sprawling backward into the dirt.

"You're back!" she cried. "You're back, and I'll never let anything bad happen to you again, okay? I'll bring you here as often as you need, and I'll never get mad at you for eating Mom's shoes or deny you the good Starbursts or forget to take you for a walk ever, ever again, okay?"

He looked at her right in the eyes then. Like he'd heard her promises and he intended to make sure she stuck to every one of them.

"Okay, okay," she said, rubbing him behind the ears and obliging when he rolled over for his favorite belly scratches.

"But we gotta go back, buddy," she said seriously. "Dante is still there with the monster we had to fight to get this thing, and he needs our help."

Bruto cocked his head, then got to his feet, every muscle tense, like he was just waiting for her to tell him which way to go.

"Come on," she said. "One more fight, and then we go home."

He raised an eyebrow at her.

"Yes, for more Starbursts than you can possibly eat."

They ran together this time, back to the hilltop where Dante was barely holding his own even though the massive rock monster was missing some of its right leg and a piece of its left.

Pao wasn't sure where to begin without a weapon. But, to her surprise, Bruto beelined straight for the battle without looking back.

Not about to be outdone by a puppy, she half ran, half limped to Dante's side. He looked worse off since she'd left him, with a fresh cut bleeding on one cheek and his left arm folded in like he was cradling it.

"He's okay?" Dante asked, and Pao nodded, feeling another tear escape.

"Good as new, it seems."

"So does that mean we can get out of here now?"

Pao wanted nothing more than to scream *YES!* at the top of her lungs and turn tail for home, but something was stopping her. Obviously the chupacabra puppies needed this strange organism to survive—Bruto's illness had proven that. So what would happen to the others if Pao and Dante left without giving the chupes access to the rest of the flowers?

"You're thinking about the feral monster puppies, aren't you?" Dante asked, grimacing from the pain, his club hanging from one hand.

Pao nodded.

"Well, it looks like you're not the only one."

Pao turned to where Dante was pointing. At the riverbank, Bruto had approached the other puppies and was whining and barking at them like he was trying to get them to do something.

After almost a whole minute of this, the giant seemed fed up. It launched a boulder into the mass of puppies, scattering them. But in the process, it knocked itself over—its balance being severely compromised by its missing leg.

Pao watched in wonder as the puppies took up the same positions as before, taunting the monster from below. They wanted to lure it into the water like they had with the smaller rock creatures, she realized.

But could they do it?

The monster was clearly furious, swiping left and right as it fought its way back to a standing position. The puppies were waiting, ready to bait it into the same roll that had been the demise of the smaller stone creatures.

But Pao was doing calculations in her head. The massive rock giant wasn't as rotund as the smaller ones had been. Also, it was much heavier. It would take a more severe angle to make this one roll at the right speed.

Lastly, its protruding left leg was too efficient at stopping it and pushing it back up.

They would fail, she realized with horror. The giant would crush the puppies before they could get out of the way, or it would get back on its feet and pummel them mercilessly with those powerful stone limbs.

Unless Pao did something to help.

"Let me see the club!" she said to Dante. "I can end this. . . . Could I use it, please?"

"Pao, whatever you're going to do, just—"

"I'll be careful," she said in a rush as the monster got into position, the puppies waiting for their chance with those hopeful eyes and that pounce pose she knew so well. "But there's not much time."

Dante looked into her eyes for a long moment, then handed her the club. "Come back in one piece, okay?"

"Okay," Pao said, smiling at him. Then, yet again, she ran.

Once she reached the top of the hill, she cupped her hands around her mouth and shouted at the top of her lungs. Nothing coherent, just sounds, but it was enough to make the monster turn around.

Just as Pao had hoped, it made for her, enraged by the glinting club she held over her head, the one responsible for its near-defeat.

The chupacabra puppies waited as it lumbered behind Pao, who shouted and waved the club, taunting him like a matador would a bull.

She would have to time it perfectly, she knew, and even then it was a long shot.

The monster reached her and pulled back its arm to swipe. Without hesitation, Pao darted between its legs and swung the club as hard as she could into the left one. She yelled in triumph when the limb shattered and the monster was sent falling backward.

Without its leg under it, the giant rolled, just as Pao had envisioned, barely missing the puppies as it careened into the water. It landed with an almighty splash that came up on the bank like a tidal wave, soaking the chupacabras. Several of the lizard-dog creatures jumped in after the monster, biting off the tentacle-like flower stems with ease.

They dragged the meaty petals to the bank, where the rest of the pups descended on the growths rabidly, ripping and tearing and chewing and wrestling over the best pieces until they were all covered in the sticky red goo. Pao hoped this meal would sustain the chupes for a long time.

She descended gingerly from the hill, her limbs aching but her spirits high.

Dante met her alongside the strange crater where the monster had pushed its way out of the earth.

"Pretty cool," he said, smiling from ear to ear and bumping her shoulder with his.

"Thanks," she said, bumping back.

"I can barely even see him in there," Dante said, squinting into the mass of wriggling green-eyed beasts.

"I can," Pao said with a hint of pride in her voice.

"Pao . . ." Dante said slowly. "Have you considered the fact that you just saved a bunch of . . . well . . . monsters?"

Sighing, Pao waited a moment before she replied. Sure, she'd considered it. She'd fought full-grown chupacabras before, and they were fearsome enemies. But weren't there times when she felt like a monster, too? Wouldn't Bruto still be one, if she hadn't taken a chance on him?

"Monsters are made, not born," she said finally. "Maybe these chupes will remember what happened today. Maybe it'll change them."

"Or, then again, maybe it won't," Dante said skeptically.

"Yeah," Pao said. "But I'd rather hope, you know?"

Dante was quiet, but it was a thoughtful kind of silence.

As the moon began to set, Pao—remembering her mom's impending return from work—whistled for Bruto.

For one heart-squeezing moment, nothing happened. The chupe puppies wrestled in the red goo and the mud left behind by the monster's tidal splash, looking like one big, happy litter. There was no sign at all that one among them had a name. A home. And a little dog bed that was only half chewed to bits.

What if he doesn't want to come back? Pao asked herself. *What if he's finally found where he's supposed to be?*

But before she could even finish thinking it, one of the pups detached from the rest, shaking mud and red stuff everywhere before loping over to Pao and Dante with a goofy, tongue-flopping puppy grin on his face.

Pao's heart returned to its rightful size and glowed with a warmth she knew would be with her as long as Bruto was. He was her family now. For better or worse.

"Come on, boys," Pao said, scratching Bruto's ears and then punching Dante lightly on the arm. "Let's go home."

"Time for a 'sneaking in,' as my abuela would say?" Dante asked with a smirk.

"Yeah," said Pao. "And after that, we have quite a story to tell her."

The Loneliest Demon

SARWAT CHADDA

"SIKANDER AZIZ! I CHALLENGE you to a duel!" the demon yelled from the deli doorway. "To the death! Choose your weapon!"

"Ya Allah! You again?" I said, pausing from filling the pita. "Get lost! I'm not interested!"

The demon glowered, or I think she did. I was too busy spooning Cairo sauce over the falafel to study her face. You can't just stuff a pita. There's an art to making the perfect—

"No use hiding from me, puny mortal!" The demon wasn't finished, unfortunately. "You have a date with destiny!"

"Did she just call me a 'puny mortal'?" I asked Mama.

She shrugged as she poured out the coffee. "Every morning this week, habibi. You really need to do something about your friend."

You would have thought a demon at the door would have attracted some attention from our customers, but, hey, this was New York. They'd seen it all before, and the lunchtime crowd was only interested in getting their food fresh, hot, and fast.

"She is not— Hey! Off the table! I just polished that!"

The demon's eyes burned as she stood on the gleaming white surface I had spent *all morning* cleaning. "Come outside and face me!" she said. "Or are you a coward?"

"Off the table!" I shouted again.

Her fangs flashed white through her snarl, but she reluctantly climbed off.

One customer looked over his shoulder. "I love cosplay. That mask is fantastically hideous."

"She's a demon," I muttered as I tore off a strip of wax paper and, with a fold-tuck-fold-tuck-tuck, slid his sandwich over the counter. "That'll be a Lincoln."

"A demon?" He handed over the five-dollar bill, then nodded slowly. "Oh yeah, out of *Sabrina*. Season three."

Isn't it amazing how people can be so blind to what's in front of them? "We're getting ready for Comic Con," I said.

The demon growled at me from the door, which she was now holding open as Mrs. Feldman shuffled in with her walker.

"Where's Sargon?" I looked around for the large tabby cat that had made his home here. "Isn't he supposed to be protecting us?"

Mama rolled her eyes upward. "On the roof. Catching some sun."

Typical. What was the point of having a cat that magically turned into a giant winged lion if it couldn't prevent a demon from upsetting our customers? Or at least those customers that weren't trying to get selfies with said demon.

"Fine." I met the demon's furious gaze. "You, around back. You're upsetting people."

She looked at the line with a sneer. "They should be cowering at my feet. I, who was the doom of Nippur and the calamity of Lagash."

"Whatever." I'd heard it all before, when Nergal, the ancient Mesopotamian god of plagues, had decided to visit with his army of demons.

Mama patted my shoulder. "Don't take too long, Sik. The sisters at St. Margaret's will need their lunch soon."

"In case you missed it, Mama, there's a demon here that wants to kill me."

"She wouldn't be the first." Then Mama clapped and said to the customers, "Okay, who's next?"

Baba was in the kitchen, kneading pita dough. He glanced up as I walked to the back door. "Girl trouble again?"

"It's a demon. One of Nergal's. The last, I hope."

"You could take the shovel," Baba suggested.

Plenty of stores have something tucked under the counter in case of trouble. Mr. Georgiou across the street has a good ole baseball bat, and Bronski at the convenience store keeps a set of nunchucks handy, despite having knocked out his front two teeth the one time he tried to use it. We have a shovel. But it's a *special* shovel.

"I think I can handle this one myself." I pushed open the back door to the alleyway.

The demon sprang off the dumpster as I appeared. "So, you are not a coward after all."

"Can we just get this over with? I've got a Dungeons and Dragons game with the guys later, and I can't miss this session. We're exploring the Catacombs of Doom."

"*I* am your doom!" snapped the demon. "Or I will be, in just one minute!"

As demons went, and I did have some experience with them, she was not exactly the most impressive I'd ever seen. In fact, she was without a doubt the *least* impressive, especially with the hem of her coat caught on the lip of the dumpster.

"Do you want help with that?" I asked.

"No, I do not!" She gripped the coat with both hands and gave it an almighty tug. It tore in half.

Exposing her tail.

Yeah, her tail. Scaly and crooked. Demon, remember?

"May Ea curse you!" she yelled, kicking the dumpster over and over again. "Ea curse you a thousand times!"

There was about another five minutes of this and also some swearing in ancient Sumerian. Eventually, once the dumpster was well and truly battered, she threw off the remains of her coat and swung around to face me. "Now you die, Sikander Aziz."

Last fall, when Nergal invaded Manhattan, he brought fourteen of his demons with him. I'd found two of them right here, in the dead of night, snuffling around in the trash, eating leftovers and rats. Over the following weeks I'd battled the rest with the help of Ishtar, the Mesopotamian goddess of love and war, and her adopted daughter, the literally ass-kicking Belet.

Nergal and his demons were long gone now. All but this one, apparently.

The thing was, I didn't even remember her. The rest had attracted all my attention, being bigger, more terrifying, more . . . demonic. "Who are you, again?"

She was short and spindly, not the right combination to induce terror in mortals, even puny ones. Her tail poked through a hole in the back of her kaftan, and she had little horns—studs, really—sticking up through her bristly red hair. She glared constantly from under a thick, cliff-heavy brow, and a pair of short curved tusks jutted from the sides of her mouth.

She puffed out her skinny chest. The sight made me want to give her a free meal with lots of carbs and protein. "I am the dread Rabisu, the terror of Nimrud, whose very name makes cow udders shrivel and flowers wither on their stalks. Wherever I walk, death and misery follow. I claimed souls upon the battlefield of . . ." She frowned. "Anyway, somewhere important. Lots of people died. And camels. I remember camels."

"Yeah . . . Rabisu. You're the demon of bad backs, aren't you?"

"Demon of *deformities*." Her glare increased a thousandfold. "Go on. I dare you to laugh. Bad backs are a curse for millions."

I couldn't trust my mouth, so I just nodded and made agreeable noises that were not like laughs *at all*.

"Bad backs are a thing!" Rabisu yelled. "Do you know how many work hours each year are lost because of poor posture?"

She wasn't making this easy. A little, teeny-tiny *hee* slipped out. Then I closed my eyes and thought about something sad—the Mets' most recent blowout loss—and I stood up a little straighter. I did spend a lot of my day hunched over food trays. "We talked about this yesterday, and I thought we came to an understanding. You can't kill me."

"Ha! Do you think I give a fig about your mortal laws?" She snapped her fingers. "I am a demon!"

"So you've said. But that's not it. You can't kill me, because I'm immortal."

She paced back and forth, frowning. "The effects of that flower you ingested should have worn off by now."

I shook my head. "Sorry to disappoint, but I really can't—"

"Diiie!" she screamed. And charged.

She went straight into the trash. There was no need for any clever moves on my part—no backflips or cartwheels or karate chops. I just stepped to the side, and she barreled through, taking out all three cans in a ringing percussion piece I'd call "Demon in the Trash." It was loud and tuneless but full of passion as Rabisu fought her way through the now-scattered leftovers, slipping on hummus and getting up to her elbows in sauces. There was an onion ring dangling from her nose.

The rear door of the deli swung open as Mama barged through. "Ya Allah, Sik! What have you done?" And in typical Mama fashion, she rushed over to the demon and gently helped her up. "Bismillah, are you hurt?"

"Don't help her! She's a demon!" I snapped. But one frown from Mama had me lifting Rabisu out of the pile of slimy leftovers. I picked off the onion ring. "Next time you charge, don't shout a warning beforehand. You totally lose the element of surprise."

Rabisu shook me off and picked the cabbage out of her hair. "I . . . I just . . ." Tears began to swell in her beady red eyes. She sniffed loudly.

Mama patted the demon's claw gently. "Why don't you come inside, habiba?"

I looked at the mess. How had Rabisu knocked over all three cans? She must have flown at them sideways. "In a minute. I just need to sweep—"

"I wasn't talking to you, Sik," said Mama, handing Rabisu a clean dishcloth to wipe herself off with. "I was talking to your . . . djinn."

Yes, Mama called her a "djinn." Since she'd been raised in Iraq, that's what she called these supernatural creatures.

"Shukran," said Rabisu, taking the cloth and practically vaporizing it with a massive, snotty blow. She offered it back, but Mama shook her head, grimacing. Then, quite casually, Rabisu stuffed it into her mouth and started chewing.

Mama winced as she straightened up. "I really need to start doing Pilates."

But even Mama's back troubles didn't cheer up Rabisu. Instead, the demon looked at her, tears running down her cheeks. "I can't exact revenge on your son. I'm so useless. What am I going to do now?"

Mama jerked her head toward the door. "Come in and clean up first. Then we'll figure it out."

Rabisu nodded miserably. I took a moment to give Mama a reality check. "You know she was one of Nergal's horde, don't you?"

"And you're going to hold that against her forever? Nergal's gone, Sik. Look at her," said Mama, sighing. "She's lost and alone in a strange city. I know how that feels."

"It's not my—*our*—problem, Mama. Just give her the Number Five special with all the toppings and send her on her way. That would be more than generous for someone who wants to kill me."

"Shame on you, Sik. The djinn needs our help. We have a duty to offer it." Mama put her arm over the demon's shoulder and led her inside. "You know where the broom is."

That's right. Mama took a creature from the darkest netherworld into our home and left me to clean up! Just as the door closed, I shouted, "She can't have any of my stuff!"

Which, of course, meant she totally could. Half an hour later, Rabisu walked into our upstairs apartment kitchen freshly showered and wearing my favorite Nirvana T-shirt. And also my best pair of jeans, her tail twitching out of a hole in the back that *hadn't been there before*. She saw me glaring. "What was I supposed to do? My tail needs room!"

I looked over at Mama, who shrugged as she laid out a plate of freshly made baklava. "They were getting too small for you anyway, Sik."

I reached for some baklava . . . only to find the plate empty. Rabisu met my accusing gaze, flakes of pastry covering her face from her snout all the way to her hairy chin. "Oops. Were those for sharing?"

We needed to wrap this up before the monster cleaned out the whole kitchen. "What do you want?" I asked her. "Aside from me dead?"

Rabisu's gaze dropped. "They left without me."

"Who?"

"Mimma, Tirid, Lemnu, Miqit, and the rest," continued Rabisu, counting on her claws. "They all fled without me."

Oh wow. Oh wow. Those were names I had never expected to hear again. "You mean Nergal's other demons?"

"I just want to go home," Rabisu said with a sigh. "I thought if I offered you as a sacrifice, the Nedu gate might open, just for a little while."

Mama gazed at Rabisu with sympathy. "Where's home?"

"Kurnugi, the netherworld," I said. I didn't tell Mama I'd been there before. There are certain things one should never share with one's parents. For everybody's sake.

Mama turned to me. "We need to get her home."

I couldn't argue. Not over this. Mama and Baba had come to America as refugees during the Iraq War, bringing my older brother, Mo, in their arms and little else. Most of their friends here had also washed up on this shore, driven by storms of conflict and persecution.

Immigrants look out for one another, too keenly aware of what it is like to have nothing, not even a home. We had gathered in communities that understood, sharing old stories and new hopes. I was Manhattan-born and spoke Arabic with a New York accent, but I still felt the tug of the "old country" in my heart.

"Where is this gate?" I asked.

"At the Canal Street subway station." Rabisu sniffed loudly. "I lived down there for weeks, praying that Ea might open it up again, just for me. I explored the tunnels, too, but I couldn't find a doorway anywhere."

Canal Street. That made sense—that was how I'd gotten to Kurnugi. But the station had been closed for months. Nergal's demons had trashed it in their haste to leave.

Rabisu looked up at me, her face still thick with honey-coated flakes. "Can you help me?"

Me? Help a demon? Of all the things to ask!

But Mama's expression was no less hopeful. Every refugee dreamed of home. Getting one back to the place they loved was a victory for them all.

"I guess." I sighed. "C'mon. Let's go find the real-life Catacombs of Doom."

"What's the problem?" asked Belet, her image slightly pixelated on my phone. I was sitting on my bed while Rabisu fidgeted to the left, off-screen.

"Who says there's any problem? Maybe I just wanted to have some FaceTime with my favorite person."

Belet's quizzical eyebrow arch practically filled my small screen. "How flattering. Like I said, what's the problem?"

"Assuming that there *is* a problem, and I'm not saying there is, why do you think I can't handle it by myself?"

Her image shook as she started laughing. She glanced to the side, speaking to someone off-screen. "See, Lizzy? I told you he was funny."

"Hold on, you're not alone? Where are you, exactly?"

Belet took a deep breath and composed herself. "Visiting a family friend for afternoon tea." She then popped a cream-lathered scone into her mouth.

"How *terribly* quaint," I said, using my very best English accent. "So where's that? The Ritz? The Savoy?"

"Buckingham Palace," Belet replied nonchalantly. "Lizzy and I are catching up."

Wait a minute. . . .

"Um, this *friend* doesn't happen to be the ruler of England, does she?"

"Actually, she— What's that, Lizzy? Oh, not just England but also the United Kingdom and the Commonwealth."

"You know the queen? Really?"

"Mother's had ties with the royal family for generations. Who do you think introduced Harry to Meghan?" Belet brushed some crumbs off her shirt. "Do you want to say hello?"

"No! I can't talk to the queen! I . . . I haven't combed my hair! I . . . I smell like fried onions!"

"There's a filter for that," replied Belet. "Sorry, Lizzy. Need some privacy for this one. Do you mind? Thanks."

Rabisu tugged at my sleeve. "Well? What did your friend say?"

"Who's that?" asked Belet.

Rabisu hissed. "That's not—"

I quickly pressed the phone screen against my chest. "Just go and wait in the kitchen!"

Rabisu scowled at me for a moment, then huffed and left. I waited until she was completely out of sight before turning back to Belet.

Who was not looking amused. "That was a demon. One of Nergal's."

"Technically, yeah, she is. Or was."

"I knew there was a problem. Okay, give me twenty-four hours."

"For what?" Why was it that each time I tried to speak with Belet it felt like we were having two entirely different conversations?

"What do you think? It's Rabisu, isn't it? Shouldn't take long. She's not exactly big league."

"Thanks, I think. But not necessary. Don't want to disrupt your tea."

"You still have Abubu, right?"

"Downstairs," I confirmed. "Baba doesn't want me keeping a shovel in my bedroom."

"You did explain to him that the shovel happens to be the most powerful weapon in existence?"

"It's still a shovel, Belet."

Belet sighed. "So, you called me to get a few pointers? Okay, since this is your first demon kill, I suggest you do some stretches first. Loosen up the arms and shoulders with a few rotations and swings. Get the blood flowing." She raised the phone over her head so I could get a better look. "Then get a firm two-handed grip on Abubu and bring it down with a big swing. Power comes from the core. Exhale sharply. Dynamic—that's the key."

"I am not killing anyone with a shovel."

"Fine. Terminate her with extreme prejudice. With a shovel." Belet drew closer to the screen. "I could come. It's really no bother."

"La, shukran. I don't need you here."

"Oh." Belet stiffened and her mouth made that thin, hard line it always did when she was having violent thoughts. "I see how it is. After all, you're Sikander Aziz, a bona fide hero to the masses."

Belet was brought up in England and has this accent that's fresh from *Downton Abbey*. Everything she says sounds sooo polite, it's hard to know when she's being sarcastic. This was one of those times.

"Rabisu wants to go back to Kurnugi. I'm gonna help her."

Belet shook her head. "Of course you are. Honestly, I don't know how you've survived this long."

"Technically, I died twice in the last year, remember?"

She frowned. "Twice? There was the train. . . ."

"And also the time I fell six thousand feet from a chariot drawn by two winged big cats."

It's a long story. Unbelievably, all true.

Belet nodded. "Ah, yes. And how is Sargon? Are you looking after him?"

"He sleeps and eats, then sleeps some more. That's about it. So he's doing great." I glanced over my shoulder, making sure Rabisu wasn't nearby. "So? How do I get her back home?"

"You can't. There are rules, Sik, and Rabisu knows them. She's stuck here."

"Come on, Belet. There's always a way. *I* did it."

"Nergal destroyed the netherworld gates before you . . . took your trip. They've been rebuilt since then. Queen Erishkigal won't allow unauthorized travel in and out of her domain. And my aunt's vindictive. She's still furious that Nergal broke out of Kurnugi, and if she got word that Rabisu is on the loose, she might do something . . . drastic."

"How drastic?" I'd met Erishkigal during my trip to the netherworld. It hadn't been pleasant.

"She once hung my mother, her sister, from great bronze hooks as decoration for her throne room, so pretty drastic," said Belet. "Uh-oh. You've got that look on your face."

"What look? It's entirely innocent!"

"No. It tells me you've got some stupid noble notion in your head. You're going to help this demon get back to her home, no matter what. You feel sorry for her because she's a refugee. Am I right?"

"Why should demons be any different?" I said, more to myself. "Can you tell me what to do?"

"Speak to my brother," Belet replied.

Okay, I think my mouth dropped open. "Since when do you have a brother?"

"I have dozens of siblings. I'm not the only person Mother

adopted, remember? Wars tend to produce orphans. Mother found Petar in Bosnia."

"Petar? How's he going to help?"

"He's a dealer in rare items."

"We talking about ill-gotten gains from ancient tombs? He handy with a bullwhip?"

The local AMC was having an Indiana Jones revival. I love them all, but my favorite is the third one, *Indiana Jones and the Last Crusade*. (Or *Last Jihad*, as I like to think of it.)

"He's the family historian and our family has plenty of that. Maybe he can help, but it's a *big* maybe. I'll text you his address. Ma'a assalamah, Sik."

"Yalla bye." The screen went black.

The door swung open and Rabisu marched straight back in. "Missing your girlfriend?"

"Belet is not my . . . She's just a friend."

Rabisu rolled her eyes. "What did she say? Aside from offering to kill me."

"Anyone ever tell you that eavesdropping is bad manners?"

She pointed at her stubby horns. "Demon, remember? Bad is what we do."

A text from Belet popped up on my screen, with an address. It was immediately followed by another message.

You sure you don't want me to come and kill your demon?

"What'd she say?" asked Rabisu as she looked over my desk, flicking through the books and checking out the drawers.

"She wishes you good luck. Hey, get your paws off my stuff!"

"Ew, Gilgamesh." Rabisu picked up a small clay statue of a heroic-looking bearded man from my shelf, then carefully slid a ring off his outstretched arm. "What's this?"

I sprang off the bed and plucked it from her claws. "Definitely not yours."

"It's a royal seal, isn't it?" Rabisu's eyes narrowed with simmering anger. "Gilgamesh is nothing but a big bully. Always throwing his weight around. As well as my friends. Hurled poor Miqit over the palace at Uruk once—right into the river."

"Into the river's not too bad."

"Unless it's full of crocodiles."

The ring was big and heavy, practically a bracelet. I traced my finger over the design on the front: a king facing a lion. And Rabisu had guessed right—Gilgamesh himself, the ancient Mesopotamian king, had given it to me. It was more than a piece of jewelry—it was proof that the wearer had the king's authority.

But Gilgamesh had given up his kingdom. He'd become a gardener and turned his legendary sword, Abubu, into a shovel. He wasn't going to help us out with this one.

I slid the ring back onto the statue's arm. "C'mon. Let's go soak up some history."

"Your girlfriend gave you the wrong address," said Rabisu.

"She is not my anything." I checked the street sign against Belet's text message. It matched. We were down an alley off Schuster Street, just north of Penn Station. Should I call her again? Best not. I reckoned it would be bedtime at Buckingham Palace.

Plus, I knew her. She didn't make this type of mistake.

"The House of Heroes?" Rabisu's snout wrinkled as she read the hand-painted sign over the big storefront. I wondered how she had learned to read, especially English. Did demons go to school?

I wasn't a huge comic book geek, but even I recognized the Jack Kirby print hanging in one of the windows, with Captain America all but bursting out of the heavy silver frame. Opposite it was an original page from *Watchmen*. This week's releases also sat in their own frames. The owner took his comics seriously.

"C'mon, let's go in and browse," I said.

The doorbell chimed as we entered, its sharp bright sound bouncing off the bare brick.

The House of Heroes wasn't just a comics store—it was a shrine dedicated to the modern gods. On a shelf behind the counter stood the pantheon of superheroes, in the form of figurines. Collectibles—the first issues and first appearances—lined the walls, high up and in gold, silver, or bronze frames, depending on the era. None had price tags—if you needed to ask, you couldn't afford it.

The other customers maintained an almost religious silence. They browsed the shelves and stood back to admire the original art. One pair took selfies with a life-size statue of the 1960s Batman.

"Ah, some new pilgrims! Welcome! Welcome!"

A guy came out from behind an oak bookcase filled with graphic novels. He was in his mid-thirties, I guessed, and wore a three-piece suit, the material printed with random comics panels. I spotted the Joker on his left lapel and Doctor Doom on the right. Spider-Man climbed up one sleeve and Aquaman surfed down the other.

"Petar?" I asked.

He held out his hand. "Salaam alaikum, Sik. Belet told me to expect you."

"Waa alaikum salaam," I replied, shaking it. I turned to Rabisu. "And this is—"

"The legendary Rabisu." He bowed. "I am honored to meet the demon of deformities."

Rabisu blushed all the way up to her stubby horns. Okay, he was a charmer. His mother *was* the goddess of love and war, after all.

"Belet said you might be able to help us." I peered at a selection of photos in one of the glass cabinets. There was Petar posing with Stan Lee. And him cosplaying Professor X at Comic Con one year. But there were plenty of much older ones, including . . .

"Is that Ishtar?" I asked. "Who's that with her?"

"Mom's with William Marston, better known as the guy who created Wonder Woman."

"I guess she might have helped inspire him?"

Petar grinned. "Superheroes aren't new. What else was Heracles? Or Cú Chulainn? I've spent my whole life studying the legends, the mythologies of the world, modern and ancient.

You see the same archetypes over and over again. It goes both ways, of course. The Norse god Thor inspired the superhero, and Superman's origin is from the Five Books of Moses. Just swap a reed basket for a spaceship." He walked over to a full-size four-color splash page hanging in a place of honor between covers of *Superman* and *The Hulk*. "And then we have the OG superhero."

There was no mistaking who it was. The deep brow, the thick ringlet beard, the tasseled kirtle, and the lion in his grip. I'd seen a thousand versions of his portrait over my lifetime, but none had the dynamism of comic book art. "Gilgamesh."

Petar pointed toward a side door. "I want to show you something."

But Rabisu stamped her foot hard. The sound was like a cannon shot, shocking the few shoppers from their comic books. Who dared violate the sacred peace of this temple?

"I don't care about all this printed . . . toilet paper!" she declared loudly.

There was a collective gasp from all corners. I sensed the simmering outrage. She might as well have wandered into the Louvre and complained that the *Mona Lisa*'s smile was "a little wonky."

Petar wasn't offended, though. He just nodded thoughtfully. "I understand, Rabisu. But it'd be better if we talked in private. I have an idea or two about your travel problem."

Travel problem? That was one way of putting it.

In the back office, floor-to-ceiling murals from ancient Egypt, classical Greece, Mesopotamia, the Mexica, and the

Middle Kingdom covered the bare brick. Gods, heroes, monsters, kings, and queens enacted the legends and tales of their worlds. There was also a triptych displaying the crucifixion and resurrection.

Petar sat down with a huff on a tall stool beside a large desk and gestured to the wall of artwork. "What does this remind you of?"

I smiled. "They're comic strips."

An old-fashioned drawing board stood in the corner. Racks of reference books were within easy reach, and there were shelves holding pots of art brushes and paints. An unfinished page was pinned to the board—I could make out just a few faint outlines. "You draw?"

"I've been working on one big project for quite a while." He swiveled around to his desk and flicked on the table lamp. Its light fell upon a large leather-bound book, and by large I mean poster-size.

"What's this?" asked Rabisu.

Petar smiled proudly at it. "Take a look."

I opened the cover to the first page.

The lettering was in gold and surrounded by colorful panels of action, the blues sparkling like crushed sapphires, the reds deeper than blood, and the greens almost alive. Vines twirled around the narration, and the borders were minutely detailed knot-work.

Rabisu drew her claw slowly along the title. "*The Further Adventures of Gilgamesh.*" Then she lifted her finger and shook it, as though the page had burned her. "Bah."

"Volume twelve," added Petar. "This covers all his activities during the twentieth century, in both world wars."

"But Gilgamesh told me he laid down his sword long ago," I said. "He said he stopped fighting."

When I'd first met the legendary hero and he'd revealed himself as a pacifist, I'd been angry and disappointed. I'd even felt a little betrayed, because we'd needed an ultra-kick-ass warrior to help us defeat Nergal. Looking back on it now, though, I realized Gilgamesh had a grander perspective than most.

Petar tutted. "You think fighting's all that matters? Gilgamesh was in the thick of it from start to finish." He peeled the pages back to roughly midway through the book. "Look here."

Gilgamesh was huge in real life, but in the illustration, his proportions were mythic. He was carrying six children on his shoulders, all pale and frightened, while cradling a dozen in his arms. Clustered around him were many more—thin and desperate-looking, their coats marked with yellow stars—as they all crept through the gray ruins of a city.

"Warsaw, 1942." Petar turned the next few pages. There was a panel of Gilgamesh holding up a collapsing ceiling while rescue workers dragged a cowering family from the ruins. "Hiroshima, two days after they dropped the bomb."

I looked at the picture. "So Gilgamesh didn't take sides?"

"Of course he did. The side of the innocent and the helpless." Petar drew his finger down the thick column of pages. "And that led him to be involved in this. This is what I wanted to show you both."

It was a full-page panel of a vast building site, with the skeletal steel frame of a tower rising in the background and the sky filled with international flags. Gilgamesh, bare-chested, his workman jeans stained with dirt, stood with his shovel resting on his shoulder while dozens of construction workers went about their duties.

There was something familiar about it. Definitely New York. "What building is it?"

"The United Nations," said Petar. "That's your answer. You still have Gilgamesh's ring?"

"At home," I said. "Why?"

"Gilgamesh's seal allows the bearer passage through his kingdoms. And he was the ruler of Kurnugi, at least for a little while. I know a way—"

Rabisu clapped. "Then I'm almost home! Get the ring, mortal! Hurry!"

"So, I pick up the ring and then what? Order an Uber?"

"Not quite." Petar grinned. "Go get the ring, and then meet me at the UN."

"Why?" I asked. "What's there?"

Petar arched an eyebrow, looking a lot like Belet. "You'd be surprised."

Don't you hate it when people say that?

We met Petar an hour later in the UN's vast, sunlit visitors' lobby. "Gilgamesh helped dig the foundations of this place in 1945. World War II had been rough, and he wanted to be part of rebuilding the peace. He made a few modifications to the building plans, which you can access by using his ring."

A school group charged past, waving their quiz sheets, filling the lobby with screams and laughter as they flooded the exhibit area.

"Follow me," said Petar as he led us across the lobby to the elevators. This time of day the place was packed, with a dozen people waiting at each car. Petar had said that wasn't going to work—we needed one to ourselves. I joined the back of one line and coughed loudly. Petar got the hint. "Don't worry, Sikander Aziz. The Commission for Highly Infectious Diseases has a special room set aside. I'm sure it's not the same pox as last year. Everyone was cured, weren't they?"

I coughed even louder. "It's not me I'm worried about—it's my friend. Look what's growing out of her head."

The group of waiting passengers slowly turned and stared at Rabisu, and her horns. She scratched them. "They just appeared last night. And you won't believe what grew out of my bottom. Look!" She wiggled her tail.

A second later we had the elevator to ourselves. The doors slid open.

"I'm sorry you're in a rush to get home," Petar said to Rabisu. "I would have loved to have drawn you. But you are definitely going in my next graphic novel." He held out his hand to the demon. "I suppose this is where we say good-bye."

Rabisu stared at it. "Won't you be needing it? And I've already eaten."

I thanked Petar and stepped into the elevator, slipping the ring on my finger. Nothing about the car looked different. The buttons didn't have any obvious labels like LOWER LEVELS OF HELL or NETHERWORLD. "Which floor is she going to?" I asked him.

"I don't think it makes any difference. Just press a button and step out before the doors close."

Beside me, Rabisu closed her eyes and breathed deeply. "I can almost smell the brimstone already. Home, sweet home."

"I guess this is good-bye for me, too." My finger hovered over the panel. "It's been, er . . . interesting."

Rabisu squinted at me. "Just press a button, will you?"

"Please, Rabisu, don't get all sappy on me now." I punched a number and leaped out. "Yalla bye."

We stood facing each other expectantly, me out in the lobby and Rabisu in the elevator, primping her hair. I waved. "Have a great time. If you feel the urge to contact me, fight it."

"Of all the mortals I've known in my long, long life, you are by far the most average," she said.

"And of all the demons I've met, you are by far the *nicest*," I answered. But she just nodded. I guess demons can't be friends with the likes of us.

I tapped my foot. "So, good-bye. Again."

"Whatever. The doors aren't closing." Rabisu started pressing all the buttons. "Come on, you stupid machine!"

"Hey! Give it a second!"

She snapped her fingers. "Give me the ring. Let me do it."

"Aaand no way, ever." I gazed up at the overhead indicator lights—they were working fine. "Something's gonna happen, trust me."

Rabisu pounded the panel. "Nothing's happening."

"Out of the way, Rabisu." I reentered the elevator and looked at the now-dented control panel. "You've broken it. We'll need to try another—"

The doors closed.

"Oh no," I moaned. "Not again."

The elevator's ceiling lights blinked, changing to a hellish red, and the elevator shook, picking up speed as it dropped.

"What are you doing?" yelled Rabisu. "Get out!"

"What do you think I'm doing?" I slammed my palm over the buttons, all of them. But there was no stopping our fall.

"By Ea! What if a demon sees me with you?" Rabisu said, horrified at the prospect of social death.

"Strangely enough, that prospect doesn't appeal to me, either."

"Why not?" snapped Rabisu. "Oh, I get it. I'm not good enough to hang out with the great and amazing Sikander Aziz!"

"Why are we even having this conversation?" I punched the panel. "Why won't it stop?"

And then it did, hard, throwing us both to the floor with a calamitous *bang* as the lights exploded, leaving us in darkness.

"Sik?" whispered Rabisu.

"Yeah?"

"Is that your elbow in my face?" she asked.

"Is that your foot on my head?" We clambered unsteadily back to our feet. "You think we've arrived?"

Red light seeped in from the crack between the dented metal doors, and a cold breeze raised goose bumps on my skin. "Go on, open the door."

"Why me?" She did not look happy. "What's that noise?"

It took a second, but then I heard it—a distant, hollow drumbeat. The elevator quaked with each *thud*, which echoed straight through me. The sound made me nauseous, as if it was vibrating at some awful, fearful frequency. It reminded me of a . . .

"It's a heartbeat," I whispered.

Rabisu stared at me, terrified, which freaked me out. What did a demon have to be scared of? I strained my ears more and realized the sound wasn't coming from a single entity.

Several somethings were waiting just outside the doors and, judging by Rabisu's terrified expression, they weren't the demonic *Welcome Home, Rabisu!* committee.

"It can't be," whispered Rabisu, her eyes widening with each passing second. "They were banished forever."

The doors started creaking, as though struggling to open.

"We have to leave! Now!" Rabisu yelled.

I wasn't about to disagree. I leaped over to the damaged control panel and started pressing the buttons with Gilgamesh's ring. "Come on! Take us anywhere else!"

Whatever was out there blocked the eerie scarlet light coming through the crack, shrouding us in utter, chilly darkness. The heartbeats were thunderous now, shaking us down to our bones. The elevator buckled more, as if it were at the bottom of the sea, being crushed by unimaginable water pressure.

"Sik!" yelled Rabisu. "Get us out of here!"

I punched the buttons harder. "How? Nothing's happen—"

The doors slid open.

I was blinded by a sudden burst of brilliant white light, and Rabisu screamed.

"No luck?" asked Petar. "It was worth a try."

Blinking the spots out of my eyes, I saw the UN's lobby, the visitors lined up to get into the elevator.

Petar put his hand on my shoulder. "Everything all right?"

"In one piece, Alhamdulillah." The panel was slightly dented but otherwise in perfect condition. Rabisu grabbed my arm. She was trembling.

"What were they?" I asked, my voice struggling to rise above a whisper.

She looked up. I'd never seen her, or anyone, so frightened. She squeezed her eyes shut. "The Anunna."

Petar grimaced. "That's not possible."

Rabisu glared at him. "I know what I heard, mortal!"

I looked from one to the other. "The Anunna? What are the Anunna?"

Petar helped make a path through the crowd while I took hold of Rabisu. Her face was drawn and pale when she said, "The Old Ones."

"I still don't get what you're talking about," I said. "Who are the Old Ones?"

"The ancient Mesopotamians believed that certain entities existed before the birth of the universe," said Petar. "Before their own gods came into being. So they were called the Anunna. The Old Ones."

We were sitting on a bench outside the UN, facing Queens across the East River. Seagulls swooped overhead, the sun was bright, and the trees lining the river were full of blossoms. Yet I felt cold and Rabisu was shivering, despite wearing my jacket.

I glanced down at Gilgamesh's ring in my palm. "I visited Kurnugi once before with no problem. The Nedu gate under Canal Street was working just fine. What went wrong this time?"

"Nergal managed to smash his way through all seven gates," said Petar. "Those gates were built to keep the different universes safe and separate from each other. The fabric of the multiverse is a surprisingly fragile thing. Maybe, in their rush, people didn't repair the gates as well as they should have. That or—"

"Wait a minute. Multiverse? What are you talking about?"

"The multiverse is a common concept in theoretical physics and, er, comic books."

I peered darkly at him. "Please tell me you are not basing your entire strategy on what you read in a comic."

"You'd be surprised how many scientists are inspired by fiction, and vice versa. You think Kurnugi exists in our reality? Remember your own visit? You only stayed there two days, yet two weeks had gone by here. Different universes, different rules."

I nodded slowly. "I didn't think about it like that. At the time me and Belet were too busy trying to save New York from Nergal's demonic invasion."

"If the Anunna ever got into our universe," said Petar, "it would make Nergal's little escapade seem like a toddler's tea party."

"Hey, toddlers' tea parties can be rough," I said. "Two-year-olds can be vicious. I still have the bite marks on my ankle from the one we hosted at the deli last week."

Rabisu was fidgeting, her claws clicking nervously. "Don't blame Nergal. My master knew what he was doing. He would never risk granting the Anunna access to our universe. This is the result of mortal meddling."

"You may be right," said Petar, frowning. "Many scientists are researching multiverse theory these days—some experimentation is undoubtedly taking place. Experiments can go wrong, and a calamity in another universe could have repercussions in ours . . . and the spaces in between, where the Anunna dwell. The Old Ones have been slumbering since the beginning of time, but if they have been awakened, they will want to visit."

A chill ran down my spine. "But with the seven gates closed, we're okay, right?"

Petar nodded cautiously. "As long as they remain closed. I'm sorry, Rabisu, but we can't get you back home after all."

"You're lying!" Rabisu snarled. "There has to be a way!"

She glared at us, pain lurking behind her anger and loneliness. How would anyone feel, even a demon, being forced to leave everything behind?

Then Rabisu sank to the floor, covering her face as she shook with dry, rasping sobs. A demon crying. Who would have thought?

Petar patted Rabisu's claw. "Seems you're here for the duration."

She looked up at him, her red eyes glowing like lava. "Duration? I'm immortal! Trapped among you pathetic humans with your petty concerns and tiny little minds! I am one of Nergal's select! The lords of Assyria built mounds of skulls in my name! What am I going to do now?"

I'll be honest, I was getting tired of her pomposity. "Set your ambitions a little lower? I'm not sure you're allowed to have mounds of skulls in New York, unless it is in the Metropolitan Museum of Art. You can get away with a lot if you call it art."

She jumped up to her feet. "Mock me at your peril, puny mortal!"

"Will you stop with that 'puny mortal' stuff?"

"You *are* puny! Where are your horns? Your fangs?" She waved her claws in front of me. "You are weak and fragile, with lives so short you measure them in mere decades!"

I folded my arms across my chest. "I've eaten the flower of immortality, remember? That makes me an immortal just like—"

Rabisu cut me off with a loud groan. She was horrified already, but now she tipped into total despair. "I'll be spending eternity with *you*?"

We both turned to Petar. He looked from me to her, then

laughed. "You'll be Best Friends Forever. And Ever. And Ever."

Rabisu burst into tears all over again.

"New York's not so bad," I said as Rabisu and I made our way back home. I'd left Petar with our thanks for trying to help and a promise to visit his store again. "In fact, it may well be the greatest city on Earth."

"How many other cities have you actually visited?" snapped Rabisu. "You never saw Alexandria during the reign of Cleopatra. That lighthouse was a beacon to the world."

"We have something like that, too."

She just grunted.

"We tried, Rabisu."

"*You* tried. Very badly. I'm not giving up. There has to be a way back. The other demons will be missing me." She smiled wistfully. "There was that one time when Sarabda planted maggots in my head when I was sleeping. They would spurt out each time I sneezed."

"Er . . . great?"

She laughed a little. "And that time Libu and Bennu threw me into a lake of molten iron! I was a blackened skeleton for a decade. Good times."

"You demons sure know how to entertain yourselves."

She nodded vigorously. "See this tail? Used to be six feet long." She swished it back and forth. "Sidana bit it off. He was jealous that mine was longer."

"And you didn't mind?"

She stopped. "Why should I? They were my friends."

"*Toxic* friends."

"Toxic ones are better than none at all," she muttered. "You wouldn't understand."

Mo's came into view. Home at last. The sun had passed overhead, but I could see that customers still crowded the counter, and Mama and Baba were in full swing.

Rabisu stood at the corner, gazing up and down Siegel Street. Looking lost and very alone.

But how had she become my responsibility? She'd wanted me dead this morning. Meanwhile, Mama and Baba were being run ragged. They needed an extra pair of hands. "You can stay with us for a night or two, Rabisu, figure out what you want to do. But I have to work. Okay?"

She just shrugged.

"When you're ready to come inside, the keys are in my jacket. Just let yourself in through the back and head upstairs."

"So the customers don't see me?" Rabisu dangled the keys on her claw. "Fine. I don't care."

"It's not . . ." Oh no. The nuns from St. Margaret were here. Had something gone wrong with their earlier order? "My parents need me."

I crossed the street quickly, already rolling up my sleeves. I glanced back to see Rabisu still standing at the corner, looking glum and hopeless. I gestured sharply to the side alley, then swung the deli's front door open and barged straight into the bedlam. Customers were shouting, waving at the menu on the wall, wanting more of this, less of that. Mama was collecting money and handing out paper bags while Baba was slicing strips of lamb off the spit. The nuns were sitting at the window tables, waiting for their orders. I slipped under the counter and washed my hands.

"Sik! You're back! Did your djinn get home?" asked Mama as she dripped Manhattan sauce over some falafels.

"Not exactly. She'll be sticking around here for a little longer."

But before I could explain further, a guy snapped his fingers. "Hey! I'm waiting here!"

This was more like it. I didn't need any multiverse drama. This was the only world I cared about. I knotted my apron and turned to face the action. "Then it's lucky you're up next."

We pushed out the last diner at ten. Baba handled locking up while Mama and I headed upstairs, exhausted, but in a good way.

"Go ask the djinn if she wants some food," said Mama as she headed to our apartment kitchen. "I'll put something together."

Typical Mama. She wanted to feed *everyone*.

"She's not a djinn, Mama. She's not going to be granting anyone's wishes."

Rabisu couldn't even make her own come true. But there was nothing we could do about it tonight. I strolled to my bedroom door and knocked. "Hey, Rabisu, you hungry?"

No answer.

"Fine, go ahead and sulk," I shouted through the door.

"But I'll have to come in later for my pajamas!" I turned back into the kitchen.

"Problems?" asked Mama as she handed me the onions.

"I'm trying to help her, but she wants the impossible." I slid the big chopping knife from the block and set to work. "And she acts like it's my fault."

Mama smirked as she picked her way through our jars of spices.

"What?" I asked.

"Oh, nothing, habibi." She smirked even more. Parents shouldn't be allowed to smirk. "Nothing at all."

"It's impossible, Mama. Totally impossible."

"If you say so."

I knew what she was thinking. Sure, I'd done a few impossible things in the past, but this was different.

Wasn't it?

I flicked the chopped onions into the cast-iron skillet and looked back at my room. Light slid from under the door. A moment later I was there, tapping gently. "Rabisu? Can we talk?"

No answer.

"Let me in. Maybe we can work something out."

Still no answer, but I felt a light, cool breeze around my ankles. I heard a car horn outside, and the laughter of a couple passing by.

"I'm coming in." I turned the handle.

Rabisu was gone. The window to the fire escape was wide open. Had she just run away? The room was its usual lived-in mess, and the jacket I'd loaned her was lying on the floor. I picked it up and dusted it off. *At least she left the keys behind*, I thought with relief as I took them out of the pocket and tossed them onto my desk.

When my eyes swept my Gilgamesh statue, I remembered that his ring was in the other pocket.

Only it wasn't.

I double-checked the pockets, all of them. I threw the jacket on the bed and checked my jeans. No luck. The royal seal was gone.

"Ya Allah . . ."

Rabisu had taken it. And I knew exactly why.

Despite everything Petar had said, she was going back to Canal Street to open the Nedu gate.

I should have known. Gilgamesh's ring was the royal seal—it gave the wearer access to *anywhere*. Of course Rabisu would use it!

I sprinted toward the Fourteenth Street subway station, shovel in hand, dodging my way past the usual Friday-night crowd.

I needed to get to Canal Street. The subway station was closed for repairs, because Nergal had turned it into his base of operations during the last days of the plague. So I'd have to get out at Spring Street and run the rest of the way. Fast.

How much of a head start did Rabisu have? The stars were still in the sky and Manhattan wasn't on fire, so I doubted the Anunna were here yet, but I had a really bad feeling about . . . everything.

Lungs bursting, I barely managed to jump on the E train just before the doors slid shut. Only two stops. I'd be there in ten minutes. How much could go wrong in ten minutes?

Turns out, *plenty*.

We'd been traveling a minute before the subway lights flickered and died. The train rattled to a halt. No one freaked out—New Yorkers have a weary familiarity with the temperamental nature of their public transportation system. And plenty of light still filled the car from dozens of phone screens. There was a long silence as everyone waited for the power to come back on, and when it didn't, the mutterings and complaints started.

"And this is why I pay my taxes?"

"I knew I should have taken a cab. . . ."

Maybe it was just a coincidence that the power failed just as a gate to another universe was about to swing open. *Sure*.

The weirdness built up slowly. First there was a tremor that flipped my stomach. Then my nausea grew stronger—the sort of belly churn you get while riding a roller coaster right after eating a huge plate of cheesy nachos. People around me turned green. One clutched her stomach, gasping as she tried not to hurl. The ripple became a wave, rolling over us again and again. A deep, ominous grinding shook the car, and someone screamed. As the wave of sickness rose, so did the panic.

"I can't breathe! I have to get out!"

"What's happening? Why won't someone do something?"

"Hey, pal! Watch where you're puking!"

The grinding grew deafening, and people started pulling at

the doors, shoving one another out of the way in desperation.

I flipped the shovel. "Outta the way!"

I smashed it against the window. Now, considering it was the legendary Abubu, the Sky Cutter, a weapon capable of slicing the heavens, the result was remarkably mediocre. A big crack did open up across the pane, but I'd expected an explosion, or at least a lightning bolt.

Maybe it needed charging?

"Hit it again, kid!" shouted someone from the dark. "And put some real muscle behind it this time!"

Everyone's a critic. . . . But the second time worked like a charm. The window flew straight out of the frame. I didn't wait but jumped onto a seat and climbed out of the opening before there was a rush. I scrambled out onto the track and paused, letting my eyes get used to the darkness.

The grinding noise had become a dull, heavy pounding. It echoed all around me, through me, like the deep bass at a rock concert.

I peered into the tunnel ahead, through the orchard of steel columns that lined all the converging rail tracks. The thrumming made me sick, and my eyes ached as they tried to penetrate the black nothingness. Any sensible person would get far, far away from that source.

Me? I tightened my grip on the shovel and headed straight toward it.

What was the worst thing that could happen? I'd been crushed under a train and had woken up with only a few scratches.

I'd been to the netherworld, where I fought giant monsters—one underwater, no less. And I'd sky-fallen six thousand feet to face-plant on Seventh Avenue . . . only to get up and walk away, no harm done.

Despite all that, I felt small, fragile, and terrified. The Anunna were a whole different level of horror, and if they got through this tunnel, it would mean the extinction of *everything*.

"Good thing I've got you, Abubu." Great, I was talking to a shovel.

It might have been my imagination, but the shadows created by the emergency lights seemed to come alive, as if creatures from other dimensions were already casting their black silhouettes on my world. I felt their desperation, their hunger. What I'm trying to say is, I was scared out of my mind.

Scared and so very alone.

The subway tracks glistened with frost, and the temperature dropped with every step. Heat—no, life itself—was being sucked out of our universe.

I tripped over something. I'd been so mesmerized by the light patterns that I missed the lump right in front of me. Someone had dropped a bundle of . . .

"Rabisu?"

She was curled up in a fetal ball, and she refused to move. "Run, Sik," she croaked. "Just run."

"What happened?"

I helped her up, and she looked in bad shape. She was covered in weeping sores . . . but as I peered closer, I realized they were fresh brand marks. Symbols had been burned into her skin. And they still glowed.

"You need to get out of here," I said. "Follow these tracks back, and you'll end up at 14th Street. Get to the deli—Mama will take care of everything."

"What about you?"

Yeah, what about me? "The Anunna, are they here?"

She shuddered. "I used the ring to open the gate, but I didn't realize that the Anunna were already waiting in the space between our realm and Kurnugi. When I tried to close the gate, they overwhelmed me. I managed to escape, but not before . . ." She looked at the marks on her blistered flesh.

"Where are they now?" I asked.

"I don't think they've come through yet. They're still trying to understand your world. That's why we've got to—"

Suddenly, it hit me. "The ring," I demanded. "Do you still have it?"

"I . . . I must have dropped it back there," Rabisu said in a small voice.

"We need to find it. That's the only chance we have of closing the gate."

"There's no way, Sik!" Rabisu began pulling me along. "We have to run!"

"You go. I'll see you later." I pushed my lips into a smile. "Inshallah."

"Why are you doing this? Why are you being nice to me?" asked Rabisu. "Why don't you hate me?"

"What good would that do?"

"None at all." Rabisu dusted herself off. "But I'm not going to be upstaged by a puny mortal. If anyone's going to save the universe, it should be a demon. We've been around longer."

So that's how one Muslim kid and one demon went off to save all existence, armed with only a shovel.

The dimensions lost all sense. I didn't know which way was left or right, up or down, both inside and outside of me. Was I really here, or had I been here sometime long ago, or was I far, far, *far* in the future?

Great waves of fear crashed over me, reminding me what a small, insignificant speck I was. I was about to face powers that had been ancient before the light of the universe first shone.

Rats came screaming out of the dark tunnel mouth, clawing and climbing over one another in their rush to escape.

I gripped my magic shovel tighter.

"It could be worse," said Rabisu.

"I can't imagine how," I replied, sincerely regretting every life decision that had led me here.

The Old Ones were coming through. I could sense their mindless, pure rage. They were desperate to get out and wreak revenge for their imprisonment, like the djinn in the *One Thousand and One Nights* story who'd been kept in a bottle for centuries.

The curtain of darkness in the tunnel ahead gradually opened to reveal an eerie, star-filled backdrop.

No, not stars. *Eyes.*

They peered out of whatever empty universe they lived in. Then crooked limbs, struggling to take solid shape, reached through, eager to rip our world apart.

Not if I could help it.

The first creature to clamber through was spindly, a whirling mass of legs, claws, and gibbering mouth laced with yellow spittle. It cartwheeled toward us, its claws striking sparks on the metal tracks, building up speed until it catapulted itself at me.

I swung Abubu.

Lightning bolts erupted on impact. The air was suddenly thick with the smell of burning ozone as the creature disintegrated in an explosion of blinding light.

The rip in the universe grew wider as more beings came through. The Anunna had never been in physical forms until this moment, and they didn't know how bodies were supposed to work. So each was more grotesque than the last.

"The ring!" I cried to Rabisu. "Where did you drop it? It's keeping the gate open for them!"

"Over that way!" She pointed to the middle of the seething horrors.

Of course it had to be there.

Her eyes blazed with fevered determination. "Ea, bless me. . . ."

"Allahu Akbar," I whispered, focusing on the nightmares facing us.

But beyond them, in the distance, a small star pulsated with golden light.

"See that light, Rabisu? I'm not sure, but I think that's the Anunna's heart. Maybe the ring is near there."

We charged. I swung Abubu at every monstrous face, claw, tentacle, whatever. The tunnel rumbled with thunder as lightning burst with each shovel blow, ripping open the darkness and driving the creatures back, at least for a moment.

We left our universe to stumble into a space that was a blurred clash of realities. The intersection of the multiverse. I raised the shovel high, feeling its energies multiply as it hurled violent sparks in all directions.

"Hey!" said a kid, who went flying past me on the back of a unicorn. "Watch where you're swinging that thing!"

And then he was gone. "Hey, Rabisu, did you just see—"

"Someone ride by on a multicolored unicorn?" She shook her head. "No. Absolutely not."

"Me neither," I said. There was only so much weird you could handle in one day.

Focus, Sik. Focus on the problem right in front of you.

The Old Ones surrounded us, vast entities that fed nightmares straight into my mind. It was like standing in front of a tsunami, an unstoppable force that obliterated everything.

Rabisu's claws dug into my arm. Tears streamed down her cheeks as she pointed ahead to the pulsing golden light. "Look! There it is!"

The *ring* was causing the glow. It throbbed within the transparent head of one of the Anunna. The creature was taking shape as it approached our universe. It had spent eternity in exile and was sluggish as it slowly awakened.

The monster reached down for me, hands sprouting out of hands, fingers transforming into tentacles, bony talons, pincers . . . Whatever it could think of, it could be.

I slammed Abubu into the columns of fingers that were closing around me. The hand recoiled, its flesh blackened by the lightning discharge.

How was I going to reach the ring? It was hundreds of feet above me.

"Sik! Help!"

The Anunna had Rabisu clutched in its other hand. I clambered over twitching tentacles and sliced through them with a single swing. "I can't get to the ring, Rabisu. It's too far away."

Rabisu snarled as she confronted the gigantic creature. "I've had to face big bullies my whole life. That ends now."

You had to admire her determination.

"They all laughed at me. Miqit, Tirid, Sidana, and the rest. I was always the victim of their pranks. Just the demon of deformities. What use was that?" She looked at me. "I lied about the mounds of skulls. No one ever built them for me. Not even a little one."

"I really don't know what to do with that information right now, but thanks for sharing."

Rabisu glared at the looming Anunna as it raised her to its eye level.

"It's now or never," I muttered.

"Then it better be now," said Rabisu. She reached out into the air, slowly clenching her fists, and twisted.

The Anunna's scream smashed into us with the power of

a sonic boom. Its body buckled and it fell to its knees. Rabisu tumbled out of its spasming hand.

"That's right!" she yelled. "It hurts, doesn't it?"

"What did you do?" I asked.

She grinned victoriously. "Slipped a few of its discs. Your back goes, everything goes."

But the Anunna was already changing, re-forming into a gigantic slug the length of a freight train. And slugs don't have spines.

Rabisu pushed me forward. "Now, Sik!"

The ring was pulsing like the heart of a sun. Great beams of golden light cut through the surrounding darkness, momentarily revealing the other Anunna, all getting closer. I clambered over the mutating slug, slipping along its bloated, slimy body. The heat coming off the king's seal was blistering. My clothes smoldered and wisps of smoke trailed behind my every agonizing step.

On the face of the glowing ring I saw the symbols of rule—the great king and the lions beside him. Waves of heat washed over me, setting fire to my hair. My skin blistered as my blood boiled. I raised Abubu one last time. . . .

The ring went supernova as I struck it, bursting into a million shards of light. The world imploded around me. I fell, tumbling over and over, through different realms, worlds with other monsters and other heroes. Too many to count. But they were there.

Then the darkness engulfed me.

"Sik?"

Someone patted my cheek. Actually, it was more like a slap.

"Ow," I muttered. Then I slowly opened my eyes. "Salaam, Rabisu."

She hugged me. It hurt pretty much everywhere, but I hugged her back.

Subway trains rumbled in the distance, and dust blew down the tunnel leading to Canal Street. My shovel lay across the rails.

"Alhamdulillah, I think we might have saved the day." I slung my arm over Rabisu's shoulder. "Help me up. I also think I wrenched my back."

"That wasn't me," she blurted. "Honest."

We got off the tracks and I limped over to a bench, collapsing on it with a long, weary sigh.

Rabisu gazed down the empty track. "It's over. I'm never going home."

"I'm sorry, Rabisu." I stood up. Wow, how could I feel this broken? "Maybe we'll find another way, just not right now." I ran my fingers through the burned stubble that had once been my hair. "Mama's gonna freak when she sees me."

Rabisu nodded. "You should get back to her."

"Now, that sounds like an excellent idea." I held out my hand. "You coming?"

Rabisu ended up staying with Petar for the next few days. I ended up staying in bed. Mama had freaked, just as I'd predicted. She'd also gotten out the clippers and given me a brutal once-over, leaving me practically bald. I passed on her offer to paint in my eyebrows with her mascara stick.

But on the third day, Rabisu appeared at the deli doorway with a knapsack and a package. Sargon growled as she came in, then purred when she tickled him under his chin. She sat at a table, and the cat found a comfortable spot on her lap.

I brought over a plate of baklava and a smoothie. "You heading somewhere?"

She rubbed the cat's ginger belly. "You know Sargon killed some of my best friends? And I mean tore them from limb to limb and ate their entrails."

He just purred louder.

Rabisu slid the package across the table. "Your Nirvana T-shirt. Washed and mended."

"What's your plan, Rabisu?"

She sighed as she looked out at the sunlit street. "Petar showed me some of his comics. You humans have a history built on heroes. You have so much stacked against you. You're fragile and short-lived and yet have such grand hopes. Perhaps I should get to know you a little better."

I reached behind the counter and took out a package of my own, wrapped in wax paper and tied with red string. She stared at it as I put it in her hands. "I've never had a present."

"Why don't you take a—"

She ripped it open with a single slice. That's the great thing about having claws. She unfolded the T-shirt and held it up. "Who is she? A goddess?"

"You could call her that. The goddess of America."

"The torch isn't bad, but she'd look better with an ax." She turned the T-shirt around and gazed at the text on the back. "What does it say?"

I could recite the poem by heart, but I didn't. No need to go into the whole Mother of Exiles thing and her offer to the huddled masses yearning to be free. The message was simple.

"Welcome to America, Rabisu."

My Night at the Gifted Carnival

GRACI KIM

I HATE WAITING IN LINE.

My legs get sore, I get fidgety, and I almost *always* need to use the toilet. What's even worse, though, is when you're waiting in line to go somewhere you don't want to go.

Like I am right now.

"Riley, look!" my sister, Hattie, squeals as she points to the winged horses that are doing aerial figure eights around the Ferris wheel. "No freaking way! There are cheollimas flying over there! They're so cool! Do you see?"

I do see them. In fact, there even seems to be a rogue unicorn among the cheollimas, carrying a kid in a trench coat and totally messing up their formation. Wow. Unicorns in California?! The carnival has really upped its game this year.

"Yeah, I guess they're all right," I say quietly, trying to dampen my enthusiasm.

Instead, I focus on the *really* long line that Hattie and I are standing in with our classmates and chaperone from Saturday

School (basically a school for witches, except you only go once a week), waiting to get our tickets to enter the Gifted Carnival. The fair comes to Los Angeles only once a year, and it's hands down Hattie's favorite day on the entire calendar—even more so than her own birthday.

I mean, it makes sense. Who wouldn't like a night full of magic? And let's be clear—I'm not talking about the Las Vegas–magician, sleight-of-hand kind of magic. I'm talking about the *real deal*. The carnival is the one time of year when the witch clans' secret gifts can be displayed in public for the non-gifted population—we call them *saram*—to see. Not that the saram know any better, of course. To them, the spells are just elaborate illusions designed to wow the crowd. (And just to be safe, the organizers spray the saram attendees with a light mist of Memoryhaze potion right before they leave.)

But members of the gifted clans know the truth. Real magic exists right here, right now in California, and it's powered by our ancestor patron goddesses, who live in the Godrealm.

Hattie grips my arm. "OMG, is that Joon at the ticket booth already?"

Sure enough, our college-aged chaperone has somehow charmed his way to the VIP TICKET HOLDERS ONLY window, which means the thirty of us will soon be able to jump to the front of the line.

From where we're standing, I can see Joon rubbing the sacred glass charm on his bracelet against his opposite wrist. I'm too far away and it's too dark to see it, but a symbol of the two suns and two moons—the mark of the gifted—will have appeared on his wrist by now, glowing in his clan color. Showing one's activated mark is how initiated witches prove their affiliation to a clan. Kind of like a built-in ID card on your skin.

The ticket attendant passes our chaperone a thick stack of carnival maps, and then, with a wide grin, Joon waves at us to join him.

"It's your lucky night, guys!" he calls as we rush over to the entrance. "You'll probably get an extra hour in here, thanks to me."

My classmates cheer in delight, and Hattie pumps her fist in the air. I, on the other hand, look down at my feet and frown.

Don't get me wrong. Objectively speaking, the Gifted Carnival is amazeballs. Enchanted snacks, mythical creatures walking (or flying) among us, performers from all over the world . . . What's not to like? And I respect magic more than anything. No, I *revere* it. Our parents are healing witches from the Gom clan, and Hattie will be formally initiated when she turns thirteen next summer. To me, there's nothing more beautiful and selfless than healing someone with the power of the divine.

But here's my truth bomb: I, Riley Oh, am a saram. I was adopted, which means that, despite being raised in a family of witches, I don't have an ounce of magic in my blood. And I won't lie. When I take a bite of those magic-dipped corn dogs, which makes my favorite K-drama star appear as a life-size apparition in front of my eyes (it's Lee Minho, if you're wondering), I feel like magic is within my grasp, too.

And that is *precisely* the problem. Every year the carnival fills me with the promise of magic, only for it to be rudely ripped away as soon as I leave the sparkling lights of the fair. For the other gifted kids, this place is a taste of the sweet future to come. For me, it's a sour reminder of everything I'll never have.

"Are you thinking too much again?" Hattie asks me, taking two copies of the map from Joon and dragging me through the entrance. "Try to live in the moment for a change. I mean, look around, Rye. This is the best place on Earth!"

I scan the surroundings, and the carnival washes over me, one wave after the other, leaving me dizzy and overwhelmed. First, it's the bright lights—the vibrant reds and yellows and oranges—calling out from the maze of stalls and rides. Then it's the sounds of balls hitting coconuts, people screaming on the haunted house ride, and calliope music singing out from the carousel. The dragon roller coaster is whizzing past in the distance, little kids are running around with cuddly toys so big they have to drag them on the ground, and I can smell something warm and sugary and buttery in the evening air. And that's just the *normal* carnival stuff.

In every nook and cranny of the fair, enchantments hide in plain sight. A boy walks past with a glow-in-the-dark butterfly painted on his cheek, and it's flapping its wings, getting ready to take off. A girl's eyes widen as her tiger plushie nestles into her neck and whispers something in her ear. Two kids watch in awe as their helium-filled kangaroo balloons have a full-on boxing match. And don't even get me started on the food. . . .

"I wish we could come here *every* day!" Hattie squeals, gripping my arm. "We are going to conquer this place, amirite?"

A sigh escapes my mouth. I love my sister more than anything, but it's hard for her to understand. It's not that I don't *want* to have fun. This place is magic—literally! But I have to keep my distance from it to protect myself. I don't want to get hooked only to have it taken away for the other 364 days of the year. Imagine discovering ice cream and falling in love with its refreshing, sweet, melt-in-your-mouth goodness, only to realize you can taste it just once a year, while everyone else you know gets to eat it daily. . . . Yep, I'm pretty sure they call that torture.

"All right, everyone, gather around." Joon calls the class over to huddle near the Lost and Found booth, and he holds up his carnival map. "Before you go wild and I lose you all, let's do some housekeeping."

Hattie passes me one of the maps and I unfold it reluctantly.

Joon points to the clusters of portable potties. "I know this place is exciting, but don't get greedy trying to cover so much ground that you forget to relieve yourselves, okay?" he says. "It's important to go when nature calls. And, for Mago's sake, please don't do anything stupid that will get you hurt." He moves his finger to the section on the map with a red cross on it. "But if at any point you're injured or need medical attention and you can't find me, make your way directly to the Gom tent."

Our parents would normally be volunteering at the healers' tent with many of the other clan members, but they're at a Witches Without Borders conference in New York this week.

"Now, if you lose something, or find something that's not yours and want to return it to its rightful owner, your best port of call is this place." Joon waves to the Lost and Found booth behind him. Then he points to the back of his map, where there's a small section of carnival-specific spells, printed only on copies for gifted visitors. "Or you could try to find an initiated witch to cast the return-to-owner spell."

I look down at my map, which says that the incantation should send any item to its proper place. After that is the puke-prevention spell, for those "fast ride aficionados with sensitive stomachs," and the walkie-talkie spell, which allows witches to communicate with one another via telepathy as long as they're within the boundary of the carnival grounds. *Wow.*

For a second, I totally geek out. I might keep my distance from practical magic, for obvious reasons, but the theory of spellwork is my jam! I've pretty much memorized all the words to the healing spells my eomma and appa use at their Traditional Korean Medicine Clinic. If I had my way, I could spend *hours* pulling apart and studying these incantations. I've never heard of a location-restricted telepathy spell before!

But as quickly as the thrill comes over me, I shove it—along with the map—into my back pocket. With so much temptation all around, even spell theory is dangerous territory tonight. I've got to keep my cool. Besides, since none of our classmates are thirteen yet and so haven't been initiated, these spells are just that—theory.

"And, no matter how much fun you're having, we all meet back here at ten p.m., got it?" Joon folds up his map. "Finally, and most important, enjoy! Those of you who want to check out the performance tent first, come with me."

I look over Hattie's shoulder at her map, wondering how to craft a route that would avoid as much magic as possible.

But she has different plans for us.

"We're going with Joon," she announces, dragging me behind her like one of those big plushies. "There's supposed to be an amazing international troupe performing tonight. We have to check it out!"

By the time Hattie and I are seated ringside in the performance tent, we've already become separated from Joon. We took too long at the food stalls, because Hattie was adamant about trying *everything*. Now her hands (and mine) are full of her snacks and drinks, and our chaperone and classmates are nowhere to be seen.

Okay, fine—I'll admit that even I was tempted by the deep-fried choco pies that promised to make me fluent in Elvish, Parseltongue, *and* Klingon for an entire hour. The Tokki clan are infusing witches who have the power to imbue magic into consumable substances, which is why they run all the food stalls at the fair.

Hattie takes a sip of her Yakult slushy and then squeals. She opens her palm, looks up at the ceiling of the tent, and then stares at her cupped hand in awe. "OMG, Rye, you have to try this. It's snowing in here!"

She passes her drink to me, but I shake my head, even though I would like nothing more than to live out my best Olaf life. "Um, that's okay."

"What about this?" She pinches a puff of the glittery

rainbow-colored cotton candy I'm holding for her and pops it into her mouth. Her eyes go wide before she erupts into a fit of giggles. "Whoa! Riley, you have a Haetae horn on your forehead!"

"Wait, *no way*!" Even though I know it's just an enchantment, my hand leaps to my brow. Wearing the horn of a divine lion beast, even if just temporarily, would be *awesome*.

Then I realize I'm doing exactly what I promised I wouldn't. I'm letting myself get swept up by all this spellcraft.

I exhale deeply and shake my head. "Thanks, Hat, but I'm fine. You can have all the food."

She pauses before taking the cotton candy and the spicy rice-cake skewer from me, putting them at her feet. Then she reaches out and squeezes my hand. "Sorry for pushing it," she says quietly. "I hear you, and I get it. Let's just enjoy the show."

I smile at her gratefully. She really tries to make me happy, and I love her for it.

A hush moves through the crowd as a tall, slender woman wearing a long, flowing silver dress steps into the center of the ring. With her huge cat eyes and big lips, she kind of looks like a Korean version of Angelina Jolie. Her shiny hair flows down her back in thick, luscious curls, and she moves with such poise that it looks like she's being carried by clouds. She bows deeply before addressing the spectators.

"Good evening, everyone!" the ringmaster announces in a deep, velvety voice. "Welcome to the one and only Gifted Carnival, the place where the impossible is possible and your dreams become reality!" She raises her arms to the sky with the grace of a ballet dancer and claps once. The sound brings an explosion of shiny confetti, raining down onto the audience like a shower of jewels.

The crowd roars with excitement, and my heart flutters inside my chest. Stupid heart. What a traitor.

"Tonight, you will meet the strongest woman you have ever seen, you will listen to the wisest man you have ever heard, and you will see things that will make you question your very eyes," the woman says, her face radiant under the lights. "But don't be alarmed. For magic is all around us, in me and in each of you. You just need to *believe*."

She twirls, and her dress glistens as if it's covered in little diamonds. Then she whirls faster, like a spinning top, and when she turns back to face us, she is no longer there. She has been replaced with a different woman in a sequined leotard, sporting a side shave that's been dyed electric blue. She has a rectangular face and is so short and stocky that she's almost as wide as she is tall. She's as solid as a tank.

"G'day, good people of Los Angeles!" The blue-haired performer strides toward a grand piano that has appeared on the opposite side of the ring. "Have ya ever fancied yourself strong? Ha! Well, ya haven't met *me* yet! I'm Strongwoman Cho, and I've come all the way from Australia to *lift* ya socks off!"

A spotlight draws our attention to the piano. The lid opens, and the silver-robed ringmaster climbs out, elegantly extending her limbs as she stands on top of it. She waves to the audience with the graceful flair of a showperson.

The crowd gasps, and we watch with anticipation as

Strongwoman Cho picks up the piano by only one of its legs and holds both the instrument and the ringmaster up over her head with impossible ease. She sports a proud grin, and I wonder how it feels to have all that strength at her fingertips. How confident and self-assured she must be, knowing she was chosen by the goddesses to wield their divine power. *Sigh*.

The audience breaks into applause, and a boy sitting behind us asks his friend in disbelief, "How did she *do* that? She's so *tiny*!"

Hattie winks knowingly at me. The boy must be a saram—but obviously not one who was raised in a gifted family like me. If he was, he would surely have guessed the strongwoman is a Miru. Witches from the Miru clan are protectors, blessed with superhuman strength or speed, which is why they guard the entrances to our sacred places and secret portals.

So, truth bomb #2: I would never actually say this to my parents, but sometimes I think it would've been easier if I'd been raised in a saram family and was blissfully ignorant of the existence of magic. At least then I wouldn't know what I was missing out on. . . . Instead, I know too much.

For example, my educated guess is that the ringmaster—judging from her beauty and her ability to conjure that confetti shower—is an illusionist witch. The Gumiho clan can perform glamour magic, which means they can make people see what they want others to see. Definitely a useful skill when you need to get dressed up but can't be bothered to change out of your pj's.

Sure enough, when Strongwoman Cho finishes her act, the

ringmaster returns to the ring, inviting an audience member into the spotlight. Just as I suspected, she is a Gumiho witch, and she uses her glamour magic to turn the volunteer into the spitting image of Billie Eilish. The crowd goes wild, and the witch does a few more transformations before inviting a third performer to the stage.

"And, for the most astounding act tonight," she announces, "prepare to be amazed by the man who sees and knows all. Put your hands together for Wise Man Nam!"

A man steps confidently into the ring wearing a summer-style hanbok in navy and ivory, reminding me of a blueberry-and-cream pie. He looks like he might be in his thirties, and he's so tall and skinny that he sways like a blade of grass in the wind when he walks. Wise Man Nam and Strongwoman Cho must be quite a sight when standing together.

"Can I have another volunteer from the audience?" he asks. His voice is heavily accented with a German lilt.

He is passing our block of seats, scanning the crowd for a willing participant, when his gaze lands on me. Ugh. I shrink in my chair, trying to disappear altogether.

"What about you?" he asks, extending his open palm to me. "You look like someone who seeks answers. Come with me, and I will give them to you. Your fortune, your luck, your future—I can reveal all."

I shake my head fervently. "Uh, no, nope, definitely not. Not a chance."

The crowd boos, but there's no way I'm going up there. It sounds like he's a Samjogo—a seeing witch, which means he's able to divine truth from merely touching an object or person. The last thing I need is for him to divulge my deepest, darkest secrets to the entire audience.

He gives me a small, polite smile. "That is fair. Any willing volunteers who *would* like to be read tonight?" He moves on to pick from the numerous other people practically jumping out of their chairs.

Hattie whispers in my ear, "Rye, I need to pee. Like, *really* bad."

I look over at her, and she is shaking her leg impatiently while nibbling on the candy charm necklace we got from one of the snack stalls. The stall owner promised that each of the glittery heart-shaped candies would taste like one of our favorite memories.

"I think I need to go right now. Stay here. I'll be back soon, okay?"

I take out my carnival map and point to the closest cluster of potties, which happens to be halfway between here and the food stalls. "Fine, but be quick about it!"

Hattie runs out of the tent as Wise Man Nam invites a girl about my age to join him. Her dark hair is in two long pigtails hanging down her back, and she's wearing a tartan skirt, a black velvet choker, and shiny purple boots with thick black soles. The man's tall frame towers over her, and he raises his two big hands in front of her face. "Aracely, was it? Thank you for coming into the ring. Now, may I?"

The girl nods eagerly.

The witch places his hands over the volunteer's eyes and

then closes his own as if watching a video play in his mind's eye.

"Ah, yes, I see that you have come tonight with your mother and little brother. And it's your brother's birthday. Happy birthday, Mateo!" he says with a wide smile.

The girl gasps. "How did you know his name was Mateo?!"

The Samjogo throws his head back in concentration. "I can also see you had chilaquiles for breakfast today. You gave your dog some cake before you left the house—against the wishes of your mother. *Tsk-tsk*." The audience laughs. "And your dream is to become a professional trivia player. Now, *that* is an interesting thing to aspire to."

"Wow, how did you know?!" The girl giggles with delight at the witch's accuracy, and the crowd roars in encouragement.

"Hmm, as for tonight," the seer continues, "I can see that after this show, you will—" He halts in mid-sentence. He frowns and drops his hands from the girl's face. "That cannot be right," he mutters. "There's nothing there. . . ."

The girl shifts her weight uncomfortably, and the audience quiets down. What does he mean, *there's nothing there?* A weird shiver runs down my spine.

The Samjogo's eyebrows knit together as he studies the girl's face, but he doesn't say any more. Eventually, the ringmaster returns to usher Wise Man Nam and the girl out of the spotlight. In their place, she invites Strongwoman Cho back into the ring to show off her superhuman strength again—this time by lifting a three-horned rhino that the Gumiho witch conjures.

To my utter dismay, I get completely sucked in. Like *really* sucked in. I don't even notice the time passing. I mean, how many times in life do you get to see a two-headed orangutan, a winged whale, *and* a rainbow-striped elephant get lifted by a woman shorter than you?

When the show is over, I lean over to Hattie to sheepishly admit how good it was . . . only to keel over and bang my elbow on the empty plastic chair.

Wait, where is she?

That's when I realize: My sister went to the restroom and never came back.

"Hattie?" I call out, tugging on the doors of the portable toilets. "Where are you?!"

The stench is next-level gross, and I don't understand why some folks don't lock the door before they do their business (Seriously, people, we're in a public place!), but I don't even care right now. These toilets are the closest to the performance tent, and I can't see why Hattie would have gone to the ones farther away. And it's not like my sister to say she'll be back and then just disappear. Especially not when there's a magic performance to watch and more enchanted food to eat. Something isn't right. . . .

I pace back and forth between the tent and the toilets, trying to figure out what might have happened. Maybe she got sick from the food and went to the Gom tent to get healed? I take out my map to study how far away the healers' area is, when something sparkling on the grass in front of me catches my eye.

I pick it up and hold it up to the bright carnival lights. It's small and heart-shaped, with glittery specks swirling inside its casing. I wipe it against my top to get the dirt off, and when no one's looking, I take a quick lick.

I frown. Just as I thought. It has a sweet, butterscotch-y flavor, with a lingering aftertaste of our first family trip to Korea—one of my favorite memories. It's definitely a charm from one of those enchanted candy necklaces Hattie bought from the snack stall.

My eyes land on another heart shimmering on the ground a few yards away. I hurry to pick it up, only to realize there's another after that. And another, and another . . .

My breath hitches in my throat. This is a *trail*. Hattie must have left me these candies as a clue. I swear, she's a Korean American tween Bear Grylls or something. She's unnaturally cool under pressure—which is basically the complete opposite of me.

Channeling my inner Hattie, I follow the string of candies until I find myself at the entrance of a small unmarked tent behind the toilets. I groan. Of *course* it leads to a creepy-looking tent in the shadows. It's the absolute last thing I want to do, but thinking of my sister, I take a deep breath and step inside.

It takes a moment for my eyes to adjust to the darkness. The only light is coming from a few small lamps sitting on chests and crates of various sizes that are stacked like Tetris pieces. This storage area is so eerily quiet, the hairs on my arms rise to attention. Some dust tickles the back of my throat, and I let out a little sneeze. I quickly cover my mouth with both hands. If Hattie led me here purposely, she might be in trouble. I have to be careful.

Weaving through the containers, I tiptoe toward a weird patch of fog lingering in the back of the tent. Let's be honest, walking into a mysterious haze in a dark, dusty, unmarked tent can't be a good idea (non-weather-related mist is *always* bad news as far as I'm concerned). But I know it's precisely what Hattie would've done. So, with great reluctance, I venture forward with my heart in my throat. Ugh. She'd better have a good reason for being here!

Immediately, I shiver and wrap my arms around myself. The temperature has plummeted, as if I just walked into a freezer. My teeth start chattering, and I take a nervous glance around . . . only for my jaw to drop to the ground.

I'm no longer in the same tent. Sure, it still has heavy tarpaulin walls and sloping drapes that stretch high into a multi-peaked ceiling. There are still chests and crates stacked up like Lego pieces. But now the tent is *humongous.* So giant, in fact, that in addition to the storage boxes, a weird glass cube the size of a small house is sitting smack-bang in the center of the pavilion. Its walls are frosted white, and when I cautiously approach to wipe an area clean with my T-shirt, a thin layer of snow flakes off and falls silently to the floor. I realize the cube is not glass at all—it's made of *ice.*

I peek through the window I made and nearly pee my pants. Inside, there are four eerily real-looking wax figures—all kids—standing in a circle, facing one another. They're covered in tiny icicles as if they were snap frozen like peas, and their arrangement reminds me of Stonehenge.

They all have a symbol of a snowflake stamped on their foreheads, and the same thin red rope is tied around each of their necks, leashing them together. It seems, from their positions and the extra thread coiled on the ground, that they're missing two more figures to complete the band.

I shudder. *What in the three realms* is *this?*

Something moves above their heads, and I nervously glance up. A robotic-looking hand made of ice is hanging from the top of the cube like an ominous chandelier about to drop at any minute. My eyes are drawn to a dark patch in one bottom corner of the enclosure, and when I look carefully, I see that it's a giant hole—large enough for all four of those wax figures to fit through, and then some.

I breathe out sharply.

A case of figurines. A hanging hand. A chute.

It looks just like one of those claw machines at the arcade—except that instead of cute little toys, this contraption is designed to pick up life-size humanoid statues. Argh. *So weird!*

Everything in my body tells me to run away from here, and fast. Whoever the designer of this twisted game is, I don't expect them to be the type to be lenient toward trespassers. As I turn to go, I notice that one of the figures looks familiar. The two long pigtails draping down her back. The tartan skirt and choker. The shiny purple combat boots with the super-thick soles.

Terror grips me like brand-new Velcro. I've seen this girl before. She was the Samjogo's volunteer from the magic show.

Her name was Aracely. She's not a wax figure *or* a statue—she's a *real person*! Is this what the Samjogo seer had meant when he'd said there was "nothing there" in her future? Was she . . . *dead*?

My sister's round, smiling face pops into my mind, and panic swirls in my gut. Could Hattie somehow be caught up in this? Could she be the next victim of this freaky claw machine?

In a frenzy, I forget all about needing to be stealthy. I start running around the room, screaming my sister's name. "Hattie? Hattie! Are you here?!"

I circle the cube, look in every unlocked chest, and search behind every stacked crate. When I can't find her anywhere, I return through the mist into the original dimly lit tent.

Just when I'm convinced she isn't anywhere near, I find her. Hattie is lying in the shadow of an open crate full of squirming dragon plushies, and she's blinking slowly as if just regaining consciousness. Her face is as white as steeped rice.

"Riley . . . ? You found my candy trail!" She winces. "Ugh. My head."

"Hattie!" I fall to my knees. "Are you okay?!"

I gently help her to a sitting position, and she rubs her temples. "I've got a splitting headache, but I'll live."

"What happened?! Why did you come in here? I've been looking *everywhere* for you!"

She looks apologetic. "Sorry, sis. I was coming back to the performance when I heard someone cry out for help. I knew it could be dangerous, but I couldn't ignore it, you know?"

I frown, but I get it. Our parents are healers. Our clan motto is Service and Sacrifice. Helping people is in her blood.

She continues. "So I left the candy trail just in case and followed the sound inside. But then I saw *her*." She shudders and her eyes cloud with fear. "I tried to run away before she saw me, but I tripped and hit my head on the side of the crate. I must have knocked myself out."

"Who did you see?" I ask apprehensively, not really wanting to know the answer. Ignorance and denial are some of my closest friends.

Hattie's lip quivers and she lowers her voice to barely a whisper. "It was the Dalgyal Gwisin, Rye. I saw her with my own two eyes." She grips my hand so tight, my fingers tingle. "She had this weird snowflake mark on her forehead and was *way* scarier than I ever imagined."

I gasp. *No. Freaking. Way.*

Any child who has ever sat around a bonfire at gifted camp and heard ghost stories knows about the Dalgyal Gwisin. She's the *worst* kind of evil spirit that haunts children, giving kids nightmares and preventing parents from turning off the lights at night. Except, unlike a lot of the subjects of campfire stories, the Dalgyal Gwisin is *real*. Her name means *egg ghost* in Korean, but don't let the cute name fool you. She wears a white mourning hanbok, has long black hair falling down her face, and hides in the shadows, only to jump out when you least expect it. . . .

Speaking of her face, it has no discernible features—only creepy contours where her eye sockets, nose, and mouth should be (hence the name egg ghost). And if you think not having features can't be that frightening, just think of Voldemort's noseless face. Petrifying, right? Well, now multiply that by five and you've come somewhat close to the horror that is the Dalgyal Gwisin.

"But I thought she was locked away for good after her last escape," I respond, willing it to be true. "How could she be *here*? In the Mortalrealm?!"

The story goes that the Dalgyal Gwisin was originally a mortal woman who was desperate to have children. When her one and only child died, she became enraged by the injustice and went on a killing spree of countless innocent kids—she wanted other mothers to feel her pain. Upon her death, the seven judges of the Spiritrealm sentenced her to spend all eternity in one of their hells, forbidding her from ever being reincarnated back to Earth. Despite this, she has unfortunately become infamous over the years for escaping the underworld's prison system, returning to the world of the living to haunt poor, unassuming kids. Basically, she's bad news.

Hattie gingerly rises to her feet, testing her balance. "I know, but she must have escaped again, because it was definitely her. And she was carrying this weird glass hammer thing that had bells on it. I saw her use it to hit some kids on the forehead, and they froze on the spot."

"I saw those kids." I tremble, remembering the symbol on Aracely's forehead, and the icicles coating her too-still body. "They're trapped in that claw game thing." I point to the mist, which is roiling like dry-ice vapor.

"That's crazy! Do you think they're still alive?"

"I don't know, but we have to help them," I blurt out on Gom autopilot, and immediately regret it. Just the *thought* of meeting the Dalgyal Gwisin in real life scares the living dokkaebi-lights out of me. Not to mention that getting involved in this rescue mission would be the exact *opposite* of keeping my distance from magic. It would be running headfirst into the fire—a fire that I won't be able to put out.

Hattie nods with determination in her eyes, already pulling me toward the exit. "You're right. We can't just leave them in there. We could be the only ones who know they're trapped." She looks back at me over her shoulder. "We need to go find Joon. He'll know what to do."

It takes us a while, but we eventually spot Joon by the Ferris wheel. He's looking a little anxious standing there, observing a bunch of our classmates as they ride the wheel. At the same time, he's keeping an eye on Jennie Byun—another classmate and probably my least-favorite person in the entire world. Jennie and her loyal sheep are striking up a conversation with some kids I don't know. The strangers are probably saram, and from what I've learned about Jennie over the years (which, I can assure you, is nothing good), I can only imagine what mischief is going to ensue. Joon is smart for watching her.

Hattie taps our chaperone on the shoulder. "Excuse me, Joon. Do you have a minute?"

He turns around and gives us a tired smile. "Hey, you two. What's up?"

"Um, well, it's kinda a long story," Hattie starts, "but basically, the Dalgyal Gwisin is here at the carnival, and we think she's trying to hurt people. We found an unmarked tent where there's this huge ice-claw thing, and she's trapped four kids inside, and—"

"That's impossible." Joon cuts Hattie off mid-sentence and shakes his head. "First of all, the carnival staff are meticulous about security, so they'd know if a malevolent spirit somehow got inside its boundaries. And second of all, the Dalgyal Gwisin—as notorious as she is—doesn't *actually* have the power to do anything. Not physically, anyway. She definitely wouldn't be able to trap kids inside a tent. She's all haunt and no hurt, if you know what I mean."

I feel my eyebrows meet in the middle. That's all well and good, but Hattie wouldn't lie about seeing her, and I definitely didn't imagine those four kids—especially not Aracely—frozen and tied up with that red rope. The Dalgyal Gwisin must have figured out a way to interact with our world.

"But we saw it with our own eyes," I say, feeling annoyed by his dismissal. "The Samjogo witch in the show said that the girl—"

"Look, it was probably just a bored Gumiho creating some illusions for a laugh," Joon says flippantly, not letting me finish. "And why were you snooping around, anyway?"

My frustration pops like bubble wrap. Why won't he listen to us?! We're asking for his help, and he won't even hear us out.

Luckily, Hattie—as always—is one step ahead of me. "Yeah, you're totally right, Joon. It was probably just an illusion. Silly us." She shrugs. "*Anyway*, random question for you, since you're here," she continues, skillfully pretending to change the subject. "What do you know about a glass hammer that has little bronze bells attached to it? And what about the symbol of a snowflake that might get stamped onto someone's skin—say, on a forehead?" She pauses. "But I mean, if you don't know what I'm talking about, that's cool, too. We can't expect you to know all the things. It's probably a real-adult question, anyway. We can ask our parents when we get home."

I try my best to hide my proud grin. My sister is making Joon think we respect his authority, while at the same time milking him for the answers we need. I wish I had even an ounce of Hattie's boldness. She is #confidencegoals.

"Well, hang on a second," he quickly says. "It *is* ringing a bell, actually—pun intended." He grins, then scratches his jaw, deep in thought. "We covered this a few years back, in the class about the afterlife. Basically, as you know, when we die, we go to the Spiritrealm and get tried by the seven judges in their respective courts for any crimes we committed in life. Only once we've served our time—if any—can we go to the heavenly Cheondang, and then eventually apply to be reborn."

Hattie and I both nod. That's just Afterlife 101. All gifted kids know that.

"What you might not know is that each of the seven judges has a special gavel that they use in their court when sentencing bad souls to their respective hells. If my memory serves me right, I'm certain those hammers have little bronze bells on them."

Hattie and I share a look.

"Oh, is that right?" Hattie coos, smiling sweetly. "How interesting! Go on. What else?"

"As for the symbol, I'm guessing, if it's related to the gavel, it's probably the mark of the Hell of Infinite Ice. I've heard each hell has its own insignia, and it basically doesn't come off until you've served your time. It's a way to make sure prisoners don't get mixed up between the hells, and to ensure they don't escape, I guess."

Whoa. I squeeze Hattie's hand. The Hell of Infinite Ice must be the prison the Dalgyal Gwisin escaped from. That would explain why everything looked like a scene from *Frozen*.

But why did she brand the kids? They aren't newly arrived souls in the afterlife seeking judgment—they are living beings. And more importantly, how did the Dalgyal Gwisin come to be in possession of the hell gavel in the first place?

A piercing shriek rips me out of my thoughts. I turn toward the sound to see that Jennie and her followers have turned one of the poor saram kids into a pig. Jennie is snickering while the other saram kids scream and shout, pointing at their friend in horror. I'm guessing Jennie bought a transformation potion from the Enemies & Lovers stall as a practical joke. Ugh. Of *course* she did.

Joon groans and pulls his hands down his face. "I *knew* I shouldn't have taken my eyes off her." He mutters some other words under his breath, which I'd rather not repeat. "Sorry, guys, I better go do some damage control. Stay away from that tent, and just have fun, okay? See you back at the entrance at ten."

Hattie and I watch a frazzled Joon hurry off to deal with Jennie's antics, and my heart drops. Because I know my sister, and I can guess exactly what she's going to say next.

Sure enough, Hattie turns to me and gives me her best boss face. "I know you're not gonna like this, Rye, but it looks like we're on our own. It's up to us and us alone to save those kids."

I've mentioned this before, but I prefer to keep my distance from magic. I've organized my life carefully so that, despite living in a family of divine healers, I've never had to get involved in anything that might give me false hopes about my magic-less future. I've done it mostly to avoid disappointment.

But I've also done it because if I was a mug, it would say KEEP CALM AND STAY INVISIBLE in big bold letters. I keep my head down and stay out of trouble because I don't want to draw attention to the fact that I'm a saram living in the gifted world. The witch community upholds its purity and secrecy above all else, and I am a threat to all that. Being a wallflower is in my best interest.

And *yet*.

Somehow, here I am. At the Gifted Carnival, surrounded by magic and witches galore, working with my sister to save four people from the evil grip of the Dalgyal Gwisin, who escaped from an afterlife prison with a mystical tool that can sentence a soul to the Hell of Infinite Ice. **Takes a big breath** How the hells did this happen?!

I want to argue with Hattie, I really do. I'd like to tell her to count me out, and that if she wants to save those kids, she's on her own. But she knows as well as I do, you can't ignore your upbringing. As Gom, serving others is our duty. If someone is in need, and we have the power to help, then sitting back and ignoring the call is not an option.

That's how Hattie and I find ourselves loitering around the entrance of the restricted staff-only tent, trying to figure out whether we might be able to sneak in. I may have agreed to the rescue mission, but there's no way we're doing it alone. We need help.

"So, what I'm thinking," Hattie whispers to me, as we hide behind an unsuspecting kissing couple, "is that we go in there and convince Strongwoman Cho to help us. If she was strong enough to lift a piano, surely she could break through the ice and get those kids out, right?"

I bite my lip but nod reluctantly. "I mean, yeah, I guess it's the best—or only—idea we've got."

Hattie steals a quick glance at the tent's monitored entrance and her eyes brighten. "And I believe we've just been handed our golden ticket."

I follow Hattie's gaze to see that the guard watching the tent has momentarily left her station.

"It's now or never. Let's make a run for it!" Hattie whispers.

Holding my breath, I scurry behind Hattie and manage to slip inside the open tent flap before the guard or any bystanders realize we've snuck in. I'm sweating buckets, and I can't believe I'm doing this. Breaking the rules and risking getting caught is so far out of my comfort zone, I don't even know who I am anymore.

Hattie, on the other hand, strides confidently toward the

buffet station and stands there, scanning the tent for the Miru witch's face. There are at least forty people in here, eating at the tables, lounging on the sofas, and watching the big TV they've set up in the back. I even see Wise Man Nam taking a nap on a recliner. None of them seem to notice, let alone care, that two random kids have come in.

"OMG, there they are!" I whisper at Hattie, pointing to two figures sitting at a small table in the far corner. Strongwoman Cho is with the Gumiho ringmaster, eating what must be a late dinner. The Miru is in a tracksuit, and the illusionist is wearing jeggings and an oversize T-shirt, both of which are far cries from their shiny stage outfits, but I'm certain it's them.

Before I can register what's happening, Hattie has dragged me over and is relaying the full Dalgyal Gwisin situation in minute detail, while I stand awkwardly behind her, wondering if the LA galbi they're eating is enchanted or not.

"And why should I believe a word you're saying?" Strongwoman Cho asks when Hattie finishes, leaning back in her chair and digging at her teeth with a toothpick. "Ya sneak into our private area, disturb my tea, and now ya want me to go save some ankle-biters who are stuck in an Esky as big as a house?" She chortles. "Good on ya, mate. A bloody good prank, if I ever heard one."

"It's not a prank!" Hattie argues, putting her hands on her hips. "You have to believe us!"

The strongwoman signals to the guard, who's finally returned to her post, and turns her back to us. "Drop the act, kid. Get outta here before I really get peeved. I'm knackered and don't have the energy to deal with you."

The guard puts her arms around our shoulders and starts guiding us toward the exit. I'm stunned. What is *with* adults not taking us seriously tonight? We might as well be wearing Christmas lights on our Pinocchio noses, the way people think we're lying.

Then, as the exit gets closer, it dawns on me that we have just lost our one chance to save those kids. My last opportunity to help Aracely get back to her brother and mom and cake-loving dog.

That's when I get an idea.

"Wait, stop!" I shout, ducking under the guard's arm to swivel back toward the two performers. "If you don't believe us, then let's get Wise Man Nam to read us." I point to the Samjogo witch still dozing on the recliner. "If he proves we're telling the truth, you *have* to help us. Innocent lives are at stake."

Strongwoman Cho scoffs and throws her toothpick on the floor. (Yuck. Personal hygiene issues, much?) But the ringmaster studies my face carefully.

"Maybe we should hear them out, Cherry Blossom?" the Gumiho murmurs softly.

Hattie and I stare at Strongwoman Cho. Her first name is *Cherry Blossom?*

The Miru witch flexes her thick, cord-like biceps as if inviting us to fight. "My eomma named me after her favorite flower. Got a problem with that?"

We both avert our gazes. After seeing her superhuman strength in action, the last thing I'm going to do is question her mom's choice in baby names.

The ringmaster raises her eyebrow, and Cherry Blossom sighs, reluctantly heading toward the recliner where the seer is napping. "Fine, I'll give ya a chance," the strongwoman says, throwing us a warning look over her shoulder. "But know that if you're pulling my leg, you'll both be banned from the carnival forever. I'll make sure of it."

She leans over and shakes Wise Man Nam's shoulder. "Jangsoo, ya got a minute, mate?"

He sits up and yawns. "Yah, yah, I'm awake. Everything good?" His German accent is even stronger than before. He peers behind Strongwoman Cho, and his eyes land on me. "You," he says curiously. "I remember you from the show. Refused to volunteer."

I clear my throat. "Sorry to disturb you, but my name is Riley Oh. This is my sister, Hattie, and we want you to confirm we're telling the truth about what we saw. The Dalgyal Gwisin is imprisoning kids at the fair—including one of your volunteers today—and we need your help to save them."

"It's that young girl Aracely, isn't it?" he asks straightaway, his forehead creasing with concern. "The one with the . . . Ah, what do you call those things? Horse tails?"

"Pigtails," the ringmaster corrects.

"Right, yes, the one with the pigtails."

I nod to confirm his suspicions, and he shakes his head. "I *knew* there was something strange about her reading."

He stretches his long legs and stands up, making us crane our necks to see his face. "Right, then, we will *do this thing*, as you young Americans would say." He slides his wrists together to activate his gifted mark, and as the symbol glows purple, he puts his hands over my eyes and Hattie's. He hums quietly in concentration, and a minute later, he removes them, exhaling deeply.

"I am afraid these girls are speaking the truth," he says to the two witches. "It is definitely the Dalgyal Gwisin—she has somehow become a tangible being in this realm. She has also created some unearthly contraption that I believe will deliver her and her victims through the chute directly to the Spiritrealm. It is quite impressive, in fact."

The ringmaster nods once and turns to us. "Well, that's it, then. Lead the way, ladies. I suspect we'll need to move fast to help those poor children."

Hattie and I squeeze each other's hands, grateful to have finally enlisted some witches. Now we actually have a chance! Even Cherry Blossom reluctantly admits she was wrong and trails us out of the tent.

As we hurriedly lead the three witches to the ice claw machine, I say a little prayer to Mago Halmi—the mother of all creation. *Please keep Aracely safe until we get there. Please let her be okay. . . .*

When we reach the unmarked tent, nothing has changed. There's no sign of the Dalgyal Gwisin (thank Mago for that . . .) and the four kids are still inside the claw machine, looking just as creepy as before. I'm glad to see them, though—not because I want them to be frozen, but at least they haven't gone down the chute yet.

"So, do you think you could break through the ice?" I ask Cherry Blossom, who is tapping the cube with her knuckles. It's so thick it might as well be solid brick.

She smirks. "Ya call that a question?" She cracks her neck and then Taegwondo-kicks the frozen wall. There is a thundering *crack!* and the ice splinters under the pressure. She studies the fissures, then gives the wall a little nudge with her shoulder. The ice simply gives way, falling to the ground like shards of glass, leaving behind a jagged opening the size of a small door.

"*Whoa!*" Hattie and I breathe out in unison, making the frigid air steam up in front of our faces. Strongwoman Cho is *good*. This is going to be a piece of cake!

All five of us make our way toward the Stonehenge circle through the newly made entrance, and I shudder when I see Aracely's face up close. The snowflake mark is clearly visible in the middle of her forehead, between her eyebrows. And I didn't notice before, but now I see that her eyes are wide and her mouth is hanging open as if she was in mid-scream when she got immobilized.

The ringmaster also studies the four kids, and she runs her finger down the icy cheek of one of the boys. "Poor, poor children. They must have been so frightened."

I swallow the lump in my throat and finally voice the question I've been too scared to ask this whole time. "Do you think they're still . . . ? You know . . . I mean, they aren't . . . Are they . . . ?"

I trail off, and thankfully, the ringmaster knows what I'm trying to say.

"They're still alive, yes," she says, placing a hand on the frozen boy's wrist. "But their pulses are weak. We need to reverse whatever was done to them, and fast."

"It was the hell gavel," Hattie says, shivering from the cold and probably also the memory. "I saw her hit the kids on the forehead with it, and suddenly they got those forehead tattoos and became these ice statues. Like they'd been put under a freaky locked-in spell or something."

The ringmaster frowns. "Hmm . . . If the hammer is to blame, the only way we'll be able to awaken these kids is to use it on them again. To undo the sentence placed on their heads—literally."

I grimace. The only way we're going to get our hands on the gavel is if we come face-to-face with the Dalgyal Gwisin. And I was really hoping to avoid that scenario at all costs. . . .

"Well, first things first. I guess we better get them kids outta here and to a safe place," Cherry Blossom says, removing a flip knife from her back pocket. She goes to cut the thin rope joining the kids together, when Wise Man Nam suddenly gasps.

"*Oh no.*"

We all turn to him. He's looking severely pale as he stares down at the red thread in his open palm. "This is bulgeun-sil," he says quietly.

"What's bulgeun-sil?" I ask, peering closer at the cord.

Hattie shrugs. "It just looks like a red string?"

He shakes his head. "It is the Red String of Fate. It is made from the fibers of the Tree of Fate, which only grows in the Spiritrealm. And when it is used to tie souls together, it binds their destinies." He pauses as if deep in thought, and then he grimaces. "I believe the Dalgyal Gwisin is trying to tie these kids' fates to her own and take them down to the hells with her. So she can finally have the children she has always wanted by her side, for all eternity."

I shudder and move closer to Hattie. The ghost is trying to sentence these innocent mortals to an eternity of torture with her so she doesn't have to be alone? *What the hells!* No wonder she was condemned by the judges to never walk the earth again.

"That makes sense," the ringmaster says, touching the insignia branded on Aracely's forehead. "She already completed the sentencing using the hell gavel, which means if she took the children down the chute while tied to her, they'd bypass the regular court process and be expedited straight to the Hell of Infinite Ice. It's an evil plan, but clever."

"And bloody sneaky," Cherry Blossom adds. "Don't forget she somehow managed to nick the gavel on the way up here, too. I can't see a judge just handing it over to one of their most notorious prisoners. Nah, yeh, she's committed if nothing else. Ya gotta give her that." She resumes the task of cutting the bulgeun-sil with small, swift movements.

"So we move them to safety, and then what?" Hattie asks, helping me remove the remains of the string from around their necks. "We'll need to get the gavel from her to wake them up. But I'm getting the impression she's not just going to hand it over, even if we say please."

"The ankle-biter's right," Cherry Blossom says. "We need to kill the Dalgyal Gwisin."

"But you can't kill a soul that's already dead," the ringmaster explains.

My heart drops. Then what are we going to do?!

"If only there was a way we could lure her in willingly," Jangsoo murmurs. "Then we could take the gavel from her and keep her prisoner until we figure out the rest."

For some reason, the image of the ringmaster turning a volunteer into Billie Eilish pops into my mind.

And suddenly, it comes to me.

"Wait, what if we made it seem like she was still in control?" I muse out loud. "If we made it *look* like the kids were still in here, when really they were just an illusion. Then maybe she'd return to the Spiritrealm of her own accord, thinking she'd gotten what she wanted."

Cherry Blossom gets a mischievous gleam in her eye. "And if she doesn't go willingly, I reckon I could give her ghostly butt a good kick down the chute."

The ringmaster nods. "That could work." She rubs her slender wrists together and smiles gently. "And I know just the illusion spell for the job."

Soon, the cube has been glamoured to look like it contains exact replicas of the four kids, while Cherry Blossom carries the real people like mannequins over her head, one by one, and hides them behind a block of tall crates.

The ringmaster is putting the finishing touches on the door-size hole in the ice, making it appear intact, when two young voices scream out from behind the mist.

"Ouch, you're hurting me!"

"Where . . . Where are you taking us?"

I grip Hattie's arm. *She's back.* And it sounds like she's brought two more victims to complete the circle.

"Everyone, hide!" the ringmaster whispers, and we all scurry to duck behind any object we can find. Hattie hides behind a large chest, and I find a tall coffin-like box to conceal me. My pulse is racing so fast my head is pounding. Can hearts wear out from beating too hard? I hope I never have to find out. . . .

Or maybe I will. From my hiding place, I see a figure with long, wavy black hair, dressed from head to toe in a mourning-white hanbok, appear through the mist. The train of her dress floats behind her, and she glides in all ominous and eerie, like she's some kind of sick zombie bride.

Her head is angled down so I can't see her face (phew!), but her skin is chalk white, and she is dragging two kids behind her, tied together with bulgeun-sil. The thread doesn't look very strong, and yet the boy and girl don't seem to be able to escape its hold. She pulls their two struggling bodies toward the circle of frozen children. Well, the illusion of them, anyway.

Just before she arrives at the ice structure, the ghost pauses. For a second, I worry she can see through the illusion disguising the hole in the wall. Is she immune to Gumiho glamour magic? Has she figured out our trap already? But then she reaches into the skirt of her hanbok and pulls out a transparent tool that has a cluster of small bronze bells attached to it.

The hell gavel!

Stealthily, I widen my eyes at Hattie and our performer friends, nodding toward the little hammer. *That* is our mission. We need to get our hands on that thing if we want to save Aracely and the other frozen kids.

"Please don't do this!" the girl cries, as the boy next to her starts sobbing. "Please let us go!"

The Dalgyal Gwisin ignores the pleading. She raises the gavel and brings it down on the girl's forehead with one swift and disturbing motion. The force of the movement blows the ghost's stringy black hair out of the way, finally giving me a dreaded glimpse of her face.

I scream.

I know I shouldn't. But you don't understand how terrifying it is to look into a face without features. There are no lips—no gap where the mouth should be. No nose—not even two holes for the nostrils. And her eye sockets are just sunken shadows, as if someone has erased the very thing that makes her human. Looking at her makes me feel breathless. As if, somehow, her lack of openings is suffocating me, too.

And now this monstrosity knows I'm here.

She whirls toward me. And despite her lack of eyes, I'm certain she sees me. Her skin stretches unnaturally over the area that would be her mouth, all taut and thin, as if she's trying to shriek when someone has stitched her lips together.

She lowers the arm holding the gavel and lets go of the bulgeun-sil leash. Her attention having been diverted from her two new prisoners, she starts coming for me instead.

"Run!" I scream at the boy. It's too late for the girl, who is frozen stiff. "Run away while you can!"

He doesn't need to be told twice. The boy leaves through the mist so fast, you'd think a Gumiho had just performed a disappearing spell on him.

The Dalgyal Gwisin picks up speed, too, approaching me with undivided interest. As she nears, she swings her icy tool at the wrist, like a baseball player stepping up to bat. Unfortunately for me, my head is her ball.

I try to move. I need to run *now*. But my limbs are useless, paralyzed by fear. I realize I'm going to be turned into an icicle and taken to the Hell of Infinite Ice for all eternity. *Gulp*. I guess this is how it ends for me. This is how I sign off. At least I had a good life. . . .

That's when I hear it. My sister's voice.

"Hey, Egg Face! I'm over here!"

Hattie leaps out from behind the large chest and races toward the Dalgyal Gwisin at full steam, diverting attention away from me.

"Hattie, don't!" I scream, just as the Gwisin swivels toward my sister and cleanly strikes her forehead with a shrill cry of the bells.

Hattie immediately freezes in place, her eyes paused in defiant mode, and the weird insignia materializes on her forehead.

"*Nooo!*" I cry. "Not Hattie, too!"

I attempt to run toward my sister, to pull her rigid body to a safe place before she falls and shatters—or worse, before the ghost takes her down the chute for good. But the Dalgyal Gwisin is more furious than ever. She clenches her fists tight against her body, and a frosty white fog starts to billow and whirl around her like a blizzard. It spreads like smoke, and then she turns her empty eye sockets back on me.

"Leave her alone, ya bitter hag!" Cherry Blossom yells, throwing a giant crate straight at the ghost's head. It hits her with surprising power and slams her to the ground. Splintered wood flies everywhere. Unfortunately, it doesn't deter the Dalgyal Gwisin in the slightest. She just gets back up and continues coming for me.

Wise Man Nam makes a lasso with the bulgeun-sil and tries to lob it over the Dalgyal Gwisin's head, but the thread isn't long enough and she is moving too fast.

"Look over here!" the ringmaster yells, as she glamours herself to look exactly like me. "You've got the wrong girl! I'm here!" She's trying to confuse the ghost by creating a decoy.

They're all good ideas, and I am grateful for all of their interventions. But like the ringmaster said, you can't kill a soul that's already dead. The strongwoman's throwing efforts are futile. Distracting the ghost doesn't seem to be working, either. It's clear the Dalgyal Gwisin only has eyes (or in this case, no eyes) for *me*.

With adrenaline pumping through my veins, I turn and make a break for it. The good news is that my legs remember how to work again. *Thank the goddesses!* The bad news is that I'm a klutz and I immediately trip over a piece of splintered wood, falling flat on my face. *Oof!*

I get on all fours and start crawling. I'm surprised I can even manage that, to be honest. And the weird swirling ice storm is everywhere now, so it's impossible to see where I'm going. The polar blast infiltrates my nostrils and fills my lungs, leaving me coughing and spluttering. In a desperate attempt to breathe, I flip over and start crab-walking backward as quickly as I can.

I'm faster than I expected. But then my back hits a solid surface. It's the ice wall of the claw box, and the blood drains from my face. I am stuck between a ghost and a hard place. And there is nowhere else to hide.

The Dalgyal Gwisin knows it, too. Despite the continual onslaught of wooden crates and heavy chests being thrown by Cherry Blossom, and the other two witches' renewed attempts to get the ghost's attention, she leisurely glides toward me with ominous smugness, the gavel swinging in her hand. She inches ever closer, her creepy long hair wafting behind her as if she's in a sappy shampoo commercial.

I realize that *this* time, I really am done for. I am going to remain a twelve-year-old in the hells forever. And as I admit defeat, I tell myself that the Dalgyal Gwisin had no choice. It's not her fault she became this wicked ghoul. She lost her child, and grief turned her into a monster. Now she's desperate to find replacement kids. Who could blame her? At least I'll be with Hattie. Maybe the hells won't be *that* bad?

Suddenly, Joon's words from the start of the evening echo in my ear. *If you lose something, or find something that's not yours and want to return it to its rightful owner . . .*

A spark of hope races through my body.

That's it! How did I not think of this earlier?

I reach into my pocket and pull out the carnival map. I turn it over to the small section of carnival-specific spells and scan it for the magic words. *Yes!* Joon had said that we could try finding an initiated witch to cast the spell on our behalf. This has to work!

As the Dalgyal Gwisin picks herself up from yet another knock in the head (thanks, Cherry Blossom), I yell out to the three initiated witches in the room. "Grab her and repeat after me!"

The three witches all regard me with perplexed expressions.

"Just take my word for it," I plead, as my attacker closes in. "Please!"

The three of them hesitantly take a step toward the ghost, but frankly, it's not fast enough.

"Do it *now*!" I scream.

The witches immediately spring into action.

Swallowing my heart back down my throat, I start reading the Korean words to the return-to-owner spell, shouting them out at the top of my lungs for the witches to recite:

"The thing I have for all to see,
Does not in fact belong to me.
With haste return to owner, please,
And finally put my mind at ease."

The hem of the Dalgyal Gwisin's hanbok grazes my leg, and she raises the hell gavel above her head, the tiny bronze bells ringing shrilly with the motion.

As soon as I hear the three adults chant the final word of the spell, I clamp my eyes shut and huddle into a ball. I don't dare breathe. This better work! Otherwise, I am seriously going to need some long underwear.

Fortunately, the next words I hear belong to Cherry Blossom.

"Bloody hells, it worked!" she exclaims. "It actually worked!"

I carefully open my lids to see the gavel mere inches from my face. I shudder, quickly squirming out from under the curtain of ghostly hair. From a careful distance, I watch the Dalgyal Gwisin start fading away. It's like a pause button has been pushed on her, and someone is rubbing her out, bit by bit, using an invisible eraser.

"How clever to use the return-to-owner spell!" the ringmaster comments, looking at me admiringly. "You knew we couldn't kill her, but she could be returned to her custodian, to her rightful place in prison."

Wise Man Nam nods approvingly. "Indeed, since she technically belongs to the Hell of Infinite Ice until she finishes her sentence. *Wunderkind!*"

I rub the back of my neck shyly. "Thanks, I guess?" I mutter. I've never been good at receiving compliments.

"Uh, guys?" Cherry Blossom says, pointing at the gavel, still in the Dalgyal Gwisin's hand. "Sorry to burst the bubble, but it looks like that *thing* is being returned to its rightful owner as well."

I watch in horror as the only item able to bring my sister and Aracely and the rest of the kids back to life starts losing its solid form.

Cherry Blossom turns toward the giant walls of ice that have started melting. "Crikey—by the looks of it, the claw machine is going buh-bye, too. . . ."

"Not a chance in *hells*!" I cry, as I leap to snatch the gavel. Then, wielding the judge's tool, I run faster than I've ever run before, to Hattie first, then to Aracely, and the other four kids, hitting the insignias on their foreheads and releasing them from their torturous sentence in the Hell of Infinite Ice.

By a very narrow margin, too.

Just as the last boy wakes from his icy slumber, the hell gavel gives a final jingle of its bronze bells before dissipating from the Mortalrealm completely.

"Riley! You saved me!" Hattie cries, leaping into my arms and hugging me close. "You saved us all!"

A bit dazed but alive, the other kids crowd around me, grateful tears falling down their cheeks. "You're a hero!" Aracely exclaims.

"They're right," the ringmaster agrees. "If it weren't for you, these children might not have lived to see another day."

Cherry Blossom nods in agreement and has the decency to look a little sheepish. "No hard feelings about before, aye? You're not half bad, as far as kids go."

I laugh, and Wise Man Nam extends his arm for a congratulatory handshake. "Indeed. Your parents must be so very proud of you." He looks down at my hand and pauses, as if a reading has just come through. "And I hope you know—you are *made* for magic. I can feel it in your essence."

The comment worms into my chest and buries itself into such a deep crevice that I don't think I'll ever be able to remove it again.

Hattie squeezes my hand and whispers into my ear. "You hear that, sis? It's what I've always said. You were born to be gifted, and one day we will find a way to make you a Gom healer, too. Whatever it takes, we'll make it happen. Together."

As my sister pulls me in for another bear hug, a switch flicks on in my head. You see, I've always avoided magic because of the fear of wanting something I could never have. But perhaps there could be another way. Maybe there is a future in which I could *earn* my gift—a different path I could take to acquire magic and dedicate myself to helping others.

I don't know how exactly I'll do it. But we didn't know how we were going to save these kids today, and we still found a solution. So maybe there's hope yet . . . ?

As the intention settles into my mind, I realize that I have never wanted anything more than to become a healer like my parents, and to make them proud of the daughter I've become.

I give Aracely a warm hug good-bye, though I know, after

she gets misted by the Memoryhaze at the exit, she's not going to remember me or the Dalgyal Gwisin. The three witches invite Hattie and me to visit them one day in their respective cities of Honolulu, Sydney, and Frankfurt. Strongwoman Cho promises to take us to the best gifted zoo in Australia. (I mean, flying kangaroos? Why not!) It feels really good to make new friends, even if we may never see them again.

As Hattie convinces me to check out just *one* more enchanted food stall before rendezvousing with Joon to head home, it strikes me that, despite my best efforts, my sister was right about the following two things after all:

(1) One should never abstain from magical food when one has the chance.

(2) The Gifted Carnival *is*, in fact, the best place on Earth.

My Life as a Child Outlaw

RICK RIORDAN

THEY CAME TO KILL me when I was eight years old.

I was cooking a fish over the fire when my foster mother Bodbmall burst out of the woods, her breath steaming in the cold air. "They're coming!"

I leaped to my feet.

I didn't need to ask who was coming. I'd been warned about this possibility my whole life. I did what any self-respecting eight-year-old would do. I dropped my fish, snatched up my spear, and said, "We can take them."

Bodbmall hissed in exasperation.

She didn't scare easily, being a druid and a hunter, but now her eyes were bright with alarm. Her unsheathed sword glistened red. Droplets of blood splattered her white woolen smock and the bleached rodent bones braided into her long black hair. She'd had to fight her way back to camp.

"There are *fifty* Clan Morna warriors right behind me," she said. "Don't be thickheaded!"

I was not impressed. "I stunned a duck on the lake when I was six. I can handle—"

"These are NOT DUCKS!" Bodbmall yelled. "Why is it always ducks with you? Just because you could—" She froze, listening. I heard nothing unusual, but Bodbmall had ways of hearing that did not involve her ears.

"We're out of time," she snapped. "I'll try to hold them off. You run! Don't come back!"

"*Don't come back?!*"

"We'll find you when it's safe," she promised. "Go!"

Her tone told me that further argument would be useless and possibly fatal.

I bolted through the trees, jumped a ditch, and made it half a league upstream before I smacked straight into my other foster mother, the Líath Lúachra—the Gray One from Lúachair.

She was called the Gray One because she was gray. It was not the most imaginative nickname. Her long ashen hair was braided with pieces of glass, because she had a weakness for shiny things. Her face was as hard and withered as a corpse pulled from the bog. On the left side of her nose was a wart the size of an egg, which I would sometimes watch, fantasizing about what might emerge when it hatched.

Like Bodbmall, the Líath Lúachra was a retired fénnid—a hunter-warrior of unrivaled skill—which meant she should have been able to run through the forest without disturbing a single branch or stone. But she'd gotten stubborn in her old age. She felt like she'd spent enough years yielding to the wilderness. Now she expected the wilderness to yield to her. Because of this, her gray cloak was always ripped and tattered. You could see the progress I'd made as a tailor over the years just looking at all the tears she'd forced me to mend.

"You dolt!" She grabbed my shoulders. "The Mac Mornas are coming!"

"I know!"

"Then what are you doing, senseless boy?"

"Running away!"

"Good!" She sighed with relief. "But not upstream. You'll run right into them. Head east. We'll find you someday."

Someday?!

I swallowed the lump in my throat. I didn't want to cry in front of the Gray One, but I'd always liked her best. She insulted me with more tenderness than Bodbmall did.

"Good-bye," I said.

"Foolish child."

Then I was gone.

Even at eight, I could run fast. I'm not bragging, but I could race a deer through the forest and win. The Líath Lúachra had recently informed me that not everyone could do this.

I had no one to compare myself to except my foster mothers, and they were getting old and losing their speed. I assumed most other eight-year-olds could outrun wild animals or throw a spear with enough precision to clip the wings of a duck without killing it, but no. Apparently, I was special. Then again, I suspected most eight-year-olds didn't grow up in a tent in the wilderness, hiding from assassins, so maybe being special was overrated.

Somewhere behind me, a deep voice wailed in pain—probably a Mac Morna meeting the sharp end of the Líath Lúachra's knife. I hoped he'd die slowly. I also hoped my foster mothers got away safely. Both were tough fighters, and Bodbmall had her magic, but against an army of seasoned warriors, there was only so much two bad-tempered old ladies could do.

The woods around me fell eerily quiet. Bodbmall had trained me to move like a fénnid. No twigs snapped under my feet. No branches broke. No birds startled from the trees. I could hear my own breathing, but that was all.

After half a league, rain began to patter against the leaves. This was good. It might obscure my tracks. Slíab Bladma, the mountains where we lived, had lots of places where I might hide—dense thickets, caves, ravines with hard-to-find entrances. The area was a favorite of bandits, deserters, murderers, and other folks who didn't want to be found, like my foster mothers and me. Usually, this worked in our favor. Anybody who came looking for us would have to fight their way through a bunch of our ornery neighbors.

But Clan Morna had managed to find us nonetheless.

The more I thought about that, the angrier I got.

I wanted to double back, surprise my enemies, and cut off their heads. Only two things stopped me: Bodbmall had ordered me not to return, and I didn't have a sword.

You can't really cut off someone's head with a spear. I'd spent a lot of time practicing on deer carcasses I'd found in the woods.

I waded through an ice-cold stream to mask my scent. I

hadn't heard any dogs yet, but I was sure my enemies would have some. I'd have to keep running until nightfall before I looked for a hiding place.

I was used to these woods. I thought I knew every rock, tree, and creek within two leagues of our camp. This made me careless. I only realized I'd ventured into unknown territory when I leaped over a log and tumbled off a cliff.

Fortunately, a donkey broke my fall. I bounced off its saddle packs before landing in the middle of a group of travelers. Unfortunately, when I hit the ground, I cracked the back of my head on a rock.

My vision swam. Half a dozen mangy, smelly old men scowled down at me.

"Look at this, now," one of them said. "It's raining children."

Then I passed out.

When I woke, I found myself draped over the donkey, plodding along a dirt path in the dim evening light. My head throbbed. My throat burned with thirst. My skin itched, but I tried not to move or make a sound.

I wasn't sure why the travelers had taken me with them, or why they'd even bothered to keep me alive. The likeliest reason I could think of was to sell me into slavery, but my hands weren't bound. As far as I could tell, neither were my feet. I decided to pretend I was still unconscious, just in case. I'd save my strength and wait for a chance to escape. Better to ride the donkey than walk.

I tried to glean clues from what the men were saying, but they didn't reveal much. Their feet hurt. They were tired and hungry. They hoped to find a farm or a village soon.

I wondered how long I'd been unconscious. Judging from the pace of the donkey, we must not have traveled far, but even if I found my way back to my foster mothers' campsite, Bodbmall and the Líath Lúachra would either be long gone or dead.

My eyes stung.

I forced myself to think of other things: how to get revenge on Clan Morna, how to escape my captors, and why this donkey smelled like rotten eggs. I guessed his hooves had thrush, which meant his masters were careless. I hoped they were just as careless with their prisoners.

We stopped for the night at the banks of a river.

"Sorry, lad," said one of the men, "but you're lying on our camping gear."

He pulled me off the donkey. I think he was surprised when I landed on my feet and made a run for it.

I should have been away in a flash, but my legs were half asleep. I chicken-walked ten steps and fell flat on my face.

"You can run if you like, boy," said the man, leaning on his walking stick. "But you'll miss dinner. Aren't you hungry?"

My heart pounding, I took measure of my captors for the first time. Walking Stick had a bald scalp with a greasy streak of black hair on either side, pulled back in a pigtail so he looked like a gray heron. Despite his pockmarked face and rotten teeth, his eyes twinkled in a friendly sort of way. From the sonorous tone of his voice, I guessed he was a singer, or maybe a seanchaí—a professional storyteller.

A second man was covered in red welts and had tufts of white hair like a half-plucked hen. Around his waist, the pockets of his burlap apron bulged with leather scraps, spare shoe soles, and cutting implements. A cobbler, then.

The other men also carried an assortment of tools and skin diseases. The muscular, warty fellow had a blacksmith's hammer hanging from his belt. The skinny young one with boils on his neck carried several musical instruments: a harp, a tin whistle, and a bodhrán with a drumstick. The poxy fifth man had a leather cord garlanded with pots, pans, and other tinsmith's wares over his shoulder. The last man had a purple skin rash. His fingers were black with pitch, so maybe he was a thatcher.

In other words, I hadn't fallen in with slavers. I'd been abducted by áes dána—traveling craftsmen.

This didn't reassure me. The Líath Lúachra often grumbled that áes dána were just as bad as bandits, only they would sing you a song or fix your pots before they robbed you.

"Sorry for carrying you off," said Walking Stick. "But Slíab Bladma was crawling with warriors. They were killing everyone they could find. We couldn't leave a helpless child behind."

"I'm not helpless," I said, my lower lip trembling. "I'm a fighter."

The plucked-hen cobbler whistled. "Good to know. Did we take you away from the battlefield, then?"

I gulped down a sob. "I *am* a fighter. One time I stunned a duck."

To their credit, none of them laughed.

"Well, now," said Walking Stick. "That's a story I'd love to add to my repertoire. Since it's dark, perhaps you'd share dinner with us? We don't have much, but there's salted pork and some fresh brown bread our last clients made for us."

I licked my lips. I didn't trust these men, but I did have a weakness for fresh-baked arán donn.

"Unless you've got someplace else to be," added Walking Stick, furrowing his brow. "Did you have family in Slíab Bladma?"

I noticed he said *did*, not *do*. If the Mac Mornas were clearing out the woods, there wouldn't be anyone left in Slíab Bladma to return to. By carrying me off, these áes dána probably figured they'd saved the life of an orphan. In a way, they were right.

Walking Stick took my silence for an answer. "Well . . . you're welcome to travel with us as long as you like. You can make the campfire. And you can protect us from any aggressive ducks we might come across."

I stayed for dinner. I promised myself I would leave first thing in the morning, though I had no idea where I would go.

I made their campfire. I wasn't going to accept charity, so I also caught a rabbit to add to our dinner. That seemed to impress them. The fools had discarded my spear, thinking it was just a child's stick (which it was, I suppose, but that's beside the point). Still, I was able to catch a wild hare with my bare hands easily enough. Rabbit stew was much better than salted pork.

We huddled around the campfire—me and the six sorry-looking artisans. They explained that they'd been exposed to mange about a week earlier, which was one reason they were covered in scabs and rashes and their hair was falling out. It also explained why I felt so itchy after lying on their pack animal all day.

Walking Stick's name was Futh. As I suspected, he was a seanchaí, always on the lookout for new stories to tell. His brother Ruth was the tinsmith with the pots and pans. Regna was the cobbler. The big blacksmith was named Madhfeá. The man with the pitch-stained fingers was Ailbe, a builder and roof thatcher. The skinny musician with the boil-covered neck was Rogein. If the donkey had a name, I didn't catch it.

"I'm Demne," I said.

I felt safe giving them that much, since Demne was a common name. I didn't tell them my background or parentage, though. Clan Morna had put a high enough price on my head to tempt even the kindest craftsmen.

The áes dána didn't pry with questions. They were too busy enjoying the rabbit stew.

After dinner, the boil-necked young musician Rogein sang for us. He had a soothing voice, which sounded even better if I closed my eyes to avoid looking at his infected sores.

"Very nice, Rogein," said Futh after the first song. In the dark, his black streaks of hair and sharp nose made him look even more like a heron. "Would you favor us with 'The Battle of Cnucha'?"

My shoulders tensed. I studied the seanchaí's face, wondering if he had guessed my identity, but Futh paid me no mind.

Rogein began.

Bodbmall and the Líath Lúachra had told me the details of my infamous father's death, but I'd never heard them put to song. Somehow, the music made the story even more painful.

My father, Cumall, had once been chief of the Fíana—the great roving band of hunter-warriors who kept peace between the tribes, defended the isle from invaders, and answered to no one except Conn, High King of Tara. Then Cumall fell in love with my mother, Muirne Fair-Neck, and everything went to pig manure.

Muirne's family wouldn't agree to a marriage. They pointed out the annoying technicality that my father was already married. Cumall didn't care. He dumped his wife and abducted Muirne, breaking all rules of polite society and making hundreds of enemies.

The high king ordered Cumall to give Muirne back. Cumall refused. He rallied those fénnidí who were still loyal to him and went to war against basically everyone else in Ireland. My father's enemies were led by Clan Morna, who wanted control of the Fíana for themselves. The Battle of Cnucha did not go well for my dear old dad.

At this point in the song, Futh joined in, startling me with his rich baritone.

I got to hear about my father's decapitation in two-part harmony.

Outnumbered ten to one, Cumall still might have prevailed, but he was betrayed by his own lieutenant. This man—never named, just called "the Traitor"—had been entrusted with my father's corrbolg, his magical bag of wealth. In the midst of the battle, out of greed or spite, the Traitor wounded my father and ran away with the corrbolg, leaving Cumall vulnerable.

The enemy leader, Aed mac Morna, cut off my father's head. Cumall's allies fled. Aed became leader of the Fíana, except his name wasn't Aed anymore. One of my father's men had stabbed Aed in the eye, so from then on he was known as Goll (One-Eye) mac Morna.

Not being the forgiving type, Goll put a price on the heads of all Cumall's offspring, including the child Muirne Fair-Neck carried in her womb. . . . Me.

I'd been marked for death since before I was born.

Rogein and Futh sang the mournful refrain:

It was by Goll that great Cumall fell,
In the battle of Cnucha of the battle-hosts,
For this did they fight the hard battle:
For leadership of the Fían of Ireland.

Even at eight years old, I could tell it wasn't great poetry. Still, it filled me with sorrow. If my face hadn't been hidden in shadows, the áes dána might have thought I was crying. Of course, I wasn't. It was just smoke and cinders in my eyes.

That night, I dreamed of my mother.

I only had one memory of her. When I was six years old, she came to visit me at my foster mothers' campsite. I didn't know who she was, because I'd been placed with Bodbmall and the Líath Lúachra for safekeeping soon after I was born. I was a little shocked when she grabbed me and started weeping. We sat by the fire for hours, she holding me in her lap, squeezing me so tight I could hardly breathe. She sang me lullabies I was much too old for.

I remember she smelled of roses. Her red brocade dress was richer and softer than anything I'd ever touched. And she was very pregnant. I remember thinking there wasn't enough room in her lap for both me and the unborn child, who kicked from inside her belly as if telling me to shove off. My mother wept and kissed me. Then she left again.

Only afterward did Bodbmall explain. Muirne Fair-Neck had remarried. Her new husband, the king of Lamraige, was powerful enough to keep her safe. Otherwise, Clan Morna would've never stopped hunting her. But she couldn't do anything for me except keep me hidden away. She returned to her castle to raise my little half brother.

That was the last time I saw her.

When I woke the next morning in the áes dána's camp, I decided I might as well join them on their travels.

You may wonder why. They were mangy and poor. They were out of arán donn. Their donkey smelled of rotten eggs. But even for a boy of my great skill, surviving alone would be difficult with Clan Morna after me. If by some miracle

Bodbmall and the Líath Lúachra were still alive, they would find me eventually no matter where I went. Fénnidí were the best trackers in the world. In the meantime, playing servant to a group of artisans was as good a disguise as any.

I knew it would only be temporary. I swore to myself I would not get too attached to these fellows. After all, people left. People died. Even at eight, I understood this.

It's a good thing I did, given what happened.

We spent five or six weeks together. I didn't count the days, but it was long enough for all my hair to fall out and a scabby red rash to cover my body.

The áes dána found this very amusing.

"We'll call you Bald Demne from now on!" Ruth cackled, as if he'd never looked at his own reflection while polishing his pots.

At last, the miserable itchiness subsided, or maybe I just got used to it. My hair grew back in uneven tufts. Where it had been brown before, it was now so blond it was almost white. My advice for those seeking to change their appearance: Get yourself a variety of skin diseases. They do wonders.

We traveled through the Crotta Mountains, going from hamlet to farmstead, trading our services for food, ale, or shelter. It was pretty country—a patchwork of lush green valleys nestled between hillsides, dotted with goats and wildflowers. But after living in the woods for so long, I felt uneasy in the wide-open terrain. I kept glancing at the ridges above us, wondering when a war party of Mac Mornas might appear or—if I was feeling optimistic—whether I might spot my foster mothers coming to reclaim me. I whittled myself a new spear, just in case the Mac Mornas found me first.

In the meantime, I learned what I could from the áes dána. By the end of a month, I could cobble a shoe, fix a pot, tell a story, bang the bodhrán, and play a few tunes on the tin whistle. I could thatch a roof and turf a wall. I also cured the donkey of his thrush, because áes dána are idiots when it comes to proper donkey maintenance. My six tutors must have been pleased with my progress, because they kept feeding me.

"You've got a future as an artisan, lad," Futh told me. "Stay with us, learn a craft, and no one can ever make you a slave."

"Legally, anyway," Ruth muttered.

Futh silenced him with a scowl. "It's not a bad life, being áes dána. No lord controls you. You can travel anywhere you like, and you're entitled to the same safety and hospitality you'd get at home."

That last part didn't mean much to me. The only home I'd known was a moving campsite, and I certainly didn't associate it with safety or hospitality. Nevertheless, I nodded as if giving Futh's idea serious consideration.

About the fifth week of my apprenticeship, we started hearing rumors of a man who was killing and looting throughout the countryside.

One farmer, after we'd cobbled his shoes and fixed his roof, paid us with this advice: "You're all going to die. Turn around while you can."

Futh frowned. "Robbers ahead?"

"Just the one," the farmer said, "but he's enough."

"Hmph." Madhfeá crossed his enormous arms. "I'll crush this reaver's head."

The smith was the muscles of our group, and he was used to getting his way. Everyone was intimidated by him, except the donkey.

The farmer looked doubtful. "Well, good luck with that." He walked back into his newly thatched house with his newly cobbled shoes.

We carried on, because we had little choice. We were traveling a lonely road through the northern marches of Leinster, almost to the kingdom of Ulster. There was nothing on either side of us but rocky fields and barren mountains. If we turned back, we'd have to retrace our steps for at least a week, through country we'd already picked clean for business, which meant we'd starve. Our only option was to forge ahead and hope for the best.

We'd heard that the woods of Fid Gliabe was a few leagues to the north. It had a reputation for being a hideout for thieves. That sounded promising to me. Even thieves need their pots fixed and their knives whetted.

The next night, we camped in the shell of a burned-out farmhouse.

The day after that, the reaver found us.

The most humiliating thing was he didn't even try to hide his intentions. We'd reached the crest of a hill when Ailbe the thatcher pointed with one pitch-stained hand and said, "Who is that?"

In the valley below, a single man barreled up the road toward us, a spear resting on his shoulder and a sword buckled at his waist. He was so hairy and so completely wrapped in fur skins, I might have mistaken him for a red bear if it weren't for his weapons and his bronze helm.

We had plenty of time to turn and run. I doubt it would have mattered, but we could've at least tried. Instead, my six mangy chaperones just stared in amazement as the reaver got closer and closer.

"Nobody reaves this way," Futh said, as if his storytelling sensibilities were offended. "You *never* charge uphill toward a large group in broad daylight. You're supposed to hide in the bushes and ambush people at night!"

I was too busy tugging my spear from the donkey's saddle packs to argue.

Madhfeá hefted his blacksmith's hammer. "It's only one man. I'll handle this."

That was the last coherent thing he ever said. The last incoherent thing was "AACCKKHH," as the reaver's spear pierced his heart.

It takes a great deal of strength to throw a spear fifty feet and drive it through a man's chest. I didn't know that at age eight, but I know it now. Madhfeá was dead before he hit the ground. My other five companions stood frozen in horror as the plunderer drew his sword and charged. The áes dána stood no chance. Against a savage killer with a broadsword, there really isn't much you can do with a bodhrán and a collection of cooking pots.

My friends' screaming filled my ears as I freed my spear. Just as the donkey panicked and ran, I turned to face the reaver. I was too late to help anyone. He was pulling his blade from the belly of poor Futh, his sixth victim. I screamed and jabbed the killer in the back of his thigh.

The reaver howled. He spun toward me, the torque of his body wrenching the spear from my hands. I was fast and strong for an eight-year-old, but I'd never fought a grown warrior in actual combat before. I tried to dodge, but he kicked me in the chest with his good leg. I stumbled backward over the bodies of my companions and landed hard on my butt. My ribs felt like knife blades in my flesh when I breathed.

The raider stood glowering over me, the point of his sword at my throat.

His eyes, red-rimmed and bloodshot around pale green irises, reminded me of bog rosemary in bloom, and his gaze was just as poisonous. He stood well over six feet tall, a giant to me. Around his neck gleamed a bronze torc like the heroes wore in Futh's stories, though Futh wouldn't be telling those tales anymore, seeing as his blood now decorated the reaver's fur cloak.

"You're just a child." The reaver sounded offended. "How did you manage to wound me?"

I spat at him, though most of it ended up on my shirt. "Let me up and I'll finish the job."

I hoped the comment would intimidate him, or at least anger him enough to make my death quick.

Instead, the reaver threw back his head and laughed. "I like you. What's your name, boy?"

"None of your business."

"Well, None-of-your-business, I'm Fíacail the Reaver, son of Codna."

I scowled. "Your name means *Tooth?*"

"No! It's *Fíacail* with a fada mark over the *i*, not *fiacail* like *tooth*. Totally different."

"Sounds the same to me."

His expression darkened. "Would you like to live or die?"

I glanced at the bodies of my six áes dána friends. They had been good to me, and their sudden deaths hurt as much as my ribs. I wanted to kick Tooth in the teeth.

On the other hand, I'd grown up around death. I'd gutted enough deer to not be shocked by blood or entrails, even when they belonged to people I'd shared breakfast with a few hours before. The practical side of me won out.

"I suppose I'd prefer to live," I told the reaver.

"You have relatives?" he asked hopefully. "Anyone who could pay a fine ransom?"

I thought of my mother, Muirne, now living in her new husband's keep. My half brother would be two years old.

"No one," I said. "Just two foster mothers, and they won't pay you anything for me."

"Who are these cheapskates?"

I pushed the point of his sword away, because it was making me go cross-eyed. "The druidess Bodbmall and the Líath Lúachra."

Fíacail's head snapped back. "*Those* old hags?"

He seemed to chew on this information. I wasn't surprised

that he knew my foster mothers. In their heyday, Bodbmall and the Líath Lúachra had made quite a name for themselves as they roamed Ireland, working magic, hunting monsters, and killing any man who dared lay a hand on them. I wasn't sure whether my connection to them would make Fíacail more or less likely to cut my throat.

"Well," said the reaver at last, "that explains how you were able to wound me. They must have trained you."

"I'm better than they ever were."

"Ha! That settles it. Hand me that spear, will you?"

He meant the one that had skewered Madhfeá. It took me a while to free it, but I did not throw up from pain or revulsion. I was determined not to give the killer that satisfaction. Meanwhile, Fíacail bandaged his wounded thigh.

"Good," he said, when I handed him his bloody weapon. "Now gather up anything valuable from these corpses. You can carry the loot back to camp. Then we'll have a nice supper, eh?"

His leg wound didn't seem to bother him much. He limped along, talking cheerfully about his favorite killings that week, how beautiful the sunset was, and how you really appreciated such things after you'd just slaughtered six people.

By the time we reached his camp in a bug-infested marsh, I'd grudgingly decided that I couldn't hate the reaver. It was hard to dislike someone who clearly loved life and killing people so much. Besides, his shelter was by far the nicest place I'd ever stayed. He had a large tree trunk all to himself, hollowed out in the middle, with an opening above to let out the smoke from his fire. On the packed-earth floor, complete with an actual piss pot so I wouldn't have to stumble outside in the middle of the night, he offered me a bed of leaves with a smooth river rock for a pillow. He even smeared me with mud and bog myrtle to keep away the flies, mosquitoes, midges, fleas, and ticks. Truly, I had never known such luxury.

"Make yourself comfortable," said Fíacail. "Tomorrow, we reave."

Reaving is not as much fun as it sounds.

For one thing, nobody takes you seriously when you're an eight-year-old reaver. You run toward them, intent on malice, and they just chuckle and say, "Aw, how cute!" Then they notice the very large sword-wielding man behind you and start to scream.

Fíacail had a talent for making people scream. It hurt my ears.

Reaving is also messy. I was in charge of gathering and cleaning the loot. This was hard, time-consuming work. Fíacail would often chide me: "We can't barter this necklace if the lady's hair is still tangled in it!" or "This bolt of cloth has bloodstains! Did you try soaking it in urine before you washed it, like I showed you?"

Fíacail promised that if I did a good job with loot management, I would someday graduate to murder. I can't say I was looking forward to that. I didn't have any qualms about killing my enemies, but killing random farmers and travelers didn't sit right with me. I was wise enough not to say this to my new guardian, however.

You may wonder why I'm complaining, since my two foster mothers were fénnidí. Reavers and outlaws—same thing, right? But no. Outlaws have a code of honor. Even the high king recognizes their value as a force outside society. Reavers, on the other hand, just do what they please. They kill, die, and try to have as much fun as possible in between.

Some good came of my time with Fíacail, though. He taught me sword-fighting techniques that Bodbmall and the Líath Lúachra never had—the kind of dirty tricks a reaver needs to stay alive. He showed me how to throw a spear with greater range and strength, and deadly accuracy. (It's all in the waist.) He taught me the manly arts of belching, farting, and singing bawdy songs that I didn't understand. The six áes dána had always been too busy plying their trades or scratching their mangy bits to teach me any fun pastimes.

We must have spent many months together. I knew I was growing taller, because I had to start stooping whenever I exited the tree trunk. Still, Fíacail warned me not to get too accustomed to my plush accommodations, because someday my foster mothers would track me down. "They're not dead," he assured me. "You can't kill fénnidí that ugly."

Perhaps this was just wishful thinking on his part. If ugliness granted long life, the reaver himself would've been immortal.

After a full cycle of seasons, Fíacail's prediction came true. Bodbmall and the Líath Lúachra appeared at our camp, looking so much smaller and older I barely recognized them.

"Curse your feet, lad." The Líath Lúachra was even grayer

than I remembered, though her hair glittered with new pieces of colored glass. The egg-size wart on her nose looked darker and ready to hatch. "Did you have to cover so much ground? We've been hunting you for over a year. What happened to your hair?"

Fíacail emerged from the tree, yawning and scratching his nether regions as if the women were part of the usual scenery. "Morning. Anyone make breakfast?"

Bodbmall had braided her hair with even more rodent bones, so her head looked like a hill that an army of mice had died to defend. She studied the reaver warily, her purple-veined hand resting on the hilt of her sword. "Fíacail, you didn't kill this boy. Why?"

"Eh." Fíacail shrugged. "Too much trouble."

The Líath Lúachra nodded as if this made perfect sense to her.

Bodbmall didn't relax. "We'll be taking him now."

The tense silence told me things might get ugly. Just because my foster mothers knew Fíacail didn't mean they wouldn't try to kill him. And reavers don't like parting with their property—or anyone else's property for that matter.

Fíacail looked me over. I think he'd grown fond of me in his own murderous way, but he seemed to be weighing whether I was worth fighting over when he hadn't even had his morning eggs and sausage.

"Take him, then," Fíacail decided. "But leave the spear and other weapons. Those are mine."

"You gave them to me!" I protested.

Tooth showed me his teeth one last time. "I *loaned* them to you, Baldy."

I hated when he called me that. My hair had grown out by then, though it was still fine, white, and tufty like a buzzard chick's plumage.

"You want a spear?" he said. "You'll have to kill the owner and take it. You want mine?" His eyes gleamed in challenge.

I was so angry, I might have accepted, but Bodbmall clamped her hand on my shoulder. "Come on, boy." She steered me away through the marsh.

Behind us, I could hear Fíacail chuckling. I never saw him again, and I missed his indoor piss pot for a long time to come.

We returned to Slíab Bladma.

My foster mothers had moved their campsite to a different part of the woods, but it was the same layout as always: two hide tents, a fire pit, a creek nearby, and a ring of traps around the perimeter. It did not feel like I was coming home. The familiar setup now seemed small, like a pair of leather breeches I'd outgrown. (I hate leather breeches. They chafe terribly.)

"What about Clan Morna?" I asked.

Bodbmall frowned. Her black hair had developed new silver streaks that made her look like an ill-tempered badger. "You mean what happened last year, after you left? Well, we escaped, obviously. The Mac Mornas killed pretty much everyone else in these woods. Eventually, they moved on."

"So it's safe here now?"

"Gods, no!" said Bodbmall. "I'm sure the Mac Mornas will

be back someday. But for now, Slíab Bladma is no more dangerous than anywhere else."

In other words, my enemies would find me and kill me wherever we went, so I might as well relax.

I tried to get back into the rhythm of our old life together. I made the fires, sharpened the spears, laundered my foster mothers' undergarments in the stream. I butchered rabbits for dinner and gathered deer poop to grind with pitch so we could glue new arrowheads to our arrows—the usual chores any child would do.

But I felt restless. I was a year older, and that year had changed me. I had seen bits and pieces of the wider world, and I'd liked the roaming. Now an old man of nine, I started to ponder what I wanted to be when I grew up.

I'd always known that someday I would avenge my father, Cumall. I would kill the Mac Mornas. Then I figured I would take my father's place as captain of the Fíana, though I wasn't sure exactly what that entailed. I imagined it would involve lots of adventure and non-reavery hacking and slaying.

I often thought of the songs Rogein sang, and the stories Futh told about heroes of old—Lug of the Túatha Dé Danann, Cú Chulainn the Hound of Ulster. I wanted to be like those fellows. I liked how the áes dána described roaming from tribe to tribe, kingdom to kingdom, but I didn't want to do that while thatching roofs.

Sometimes, as I was grinding deer poop, I even felt nostalgic for my time with Fíacail. I wanted to be as fearless as the reaver. Fíacail never would have run from a fight, even if the entire Mac Morna clan was after him. I yearned for the day when I would be strong enough to meet Goll mac Morna face-to-face in battle. I'd take his other eye. Then I'd chop off his head.

I asked Bodbmall if she would teach me some druidry to make me more powerful.

"You don't *teach* druidry," she said. "You *live* it. And you, child, are not meant for that life."

I protested, until she told me that the first requirement would be to memorize the entire history of every clan in Ireland. I stopped wanting to be a druid.

I asked the Líath Lúachra to teach me more fighting skills.

"My bunions hurt," she said. "Go away."

One night after dinner, I pestered my fosterers for more information about the Battle of Cnucha, especially about the man who had betrayed my father and stolen his corrbolg. "What was his name?" I asked. "When I kill all Cumall's enemies, I would like to start with that traitor."

Bodbmall and the Gray One exchanged a wary look, just like they had when I'd asked them where babies come from.

"If the Traitor had a name," Bodbmall said, "I never heard it."

"Nor I," said the Líath Lúachra, scratching her wart. "But he got in your father's good graces as quick as a fox, they say."

Bodbmall poked the fire with a stick. "The Traitor probably ran to Greece. He'll be living like a king there with all the treasure from that bag."

This made me angry. I had no idea what kind of treasures

my father had kept in his magical pouch, but if anyone should run to Greece and live like a king, it should be me.

"I will definitely kill that traitorous thief first," I decided. "Then I will kill Goll mac Morna."

The Líath Lúachra sucked her teeth. "Well, in the meantime, you know what's good practice for killing your enemies?"

"What?"

"Washing pots. Get to it."

I started wandering farther and farther from camp.

I claimed it was because we'd cleaned the area of all the good berries and deer poop. To a certain extent, that was true. Bodbmall and the Líath Lúachra kept coming up with excuses not to change our campsite. Their bones hurt, it was raining too hard, Bodbmall had just discovered she had a geis against traveling on Tuesdays—though how she'd learned about this taboo, and how she knew it was Tuesday, I had no idea.

I was well aware that my foster mothers were just getting older and lazier. Staying in one place was dangerous, but I didn't complain. It gave me an excuse to roam farther afield and be gone longer, sometimes even staying away a night or two.

One day, I found myself at the eastern edge of the forest. The reed-choked river I'd been following emptied into a wide plain speckled with blooming yellow gorse. Atop a nearby hill stood an impressive ringfort, its stone walls bristling with stakes. Clustered around its base was the largest settlement I'd ever seen. Judging from the smoke trails of the cooking fires, there must have been a dozen buildings at least. To the south, on the banks of a small lake, about twenty boys ran around a green field, shouting at one another and waving crooked sticks.

I watched, entranced. I'd encountered a few people my own age before, but I'd never seen so many in one place.

What were they doing—fighting? Performing some sort of ritual?

Then I noticed that their attention was focused on a small white sliotar—a ball that they hit with their sticks, sending it back and forth across the green. I'd heard stories about this. They were playing iománaíocht!

Compared to my sword-fighting practice with Fíacail, or even the sparring I'd done with my foster mothers, the game of hurling looked tame to me, but the boys seemed to be enjoying themselves. They laughed and shouted insults at one another as they chased the sliotar back and forth across the field.

I couldn't remember the last time I had laughed. I wasn't sure I remembered how. But I *did* know how to run, swing a stick, and insult people. I felt a strange yearning—like hunger, except in the heart rather than the stomach.

Before I could think better of it, I emerged from the woods and marched toward the hurlers.

Their game fell apart as soon as they noticed me. I must have looked strange to them with my feathery white hair, my hide loincloth, and my skin caked with white mud to keep away the midges.

"I want to play," I announced.

They looked at one another. One of them, I supposed the

eldest, stepped toward me. He had red hair and green eyes like a fox, which made me uneasy, since foxes are tricky creatures.

"Where'd you come from?" he demanded.

I pointed to the woods.

Fox Face frowned. "Well, you smell bad. You can join Lugaid's team."

"Póg mo thóin, Mahan," said another boy, whom I guessed was Lugaid. He had dark hair and a splash of freckles across his nose. "I don't want him."

"Too late," said Mahan. "I called it first."

The group split into two teams again. The game recommenced. I didn't have a hurling stick, and nobody offered me one, so I knocked down the nearest lad and took his. Then I ran after Lugaid, trying to figure out the rules of the game as I went along.

Judging from the cries of protest, I apparently wasn't supposed to clobber members of the opposing team with my stick. That seemed silly to me. Why hold a stick if you can't wield it against the enemy?

I turned my attention to the ball. Tracking it down and hitting it with my stick was much easier than chasing deer or stunning ducks. I didn't understand why the other boys had so much trouble, or why they moved so slowly.

The game lasted about five minutes. I think it was supposed to go longer, but by that point, I'd knocked down everyone on the other team and made all the goals, so there didn't seem to be any reason to continue. The enemy team lay scattered across the field, groaning and crying. Their captain, Mahan, clutched his now-broken leg. His face was as red as his hair.

My own team captain, Lugaid, didn't look happy about winning. When he scowled, all his freckles bunched around his nose. "You'd better get out of here," he warned me, "or they'll kill you."

I looked at our opponents. Some were starting to get up. All were glaring at me.

I was confused. "Is killing someone part of the game?"

"Not usually," Lugaid said. "But today it might be. Get lost!"

I ran—not because I was scared of being killed, but because my feelings were hurt. I'd thought I was making friends.

That night, I camped in the woods nearby. I doubted Bodbmall or the Líath Lúachra would worry about me if I was gone for an extra day or two. In the morning, I crept back to the edge of the forest. I waited for the boys to return to the playing field, which they did around noon—even fox-haired Mahan, limping along on a crutch.

When I emerged from my hiding spot, the boys didn't attack me. They didn't look happy to see me, though, despite the fact that I'd bathed in the river to get rid of the mud and the stink. My captain from yesterday, Lugaid, glowered at me from under his dark bangs, silently warning me to go away.

"I want to try again," I announced.

The boys faced Mahan, waiting for his decision.

Mahan clenched his jaw so tightly I thought his neck tendons might snap. His green eyes were cold as winter moss.

"Fine," he said at last. "But this time, let's try something different. We'll pit five of our best players against you alone."

I agreed. I was just relieved they were giving me a second chance.

I tried to restrain myself. I left my five opponents groaning on the field, but I was careful not to break any limbs. I stopped scoring after ten goals, because any more would have felt like overkill.

Grinning, I returned to the group, ready to be congratulated. No one patted me on the back.

If anything, Mahan looked even angrier. "All right," he growled. "That was your warm-up. Now we'll send *ten* of ours against you."

"No problem," I said, and it wasn't. I beat them in the same amount of time.

Before I could catch my breath, Mahan screamed, "EVERYONE, GET HIM!"

The rest of the group charged me. Only Lugaid held back. The boys seemed more interested in hitting me than the ball, so I was forced to knock most of them unconscious before I made all the goals and won the match.

Only Lugaid and Mahan remained standing. Mahan limped toward me. He screamed and tried to brain me with his crutch, so I shoved him to the ground. He howled in pain.

Lugaid just frowned at me, his freckles in the sunlight too numerous to count. "Who *are* you?"

"My name's Demne."

He sighed. "Well, you've made a lot of enemies today, Demne."

My heart sank. "Is this the part where I run away?"

"Yes. And this time, don't come back."

I ran, Lugaid's words still stinging my ears.

I should've followed his advice and never gone back. Instead, I camped in the woods again that night. The following day, I returned to the playing field. How could I stay away? This was the most interesting thing that had happened to me in months. Also, if you've ever had a wound, you know how hard it is to leave it alone. You pick at it and scratch it, even when you know that will only make it worse.

Once again, the hurling match fell apart when the boys saw me.

Lugaid started toward me, but Mahan grabbed his arm. "I'll handle this."

Mahan limped over on his crutch. His fiery red hair and cold green eyes suddenly reminded me of Fíacail. The reaver had worn that same expression whenever we came back from an unsuccessful day of marauding.

"I told my father about you," Mahan growled. "He's the lord of Mag Life." He pointed to the stronghold on the hill.

"And?" I hoped perhaps Mahan's father had ordered the boys to be nicer to me. I didn't know much about fathers back then.

"I told him how you ruined our games and broke my leg," Mahan continued. "And how you claimed your name was

Demne. He said he didn't know anyone by that name. He asked me to describe you. I said you were tall and fair."

He used the word *finn*, as in bright or blond. I'd never thought of myself as finn before, especially the way he said it, like an insult. I realized he was making fun of my white hair, and perhaps how pale I'd looked when I first appeared, streaked with white mud.

"I'm not finn," I said. "My name *is* Demne."

Mahan gave me a sly smile. "Not anymore. We're going to call you *Finn*."

I didn't like that new name, but I didn't want to show Mahan any reaction. The other boys snickered, except for Lugaid, who looked at me with something like pity.

"I just want to play," I told Mahan. "I'll get it right this time."

He sneered. "Since you humiliated us, my father said that if you came back, we should do our best to kill you."

The boys circled me like a pack of dogs, their eyes full of hate, their hands tight on their hurling sticks. I realized this wasn't a game now. My heart began to race with fear. Then all twenty of them attacked, even Lugaid.

I kicked and punched, dodged and squirmed. I knocked down about seven of the boys. I could have broken their necks, but, strangely enough, I didn't want to. Even though they were trying to kill me, it didn't feel right to take their lives.

I suppose my time with Fíacail had made me think about when to kill and when to simply whack someone in the face really hard. Finally, I slipped free of the mob and bolted for the woods.

The boys didn't try to follow.

After that, I *definitely* should have stayed away.

For a while, I tried.

I went back to my foster mothers' camp as if nothing had happened. Bodbmall and the Líath Lúachra didn't seem concerned about where I'd been. I caught up on my chores. I washed more undergarments. I gathered more deer poop. But after a week of my old routine, a compulsion came over me worse than mange itch. I had to try and patch things up with the boys of Mag Life one last time.

Maybe there had been a misunderstanding. Maybe if I went back and tried to talk to them, or participated in some activity other than hurling, they would stop trying to murder me. At least Lugaid seemed nice. If I could befriend him, the others might come around. I wanted to see what the freckles on his face looked like when he smiled.

I arrived at Mag Life in the middle of a hot, humid day. The hurling field was empty. In the nearby lake, the boys were laughing and splashing, trying to dunk one another.

I'd never had much cause to swim for pleasure. Generally, swimming was something I did only when I had to rescue a stray animal from the current. Nevertheless, I knew how. And after my long, sweaty hike, the water looked inviting.

I spotted Mahan's red hair. He sat on the shore with his

broken leg, looking miserable. When he saw me, he splashed at his friends to get their attention.

"What do you want, Finn?" he demanded. "You've got some sliotair, showing up here again."

I wasn't sure what he meant. I hadn't brought any hurling balls with me. I gestured at the water. "May I swim?"

The boys laughed. They seemed to find my request hilariously stupid, as if I'd asked for all their horses and all their slaves.

"Yes, come in!" said one.

"Try to dunk us!" said another.

"Finn," said Lugaid, his voice on edge. "Just go away. Please."

I'm not sure what made me angrier—that the nicest of the boys was telling me to leave, or that he called me Finn. I jumped into the water.

Immediately, the boys surrounded me. They grabbed me, pushed me under, and held me there. The water felt nice, but not so nice that I wanted to drown in it.

I thrashed and fought. I kicked groins, broke fingers, and employed every reaver trick Fíacail had taught me to stay alive. By the time I'd clawed my way to the shore, gasping and shivering, blood had billowed in the water like red smoke. Eight boys floated facedown. Two more were towing Lugaid to the shore. His dark hair was plastered to his face. His freckled nose had been smashed. He did not appear to be breathing.

"Get the adults!" Mahan screamed. "Kill Finn!"

I felt awful. I wanted to help Lugaid, or at least stay long enough to see if he was alive. I hadn't meant to hurt anyone, especially not him. But I was learning that intentions didn't count for much. I ran for the woods.

I never returned to Mag Life.

I often thought of Lugaid, though. I wondered if his heartbroken father had pledged a blood feud against me, the way I'd pledged to kill Goll mac Morna for slaying my father. I would not have blamed Lugaid's father. From that point on, in my worst nightmares, I dreamed I was Goll mac Morna, desperately trying to explain to a furious boy named Finn why I hadn't meant to kill Cumall at the Battle of Cnucha. Sometimes, I woke up not sure of who I was.

As summer faded, I stayed close to my foster mothers' camp. Somewhere along the way, I turned ten years old. I didn't know my exact birthday—we didn't keep calendars, so it wouldn't have mattered—but Bodbmall assured me the date had come and gone.

I started to see more evidence that Bodbmall and the Líath Lúachra were getting old. Not just older—OLD. I don't know if you've observed this with adults, but they tend to look basically the same for years and years. Then, suddenly, their appearance falls off a cliff, along with their ability to take care of themselves.

One day, as the three of us were curing badger hides by the river, a herd of wild deer thundered through the woods.

Bodbmall heaved a sigh as she watched them pass. "I wish we could catch one of those for dinner."

"Yes," agreed the Líath Lúachra. "Been a long time since we had good meat."

I stared at my foster mothers in surprise. Neither of them got up to prepare for the hunt. They didn't even ask me to do it.

I'd seen them chase down deer many times before. Now they spoke about the animals as if they were clouds in the sky—impossibly out of reach. I realized they weren't just being lazy. They truly did not think they could run fast enough anymore. And being too proud to ask me, they were content to simply not have the meat.

"I'll do it," I said.

Before they could protest, I raced off.

I caught the two largest stags in the herd. I grabbed the first by the antlers and steered him into a tree, dazing him nicely. Then, seeing as I still had a free hand, I grabbed another stag and gave him the same treatment. Even stunned, they were big, lively animals. They thrashed and struggled as I towed them back to camp, but I was used to dragging heavy things: áes dána supplies, reaver loot, my foster mothers' undergarments. The stags were no match for me.

Bodbmall and the Líath Lúachra pretended to be upset, but I could see them licking their lips as they watched me butcher the animals.

"Hmph," said Bodbmall. "If we wanted your help in feeding ourselves, boy, we would've asked."

The Líath Lúachra grunted in agreement. "We don't need a man taking care of us."

My ears burned. I wasn't sure how to ask my next question, but I felt I should try. "Are you sure?"

They both stared at me. Even the Líath Lúachra's wart was staring at me.

"I mean, you're not fénnidí anymore," I forged on. "You're getting older. Haven't you ever thought of finding men? Getting married and settling down? Might be nice to have some help."

From their confused expressions, I wondered if I'd spoken gibberish rather than Irish. Finally, both women began to cackle.

"Find men?" Bodbmall scoffed.

"Get married!" roared the Líath Lúachra. "Ha!"

True, I didn't know much about the ways of marriage. I assumed women decided to live with men so they would have companions to do their chores. I thought that Bodbmall and the Líath Lúachra could use some help as they slid into their final years. As strong as I was, it scared me to think that the task might fall on me alone.

"Listen here, boy," said the Líath Lúachra. "Fénnidí only stop being fénnidí when they settle down. If they know what's good for them, they *never* marry."

I looked up from the guts of the stag. "But my father—"

"Yes, your father," she snapped. "He married, and look what happened to him!"

Bodbmall put her hand on the Líath Lúachra's wrist—a warning touch.

"I only meant," the Líath Lúachra continued, her voice

softening from granite to sandstone, "that the Fíana is one of the few places in this world where you can be free regardless of your gender. That's why we like it."

Bodbmall nodded. "That's why we'll never *not* be Fénnidí, no matter how old we get. We don't need husbands, thank you very much."

The Líath Lúachra got a mischievous glint in her eyes. "Besides, some Fénnidí care so little for gender they can change theirs at will."

My hand slipped. I almost cut off my own fingers. "*What?*"

Bodbmall frowned at the Líath Lúachra. "Don't confuse the boy."

"What's the harm?" she crowed. "We had one comrade in the Fíana who alternated every year between male and female! Perhaps you'll meet him or her someday. We had another fénnid—"

"And that's enough of that," Bodbmall said, her look so stern even the Gray One fell silent. "Boy, make sure you roast up those livers for us, eh? They're the best part."

From then on, I took over the hunting. I resigned myself to the fact that my foster mothers *needed* me. The more I did for them, the weaker and slower they seemed to get.

I tried to make peace with our new arrangement. Even if it meant I would never get revenge on Goll or the Traitor with the corrbolg, even if I never took my father's place as captain of the Fíana, I owed it to my foster mothers to care for them until they died.

But Clan Morna had other ideas.

One day, the Líath Lúachra, who still roamed more than Bodbmall did, came back to camp after being gone a week. She'd been to the nearest seaside village to trade for colored glass—as I mentioned, she had a weakness for shiny things—and had heard bad news.

"Clan Morna knows you are here." She gave me a withering stare. "Apparently, someone in Mag Life reported a boy of your description living in these woods. They called this boy *Finn*."

My face burned. "I can explain."

"Don't bother. There's no time. You need to run."

I'd always suspected this day might come. Still, I felt as if I were back in the lake at Mag Life, desperately grabbing for anything to keep from drowning. "I can't leave you two alone!"

The Líath Lúachra spat in the dirt. "Foolish child. We'll be fine. It's not my destiny to be killed by the sons of Morna."

"How can you know that?" I demanded.

The Líath Lúachra scowled at Bodbmall, who peered mournfully into the embers of our fire.

"Just go, boy," Bodbmall said. The druidess's hair had gone almost fully gray by then, so you could barely see the rodent bones in her braids. "Don't tell anyone your true identity. You're old enough to find employment now." She gestured vaguely toward the west. "Try the king of Benntraige. He's an honorable man."

So I ran, as I had two years before. Only this time, I was faster and stronger, and did not tumble off any cliffs.

I traveled west for days. I slept in caves or under thornbushes. I lived on wild berries. I avoided making campfires, because I didn't want to draw attention to myself. At last, following the directions of a roving bard, I arrived at Loch Léin, the seat of the Benntraige tribe.

The lake was a gray mirror set in a frame of rugged green hills. A modest wattle-and-daub stronghold clung to the northern shore, the smoke from its cooking fire mixing with the fog above.

No guards watched the gates. I got an audience with the king simply by walking through the door and saying, "Hello, I want a job."

The king was a kindly-looking old man. His hair and beard looked like fog that had stuck to him as he walked outside. His hall was held together by cobwebs. His roof had so many leaks it would have kept my friend Ailbe busy thatching for a whole year. Around the king stood a dozen men—all thin, elderly, and stooped.

"A job?" The king stroked his beard as if trying to remember what the word meant. "Well, lad, what can you do?"

I glanced at his dinner table, poorly laden with a few pieces of salted pork and moldy cheese. I hadn't seen such a sorry meal since my time with the áes dána. "I'm an excellent hunter."

One of his men scoffed—the royal hunter, probably.

"Give me a try," I promised. "You'll see."

The king smiled indulgently. "What could it hurt? Go hunt!"

That night I came back leading a dozen deer all tied together, spancel hoops around their legs to keep them from running at more than a slow jog.

The royal hunter's jaw nearly dropped to the floor.

The king's eyes narrowed as he considered the deer.

I expected him to say *Good job! You're hired!*

Instead, he studied my face with concern. "Who did you say your father was, lad?"

My heart beat faster. "I . . . didn't say."

The king tugged at his foggy beard. "I would swear you are the son of my old friend Cumall. You look just like him—except for the blond hair—and he was the only man I ever knew who could hunt as well as you have today. But I only know of one surviving son of Cumall—Tulcha. He's much older than you, and he works for the king of Scotland."

"I have an older brother?" I blurted out.

It was not one of my smarter comments, but I was too surprised to think straight. I'd heard that my father had sired other children with other wives. Bodbmall and the Líath Lúachra had never mentioned any of the offspring by name, and I'd assumed they'd all been hunted down and killed.

The king's face fell. "You will have to leave, lad."

"But if you were my father's friend—"

"I'm sorry, lad. Once word gets out to Clan Morna, they will come to kill you, and I will not be able to protect you." He gestured at his sorry band of warriors, who did not look capable of defending themselves from a flock of chickens. "I cannot have Cumall's son killed under my roof."

My eyes stinging, I turned to leave.

"You can leave the deer, however," the king called to me on my way out. "Thank you!"

From Benntraige, I traveled north with no real destination in mind.

I was still in shock that I had a brother in Scotland. I thought of making my way there to find him, but I wasn't sure where Scotland was. Across the sea, I'd heard. But when you live in Ireland, *everything* is across the sea.

Even if I found this Tulcha, there was no guarantee he would welcome me. He might hate me because I had a different mother. He might kick me out as quickly as the king of Benntraige had. He might have ignored me all these years on purpose for fear of his own safety, just as my mother had. That thought left a bitter taste in my mouth.

For a few days, I stayed with a shepherd's family on the windswept rocky plains of Ciarraige, helping the shepherd shear his flock. He was so impressed with my work he gave me directions to the tribe's stronghold and said I should offer my services to their king.

The king of Ciarraige's fortress was bigger than Benntraige's, and better built, but the inside was a mess. The king had about twenty warriors, all of whom looked like they could fight but none of whom could pick up after themselves. The straw on the floor hadn't been changed in years. The main room was littered with muddy boots, dirty clothes, broken armor, and crusty plates.

When I asked for a job, the king looked me over. He had

crinkly eyes, a shirt almost as messy as the floor, and a physique that I found fascinating. I'd never seen anyone with such an impressive round belly. . . . Well, except for my pregnant mother. I wondered if his kicked like hers had.

"Can you clean?" he asked.

"Yes," I said.

"You're hired."

I didn't mind the work. The king's entire household didn't make nearly as much of a mess as Fíacail the Reaver had. At dinnertime, I even got a piece of arán donn with butter that I could enjoy in the corner, and I only had to share it with two dogs and the scullery maid.

I was beginning to think I'd found a home at last when the king called to me from the dining table. "You, boy, do you play fidchell? I've beaten everyone else here a thousand times. Let's see how you play!"

I approached cautiously. Bodbmall had taught me the game using river rocks and holes in the dirt. Futh had told me stories about heroes and kings who played fidchell. But I'd never seen an actual game board before. The polished oak surface was intricately carved. The game pieces were gold for one player and silver for the other—each token probably worth more than a yearling heifer.

The king set up his gold pieces in the center of the board. Then he set up my silver pieces around the edges.

"Do you know the rules, lad?" he asked.

"Sort of?"

He smiled and patted his belly as he explained the various movements and strategies of fidchell. "It's easy to learn, but it takes a lifetime to master. Let's begin!"

I won in five moves.

The king frowned. "Well, that was unexpected. Again?"

I won the next game. And the next. I had no problem seeing four or five moves ahead, and how each of those possibilities could split into dozens more. The king, on the other hand, seemed to struggle, playing one move at a time. I felt as I had on the hurling field against the boys of Mag Life. I just didn't understand why this game was supposed to be hard.

As we played, the king's warriors gathered 'round. Some began to smile with smug satisfaction as their ruler's face got redder and redder. When he leaned forward to study the board, his belly pressed against the table, bulging around it like a giant mouth trying to eat the wood.

After I won my seventeenth game in a row, the king sat back and glowered at me.

It dawned on me then that perhaps I should have played to lose.

"Who did you say you were?" the king asked.

"Uh . . . nobody, really. Just a commoner. From the . . . Luaigni tribe, near Tara."

I'm not sure why I chose that name. Maybe I'd heard it in one of Rogein's songs, or maybe I was thinking about the boy Lugaid whom I'd almost befriended, then drowned.

The king shook his head. "No. There's only one man I

ever knew who could play fidchell the way you do. That was Cumall. You look like him, too. Who sent you here, your uncle Crimall?"

I bit my tongue to keep from crying *I have an uncle?* At least I'd learned that much from my experience at Benntraige.

But my expression must have been easy to read.

"I see," said the king. "You didn't know your uncle was alive, did you? Well, he's hiding somewhere in the wilderness of Connacht with the remainder of your father's men. Perhaps you should go look for him. I hear Clan Morna is hunting all over Ireland for you. I can't protect you from the likes of them. Off you go."

With as much dignity as I could muster, I stood and bowed. I didn't want the king to see how crushed I felt. The brown bread and butter sat heavily in my stomach as I trudged off into the night, cursing my skill at games.

That night, I slept shivering in the rain. I felt low and miserable. I had no home, no job, no friends—just a single silver fidchell piece I'd stolen from the king of Ciarraige's board out of spite.

I'd learned of a brother and an uncle that no one ever told me about, but the information didn't lift my spirits. Connacht was part of Ireland, at least, but I didn't know how to get there any more than I knew how to sail to Scotland. Even if I found my uncle Crimall, he might boot me out just like everyone else had. Or he'd take me in and I'd get him killed.

I was a walking ten-year-old curse.

The next morning, I stumbled along sheep paths until I saw

smoke in the distance and heard the clanging of a hammer on metal. That brought back fond memories of my smith friend, Madhfeá, so I walked toward the sound.

In the next valley stood a whitewashed cottage with a detached barn and an open-air smithy.

As I got closer, I saw a grizzled, barrel-chested man standing over his anvil, hammering away at a red-hot plowshare. Sparks flew across the dirt. The forge glowed behind him. The air smelled sweetly of molten iron and charcoal.

Nearby, in the shade of an apple tree, a girl about my age was churning butter. She met my gaze. Her suspicious frown, unfriendly green eyes, and tangle of turf-black hair made my heart flop in my chest like a drowning Mag Life boy.

The smith noticed me. He gestured for me to wait, because the hot blade couldn't, then quenched it in his water trough. Curls of steam rolled off his arms. He set aside his work and turned to study me. His eyes were nested under a thicket of gray-and-black eyebrows, and were as blue as thrush eggs.

"Well," he said. "Look at you."

I wasn't sure what he meant by that. I looked at myself. My clothes were speckled in sheep poop. My feet were caked in bog muck. I hadn't bathed since leaving Slíab Bladma, so I doubted I smelled very good.

The girl examined me, too, in a way that made the blood collect in my lower gut.

"Strong arms," the smith judged. "Looks like a smith's apprentice, doesn't he, Cruithne?"

The girl, who must have been his daughter, said, "Hmph."

Her scowl was entrancing. She turned back to her butter churn, but the few seconds of attention she'd given me left my ears ringing as if I'd been hit in the face with old Futh's walking stick.

"I'm Lóchán," said the man. "Chief smith of the Uí Chúanach tribe."

He swept his arm expansively, as if there were thousands of other smiths nearby not as good as he was, though all I saw was the girl, a cow, and rocky fields.

"I can't pay you anything," Lóchán continued, "but you'll get a meal every day, and you can sleep in the barn with the cow."

"Deal," I said, my eyes still fixed on the girl. If Lóchán noticed, he didn't seem displeased.

That's how I got my first real job.

The strangest thing was, Lóchán never once asked my name. Every day, he would simply say, "Son, do this, will you?" or "Son, fetch me the pig iron." I didn't complain, since every time I told someone my name, I got pushed away, somebody died, or both.

The girl, Cruithne, never asked my name either. She just called me gilla, which meant *lad* or *boy*. Coming from her, it sounded more like *pond scum*, but I didn't mind. At least she noticed me.

I'd been on the job for about a week when she pulled me behind the barn one evening. "You might as well kiss me, gilla. Nothing else to do around here."

That's how I got my first girlfriend. We were young, yes, but Lóchán could see how much we loved each other. It was obvious from the way Cruithne ordered me around, and the way I hit my thumb with the hammer whenever she came close.

"I'll give you my daughter," Lóchán announced one day, causing me to bash my thumb even harder than usual. "Though I suppose I don't know anything about you. . . ." He considered this for a moment, then gave me a charitable grin. "Well, no matter! You're a good worker, son. Do we have an agreement?"

I gulped. I looked at Cruithne, who rolled her beautiful green eyes to let me know how ridiculous I was. But she didn't protest.

"Yes," I said.

Lóchán nodded. "I only ask one thing. There's a monstrous boar terrorizing the road to Munster. Folks call it Béo. It's been ravaging the land and slaughtering anyone who tries to hunt it."

"You want me to kill it."

"Gods of the forge, no!" Lóchán cried. "I wanted you to *stay away* from it! The last thing I need is for my son-in-law and apprentice to get himself killed. Will you promise?"

I weighed my options. I liked Lóchán. I appreciated all he had done for me. But I also wanted to impress Cruithne, my new girlfriend/wife/overlord. She often complained how boring her life was here, how boring her father was, how boring I was. Killing a giant boar would not be boring. I could show her that I was much more than an apprentice blacksmith. Besides, why would Lóchán tell me about this monster if he didn't actually want me to kill it?

"I promise," I told the smith. "By the way, Dad, could you make me some spears?"

Lóchán frowned. "What for?"

"Purely for self-defense."

"Well . . . all right, then." He started on the weapons, while Cruithne shook her head and muttered under her breath how stupid we both were.

The next morning before dawn, I went hunting for Béo.

After weeks of working at the forge, my hunting skills had grown rusty. It took me hours to track down the beast, and it smelled me before I smelled it, which was embarrassing since Béo stank like a rotting carcass in the August sun.

I don't know if you've ever hunted a wild boar, but they are the meanest, trickiest, foulest animals you will ever encounter. They are also as ugly as a Leinsterman's back end.

Béo was twice the size of the largest men I had ever seen, those being Madhfeá and Fíacail. Its tusks were thicker than my legs. Its snout glistened red as a flesh wound. Its tiny black eyes gleamed with hatred, and along its back grew a forest of bristles that looked like miniature spears.

When it burst out of the bushes and charged me, my first instinct was to run. Instead, I remembered what the Líath Lúachra had told me about fighting boars: If you run, you die. I braced the butt of my spear against the ground, held my position, and let the beast impale itself.

The boar should have died on the spot. Instead, it squealed with rage and just kept pushing. It ripped the spear from my hands, and I had to jump to one side to avoid being trampled. The beast turned and charged again, never mind that it now had a wooden shaft sunk halfway through its chest. I launched my second spear, which pierced the monster in its back-left haunch. Still it limped forward, intent on slaughter. My third and last spear split its skull right between the eyes. Two more steps, and the beast collapsed dead at my feet.

My heart was hammering almost as hard as when Cruithne first kissed me. I checked myself to make sure the creature hadn't gored me. Somehow I'd come through unscathed.

I pulled out a knife I'd borrowed from Lóchán. You may remember I said you can't decapitate something with a spear. I needed to bring back proof that I had made the kill, and I could not carry the entire boar, so I spent the next hour sawing off the monster's head, which was almost as big as I was. It was gruesome work, and since I was now warmer than the beast's carcass, all of Béo's fleas, ticks, and other hangers-on migrated onto me.

At last, toward evening, I dragged my prize back to the smithy.

I expected Lóchán to be amazed and grateful. I wanted Cruithne to sob, hug me, and shower me with kisses because I had returned alive—a hero to the tribe!

Instead, Lóchán glowered. "Where have you been? You missed a whole day's work." Then he scowled at the boar's head. "What is *THAT?*"

Cruithne gagged and pinched her nose. "Disgusting!"

"It's your bridal price," I explained. Then, when they still did not seem to understand, I said, "It's the head of Béo. I have freed the land of the monster."

I discovered two things from this. First: Sometimes when a blacksmith tells you not to kill a monster, he really means don't kill the monster. Second: Women do not value severed boars' heads as bridal gifts.

That very night, Lóchán packed me a bag of supplies. Cruithne added some apples and butter. She announced that she would be marrying a herdsman in the next village. Then they both wished me a safe journey and told me never to come back.

I left, miserable and dismayed. All I'd gotten from the experience were three good spears, a fresh batch of lice, and an aversion to giant boars.

Alas, my worst heartbreak was yet to come.

I made my way toward the setting sun.

I thought this would eventually bring me to Connacht, where I could search for my uncle Crimall. Failing that, once I reached the ocean, I could throw myself in.

On my third day, I was passing through a dreary forest when I heard the sound of desolate sobbing. I feared it might be a woman of the Otherworld, a bean sídhe, because I couldn't imagine a human voice containing so much sorrow. Nevertheless, I forged ahead, curious to see who could be feeling even worse than I was.

At the banks of a river, an old woman crouched on her hands and knees, weeping over the water.

"Hello?" I called.

She turned. I still wasn't sure if she was human. She'd been weeping so hard that blood ran from her eyes along with the tears. She'd gnashed her teeth and bitten her lips until her mouth glistened with blood.

I was so rattled, the only thing I could think to say was "Your mouth is red."

"That's as it should be," the woman sobbed. "What do I need blood for? My life is over! My son has been murdered by a lone warrior, wild and terrible!"

I suppose I should have wished her a good day and kept walking. That would have spared me much sorrow. But my heart ached for the woman. I wondered if anyone would weep for me this way, should I be killed. My foster mothers were not weepers. My ex-betrothed Cruithne had never even known my name. My own mother had not seen me in four years.

"What was your son's name?" I asked.

"Glonda," she sobbed.

"That's a lovely name," I said. "I will avenge him."

"But you're just a boy."

"A boy with three good spears," I said, "and a bad temper. Tell me where I may find Glonda's murderer."

Sniffling, she pointed in the direction of where she had found her son's body. She assured me I would have no trouble locating his murderer. She was right.

I found myself at the edge of a lake nestled between two tall hills to the north and south. The only obvious path west—unless you were a mountain goat, or you were willing to travel miles out of your way—was a narrow chain of islets that ran down the center of the lake like the vertebrae of a spine. The islets looked so close together, and the water between them so shallow, that I imagined you could hop from one to the other and reach the opposite shore easily enough . . . except that Glonda's murderer had set up his camp right in the middle of the causeway.

He made no secret about his presence. A cooking fire guttered in front of his tent. A gray banner snapped in the wind. The killer himself was too far away for me to see clearly, but he was wrapped in a gray cloak, sitting in front of his fire with his back to me, as if he had no concerns for his safety.

Floating in the lake were dozens of bodies—perhaps those who had tried to challenge the warrior, or simply travelers who had tried to cross.

I gripped my spear so tightly I feared it might snap.

I hated this warrior with every drop of blood in my veins. Suddenly, he wasn't just Glonda's killer. He was everything that had stood in my way my entire life—my shame when Lóchán and Cruithne had kicked me out, my rage at the two cowardly kings who had respected my father but would not protect me, my guilt when I killed the boys of Mag Life whom I'd just wanted to befriend, my resentment of Fíacail for letting me go so easily, my helplessness as six áes dána who'd treated me kindly were slaughtered before my eyes. This murderer was Clan Morna, whom I'd never even faced, but who had made my life miserable since the day I was born. He was my mother's only lullaby to me when I was six years old, before she left me behind forever.

I marched forward. I decided that after I killed this man,

I would name the land bridge the Causeway of Glonda, so at least that poor red-mouthed mother would have something to remember her son by.

I could have thrown my spear from the lake's edge and killed the man where he sat. Fíacail had taught me well. But I wanted to look in the murderer's eyes first. I leaped from islet to islet, my feet squelching in the marshy grass.

"Hey!" I yelled.

The man rose.

His leather tent looked familiar, but many tents looked the same. His gray cloak had been ripped and resewn many times.

Unease began to build in my stomach. I assumed it was nerves. I marched ahead.

When he turned, his appearance made me falter. He had a young face but a gray beard that glittered with glass beads. His eyes were the color of cold ashes.

He said, "You."

I did not recognize his face, but his tone suggested that he knew me. He sounded resigned rather than surprised.

I might have stayed my hand. Then I saw the bag hanging from his belt—a pouch of supple white leather. I'd never seen it before, but I recognized it instantly. My foster mothers had described it. I'd heard about it in Futh's stories and Rogein's songs. It was the corrbolg, my father's crane bag, which held his treasure.

I screamed with rage and threw my spear.

The warrior dropped to his knees, a look of shock on his face, the shaft of my spear buried in his chest. I drew my blacksmith's knife and approached, ready to cut off the head of my father's traitor.

"So," the man croaked, "this is how it ends."

I stopped short. Why did I know his voice?

And his gray cloak . . . torn and mended so many times. Why did I recognize those uneven, childish stitches?

Before my eyes, the man's form throbbed like a moth pupa in its cocoon. His hips grew wider. His breasts filled out. His beard dissolved. His skin wrinkled and sagged. A large wart blossomed on the left side of his nose. He became an old gray woman, glass beads braided into her hair, her hands feebly clutching at the spear that sprouted from her sternum. My foster mother coughed blood. "Your spear arm . . . has improved, boy."

The knife dropped from my hands. The anger that had filled me a moment ago turned to horror. I wanted to run to the Líath Lúachra, but my legs would not obey.

"How?" I sobbed.

She fell sideways on her hip. The tip of the spear that jutted from her back formed a grotesque tripod holding her up. "Told you. The Morna clan . . . not my fate to die from them."

My guilt fought with my grief, each trying to drown the other. I edged closer. I hoped the Líath Lúachra was another illusion. Glonda's murderer was trying to fool me into seeing my foster mother. But no. I knew her smell, her wrinkles, the shiny beads she loved to braid into her straggly hair. It was her.

But why did she have my father's crane bag?

She followed my gaze to the pouch. She groped at it, her

fingers smearing blood across the white leather. "Yours now. Was"—she coughed hideously—"saving it for you."

My fists trembled. "You betrayed my father."

She nodded weakly.

"To save his *bag* for me?"

A heavy, painful wheeze. "More complicated than that. Someday . . . when *you* die . . . you will understand. Now go to Crimall. He will help you." Her head sagged.

"No!" Finally, I rushed to her side. "Did Bodbmall know? Did my mother know?"

The Líath Lúachra shook a string of blood from her lips, perhaps indicating *no*, or saying that it didn't matter now. "What is your name, warrior?"

"What? My name is Demne!"

Another shake of her head. "No longer. What the boys of Mag Life called you is better. . . . You are the Bright One now, a son worthy of Cumall. You are Finn mac Cumaill."

The name settled over me like a new cloak, too big and too heavy.

"Did you ever truly love me?" I sobbed.

She cocked an eye at me one last time. "Foolish child."

Then she went limp, held in place by my spear.

I buried her under a cairn of stones. I spent the night at her camp.

She left me with too many unanswered questions. Had she betrayed my father for his shiny treasures? Had she thought she was helping me somehow? And if she'd foreseen that I would someday kill her, why help raise me? Why hadn't she simply strangled me as a baby?

I still do not have those answers.

I do have the crane bag, filled with more gold and silver than I could ever spend in a lifetime. The bag's magic is such that it can carry anything, as long as I can fit it through the opening. I can carry my spears inside it. I can carry the Líath Lúachra's tent, and Lóchán's knife, and the fidchell piece I stole from the king of Ciarraige. If the opening were bigger, I'd be tempted to crawl inside it myself and disappear. No matter how much it carries, the corrbolg is as light as a bird's wing, yet it is my heaviest burden. It is all I have left of my father and my foster mother.

I didn't try to find Bodbmall and seek answers from her.

Rather, I did as the Líath Lúachra instructed. I continued west to find my uncle Crimall and the remnants of my father's band of Fíana. Perhaps they could tell me more.

What happened next is a tale unto itself: how I found those men, how I earned my magic and poetry, how I first encountered the spirit folk of the Síde, how I finally came face-to-face with Goll mac Morna. All that happened in my eleventh year. Perhaps we will speak of it another day.

In the meantime, I have traveling to do. The Causeway of Glonda is safe to cross now, but if you choose to do so, be warned: I cannot promise what you will find on the other side.

Finn's Guide to Irish Names

THESE ADVENTURES HAPPENED BEFORE the English colonizers came to our land. From the moment they arrived, our language began to die like a poisoned tree. Over the centuries, they took away our alphabet, along with everything else. They made us write our names in English, which has no letters for many of the sounds we needed. Then they made fun of us because we spelled our names strangely.

I have recorded this tale in the colonizers' tongue, but you have to meet me halfway. At least learn to say our names with the spellings we choose. I don't have time to teach you all the rules of Irish. Just know that the spelling makes perfect sense . . . just not the sense the English have trained you to see.

Below are some names and how to say them properly. However, be aware that Irish folk today don't pronounce things the same way I did back in the ancient times, and people in different parts of Ireland pronounce things differently. That shouldn't shock you. Languages are always changing, like the seasons, or the genders of fénnidí.

You may also ask: If this story happened so long ago, how I am speaking to you now in your own tongue? That, too, is a tale for another time. . . .

Note: When you see "kh," make a sound like clearing your throat just a little.

Aed (EE-th) a man's name that means "fire." It was Goll mac Morna's given name.

áes dána (ice DAWN-uh) "people of the gifts." Traveling craftsmen and artisans.

Ailbe (ILL-buh) the given name of my thatcher friend

arán donn (uh-RAWN dawn) heavy brown bread, still a staple food in Ireland

bean sídhe (ban SHEE) a woman of the spirit world. Known today as the banshee.

Benntraige (ban-TREE) the tribe that lived in modern-day Bantry, County Cork

Béo (bee-OH) the name of a monstrous wild boar

Bodbmall (BAWTH-mall) my first foster mother, a druidess

bodhrán (bow-RAWN) a traditional Irish drum

Ciarraige (keer-EE) the tribe that settled in modern County Kerry

Cnucha (NOO-kha) the modern-day hill of Castleknock, County Dublin, where my father, Cumall, died in battle

Codna (CAWD-nuh) the father of Fíacail

Connacht (CAWN-akht) one of the four ancient kingdoms of Ireland

corrbolg (kor-BALL-ug) crane bag. The magic crane-leather pouch that held Cumall's treasure.

Crimall (KRIH-mull) my uncle, brother of Cumall

Crotta (CRUH-tah) now called the Galtee Mountains, County Tipperary

Cruithne (KRIH-nuh) the daughter of the blacksmith Lóchán

Cú Chulainn (koo KHULL-an) the most famous hero of ancient Ireland, champion of the kingdom of Ulster

Cumall (KOO-mull) my father, formerly captain of Ireland's Fíana

Demne (DEV-nah) my given name

fénnid (FAY-nid) (**fénnidí**, *pl.*) a hunter-warrior, an outlaw, and a member of the Fíana

Fíacail (FEE-uh-kull) the name of a notorious reaver

Fíana (FEE-uh-nuh) a band of outlaws that roamed Ireland, keeping peace between tribes and protecting the land from foreign invasion

fidchell (FID-khell) an ancient board game, something like chess. Its name means "wood sense."

Fid Gliabe (fid GLEE-buh) a forest in the kingdom of Leinster

finn (FIN) fair, bright, blond

Futh (FOO) the name of my storyteller friend

geis (GESH) a personal taboo or restriction. Break it, and bad things will happen.

gilla (GILL-uh) the term for a boy or lad

Glonda (GLAWN-dah) the name of a deceased young man

Goll (GAWL) a name that means "One Eye," given to Goll mac Morna after the Battle of Cnucha

iománaíocht (ih-MAWN-ee-akht) the game of hurling

Lamraige (LAH-muh-rig) the kingdom of Gleór Red-Head, my mother's second husband

Leinster (LIN-ster) one of the four ancient kingdoms of Ireland

Líath Lúachra (LEE-ah LOO-khra) the Gray One of Lúachair, my second foster mother

Lóchán (low-KHAWN) a blacksmith who took me in (for a while)

Loch Léin (lokh LAIN) now called the Lakes of Killarney, County Tipperary

Luaigni (LOOG-nee) one of the largest ancient tribes of Ireland

Lugaid (LOOG-ud) a popular ancient Irish name. One of the boys of Mag Life.

mac Cumaill (muh-KOO-wool) son of Cumall

mac Morna (mack MOURN-nah) a son (or clan member) of Morna

Madhfeá (MAWTH-ah) the name of my blacksmith friend

Mag Life (mawg LIFF-uh) a plain on the banks of the River Liffey, County Kildare

Mahan (mah-HAWN) a common Irish name, one of the boys of Mag Life

Muirne (MWEER-nuh) the name of my mother

póg mo thóin (poh-g muh HONE) "Kiss my posterior." Use this phrase only if you want to start a fight.

Regna (RAY-nyuh) the name of my cobbler friend

Rogein (ROH-gan) the name of my musician friend

Ruth (ROO) the name of my tinsmith friend

seanchaí (SHAN-uh-hee) a traditional storyteller

Síde (SHEE) the Otherworld, the world of spirit folk who live under the hills

Slíab Bladma (shleev BLAHD-mah) today called the Slieve Bloom Mountains, County Laois

sliotar (SLEE-cher) (**sliotair**, *pl.*) a ball (or balls) used in hurling

túath (TOO-ath) a tribe

Túatha Dé Danann (TWAH-thah day DAN-nahn) the Tribe of the Goddess Danu, Ireland's immortal god-folk

Uí Chúanach (oh KHOO-nah) the tribe that lived in modern-day Coonagh, County Limerick

About the Contributors

Carlos Hernandez has published more than thirty works of fiction, poetry, and drama, including *Sal and Gabi Break the Universe*, for which he won a Pura Belpré Award from the American Library Association, and its sequel, *Sal and Gabi Fix the Universe*. Carlos is an English professor at the City University of New York, and he loves to both play games and design them. He lives with his wife, Claire, in Queens, New York. Follow him on Twitter @WriteTeachPlay.

Roshani Chokshi is the author of the *New York Times* best-selling Pandava series, which began with *Aru Shah and the End of Time* and was inspired by the Hindu stories her grandmother told her. Rosh also wrote the *New York Times* best-selling YA books *The Star-Touched Queen, The Gilded Wolves*, and *The Silvered Serpents*. She studied fairy tales in college and once had a pet luck dragon that looked suspiciously like a Great Pyrenees dog. Roshani lives in the South and says *y'all*, but she doesn't really have a Southern accent. Her Twitter handle is @roshani_chokshi.

J. C. Cervantes is the *New York Times* best-selling author of *The Storm Runner, The Fire Keeper*, and *The Shadow Crosser*, a fantasy adventure trilogy based on Mesoamerican mythology.

Jen grew up in San Diego and was fascinated by stories about Maya gods, impossible adventures, and all things magic. She now lives in New Mexico, where she is creating more tales, including a spin-off of the Storm Runner series. Follow her on Twitter @jencerv and Instagram @authorjcervantes.

Yoon Ha Lee is the *New York Times* best-selling author of *Dragon Pearl*, winner of a Locus Award and the Mythopoeic Award. He has also published several books for adults, including a standalone fantasy entitled *Phoenix Extravagant*, and the Machineries of Empire space opera trilogy: *Ninefox Gambit*, *Raven Strategem*, and *Revenant Gun*. Yoon draws inspiration from a variety of sources, e.g. Korean history and mythology, fairy tales, higher mathematics, classic moral dilemmas, and genre fiction. His website can be found at yoonhalee.com and his Twitter handle is @deuceofgears.

Kwame Mbalia is the *New York Times* best-selling author of the Tristan Strong trilogy, which incorporates elements from African American folklore and African mythology. He received a Coretta Scott King Author Honor award for the first book, *Tristan Strong Punches a Hole in the Sky*. The book was also named to best-of-the-year lists compiled by *Publishers Weekly*, the Chicago Public Library, and the *New York Times*. Kwame lives with his wife and children in Raleigh, North Carolina, where he is currently working on two new series. Follow him on Twitter @KSekouM.

Rebecca Roanhorse is a Black Indigenous (Ohkay Owingeh) writer of speculative fiction, including *Black Sun*, *Star Wars: Resistance Reborn*, *Trail of Lightning*, *Storm of Locusts*, and a Nebula- and Hugo-winning short story, "Welcome to Your Authentic Indian Experience." The *New York Times* best-selling *Race to the Sun*, inspired by Diné stories, was her middle grade debut. Rebecca lives in Northern New Mexico with her Navajo husband and their daughter. Follow her on Twitter @RoanhorseBex.

Tehlor Kay Mejia is an Oregon native in love with the alpine meadows and evergreen forests of her home state, where she lives with her daughter. When she's not writing, you can find her plucking at her guitar, stealing rosemary sprigs from over-grown gardens, or trying to make the perfect vegan tamale. She is the author of *Paola Santiago and the River of Tears* and *Paola Santiago and the Forest of Nightmares*, based on Mexican folktales, as well as the YA fantasy novels *We Set the Dark on Fire* and *We Unleash the Merciless Storm*. Follow her on Twitter @tehlorkay.

Sarwat Chadda, a first-generation Muslim immigrant, is the author of *City of the Plague God*, a novel based on Mesopotamian mythology. As a lifelong gamer, he decided to embrace his passion for over-the-top adventure stories by swapping a career in engineering for a new one as a writer. That resulted in his first novel, *Devil's Kiss*, back in 2009. Since then he has been published in a dozen languages, writing comic books, TV shows, and novels such as the award-winning Indian mythology–inspired Ash Mistry series and the epic high-fantasy Shadow Magic trilogy (as Joshua Khan). While he's traveled far and wide, including to Africa, the Middle East, and Asia, he's most at home in London, where he lives with his wife, two more-or-less grown-up daughters, and an aloof cat. Drop him a line on Twitter @sarwatchadda or Instagram @sarwat_chadda.

Graci Kim is a Korean Kiwi diplomat turned author who writes about the magic she wants to see in the world. Her middle grade debut, *The Last Fallen Star,* is the first book in the Gifted Clans trilogy, inspired by Korean mythology. In a previous life she used to be a cooking-show host, and she once ran a business that turned children's drawings into plushies. When she's not lost in her imagination, you'll find Graci drinking flat whites, eating ramyeon, and most likely hugging a dog (or ideally, many). She lives in New Zealand with her husband and daughter. Follow her on Twitter @gracikim and Instagram @gracikimwrites.

Rick Riordan, dubbed "storyteller of the gods" by *Publishers Weekly,* is the author of five #1 *New York Times* best-selling middle grade series with millions of copies sold throughout the world: Percy Jackson and the Olympians, the Heroes of Olympus, and the Trials of Apollo, based on Greek and Roman mythology; the Kane Chronicles, based on ancient Egyptian mythology; and Magnus Chase and the Gods of Asgard, based on Norse mythology. Rick collaborated with illustrator John Rocco on two #1 *New York Times* best-selling collections of Greek myths for the whole family, *Percy Jackson's Greek Gods* and *Percy Jackson's Greek Heroes*. His latest book is *Daughter of the Deep*, a modern take on the Jules Verne classic *20,000 Leagues Under the Sea*. Rick is also the publisher of an imprint at Disney Hyperion, Rick Riordan Presents, dedicated to finding other authors of highly entertaining fiction based on world cultures and mythologies. He lives in Boston, Massachusetts, with his wife and two sons. Follow him on Twitter at @RickRiordan.